Praise for *The French House*

'A raw and honest love story, filled with a wealth of historical detail. The French House is a powerful depiction of the brutal intricacies of island relationships and loyalties in a time of war'
FIONA VALPY, bestselling author of
The Beekeeper's Promise

'Deeply involving . . . A fantastic debut by a gifted storyteller'
JILL MANSELL, bestselling author of
And Now You're Back

'A story of fraught secrets and tested loyalties, of family and friendship, and of a love that once reignited, refuses to die. I found this beautifully told tale hard to put down'
ANITA FRANK, award-winning author of
The Lost Ones

'Heart-wrenching . . . A truly special novel'
LOUISE FEIN, author of *People Like Us*

'An accomplished and atmospheric debut . . . I really enjoyed this uncliched yet deeply moving love story'
TRACY REES, bestselling author of
The House at Silvermoor

Jacquie Bloese grew up on the Channel Island of Guernsey. Her interest in travel, languages and other cultures led to a career in educational publishing, a job which has taken her in and out of classrooms all over the world. After many years in London, she now lives in Brighton with her partner. *The French House* is her first novel.

jacquiebloese.com

 @novelthesecond

 @jb_writer

JACQUIE BLOESE

The French House

HODDER

First published in Great Britain in 2022 by Hodder & Stoughton
An Hachette UK company

This paperback edition published in 2022

1

A CIP catalogue record for this title is available from the British Library

Paperback ISBN 978 1 529 37735 4

Typeset in Plantin Light by Hewer Text UK Ltd, Edinburgh
Printed and bound in Great Britain by Clays Ltd, Elcograf S.p.A.

Hodder & Stoughton policy is to use papers that are natural, renewable
and recyclable products and made from wood grown in sustainable
forests. The logging and manufacturing processes are expected to
conform to the environmental regulations of the country of origin.

Hodder & Stoughton Ltd
Carmelite House
50 Victoria Embankment
London EC4Y 0DZ

www.hodder.co.uk

'But though I wanted to hear,
I did not want to listen.'

Deborah Levy, *My Muse Appeared to Me in a Dream*

For my parents

PROLOGUE

Vancouver, 1911

The men in the boarding house have started calling Émile a sap. They greet him with kissing noises as they stumble down to breakfast, heavy with hangover, on a Sunday morning. It is the time Émile reserves for writing to Isabelle, while church bells ring for the faithful and his companions snore in their beds – it is his holy hour and everyone knows it, and if ever a boisterous back slap from one of the fellows should cause Émile to smudge or blot, they'll share a smoke later to show they're sorry.

'She must be some woman,' they say, and Émile grins and tells them she is, although recently the effort of doing so makes his face ache. It has been four months with no word and Isabelle is not the kind of woman who mislays addresses – or who gives up on a thing because other people don't like it; they are the same that way, she and him.

Nonetheless, the other evening, in a saloon in Gastown, Émile had found himself swept up into a little more than just conversation with a girl who would have made his mother tut (lips ladybird red, tatty lace shawl prone to slippage, glimpses of bare freckled skin). He had bought her drinks, flirted a little, but when, from under the table, her hand crept like a small creature across his thigh, Émile moved away, feeling a rush of shame, as if Isabelle herself was standing there, silently observing.

Now it is September and he has been in Vancouver a
year. He wakes to the screech of freight trains and the smell
of frying bacon, he walks through streets alive with unfathomable languages – Chinese, Japanese, Russian. His job at
the dairy pays thirty-five a month, with a few dimes extra
when he plays his accordion in bars for tips; his boss calls
him Mike because he says his last name is too fancy and his
first doesn't suit him; no one has heard of the tiny island in
the Channel that he used to call home. This is the new life
the advertisements promised, but the sky isn't as blue as he
remembers from the posters, and he's not ready to leave the
city for a homestead in Saskatchewan or Manitoba just yet,
not with winter around the corner and his savings still lower
than he'd like.

On the day it happens, a day that will vibrate like a chord
across the years ahead, it is Émile's first week on the night
shift and he cannot sleep. His body protests at being
coerced into lying in bed like an invalid when it's light
outside, and he is in the worst of humours when six o'clock
comes and it's time for him to rouse himself.

The street car he takes to the East Side is cramped and
noisy. A baby screams relentlessly, there is an altercation
between two men on his right and the air is blue with cursing, he steps on an elderly woman's foot and when he apol-
ogises, she regards him suspiciously and mutters something about foreign types having no manners and she
doesn't know what kind of place Vancouver is turning into.
His head aches, he feels soiled with the city and at that
moment, there is nothing Émile longs for more than to be
sitting on the bank of pebbles at Portinfer Bay, with the
sound of the sea sieving through shingle, and just a few
oystercatchers for company.

2

This week he is doing deliveries with a man from China called Lin. He doesn't speak much and when he does, Émile can only make out one word in five. When he arrives at the dairy, Lin is harnessing the horses; he greets Émile with a nod and they begin the nightly routine of loading milk churns onto the wagon to take to Pender Street for pasteurising. As they set off, it starts to rain. The streets glisten in the yellow lamplight and Émile feels the slow creep of exhaustion. He turns to Lin.

'You want to stop off at Kowalski's later?'

A year ago, he would have baulked at eating anything that he couldn't pronounce; now the plates of steaming pierogi from a hole in the wall on Keefer Street count among Émile's favourite meals.

Lin's shrug is as good as a yes. He doesn't like the food here and compares every meal they eat with those that his wife used to make in China. *She coming soon*, he says, but everyone knows that the Chinese wives never come – the authorities make them pay five hundred bucks before they even get off the boat. The unfairness of it rankles Émile. He slaps Lin's shoulder and resolves to stand him dinner.

They draw up outside the depot and begin unloading the milk. There are no street lamps and the place is in darkness. Émile has only ever been here in the daytime before. It has one of those new-fangled elevators to transport the milk down to the basement and Émile gets a childlike thrill whenever he rides in it. Lin, he knows, is scared; every time they go in, he stands rigid with one fist clenched and the other clutching his stomach, eyes squeezed shut. Even now, as they roll off the last churn, Émile can sense him drawing back.

'Christ's sake, it won't bite you,' he says, then takes pity on the fellow. Lin is twice his age and the foreman is tough on his sort – cutting their breaks short, giving them the worst shifts.

'Get the horses watered,' Émile tells him. 'I'll see you round the corner.'

The relief in Lin's voice as he thanks him makes Émile feel a notch or two better than he did when he woke up. Do as you would have done to you, isn't that what they say? It isn't easy starting up in a new country and he should pat himself on the back more than he does – isn't he putting money away every week for him and Isabelle, for the farm on the prairie with a south-facing porch overlooking the golden wheat fields, where they will sit together on warm Sunday afternoons . . . Émile yanks back the elevator door. The image he creates feels as real as a recent memory: Isabelle with a book in one hand, the other resting on the curve of her belly, which in this latest fantasy is just beginning to swell, the ring now on her finger where it should be, not hidden under layers of clothing on a piece of ribbon inside her petticoat.

The familiar metallic chill of the elevator greets him. It is black as tar and he gropes in his pocket for matches, cursing the dairy for expecting him to do a daytime job in the night-time, when he should be at home with the others, having a smoke in front of the fire and chewing the fat. But he must have left his tobacco and papers in the wagon, because he can't find any matches and he tries to recall if there's an electric light affixed to the sides of the elevator. He doesn't remember and so he steps forward into the cave-like darkness, his hand outstretched.

Later, they will tell him he fell a full fifteen feet down the elevator shaft. He supposes it was over quickly, in no more than a split second, yet time seems to lengthen and slow as a roaring starts up in his ears, a howl of sorts like a demented dog, and his legs paddle underneath him and the shock of it all is compounded by the surety that he is about to die. No homestead, no children, no Isabelle.

The ground crushes him. His body crumples. There is a ferocious pain in the base of his skull, which spreads to his collarbone and shoulders. His body is not his own anymore, he doesn't dare to move; he is fragile, broken. He opens his mouth to call for help but no sound comes out. Over and over again he tries, but if he can't hear himself, what hope is there that anyone else will, and this is Émile's final despairing thought, before the blackness overwhelms him.

He comes to three weeks later in crisp hospital sheets. There is a young, yellow-haired nurse bending over him with concern in her pale eyes. Her lips move, but Émile hears nothing. Speak up, he says, or at least he thinks he does, and the nurse turns and the ward sister appears, pushing a trolley that glides soundlessly across the tiled floor before pressing a cold instrument against the flesh of his ear. More nurses come and a doctor this time, circling him, mouths opening and closing like goldfish in a bowl – speak up, dammit, speak up, he thinks – until the truth batters him like another clout to the head. Everyone else can hear perfectly well, and it is he who can't hear a blasted thing.

I

Guernsey, 1940

É mile may not hear trouble coming, but he always knows when it's on the way. As he sweats in the greenhouse on this plump June afternoon, while the sea rails against the jagged cliffs and gusts of wind whip up the salted scent of the Channel, Émile feels as if the pulse of the island is quickening in time with his own. When the shadow of the first German plane lengthens over him and the vibrations on the glass sting his palm, he stares after it, and wonders whether he would feel more afraid if he could hear the roar of the engine. Another follows and then another and although he's seen them before, they are lower than usual, close enough for him to see the monochrome markings on the underside of the wing. A blast of warm air courses through the greenhouse and then they are gone, and all is still again.

Émile looks at his watch and curses. Maud should have been here half an hour ago: there are still a load of tomatoes to pack and annoyance curdles inside him as he picks up several of the wooden chip baskets and carries them out to the lorry. As he passes the cottage, the back door opens and his other daughter – the real one, and this he knows is his temper speaking – steps outside. She is clutching the ivory dance shoes she bought with her first month's pay packet; she has done something to her hair that he's not sure he likes, but when she smiles, the years roll back and Stella is

7

six again, skipping down to the greenhouse to collect him for tea, her hand warm in his. Now she peers anxiously down the garden, to where her sister should be and isn't. Her mouth opens and Émile waves away any real or imagined offer of help.

'Go!' he says, and she doesn't need telling again and Émile is glad to see it, because dance classes and war aren't natural companions, even here in the islands where they have been safe so far. He tries not to think of the planes as he hoists the boxes of tomatoes into the back of the lorry.

Maud arrives just as he is tying up the tarpaulin, when all the real work is over. It is almost six-fifteen; she is over an hour late, and it is maddening because now they will be one of the last in the queue at the harbour and by the time the paperwork is done and the tomatoes are loaded, the fellows in the Caves will be several rounds ahead of him and he has a thirst on him today: he'd start now if he could. And the girl isn't even making a show of hurrying, propping her bicycle against the wall, checking a run in her stocking.

'Where were you?'

'Out.' She stares at him, her eyes dark as sloes.

'Get in the lorry!'

Maud flinches but does as she's told and the smell of diesel fills the air as he starts up the engine and drives down the narrow lane, putting his foot down once they're on the main road. Maud's knuckles are clenched on the dashboard, the silence between them a hiss, a fizz. Émile knows what she's thinking, can follow her thoughts like a score of music. The less she says, the simpler it is.

You know that I always rehearse on Friday, while Ma's out cleaning because all the stopping and starting and the same song over and again makes her head hurt.

8

Yes, Émile does know this. His wife isn't fond of the accordion; he doesn't need telling.

Why is Stella's tap class more important than my accordion?

Because she's paid for the classes already, show some sense, girl!

You just want to stop me from playing.

Not true. Not true. And yet . . .

Émile brakes as they approach the coast road. From time to time, he has caught glimpses of Maud practising through the half open door of the bedroom. She wears the accordion like it is part of her and that, he knows, is half the battle. Even though he can't hear a single note, he can tell she is good, better than he was before the accident. If he watches for too long, it makes him feel peculiar, as if something is rotting inside him. Couldn't she have picked another instrument – the fiddle, the harmonica?

He sighs and winds down the window a little further. The sea is lively today, the waves capped with silver, the filtered rays of the sun turning the hump of Herm Island into more than it is, whitewashing the beaches, dusting the rocks with gold. He knows the visitors love it, but the place is overrated, if you ask him – half an hour to get there and not much longer than that to get bored once you've arrived. If he was going to take the trouble to leave Guernsey, he'd want a bit more than a pint of ale and a dose of sunburn to show for it – not that he's likely to go anywhere further than the White Rock to see off his tomatoes on the boat every Friday, these days. And, really – he presses down harder on the accelerator – it comes to something when a basket of Grade One Smooths has a more exciting future than the man who grows them.

This last thought dies abruptly, extinguished by Maud doing what she's been taught never to do when he's driving: she takes him by surprise, grips him suddenly, without warning – the truck swerves across the road as the steering wheel slips through his hands. He starts to yell, asking what the hell she's playing at, but Maud's mouth is frozen in a scream, and as Émile looks towards where she's pointing, her fear becomes his own.

Two German aircraft are hovering over the quay, above the line of lorries, and in the time it takes for Émile to thank his dizzy stars that he and Maud are not there like sitting ducks underneath them, silver pellets tumble like the rungs of a ladder from the innards of one of the planes, and the truck shakes until his teeth chatter. He is on the floor now – they are both on the floor – Maud's knee lodged in his armpit and she is trembling as he drags them both out into air which reeks of sulphur and smoke. Maud's hands are clamped over her ears, and Émile gestures towards the greasy undercarriage of the truck and begins to slide himself underneath it. For a few excruciating seconds, she doesn't move. But then the ground shakes a second time and Maud shuffles in next to him, and they lie belly-down in the dark as tomatoes tumble from the back of the lorry, the juice running in rivulets around them.

As the vibrations subside, Émile is tortured by the small things. Letty will be furious. Letty will be furious about the ruined tomatoes and will somehow attach the blame to him, as if he is personally responsible for the Germans' military strategy and when they get back home, she will make her displeasure felt for as long as it takes for him to find this month's rent, to put food back on the table. Then the ground quakes again and the housekeeping is forgotten. *If* they get back home. Letty had been dead set against them evacuating and he'd let her have her way, but it would have kept the girls safe, he sees that now. He should have insisted; he's been a fool. Émile closes his eyes. He tries to remember the last time he laughed, or felt his life was something more than early mornings and the sweat of the greenhouse, the last time he and Letty had looked at each other with even a drop of tenderness.

Maud taps his shoulder and he turns to see her crawling back out. The road is just a road again; solid, unmoveable. He follows and emerges, blinking in the sunlight. He turns towards the White Rock, absorbs the chaos of flames, the thick grey plumes of smoke on the quay where Stella and Maud used to play hopscotch every Friday as they waited for the boat to come in. Maud's face is streaked with tears and grime and a damp patch has bloomed across the front of her skirt and with it comes the forgotten smell of accidents at night-time; he remembers bedsheets soaking in a bucket, the whiff of shame at the breakfast table. Émile wants to take her in his arms and hold her, stroke her back as she sobs, but they've never been that way and he can't start now. Instead, he asks if she is all right and she nods and says she is.

Émile opens the door of the truck. 'Let's get home,' he says. 'Your ma will be worried.'

As they pull into the yard, Émile sees his wife standing on the porch. Her hair is loose and he hasn't seen it like this for years – she is luminous, beautiful in the fierce gold of the slanting sun, her hands clasped as if in prayer – and for a moment, Émile tastes hope. For once, she will be proud of him; he kept his head, protected Maud, brought her home safe. Then she steps into shadow and calls into the house and he realises that it's Stella, not Letty. It's a trick that his mind has played on him before and it is disorientating, this confusion between what is real and what is wished for – and then Letty appears, striding towards the truck in her faded housecoat, her face contorting as she shouts, and not for the first time, Émile is glad he can't hear her.

Letty pulls Maud from the truck as if from a burning fire. Her embrace is more of an assault than a hug; her body, tense with resentment and she releases Maud quickly. She jabs her index finger at the sky and then at Émile.

You saw the planes, she seems to be saying, everyone saw them. Lipreading his wife has always been a struggle – words spill like slops, shapeless for the most part, although certain phrases are well-worn, fitting comfortably in the contours of her mouth. *I'm married to a fool. What were you thinking?*

Émile pushes past her, heads towards the cottage. He looks back. Letty's shoulders are slumped, she is rubbing her forehead with the pad of her thumb – a gesture as old as their marriage. He refuses to let himself feel an ounce of sympathy: she doesn't deserve it, not today, not after what's just happened.

'All the same to you if I hadn't made it back, eh?'

She looks up. Her eyes are red. He says it again, just in case. He wonders if his voice is shaking, but in any event, it's unimportant, as she is screwing up her face and shrugging and saying, Wha'? What's that, Émile? and there is a high-pitching ringing in his ears as he goes into the house.

The kitchen table is set for tea. Slices of ham sweat on chipped plates, a bowl of glistening tomatoes covers the stain in the oilcloth. Stella appears and half knocks the breath out of him she hugs him so hard, and Émile stands a little awkwardly and pats her head.

'Shush,' he says. 'Ssh.'

Then he goes to the bedroom, closes the door and rifles through the bottom drawer of the dressing table, where Letty has taken to keeping the housekeeping money, until he finds the brown envelope he is seeking. A note and a few coppers. He counts up the loose change – barely enough for a couple of drinks, much less a round. Émile hesitates, sees once again Letty's expression of outrage, the jabbing index finger, and trembling a little, he tosses the coins back into the drawer and slips the ten-bob note in his back pocket. He's the man of the house, he can do as he pleases, there's plenty more where that came from except there isn't and he can't, at least not without feeling wretched with guilt, but it's too late now – they all know what he's doing in here. As he strides back into the kitchen, he feels the sudden dip in conversation as he might a pothole in the road and he cannot look at any of them as he leaves.

The first drink is always the most difficult; the faces of his wife and daughters seem to glimmer in the bevelled beer glass whenever it catches the light, and Émile drinks quickly to chase them away. He has barely swallowed his last mouthful before he is reaching for the brown envelope and standing a second round.

His back gets slapped, his glass clinked, satisfying even when silent. Tobacco is rolled and lit. The men shift on their bar stools, letting him in for as long as the free pint lasts. They are talking about the raid. Forty dead, fifty. They'd dropped them on Jersey too, and Sark. The landlord, polishing the bar as if his life depended on it, says something that makes everyone laugh but they're all scared; Émile sees it in their eyes. The drink makes swaggering fools of them all, when he knows most of them to be cowards, only too ready to take advantage, to cut him out of a round as soon as his back's turned.

Émile feels a hand on his shoulder. He looks up and sees Ron Martel, a cousin of sorts of Letty's. He is a short, weasely man, with a permanent thirst and a tab longer than your arm. Émile waits to be touched for a bob or two, but to his surprise, Ron throws a couple of coins on the counter and nods at Émile's empty glass.

He is being paid to listen, not the first time nor the last. The beer is sour but vaguely comforting, like the smell of home. Émile nods slowly as if in time to music, as Ron speaks, catching what words he can.

Now Ron is miming an explosion. 'Bombed!' he says. 'The French House.'

'On Hauteville?' Émile puts down his drink, does his best to concentrate.

Ron nods. He has moved on to the Germans. He turns an imaginary key in a lock and says something to Émile about his daughters, about Letty, which Émile ignores. Through the fog of alcohol, an unpleasant feeling, like grit under an eyelid, worries at him. He sees the peevish curl of Letty's lip. *For all her airs and graces, the woman's just a housekeeper. Scrubs floors same as I do, I should think.*

'Anyone in the French House,' he asks, 'when it happened?'

But Ron's desire for an audience has waned now that their glasses are empty and he looks expectantly at Émile and Émile gives him the same look back. He gets to his feet, shakes Ron's hand and launches himself unsteadily into the deserted streets.

Émile ducks down a side alley and relieves himself against the wall. He squints up at the sky, swaying a little, searching for the tilt and dip of the Plough, but the night is soupy and close and the stars are hidden. He wipes himself off and is halfway up Cornet Street before his mind has caught up with his body, and he understands where he is going and why.

He continues up the hill into Hauteville, no more than a spit away from the crooked terraces of Cornet Street, but where the houses are grand, all la-di-dah brass door knockers and freshly painted railings, and tradesmen's entrances for those the rich folk don't want to look in the eye. Émile can't remember the last time he was up here; he has no reason to be around these parts and he feels out of place, a trespasser. Ahead he can make out the bulk of the large oak tree that stands in the front garden of the French House, and as he approaches, Émile sees that the house is intact, all three haughty storeys of it, and he curses Ron Martel for not knowing his arse from his elbow and giving him a fright.

He stares at the shuttered windows, wondering if it's as grand on the inside as it seems from up front, and whether Letty's right and it falls to Isabelle to get down on her hands and knees with a rag and a tin of wax, or to beat the dust from the rugs until her forearms ache. He does not know the answer to this, nor is he ever likely to, because he and Mrs Isabelle Larch – and he raps out her married title with drumsticks in his head, allowing himself a smirk at the monotone dullness of that English surname – he and Mrs Isabelle Larch duck into shop doorways to avoid each other. Some years back, on one muggy August afternoon at the North Show, he remembers steering Letty and the girls into the jostling fray of the beer tent, such was the deep-seated unrest he felt upon seeing Isabelle approach on her husband's arm.

A flicker of light passes across a window on the top floor. There is someone up there, a woman, and the skinful he's had doesn't stop his heart turning in recognition as he sees Isabelle's silhouette in the frame – the long graceful neck and sweep of her shoulders, the mussed-up, disobedient hair that would never lie smooth: he remembers the coarseness of it brushing his cheek. She stops and looks straight at him, and Émile stares back. What remains of next week's housekeeping lies heavy as rocks in his pocket. For a moment, he thinks she doesn't recognise him and he is almost glad, because he barely knows himself anymore, but then slowly Isabelle raises a hand. His palms remain rigid by his side, but the satisfaction he gets from this small act of dissent passes swiftly, and Émile is left feeling as he always does whenever he is confronted with remnants of his life before the accident – cheated, lost, alone.

There is only one way this evening can end for him now. Lowering his head, he scoots down the hill, not stopping until he is at the top of Cornet Street. There is a lamp glowing at Céline's window and he throws up a handful of gravel, hoping to God that she'll let him in quickly – no amount of alcohol seems to protect him from the shame that descends as he loiters on the doorstep. But a few beats later the front door opens and Céline appears wearing a thin mauve dressing gown, seeming neither pleased nor displeased to see him – she delivers a curt nod and gestures him inside.

Émile follows her upstairs to her room with its cloying smell of violets. A magazine lies splayed on the rumpled bedclothes. Céline nods towards the tea caddy on the mantlepiece and shrugs off her dressing gown.

He pays with what he has left, then strips down to his underclothes and lies next to her on the bed. Céline is not a young woman and her body is beginning to pucker and sag. Émile prefers it this way – she is Letty's age or thereabouts, with the same silvery stretch marks hatching her belly, and this makes the whole business easier somehow. She reaches for him and he closes his eyes. But tonight is not like other nights and as her hand moves against him – and when that bears no results, her mouth – any lurch of desire is knocked flat and he is lying under the truck again, next to Maud, with the ground shuddering beneath them and the tomatoes split open like brains.

Céline gives up and slumps back on the bed. He feels her breath tickle his ear and realises she is saying something: she does this sometimes, forgets that he's deaf. Émile supposes this should irritate him but the truth is he likes it.

He speaks for the first time. 'Can I stay?'

Céline rolls her eyes, then holds up six fingers, and points to the alarm clock.

'Six o'clock,' she says. 'Before the others get up.' She pulls back the covers and they both climb underneath.

She turns her back to him and Émile waits a while, then eases himself towards her, tentatively resting his arm on her hip. She stirs but doesn't wake. Émile tries to let the gentle undulations of her body soothe him but although he aches with exhaustion, he can't sleep. He stares into the darkness. This day, 28 June 1940, could have been the last day of his life. His death day. And here he is, alive and not even sure he is glad about it. Hands stained black from tomato plants with a wife who barely comes near him. One daughter who loves him and another who loves to provoke. And the storm, louder tonight than it has been for some time, raging inside his head.

2

The last time Isabelle Larch was in the salon rouge at Hauteville House, she'd been Christmas Day-tipsy and behaving quite out of turn with the person she usually was. She'd kicked off her shoes and settled herself down on the red brocade chaise longue, in front of the enormous gilt mirror that was the devil to dust, and there she had lolled, sipping her employer's brandy as if she were some erstwhile mistress of the house, rather than the housekeeper, until her husband's voice crept up on her and ruined everything.

Look at the state of you, woman!

Then, quite obediently, as if he were there standing over her, she had got up, smoothed down her skirt and slipped back into the office for a top up. It wasn't like her to drink much either, but it was the day the bombs fell, and in a strange way, she had been celebrating. If the French House went, then everything Isabelle cared about went with it and as soon as the all clear sounded, she had gone there directly to see for herself, almost sobbing with relief when she discovered it intact. And one thing Isabelle didn't give in to easily was tears. But today, almost a full month later, as she rearranges the drapes, passes a duster over the mirror frame one last time, she can't help thinking that the house might as well have been blown to bits, if it were now to be turned over to the Germans to do with as they pleased.

On the landing, the grandfather clock wheezes and grumbles and begins to strike two o'clock, and almost simultaneously there is a rap on the front door. As Isabelle comes out of the salon, she sees Monsieur Corbeille emerge from his office across the hallway.

He throws her a rueful smile. 'We can't fault them for punctuality at least.'

Isabelle smooths down the collar of her blouse and goes downstairs. It is at times like these that she derives some pleasure in being tall; it goes some way to alleviating the rising tide of anxiety she feels as they knock again. Trying to corral her expression into one that is both respectful but firm, she draws back the bolt. There are three of them – a senior officer, who dips his head politely as he greets her, and two younger men, carrying attaché cases. She stands aside to let them pass and doesn't know whether it is a good sign or a bad one when, interspersed with the round of introductions, she hears them exclaim over the beauty of the place to Monsieur Corbeille – the fine detail in the carved mahogany panelling, the novelty of the china plates that tile the length of the hall. A ripple of courteous laughter follows her downstairs as she goes to the kitchen to make tea and Isabelle knows Corbeille is doing his best to charm them.

'We have to work with these people, not against them,' he'd said to her earlier that week when they'd received the letter from Grange Lodge, requesting a meeting 'regarding the future usage of Hauteville House by the Occupying Forces'.

It had never occurred to Isabelle that the French House would be anything other than exempt from the rash of compulsory evictions that were taking place all over the island. The house belonged to France, it was a museum or as good as. They couldn't just take it: it wasn't right. As she skimmed the letter, she had said so.

'I suspect our uninvited guests don't hold dead French novelists in quite the high esteem that we do, Mrs Larch,' Corbeille had said. He nodded towards the alabaster bust on the mantlepiece. 'Poor Monsieur Hugo will be turning in his grave.'

Now, she fills the kettle and lights the range, unwraps the extra ration of tea Corbeille has acquired for the occasion and gets out the teapot. She opens the kitchen window and breathes in the scented mid-summer air. Bees knock against the lavender on the patio; a blackbird lands on the urn above the pond and dips its beak into the dribbling water. The grass is getting long – the gardener had managed to evacuate just before the Germans came, one of the lucky ones. Isabelle had joined the crowds down at the harbour to see off the evacuees, had stood dry-eyed as mothers wept and fussed over their children. She had felt like a cat whose lives were running out because she had reached forty-eight and never travelled further than Jersey, and now she wonders if she ever will.

The sound of German snags on the breeze and she sees the three of them come out onto the patio. There is no sign of Corbeille. The officer gives orders to the two younger men and they set off in different directions, pacing along the paths, stopping every so often to scribble down notes. Isabelle watches as the officer stoops down by one of the rose bushes and picks up a handful of soil, frowning as he examines it. They're going to build here, Isabelle thinks in sudden horror, they're going to rip the house down and build a barracks in its place. The kettle shrieks in sympathy and she fills the teapot, arranges cups on a tray, looks out of the window once more. The men have disappeared into the bottom of the garden. They will be in the outhouse by now, taking an inventory, making another one of their blasted lists. She brings the tray upstairs to Corbeille, who she finds sitting glumly at his desk.

'I'll call you up when they're gone,' he says.

Isabelle returns to the kitchen. She goes to the dresser, which is now a temporary home to her modest book collection, and takes out a jaundiced copy of *The Toilers of the Sea*. She has started it several times, but never reached the end – she prefers Dickens to Hugo any day of the week and would freely have admitted it if anyone had ever shown enough interest to ask. As she hears the Germans come in from the garden, a hopelessness descends upon her. In the time it takes for them to drink their tea, she could be out of a job. There will be no more reading at the end of the day, once the accounts are done, no excuse to be away from home. Her brain will turn to mulch as she washes and irons and darns, buttoning and re-buttoning her lip night after night. There'll be no question of her finding another position: she'd had to fight Ron hard enough for this one.

She hears boots on the stairs overhead, the creak of the floorboards in the hallway. The front door slams.

'Mrs Larch!'

There is an urgency in her employer's voice as if he's just discovered a heap of unpaid invoices or evidence of dry rot. As she hurries up to the office, she is plagued by two familiar trains of thought: that even when you thought the worst had happened, it generally hadn't, and secondly, that there was probably no God.

Corbeille is polishing his glasses by the window. He looks up, his smile brisk and business-like, and ushers her into a chair by the desk. 'No need to look so concerned, Mrs Larch. It's not nearly as calamitous as we first thought.'

He skims a file of detailed notes. 'It's the garden they're interested in,' he says. 'They want it dug up and turned over for vegetable cultivation. Potatoes, marrows and the like. Food for the troops, so to speak. There's . . .' – he glances at a grid of figures – 'approximately a third of an acre of land, which with the right attention should yield so many pounds of produce etcetera.'

'And the house?'

'Stays as it is. Though I think we should expect a few visits of a touristic nature – the Kommandant was quite taken with the place.' Corbeille frowns. 'The De Carteret man has left us, hasn't he?'

Isabelle nods. 'I'll get an advertisement in the *Press* straight away.'

'No slackers, Mrs Larch. We don't want any problems. Squeaky clean is the order of the day. Last thing we need is the whole thing backfiring on us because the gardener knows someone who knows someone who can get a good price on the black market. In fact, I'll give them the once over myself.'

Corbeille unlocks the bottom drawer of the bureau and brings out a bottle of brandy and two glasses. Isabelle tenses. She had taken care to top the brandy up with water, but had she overdone it? How many glasses had she had that night anyway – two, three? Certainly more than she had intended, enough for her to get maudlin.

'Of course,' Corbeille goes on, 'if there's anyone you can recommend personally, do let me know.'

Isabelle looks out of the window onto the empty street. 'I knew a grower once who told me his fingers twitched whenever he went into a greenhouse of tomatoes. It was as if he could sense them ripening in his blood.'

Corbeille chuckles. 'He sounds just the ticket, Mrs Larch.'

Isabelle shakes her head. 'I've no idea what became of him, I'm afraid. It was a long time ago.'

Over the years, she has become an accomplished liar. And yet, perhaps it is only half a lie. She doesn't know what has become of Émile Quenneville, not really. She cannot reconcile the image of the half-drunk man gripping the railings outside Hauteville House on the night of the bombing, with the person who had once traced the thin blue veins at her wrist with his forefinger as she read *The Return of Sherlock Holmes* to him on a bank of shingle on Lihou Island, while her mother believed her to be at church. Nor can he be the same person who took his treasured accordion to a pawnshop so that he could buy her a ring. That man had made her feel free yet anchored at the same time, a state of mind that she hadn't experienced either before or since. Now, he seems to be just another man who drinks away his disappointment, the type of man her mother always said 'won't do at all'. It had hurt when he'd hared off down the road, yet his behaviour was hardly surprising: she has long since forfeited the right to feel anything where Émile is concerned.

Brandy glugs into a tumbler and Isabelle looks up at Corbeille.

'I think we should advertise,' she says. 'It's safer that way.' She holds up her hand as he offers her a glass. 'Not for me.'

'Are you sure?' His brow furrows: Isabelle supposes he interprets it as discomfort on her part. The drink they share at Christmas, when the awkward stumble into conversation that has nothing to do with their work always feels unnatural. She imagines him going home to his French wife, toying with a drink as he relaxes in his leather armchair. *Can't quite work her out, that Mrs Larch.*

'Positive.' Isabelle glances at the clock. If she gets her skates on, she can get the advertisement phoned through to the *Press* by four, and still have some time left to read her library book before she is expected home. 'I'll be downstairs if you need me.'

Isabelle leaves the French House at five sharp but it still takes her longer than the twenty minutes it should to walk home. Some days she feels like a schoolgirl dawdling and the closer she gets, the less she feels like hurrying. Home is a large cottage near Cambridge Park, which she inherited from her uncle, and although Isabelle is used to people telling her how fortunate she is, she doesn't feel it. The reception rooms are north-facing and starved of sunlight for most of the day. She finds the view of the park with its skeletal trees oppressive in winter and in summer the sound of children playing carries through the open windows and if her mood is low, she has to retreat to the attic where they can't be heard.

She opens the gate and walks up the path to the back of the house. She can hear male voices coming from the kitchen and it feels as if she is trespassing on someone else's life: they rarely have visitors. She takes off her hat and walks inside and her first thought is that the Germans sprout up everywhere like weeds and she's had quite enough for one day because here's another one sitting next to Ron at the table. The German gets to his feet straight away and she sees that he's a little shorter than many of them and that his hand, which she has no option but to shake, is tense.

'Leutnant Peter Schreiber,' he says.

Did he have to give them his first name? Her hand goes slack in his and for a moment she doesn't know what to do with herself, then Ron wades in and she is almost grateful.

'Leutnant Schreiber is our new house guest, Isabelle,' he says, slipping an arm around her waist. 'Leutnant, may I introduce the lady of the house!'

And then Isabelle understands and she knows that her husband only shows this much front when, underneath, he is furious. So they are to have a billet after all, and she supposes it shouldn't surprise her. The house is sizeable and close to Town with one unoccupied bedroom if you count the attic, which the requisitioning officer had done as he'd walked around with his clipboard and tape measure. Ron had done his utmost to dissuade him, told him that the roof leaked and the carpet was mouldy; it's unhealthy, he said, just a junk room. They had heard nothing since and Ron had congratulated himself several times on sending the man packing.

The German is talking and this in itself is confusing because his English is almost as good as her own, with barely a trace of an accent.

'I appreciate how inconvenient this must be for you and your husband, Mrs Larch,' he says, 'but I'll do my best to stay out of your way. I'll take most of my meals at the officers' mess.'

He wears gold-rimmed spectacles and his hair is a sandy colour. He is young – made younger perhaps by the cluster of freckles on the bridge of his nose – and Isabelle feels something turn inside her, an ancient grief that flares up every so often, like a fever.

26

'The attic's missing a few home comforts, I'm afraid,' she says cautiously. 'It can get a bit chilly in winter.'

He tells her that he's used to the cold; the winters in Hanover can be brutal.

'Your English is good.'

It slips out and she wishes it hadn't as the compliment seems to make the German uncomfortable, and causes her husband to sigh.

'I studied at Oxford,' Schreiber says, after a moment's hesitation, 'and worked in London for a while.'

How wonderful, Isabelle thinks, to be able to sum up your life in this way when you've barely reached thirty. She smiles at him. 'Then that explains it.'

Ron takes over and they talk practicalities. They will be paid ten shillings a week and extra for fuel. Leutnant Schreiber will move in this Friday. They are to carry on with their lives as they would usually, he assures them, as if he wasn't there. Isabelle avoids her husband's eye and looks out into the garden. The setting sun casts a warm amber hue over the tatty flowerbeds, turns the potato plants golden. They should make more of an effort, she thinks, do some weeding, put a table and set of chairs out there.

The German is leaving now. She notices a smudge of blue ink on his index finger as they shake hands. The back door closes quietly behind him.

Isabelle looks at her husband. It is not nearly as bad as she, at least, had feared; Leutnant Schreiber verges on the charming, but she knows better than to say so. 'He seems pleasant enough,' she says.

'*He seems pleasant,*' Ron says mincingly. His smile drops. 'He's young enough to be your son, girl.'

Sometimes, it is better not to retaliate; other times, Isabelle cannot help herself.

'What do you mean?' She moves away from him and puts on her apron, goes to the sink. There, she focuses on the running tap, the bag of potatoes waiting to be peeled.

'Nothing.' His voice behind her is no more than a shrug, and she breathes again.

'Just don't go thinking this will change anything is all,' he says, then slaps her hard on the backside. She cries out and he laughs, telling her she's skin and bone and anyone would think he didn't put food on the table, and can she get a move on with the tea: he's starving.

3

Letty scrapes a concave nub of orange lipstick across her lips and pinches her cheeks twice for colour. The afternoon sun picks out the silver threads in her fair hair, shaming her. She turns away from the mirror and tells herself not to be ridiculous – he is an old man now and she a middle-aged woman with hands worn red from cleaning and a scuffed gold band digging into the rough skin of her ring finger. She checks her purse – just enough for the bus fare into Town and back. As she leaves, Letty takes care to lock the back door, which they hardly ever do, but the rent is a month overdue and she worries that if the landlord comes, he might take the wireless.

She waits at the bus stop, her head throbbing in the hot sun. Putting on a good show for the Germans, this weather is, while tomatoes rot in the greenhouses because there's nowhere to send them anymore. She's told Émile countless times to get out there and find different work – the Germans were building heaven knows what all over the place, bunkers, tunnels, even a railway. There are ads in the paper all the time for labourers, but every day he comes home, brooding and sullen.

'Not for people like me,' he'd said last night. 'No chance' – and Letty had slammed down the colander of potatoes so hard that the window rattled. Her sisters had warned her not to marry a deaf man and she often wondered if the alternative, which she had so feared at the time, would have been as bad as she'd thought. Not that any of it mattered now. The evening of the bombing, after he and Maud had come back from the harbour and he'd mumbled some rubbish about how she'd rather have seen him dead, she should have guessed that he would go drinking with the remains of that month's housekeeping – it wasn't as if it was the first time. Sometimes, Letty wonders if things would be different if they were a normal family without kinks in their family tree; people say that blood is thicker than water for a reason, don't they? As she gets on the bus, she clings to this notion and thinks about where she is going and why, convincing herself that it doesn't need to be difficult: he has helped her before.

Around her the air sings with gossip about the Germans. Did she know – the woman next to her prods her elbow – that a whole crowd of them had been down on the beach at Port Soif at the weekend? Running about in their swimming trunks as if they owned the place! Is that right? Letty says, thinking that at this exact moment she really couldn't give a flying fig.

She gets off at the terminus and walks up Mansell Street to Trinity Square, looks quickly around her before crossing the road to his office. The bronze plaque on the door glints in the sun. *W. Le Lacheur, Esq. Wine Merchant.* She lifts the knocker and raps firmly on the painted door. Some time passes before it is opened by a woman in a lilac cardigan, hair pinned back into a grey bun, pince-nez dangling round her neck. Her expression upon seeing Letty is a reflection of everything Letty knows herself to be. Shabby. Poor. Trouble. Her insides are flipping like a Big Dipper but she wasn't dragged up on the wrong side of town with seven siblings and a mother who made liberal use of the belt for nothing, and she steps forcefully over the threshold and begins to march up the narrow flight of stairs.

'Juliette Quenneville,' she says, over her shoulder. 'I'm here to see Mr Le Lacheur.'

The woman bristles. 'Do you have an appointment?' She tuts as she elbows past Letty and hurries ahead, pointing to a chair in the dim hallway.

'Wait there,' she says, as if Letty is a dog that requires careful handling, before knocking on the door opposite and disappearing inside. In a few seconds, she is out again.

'You have to leave,' she says. But then, in the few taut beats of silence that follows, the office door swings open and Le Lacheur appears, leaning on his cane. A ruddy face from drinking, small sharp eyes, dark as the underside of a mushroom, dark like Maud's. Letty gets to her feet. He eyes her warily and she can almost hear him weighing up how much of a fuss she might make, before he nods at the secretary and beckons Letty inside.

The room stinks of cigars. A faded map entitled 'The Vineyards of France' hangs on the wall above a fancy mahogany desk, strewn with papers, behind which Le Lacheur settles himself. He lights a cigarette and leans back in his chair, lips twitching slightly beneath his silver-grey moustache, and Letty feels as if she is back in service at the farmhouse again and has been summoned to make a fire or to take away the tea things.

'Oh, do sit down,' he says impatiently, flicking ash into a pewter tray. 'What do you want, Letty?'

On his desk is a photo of his wife. She had died a few years back and Letty hadn't been sorry to hear it. The first

31

whiff of Letty's pregnancy and the woman had sent her packing.

'Those that can't have their own get all bitter inside. You're the lucky one, dearie,' the cook had said, patting her shoulder, although later Letty had overheard her saying that she couldn't understand why a pretty thing like Letty would get herself into trouble with a man with no prospects, who was deaf as a post to boot.

'We're behind on the rent,' Letty says. 'Émile's had no work since the Germans came and the greenhouse got taken over.'

'There's a war on. I can't go giving handouts to every Tom, Dick and Harriet who comes asking.' He chuckles a little.

Letty says nothing. She might be here with a begging bowl but she isn't going to rattle it, not until she really has to.

'What about those girls of yours?' he asks. 'Don't they help?'

Letty thinks of Stella sweeping up hair clippings at the beauty parlour in Berthelot Street, of the private piano lessons Maud used to give but no one wanted anymore because of the war.

'They do,' she says tightly, 'but it's not enough.'

Le Lacheur gets up and walks over to the window. 'I see that your eldest is playing at the concert at Candie Gardens in a couple of weeks? Accordion, isn't it? Can't say it's the instrument I'd rush to save from a sinking ship, but what does an old fuddy-duddy like me know!' He turns to her and smiles. 'Thought I might go along myself.'

Letty looks at him, squares him up. She doesn't want him anywhere near Maud, she doesn't want trouble.

'You leave her be,' she says. 'She's got a father.'

'I didn't say she hadn't.'

'Well, then.'

'Well, then.'

Le Lacheur's cane taps across the floor as he approaches her, his belly quivering. He takes a finger and tilts her chin towards him as if she is still the young girl without the wit she was born with, who had thought that you couldn't get pregnant if you did it standing up.

'You'll need to come back at the end of the day,' he says softly. 'When Miss Guille's gone.'

Letty hesitates. It will be over quickly – she knows that by now – five minutes of wheezing and thrusting, her on her hands and knees, staring at the rough wooden floorboards through the fraying weave of the rug. Afterwards, he will pull up his trousers and braces and take out a couple of notes from the top drawer of the bureau. Sometimes there will be extras – a pair of stockings, a packet of expensive French biscuits he's picked up on one of his trips. And it is so unfair what she has had to resort to when all she ever wanted was a respectable life with an ordinary man, and children who wouldn't shame her; to hold her head up when she goes into the grocer's, rather than have the shop fall quiet as she is told politely but firmly that they cannot allow her any more credit.

Her encounters with Le Lacheur are, mercifully, infrequent enough to have remained undetected by any of the island gossips, yet sometimes Letty wonders what difference it would make. People still talk about her and Émile behind her back, just as they had about her own mother. Her husband has a taste for the drink, they say, and beats her black and blue if she complains (this last fact being outright slander – for all his faults, Émile had never laid a hand on her or the girls); and they let the oldest one run wild, playing that accordion wheresoever she pleases, and Letty thinks they should try stopping her, because God knows she can't.

She stares at Le Lacheur. 'I've got a few errands to run in Town anyway,' she says. 'I can pop back later.'

He smiles approvingly and then taps the side of his nose, just like he used to when they'd finished in the barn and she was rearranging her clothes. It makes her feel ashamed and angry, yet a small part of her is flattered, just as she had been when she was eighteen, and she closes the door with force as she leaves, relishing the look on Miss Guille's face.

Émile stands amongst the other men at the mouth of the quarry and tries to look like someone who isn't deaf. Arms folded, head cocked the right side of respectful as a German, young enough to be his son, stands in front of them and says more than Émile thinks there is to be said about smashing up lumps of rock. He did a stint in the quarry himself before he went to Canada; it's back-breaking work that makes your ears ring into the middle of next week and the dust gets everywhere, but it's work and he can't wait to see the look on Letty's face when he gets home with a day's wages in his pocket. He has promised himself he won't go to the pub afterwards, no matter what. He is trying – God knows he's trying – to make amends for the night of the bombing but Letty's cold shoulder shows no sign of thawing and most days she won't even look him in the eye.

The line of men starts to move and he moves with it. He had kept his mouth firmly shut as he'd queued up this morning and it had paid off: all he'd had to do was show his identity card and his name was added to the list. The men are dividing off now into streams, taking different paths down the quarry and for a moment, Émile flounders: he isn't sure which way to go or why and this hesitation is his downfall, because as he glances over his shoulder, he sees a couple of Germans gesticulating. He pretends not to have noticed and descends decisively into the quarry, but one of them follows, tapping him on the shoulder. He's yet to understand the Germans, unless they're saying '*Nein*' – their lips move differently to the English – and the longer they speak and wait for him to answer, the worse it gets, so he comes clean and tells them that he can't hear.

They shake their heads and indicate that he must leave. Émile protests and tells them that he can do the work, but it makes no difference: the game is up. As he goes, he turns back and sees one of them grin at the other, while making a circling motion at the side of his head. Émile tells himself he should be used to it by now; this assumption that he lost his wits along with his hearing, but the truth is that it crushes him every time.

He gets to his bike and takes yesterday's paper from his back pocket, looks again through the job advertisements. He resists and resists but his eye is still drawn to the one he hasn't circled, the one for which he is infinitely qualified.

Experienced grower required for cultivation of vegetables in large domestic garden. Must be reliable and trustworthy. Interested parties should present themselves on Tuesday morning from 10am at Hauteville House, St Peter Port.

He can't, not if it were the last job on the island. The past is a place best left behind, and there is no point pretending otherwise. On the night of the bombing, when he'd pitched up outside the French House, he had felt like he was prodding a dead thing to see if it was still alive. Then he thinks of Letty and the silence between them that has changed in texture of late. She is not just angry about the housekeeping, there is something else buried there, something secret and unsaid, and he won't be able to winkle it out, not while he's still in the doghouse for being out of work. With a feeling that he has nothing to lose that hasn't been taken from him already, he gets on his bike and starts cycling in the direction of Town.

When he arrives at the French House, Émile props his bike against the wall next to the side entrance. The door is ajar. He knocks lightly and walks through into an alleyway that leads to the garden. There are two men waiting outside the kitchen and he nods and joins them. He can smell the garden – he catches a glimpse of a palm quivering in the breeze, a blast of colour from the flowerbeds. For a split second, Émile actually wants this job and then the back door opens and Isabelle appears. Her hair is wrapped in a mustard-coloured scarf and her mouth is painted orange and opens in surprise when she sees him. She frowns, squeezes out a half-cooked smile and adds his name to the list, before calling in the next man. So, she's not best pleased that he's here; well, apologies for the inconvenience, madam! Émile kicks at the gravel in an attempt to still his nerves.

His turn comes soon enough, too soon. Avoiding his eye, Isabelle points to his boots and he takes them off, as the other men have before him, and goes inside. His big toe protrudes through a hole in his left sock and the feeling that he shouldn't have come is compounded as he follows her into the kitchen and sees a fellow in a shirt and tie with pomade in his hair, sitting with a bunch of papers and a silver pen at the kitchen table. He knows this type – they care about money and their own comfort and not a lot else – but the man is smiling at him and gesturing towards a chair, and doesn't pay a scrap of attention to his worn socks. Isabelle pours them all a glass of water then takes a seat at the table too, and isn't this cosy, Émile thinks, almost amused, until the man starts speaking and he doesn't catch a word.

'He can't hear you,' Isabelle says. 'Mr Quenneville is deaf.'

Three decades of practice have taught Émile to recognise those words. Wishing to God he'd trusted his instincts and never set foot here in the first place, he digs his notebook and pencil stub from his trouser pocket, turns to a fresh page that does not bear witness to his and Letty's last argument about money and work, and sets it on the table.

The man in the jacket smiles again. He picks up the silver pen and writes his name at the top of the page, with Isabelle's alongside it. *M. Corbeille. Mrs Larch.* Isabelle stares at her fingernails, which are ragged and split. Émile doesn't remember this about her, no more than he does her chipped front tooth and the dark circles under her eyes. She looks like someone who hasn't laughed as much as she could have; he supposes the same could be said of him.

Corbeille is pointing towards the garden and drawing a sketch. He divides it into neat sections, labelled 'potatoes', 'marrows', 'beans'.

'It will be hard work,' he says. 'The lawn will need to be dug up, every last inch of it.' Corbeille pauses.

You'll be working for the Germans, he writes. He underlines Germans twice and looks straight at Émile. *Growing food for their troops.*

'How do you feel about that, Mr Quenneville?'

It is not a question Émile is accustomed to being asked. He stares back at the Frenchman. For some unfathomable reason, this Corbeille character seems to want to help him. Émile thinks for a moment.

'Most of 'em don't want this war any more than we do,' he says.

The response seems to please Corbeille, who nods gravely before turning to Isabelle. 'Show Mr Quenneville the garden,' he says.

Isabelle hesitates. She glances towards the window and then back at Émile, but Corbeille is not taking no for an answer and, dammit all, either the man's toying with him or Émile is within a cat's whisker of getting the job. He gets up and follows Isabelle outside.

It is a rich man's garden and no mistake, and briefly Émile forgets his awkwardness, forgets the strangeness of the situation as he takes in the stately palms, the urn trickling water into a small pond, the foxgloves and lavender, hollyhocks and rambling roses. It will be, he knows, alive with the sounds of summer, with the hum of bees, the call of thrushes and larks, blackbirds and seagulls – there was a time he could identify them all.

'He likes you.' Isabelle's lips move slowly, as she nods in the direction of the house. 'He wants someone reliable, someone he can trust.'

Émile looks at her. The woman's as pale as paper. He

38

remembers – or thinks he does – the freckles that used to dust her cheeks like cinnamon during that first long summer together, a few more every day, even with the pains she took to face away from the sun, to pull the brim of her hat low over her forehead. In the beginning, she had been scared of her mother finding out about the two of them, but not scared enough that she wouldn't slip out of church to meet him most Sundays.

'What about you?' he says.

'What?' She turns to him, confused.

'Which fellow do *you* want for the job?'

A low flush spreads across Isabelle's neck, as well it might, Émile thinks, because it'll be a fine day in hell before Isabelle de Garis actually tells him what she really thinks, not just what she supposes he'd like to hear.

Isabelle takes a set of keys from the pocket of her dress and gives him a steady look. 'It makes no difference to me, Émile.'

He catches each of the words as if she were lobbing them into a net, and he has unsettled her now, he sees that in the quick, angry strides with which she walks down the path towards the shed at the bottom of the garden. Following in her wake, ambling a little for why should he hurry, Émile decides that if the Frenchman does give him the job, he will take it, Isabelle or no Isabelle: hasn't he let her off the hook for long enough?

Émile always knew, of course. He knew as the letters became scarcer and scarcer, as autumn froze into winter and Christmas came without so much as a card. He knew long before the accident, before he'd heard his last ragtime riff and played his final tune on the accordion. It was clear that Isabelle had found someone else. Then, as the court case drew to a close, what his lawyer had assured him wasn't his fault turned out to be his fault, after all. An act of 'gross carelessness' on his part, according to the judge, for what kind of fool steps into an unlit elevator shaft? He was saddled with lawyer's fees on top of everything else, and then there was no place for him to go but back home. Émile had still retained a morsel of hope that it might be Isabelle, who would be there at the White Rock waiting for him as the ferry drew in, rather than his mother wearing her best I-told-you-so face. But his life was a far cry from a fairy tale, and of course there was no sign of her.

He had barely had time to set down his things in the cramped back bedroom before his mother told him. *She's married now*, she had scrawled at the top of the Classifieds section of the *Press*. An English fellow, apparently, a few months earlier, around the time of Émile's accident. The weight Émile carried around in his heart told him it was true, as did the taste he acquired for liquor. He would go to the Caves and sit in the corner where he used to play the accordion, and drink until he could barely remember who he was. The rounds he was cut into grew fewer because he seldom had the money to stand his own in return, and the visitors to his mother's cottage were reduced to one man from the Salvation Army, who didn't seem to mind if Émile was unwashed and hungover. He would read out passages from the Bible, enunciating like a demented goldfish words that Émile had no reason to say, like 'loaves' and 'fishes' and 'the garden of Eden'.

As weeks went by, Émile resolved to go and see Isabelle, to confront her. He got as far as finding out where she lived, a place just opposite Cambridge Park on the outskirts of Town, but when he was sober, he lost his nerve and when he was drunk, he was too wretched. Then August came and with it the North Show and Émile found himself there on the day of the Battle of Flowers when the whole island had come out, dressed in their finery, to watch the floats. He'd spent the best part of the afternoon in the beer tent, emerging only when his money had run out and the final procession was taking place, led by a brass band. He stood watching as a replica of the Eiffel Tower made entirely of red, white and blue paper flowers passed by and tried to imagine the bank holiday oom-pah-pah of the trombone, the cheer of the children as the exhibitors tossed penny chews into the crowd.

A group of lads about his age elbowed and joshed each other as two pretty girls in sailor dresses and straw hats walked by. Émile felt invisible as well as deaf and longed suddenly to be lying face down on the stained eiderdown in the back bedroom, where on those long, slow afternoons, he could pretend that life had stopped for everyone else, too.

He was about to leave when he saw them. She hadn't changed, not a bit – she wore a cream dress, cinched in at the waist and was eating a strawberry ice and her right arm was very firmly looped through that of a man in a fawn-coloured suit. A bushy moustache that resembled a ferret's tail bristled above his top lip. Isabelle hadn't seen Émile yet, she continued spooning in mouthfuls of ice cream as if there was nothing that could possibly spoil this perfect summer afternoon. She turned to the man and said something and he smiled and drawing a crisp handkerchief from his pocket, dabbed playfully at her chin. And Émile could bear it no longer. He stepped from the crowd and swerved in front of them, causing Isabelle to stumble, and her husband to scowl.

'Émile.'

The minute she said his name, a light of recognition flickered across the man's face. He took in Émile and indicated that he should move aside. Émile did not move.

'Aren't you going to introduce us?' he said.

Isabelle's ring caught in the sunlight, sparkled and shone. It had a small stone in its centre, not flashy, but for a moment it was all Émile could see. She looked as if she might cry. Her mouth opened and closed again and Émile didn't know what she'd said, but it was enough to get her husband started and he stepped forward and prodded Émile hard in the chest. His eyes narrowed. Émile could smell his stale breath and there was only one way this could end now and Ferret Tail knew it too, for all his airs and graces. A small crowd was gathering. Well, let them watch, Émile thought and he lifted his fist and swung for the man, aiming straight for his ridiculous moustache. But his hand made contact with nothing more than the soft summer air – Ferret Tail had ducked – and Émile staggered and fell.

No one helped him up. The circle of onlookers thinned quickly; there had been nothing to watch after all, just another man who had spent too long in the beer tent, turned sour with drink. As Émile got to his feet, he could just make out the retreating figures of Isabelle and her husband marching with purpose towards the 'Best in Show' tent, and it would have been as if what had happened never did, were it not for the small puddle of strawberry ice cream melting on the ground in front of him.

A couple of days later, Émile had received some post.

Her handwriting on the envelope and something other than words contained within it – the shape was bumpy, irregular. He could not open it, left it on the kitchen table and went down to the greenhouses to work, came home again and was sorry to see it still there. Eventually, once his mother was in bed, he ripped it open and the ring he gave Isabelle plopped softly onto the table, wrapped in mauve tissue paper, the note that accompanied it unapologetically brief.

I'm so sorry.

The following day, before he had time to persuade himself otherwise, Émile had taken the ring to the pawnshop. With the proceeds, he caught the boat to Herm, where he spent the day getting drunk in the Mermaid Tavern, depositing the rest in the tea caddy on Céline's bedroom mantlepiece in Cornet Street that same evening. She was the first woman he'd ever slept with and he felt sick with himself for holding out for Isabelle and then sicker still for paying for it, for taking advantage of someone like Céline with her pockmarked face and threadbare nightdress. This is who you are now, he told himself with a bitter satisfaction as he slunk past the children playing on the doorstep, cap pulled low over his face. He couldn't pretend any longer.

When Émile arrives home, there is no sign of Letty. Maud is laying the table for tea; Stella, peeling carrots at the sink.

'Where's your mother?'

Maud shrugs. Stella launches into a long and mainly incomprehensible stream of possible explanations – Émile catches 'maybe horse bus', 'maybe late', 'I don't know'. He takes the letter, signed by himself and Corbeille, and places it in the centre of the table.

'What's that?' Maud regards it with suspicion.

'A contract.' He feels himself flush. He's more accustomed to a nod and a handshake, and the relief that he has work jostling alongside resentment that he is being underpaid. Not this time. 'I've got a job.'

Stella beams. Maud looks sceptical, but then the door opens and Letty enters the kitchen like a gust of wind: her face is red as if she's been running and tendrils of her hair are falling loose from their pins.

'The horse bus was late,' she says. She takes a packet of biscuits out of her shopping bag and puts them on the counter. They are fancy ones from France with fluted edges – *Galettes de Normandie*, Émile reads on the label – and something stirs in him, a memory so old that it dissolves before he can revisit it.

'Got 'em cheap.' Letty looks pointedly towards Émile, and says something that puts him in a bad light and her in a good one.

Stella points towards the contract. 'Pa's got a job!'

'Where?' Letty's expression verges on the indignant.

'At the French House up Hauteville,' Émile says, trying to inject a shrug into the words. 'Growing veg. Looking after the place a bit.'

Letty's brow furrows. She says something about the Larch woman. 'She cleans there, don't she?'

'Housekeeper,' Émile says.

'Housekeeper!' Letty rolls her eyes. 'Why you?'

'You think I should turn it down?'

Letty pouts and gives an infinitesimal shake of the head. She picks up the contract and makes a show of examining it, but her reading was never up to much, and before long, she pushes it away. She gets up and puts on her apron, sets water on the range to boil, and a kind of peace settles over them all. There is something different about his wife tonight, Émile thinks as he watches her, something different but familiar. As they have tea, Émile asks her where she went that afternoon.

'Work, then Town,' she says and points at the ham with her fork.

Each member of his family betrays themselves in different ways when they are lying. Stella licks her bottom lip. Maud brazens it out, locking eyes for as long as she can without blinking. And Letty – Letty runs the nail of her index finger back and forth across the tip of her thumb, just as she did when they first met, just as she is doing now.

4

Isabelle wipes a duster across the living-room mantlepiece then returns the pair of china spaniels to their usual spot, arranging them so their doleful faces are turned away from her chair by the hearth and towards the window instead. She runs an imaginary sweepstake on how long it will take Ron to notice that evening and to rectify the error, and plumps for half an hour. Her husband has not been entirely himself since the Germans arrived. As they sit in the gloom of the living room after supper, he is distracted, twitching and frowning at each creak of the floorboard from the attic above, although he can't complain, neither of them can: Peter Schreiber is the quietest, most considerate of guests, too bloody quiet in Ron's opinion.

'What does he do up there for hours on end?' Ron will mutter, staring darkly at the ceiling, and Isabelle replies that she doesn't know, he's working, she expects, although she does know because she has been up to Schreiber's room when he is out and the bookshelves in the eaves are full again, just as they were in the early days of her marriage. As she browsed his collection, she had encountered more English novels than German ones – Dickens, Trollope, Austen. A library paperback of *Gone with the Wind* was tossed on the battered leather armchair by the window, in the alcove where she had once placed a crib. She imagines

Schreiber slouched there, smoking perhaps, reading away the hours, just as she had once done.

Isabelle sighs, rubs at the mirror with vinegar on a rag and sees her own reflection, sallow in the sun-starved room, the shame of her chipped front tooth. If she squints, she sees her mother in her, in the slow accretion of silvery grey hair at her crown, the faint creases like speech marks that tug at either side of her mouth. She had been no less forgiving when she saw Émile again at close quarters; he looked like a convict with his patchy stubble and thick neck, ruddy from the sun – impossible not to notice his fingers, too, stained with tomato tar. The voice in her head had been cruel as the three of them sat at the table, but it helped to still the slight tremor in her hands. It was shock at seeing him, where he had no business to be – the French House was her refuge. But Corbeille, being the man he was, had taken to him right from the start.

'He's a decent enough fellow, if a bit rough around the edges,' he had said, taking her to one side afterwards, lowering his voice through courtesy rather than necessity. 'Lord knows it's hard enough for these growers now that the Germans are here, and a man like him won't have many options.'

Isabelle's voice had died in her throat. Sensing her hesitation, Corbeille asked if she had reservations. 'If there's someone else, you'd prefer,' he suggested gently, 'the Batiste man perhaps?'

Slowly, Isabelle had shaken her head. No, she told her employer, she was sure that they had a safe pair of hands in Mr Quenneville. The matter was decided and he should start on Monday next; she would get the paperwork in order right away. Émile had flushed with surprise when Corbeille handed him the envelope containing the terms and conditions, his gaze flickering to Isabelle, but she didn't want his gratitude, didn't want him thinking she'd somehow played a part in it. She looked away as he thanked them, feeling suddenly out of her depth.

She hears footsteps on the path outside, sees the now familiar grey serge uniform pass the window. Isabelle puts down the duster and heads into the kitchen. She has noticed that their billet is more likely to stop and talk for a few minutes if it's just her at home; he is uneasy around Ron, awkward. She positions herself at the sink and takes up the potato peeler.

The back door opens. Schreiber is carrying a sheaf of papers and he whips off his hat as if it's scalding him, schoolboyish in his haste. The name he gave that she cannot call him seems to crowd the room, like strong scent. Peter, Peter, Peter. Isabelle tells herself not to be foolish. It is just a name – and a common one; it is a meaningless coincidence, nothing more.

Schreiber hovers, good manners preventing him from rushing straight to his room, Isabelle assumes. She turns towards him, recalling the photo of his mother on his bedside table, a smiling dark-haired woman in a summer dress, decorated with giant peonies.

'So hot today,' he says.

'Not a breath of wind. Water?' She pours him a glass and sets it on the table.

'Thank you.' His cheeks redden as he drinks, there is a smear on the right lens of his spectacles. Isabelle has a sudden picture of Leutnant Schreiber as he might have been aged ten, small for his age, in short trousers with scabs on his knees, hands disappearing into blazer sleeves that had been bought big for him to grow into.

He enquires after her day at Hauteville House and she cannot tell him the truth: how much it distresses her to see the gardens dug up and turned to dirt, how fearful she is still, as she prepares an inventory of the objects in each room, that the Germans will go back on their word, that the house will be requisitioned.

'There are adjustments to be made,' she says. 'Inevitably.'

'Indeed,' he says, and then he asks if it's true that Hugo brought his mistress with him from France along with his wife. Isabelle laughs and said it certainly was, she lived across the street, although she wasn't allowed in the house itself, and before long the conversation is flowing as though he is just another visitor to the French House on his holidays, whom she is entertaining with stories.

'I'd love to see it one day,' he says. 'If it might be arranged?'

Some would say she is overstepping the mark, she supposes, but she can't see the harm in it and says as much.

Schreiber glances at the clock and says he should be going; he has some work to do before the dance later.

'You're going?' Isabelle tosses a piece of potato peeling into the colander. The dance was at Candie Gardens and everyone she'd bumped into in Town this past week had spoken of little else.

'In a professional capacity.' Schreiber opens his attaché case and rummages inside, then lays the programme of events on the table. 'It may be the last one for a while, or so I heard.'

Isabelle glances at the programme, skimming the musicians. *Ursula Le Poidevin, chanteuse. Bertie Baudains and his Big Time Band.* It is pointless, of course, there is more chance of Hitler waking up one morning and declaring a truce than there is of her and Ron stepping out together at an Occupation dance. Then she is drawn to a name, right at the end, before the stern warning in red that there were to be strictly no encores, that the dance must finish at eleven.

Miss Maud Quenneville, accordionist.

His daughter, it must be. The only Quennevilles on the island, isn't that what he'd told her the very first time they met on the slipway at Pembroke on a windy Sunday afternoon, as together they picked up broken fragments of crockery from the tea tray she had just dropped? He had been playing for loose change on the slipway, trousers rolled, feet bare, his cheeks whipped pink by the wind, the Parisian waltz sweeping brazenly across the sands, not giving a tinker's damn about the day of rest. Neither had Isabelle, not that day, free to do as she pleased for a few blissful hours, her legs sand-speckled in a cream bathing dress while her mother unknowing, languished in bed with pleurisy. Émile had been nervous, jabbering a little as he emptied the coins from his cap, saying he played for the fun of it, not for the money, and could he invite her for a fresh pot at the kiosk?

Schreiber is saying something but his voice is little more than a murmur, a breeze in her ear. She had said yes to Émile that afternoon, and then she had kept saying yes after that, because there was nothing she had wanted more than to take the arm of this man who played the accordion with such spirit, to be as free as he seemed to be.

'We must enjoy ourselves while we can, don't you think?' Schreiber is looking at her quizzically before he delves once again into his case and passes her an envelope containing that week's rent.

As she thanks him, she hears the creak of the gate, glances at the clock and realises she is late with the tea. As if on cue, the German gets up and wishes her a pleasant evening, disappearing into the hall just as Ron arrives.

'Everything all right?' Ron hands his jacket to Isabelle, frowning in the direction of the hallway, as if troubled by a bad smell.

Isabelle nods towards the bulging envelope. 'Quite all right.'

Her husband settles himself at the table and counts out the coins, then picks up the programme.

'What's this?'

'There's a dance on at Candie tonight. They've extended the curfew.'

He snorts. 'That's good of them. Letting us come and go as we please on our own island.'

Isabelle lowers potatoes into the boiling water. Mashed tonight, she decides. She wants to pummel something and the potatoes will have to do.

'It'll be full of youngsters, I expect,' she says carefully. A display of reluctance may give her a better chance; her husband is a contrary man. It has worked before.

'Old before your time, you are!' He whistles tunelessly between his teeth. 'Reckon we should show the Jerries we've still got some spirit left.'

'You want to go?' She sighs. 'Oh Ron, I've got nothing to wear.'

'You've got a wardrobe full of clothes, woman!' He is jocular now; the decision is made. 'We'll have our tea and then we'll go. It's only up the road.'

'If you like,' she says, working to keep her voice even. A tiny triumph. And now if she is to satisfy this niggling curiosity she has about Émile's daughter, she must ensure that they stay until the end.

'I'll ask you to dance if you're lucky,' Ron says, and Isabelle turns her back before she has a chance to witness the wink she suspects is coming. She cannot bear it when he pretends to play nice.

Maud stands on the fringes of the dancefloor and searches for her sister in the kaleidoscope of white shirts, shiny foreheads and dresses saved for best that circles and turns in front of her. Stella had convinced her to spend most of the afternoon practising in the kitchen when she knew she should have been rehearsing for tonight, but there were only so many times you could play 'Au bord de l'eau' without going stale, and some of her best performances had been those that were spontaneous, unexpected: the encore at the end of a set. Nonetheless, half the island is here tonight, not to mention a fair smattering of Germans, and nerves have started to seed in the pit of her stomach.

She takes out the programme and studies it one more time. The small thrill of seeing her name there, asserting itself in neat cursive script, when – and this is not melodrama, she reminds herself, this is fact – when two months ago, she had almost died. She had almost died, face down in tomato pulp, under the oily chassis of her father's truck, and as the ground shuddered beneath her, she had prayed and really meant it, offering up everything that mattered. The new accordion strap she hoped to receive for her birthday. Damn the strap, the accordion itself. And then, when the bombing showed no signs of stopping, she had traded in her plans. She would stay at Amherst Infants teaching tone deaf children to sing and rattle tambourines, and it would be enough. There would be no saving to go to Europe to study music, to live a different life. She would accept what she had, she'd stop needling Pa to get his attention and resist talking back to her mother. For once, she would try, really try to fit in.

Maud looks down at her accordion case, at her father's initials inscribed in gold in the bottom corner. She would kill for a new one, for one of her own. She is a bad person, she tells herself. The bargain with God had been summarily dismissed, almost as soon as she was safely back at home and Pa had gone out drinking that week's rent money. He had not come back all night, and she had woken next morning more determined than ever to escape.

'What's the old squeezebox got for us tonight, then, Maud?'

Maud turns. It is Ozzy Ozanne, a fisherman from L'Ancresse with a knack for sourcing produce that no one else can: mackerel in May; mussels that are still plump and full of flavour in early summer. He glances around and draws her in closer.

'What is it?' Maud isn't in the mood for Ozzy. She wouldn't put it past him to whip out a soggy package of plaice from his back pocket and start to haggle.

'You and your folks fancy a bit extra, you know where to come.' He lowers his voice. 'Jerries have their eyes in their pockets, far as I can gather. I've got brill, conger – tons of conger. Competitive prices for previous customers.'

Ozzy has a lot of strut for a fisherman. Maud rolls her eyes and lowers her voice in turn. 'Don't look now, Ozzy – I said *don't* – but there's a German at the back of the hall who's looking very interested in what you might be telling me.'

'You're having me on.' Ozzy starts to turn, then thinks better of it.

'I'm not,' Maud says and she isn't, because the short German leutnant in spectacles, who she takes to be the censor, is still staring when she glances back – and is it any wonder, Maud thinks, with Ozzy swaggering around from person to person. He may as well set up a stall!

'Which one is it?'

'Schreiber. The censor. He could stop all of this in a heartbeat and I'm on in ten minutes, so if you wouldn't mind—'

'You two look very serious!'

It is Stella, flushed and breathless, her hair frizzing loose from its grips as she pivots free from her dance partner.

'All right, Stella?' Ozzy winks. 'You owe me a dance later.'

And with a nod to Maud, he disappears into the crowd.

As Bertie Baudains raises his baton for the last time, Maud picks up the accordion and walks with Stella to the side of the stage.

'You nervous?' her sister asks.

'A bit.'

'Hug for good luck?'

'If you have to.'

Stella giggles and hugs her hard, and as Maud breathes in her sister's familiar smell of talcum powder and lily of the valley scent, she marvels at how two people, drawn from the same gene pool, can be so utterly different. Maud rarely embraces anyone unless she has to; in that way at least, she and Pa are similar.

'Break a leg, Mo!' Stella grins and twirls in the direction of the dancefloor, as if drawn by an invisible thread.

As Maud waits for the band to finish, she runs through the polka in her head, visualises the crochets and quavers on the staff. She had taught herself or as good as, ever since she came upon the accordion at Old Mum's house, tucked away in the back of the wardrobe, a secret waiting to be discovered.

'Need a bit of Dutch courage?'

'Pardon?'

Maud turns. A man has crept up on her – an old one with alert brown eyes, a thatch of bushy white hair and a silver plated walking stick, which he rests against the stage as he takes a hip flask from his jacket pocket and offers it to her.

'Cognac,' he says.

'I don't usually . . .'

'Go on.'

He is about to withdraw the flask when Maud thinks to hell with it and, grasping the bottle, swigs more than she intended. It scalds her throat; she splutters and feels like an idiot when he chuckles.

'Martell's finest. Picked it up last fortnight in France.'

He must think she was born yesterday. Maud looks at him sceptically. 'The borders are shut.'

'Not if you have a special pass from the Controlling Committee,' he says. 'Folks will always want liquor and the Jerries drink like there's no tomorrow. Business isn't what it used to be, but I can't complain.'

The man fishes a card from his pocket. 'Jean Le Lacheur,' he says, handing her the card. 'And you must be Maud.'

'Yes.'

Maud stares at him. If Stella were still here, she'd be burying her face in her hanky to keep herself from laughing. *Jean Le Lacheur*, she would intone later, prancing around the bedroom. *One hundred years old and at your service, young lady!*

She studies his card. *Jean Le Lacheur, Esquire. Purveyor of Fine Wines and Spirits.* An address in Trinity Square in Town.

'Do I know you from somewhere?' As she speaks, she becomes aware that the band has stopped. Musicians jostle past her as they leave the stage. She takes out her accordion and fastens the strap around her neck.

Le Lacheur doesn't answer. Instead, he nods towards the fraying leather strap. 'Do let me know if I can be of assistance at any time.' He leans in, conspiratorial, his moustache quivering like a small animal. 'Times like these we have to stick together.'

He walks away as her name is announced and this jolts Maud back to where she is. She slips his card into her pocket and walks up the steps to the stage. There is applause and the sea of faces in front of her become foggy, indistinct, as if they are underwater. She sits, settles the accordion against her and with the familiar weight of it comes reassurance, and Maud finds herself again. Fingers on the bass, she draws out the bellows, and plays.

His daughter has inherited his talent, that much is clear, although she bears none of Émile's physical traits. She is taller, darker, slighter, more serious too but she plays the accordion as if it is her second voice, just as he did, and Isabelle wonders if she is the only person to find such deep melancholy in this spritely French ballad about walking by the riverside with a new love.

'Care to dance?'

No, she doesn't, and her husband is no dancer, but Ron is not to be dissuaded and she finds herself in the clammy centre of the rotating circle of couples, held hostage in his arms, a tight smile welded to her face.

Maud's accordion is ox-blood red, just as Émile's was, and soon they are at the edge of the stage. When she looks up, Isabelle can see the scuffed toe of the girl's right shoe, tapping out the rhythm, the case itself embossed with two gold initials, 'E Q'. Isabelle falters, loses her step for a second.

'So you can never pawn it again,' she had told Émile, remembering the knot of panic as she scoured the window of the pawnshop and her relief at still finding it there, the strange, hungry look the man behind the counter had given her as she had taken out her leather purse to pay. Then the trip to the jeweller's, where she had paid them to engrave Émile's initials while she waited.

'What's wrong?' Ron is watching her.

'Nothing.' She searches for a distraction, her eyes landing on Schreiber as they gravitate towards the back of the hall. 'He must be sweltering in that uniform! Haven't seen him have so much as a glass of water all night.'

Ron's hand tightens across her back. 'Don't think I haven't noticed,' he says.

'What?' Isabelle frowns.

'Ever since he moved in. Fussing around him.' Ron gives her a small smile. 'It's a bit late to start getting maternal, Izzy!'

She is silent for a moment. Her head starts to throb like a second pulse and she suddenly feels unbearably hot.

'Some women just aren't meant to be mothers.' He moves closer, his breath webbing her neck. 'There's no shame in it.'

Isabelle wrestles herself from his grip, gives him a little shove. He stumbles, flails into the couple behind him – there are cries of 'Watch out!' – and people turn to look. For a brief moment, the flow of the accordion slows, and she sees

Émile's daughter staring at her. Head down, Isabelle makes a path for the exit.

The night air is cool, forgiving. Isabelle leans against a tree, takes a cigarette from her handbag and lights up. Beyond the jumble of rooftops, she can just make out the dark chasm of the sea, the silvery crests of the waves. She fantasises about running through the moonlit streets until she reaches a place where he cannot find her, where she can fall asleep to the sound of surf and gulls and the rhythm of her own breathing. It is far from the first time she has thought of it; at times the force of her desire to escape is overwhelming. But she is ashamed. She cannot speak the truth about her marriage to anyone – whenever she has tried, the words shrivel and die on her tongue. And in any event, she has nowhere to go.

Inside, the accordion emits one final flourish and stops. Applause, one solitary whoop for an encore, quickly silenced. People begin to spill through the doors in a breezy cloud of chatter and laughter. And Isabelle finishes her cigarette and waits for her husband, because what else is left for her now, what else can she do?

5

There's a German coming to the French House, and Isabelle appears to have dressed up in her Sunday best for the occasion. At least, Émile hasn't seen the blue dress she's wearing before, and is that a dab of rouge on her cheeks or is she just flushed? Something's ruffled her, that's for certain. She's talking too quickly, the way folks do when they're excited or nervous; he suspects the former in this instance. It's uncommon enough for her to come and see him when he's working anyway – they avoid each other on the whole. Now she is scribbling on a scrap of paper, holding it out to him. With force, he tips a barrow load of *vraic* onto the damp earth, and the odour of dried fish, baked in the sun, and the salty tang of the sea envelops them. Isabelle's face contorts at the smell, and then, and only then, does he reach over to take the note from her.

Leutnant Schreiber, he reads. *The censor. Wants to visit the house. Might want to see the work in the garden afterwards.*

Émile picks up the rake. He can't honestly see what it has to do with him, if Isabelle wants to play tour guide to the enemy for an afternoon.

'It's a free country.' He starts to spread the seaweed across the soil and the smell intensifies. 'For some people anyway.'

Isabelle hesitates then mouths a thank you, which Émile knows he's done little to deserve. With a twinge of guilt, he watches her make her way back towards the house. It wouldn't have killed him to have held off on the tipping and spreading until she'd gone, he tells himself. The smell hit you hard if you weren't accustomed to it.

Later that day, when he is up a ladder wrestling for fruit amongst the branches of the apple tree and batting away the wasps, he catches sight of them. The German is standing next to Isabelle on the sun terrace on the middle floor of the house, pointing a camera at the view as if he's on his holidays and having a fine time of it. And Isabelle is leaning against the rail, shielding her eyes from the sun as she gestures towards Castle Cornet, Herm, Jethou, her navy dress billowing in the breeze. There's something girlish about her mannerisms as she finds amusement in whatever the German has said and turns and laughs. At that moment, Émile's desire to hear, to catch even snippets of their conversation, is fierce.

He takes Isabelle's note from earlier from the pocket of his overalls and studies it with renewed interest. *Leutnant Schreiber. Censor.* He squints at the man. So he's the fellow who spends all day deciding what people can and can't read, no matter whether it's true or not, when they sit down with the *Press* after tea of an evening. He remembers now some fuss before the concert at Candie Gardens a couple of weeks ago, a popular ragtime song that Stella had been mad about, struck out of the programme, he supposes by order of that man a few feet away who is now following Isabelle into the glass lookout.

Émile descends from the ladder and starts picking up windfalls. It is better when she keeps out the way, he decides; better for both of them. He doesn't like who he becomes when Isabelle is around. He is all shrugs and monosyllables, offhand at best and rude at worst (he still hasn't forgiven himself for the seaweed), and now it would seem he is resentful or envious or even jealous, judging by his childish impulse to chuck rotten apples at the censor as if he were a coconut shy and knock that ridiculous hat off. No, he has nothing in common with these office types who spend all day cooped up inside, throttled in a shirt and tie, and there was a time when Émile had thought Isabelle felt the same, until she'd married a bank clerk of all people.

He picks up the basket and sees Isabelle heading towards him, the German ambling a few paces behind. Let me deal with him, Émile imagines her telling Schreiber; Mr Quenneville can be difficult. He braces himself as if for a punch as she approaches and Isabelle's demeanour changes, the pleasant smile sliding from her face, her shoulders tensing. And there it comes, that feeling again.

'Leutnant Schreiber would like to inspect the grounds now.' Isabelle looks towards the pocket containing his notebook and makes a scribbling motion. 'I've told him about the notebook.'

The German steps forward and offers Émile his hand. Close up, he's a pale, speccy fellow, not as tall as some of them and not as full of himself either: his handshake borders on apologetic.

'Can you hear anything at all, Mr Quenneville?' he asks and Émile shakes his head, feeling exposed suddenly with Isabelle standing there. He remembers that this is the chap who is billeted with her, and he wonders what has been said privately between them.

'Took a blow to the head,' Émile says. 'A long time ago now.'

The German grimaces in sympathy, but Émile shrugs. It's not what he'd have wished for, he says, but you just have to get on with things; no point in spending a lifetime snivelling about what might have been. And this seems to be the cue for Isabelle to walk back to the house, and for Schreiber to take out his file and pen.

'Let's get started, shall we?' he says and Émile brushes the dirt from his hands, looks dubiously at the shine on Schreiber's boots, then does as he is told. Together, they walk up and down the length of the ruined garden, the brackish smell of seaweed causing Schreiber to get out his handkerchief. Émile points out the rosebeds sacrificed for marrows, pumpkins and swedes; the dried-up water fountain now presiding over the large area allocated for potatoes. He shows him the bucket of eggshells he scavenges from the rubbish to keep away the slugs, and then the small greenhouse, which he'll use for planting carrots and radishes in the winter if it's mild enough, as there'll likely be no fuel for heating.

Schreiber listens and nods and scribbles in his file, but for someone who's doing an inspection, it strikes Émile that he's short on questions and when he glances at the fellow's notepad, he sees not figures and notes, but a series of doodles at the bottom of the page: a long ribbon of seaweed wrapped around a shoal of fish, a man with a bushy beard, standing on a rock. Fine for those who don't have work to do, Émile thinks, and as they come to the enclosure at the foot of the garden, he nods with as much respect as he can muster and says he'd better get on. But the German pays little attention.

'What's through there?' He indicates the wooden door.

Just the shed, Émile tells him; it's where he keeps the wheelbarrow and the like.

'Do you have time for a smoke?' Schreiber takes a packet of cigarettes from his inside pocket.

Émile looks up towards the house. It's a rare thing these days that a man gets offered a smoke, even if there's a German attached to the other end of it. Isabelle can hardly come down on him for obeying orders. He shrugs and opens the door.

The enclosure is a shabby patch of land flanked by a high stone wall, with the shed at one end and a wood pile at the other; and Émile can't see that there's too much to get excited about. Schreiber, however, appears intent on exploring, walking from one end to the other, running his hand absently along the rungs of the ladder Émile has hung on brackets to stop it getting rusty, peering into the burlap sacks of leftover seaweed. Eventually, he sits on the edge of the upturned wheelbarrow and faces the sun.

Nice spot! he writes on his notepad above the doodles and Émile supposes there's something in that: it is where he starts and ends his day, eking out his tobacco ration, on the step of the shed.

'It's peaceful at any rate,' Émile says, and they smoke in silence, watching a robin wrestle with a worm on the compost heap.

They are on their second cigarette before Schreiber speaks again. 'Your daughter plays the accordion, I believe?'

He writes it down and passes the pad to Émile. *Pleasure to hear her. Candie Gardens. Accomplished!*

He'll pass that on, Émile says, thank you. Then his eyes are drawn again to the sketch of the man with the beard, and now the features fall into place and he thinks of the statue in Candie Gardens, the sepia photo on the mantlepiece in the kitchen where he had his interview with Corbeille.

'Victor Hugo.' He grins. 'Knew I recognised the fellow

from somewhere.' It seems to him that Schreiber laughs. 'Draw a lot, do you?'

'A bit,' Schreiber says. 'When I can.'

Émile draws deeply on the cigarette and leans back against the shed, his eyes lingering on the aggressive-looking eagle on the breast of Schreiber's tunic. They were an odd lot, the Germans, with their brass bands and their funny salutes. He couldn't imagine this one in front of him marching and Heil Hitlering, but he supposes he does.

'You like it here all right?' he asks. 'On Guernsey?'

Schreiber shakes his head apologetically. 'Too small. I prefer cities.'

Well, Émile can understand that. There's a comfort in not having everyone know your business. Some folk said cities were lonely, but in Émile's experience, it didn't matter whether you were on an island the size of a postage stamp or in the middle of a city, where no one knew you from Adam – life could be lonely.

'But I am lucky,' Schreiber goes on, placing a hand on his heart. 'To be here.' He starts to talk about Isabelle, how she's made him feel welcome or some such and Émile's concentration lapses. He thinks of the crack in the basement window that needs boarding up, the weeds to be hoed. But the German is starting to scribble again and there is no escape from words on the page.

Old friends? You and Mrs Larch.

Émile grinds out his cigarette under the heel of his boot. 'I wouldn't say we were friends.'

Schreiber looks startled and Émile wonders what else Isabelle has told him. That she ignored his letters and married someone 'more suitable'? That she had treated their love as if it were no more than a story in one of her library books, to be returned and forgotten when she tired of it.

Émile picks up the watering can and looks expectantly at Schreiber. But the German is not taking the hint, and now he seems to be asking Émile's permission to stay here a little longer, as if it is Émile who gets to say what's what, as if he's the one in the grey tunic with the bird of prey on his chest. The man can suit himself, Émile thinks, and takes his leave. But as he heads back into the garden, he finds himself shaking his head at the sheer curiousness of it: the German sitting on the wheelbarrow in the enclosure, with his notebook of doodles.

The afternoon passes and when Émile returns to the enclosure at the end of the day, Schreiber has gone. He goes into the shed and tidies away his tools, stores the crate of apples under the bench. He is about to lock up when something catches his eye, a piece of paper sagging over the seed trays. Émile reaches for it, holds it up to the light. It is a drawing of Maud – Maud and the accordion – and there can be no mistaking her, for although the sketch is rough, the German has captured her perfectly, the jut of her chin, which echoes neither his nor Letty's, the dark cloud of hair that never quite lays flat, the taut curve of her right arm as she draws out the bellows. His initials lie at the foot of the page, 'P.S.', and Émile stares at them and then at the two cigarettes that lie side by side next to the seed tray. He pockets them hastily before he thinks of reasons why he shouldn't.

He sits on the bench in the gloom, watching slits of dying sunlight pattern the dusty floor. What does the fellow mean by it? Is it a gift or a transaction? He studies the drawing again, half-considers taking it home to Maud, then thinks better of it, imagining the volley of questions from Letty:

Where did he get it from?

A German? A German!

Why? What business did a German have drawing Maud? What did he want with her?

And then a row would follow about the accordion, and how it was going to end up getting her in trouble one of these days. Letty would shout and Maud would scowl and say she'd never wanted the stupid drawing in the first place, and it would be tossed onto the fire, swallowed up in a lick of orange flame.

With care, Émile sets the drawing back against the wall of the shed and locks up. As he walks towards the house, he sees Isabelle through the kitchen window, hunched over a book. She's never in much of a hurry to get home, he thinks, and the light has gone from the kitchen by this time. Then the shadow of a thought, disquieting, uneasy, flits past him and Émile calls himself a fool and shakes his head to be rid of it. At that moment, Isabelle looks up and stares right back at him: her mouth parted, hand to her breastbone and, realising he has startled her, Émile ducks his head, embarrassed, and strides past.

6

When Émile arrives home, he steps into what the hairs on the back of his neck tell him has been a humdinger of a row, with Maud and Letty at its centre. It will be about the accordion most likely, he suspects, and Maud wanting to play it out somewhere and Letty getting into one of her rages and forbidding it. But no one speaks as he crosses the kitchen to scrub his hands at the sink, whereas normally they all just carry on, and Letty eyes him warily and mutters something to Maud, who slumps back in her chair with a weary expression.

'What's going on?' Émile looks from Maud to Letty, and then to Stella who is chewing her thumbnail thoughtfully.

Letty slams a pot of broth onto the table and begins to dish up. 'She's not to play that blasted accordion. Making a show of herself all over the island. You tell her!'

She glares at Émile and he frowns because 'making a show of herself' and 'blasted accordion' are not unfamiliar phrases to be found on his wife's lips, but she is more agitated than he has seen her in a long time and he wonders what Maud has done.

Jealous, Maud says to her mother, *you're*-something-*and-you're*-something-*and-you're-jealous* and with an air of provocation, she takes out a small card from her skirt pocket and studies it.

The table tilts and rocks as Letty springs to her feet. She leans towards Maud and tries to snatch the card but Maud backs up against the wall and holds it out of reach. Émile feels the air around him sing with rage as Letty barges towards her, and there is poor Stella telling them to *Stop, Stop!* and suddenly Émile has had enough. He gets to his feet and wrestles the card from Maud's grip, determined to get to the bottom of this now so that they can all have some peace.

He sits back down. As he reads the card's inscription, a buzzing starts up in his ears. He turns to Maud.

'Where did you get this?'

'At Candie Gardens. At the concert last month. He enjoyed the music, that's all!'

Her indignation at further questioning reassures Émile: Maud, at least, has nothing to hide. He looks at his wife. She is eating her soup in quick, sloppy mouthfuls; she cannot meet his eye. Émile crumples up the card and tosses it in with the rubbish.

'Be careful who you talk to,' he tells Maud. 'Your mother's right.'

Maud looks at him as if he's the biggest killjoy of all time, but mercifully says nothing. Letty starts to clear away the dishes and tells Stella to make tea. Émile picks up that day's copy of the *Press* and tries to concentrate on the headline story but the words will not stick, and all he can see is that wretched card, and that wretched man sniffing around Maud when he had no business with her or any of them.

Stella nudges his elbow. She is offering him a biscuit to go with his tea, one of the French ones Letty said she got for cheap a while back. He'd rather leave the treats for the girls, but he still feels as hungry as he did when he sat down to supper so he splits it with Stella and takes a bite. It's buttery with just the right amount of sweetness, good quality, not the broken fragments you get in Warry's that are fair set to break your teeth. He pops the rest in his mouth and suddenly the years unspool and it comes to him.

He is a young man in his late twenties, almost a decade deaf, delivering the weekly groceries to a farmhouse up in Torteval. Émile does the packing and the lifting and the sweating and the driver gets to sit on his backside and flirt with the maids – or the cook in this instance, who has taken a shine to him. The three of them are having a brew in the kitchen and eating the fancy French biscuits the master of the house, one Jean Le Lacheur, had brought back from Normandy.

Through the passageway Émile can see Letty – although he doesn't know her name yet – washing dishes in the scullery. She is standing in a shaft of sunlight and has a distracted expression on her pretty, rosy face, and he is mesmerised by the rise and fall of her bodice, which is tight and trimmed with white lace. With each mouthful Émile longs a little more for the housemaid, her smooth plump arms, the damp tendrils of blond hair that dress her neck, until the driver nudges him and Émile sees that both he and the cook are laughing at him. Letty turns then and stare, her mouth an oval of surprise, and Émile can't get out fast enough.

Émile wipes the crumbs from his mouth, sets down the *Press*. Letty and his two daughters have all turned towards the wireless, their faces set in mute concentration. The room is still. He considers asking his wife where she got the biscuits from, then decides to wait. Not in front of the girls.

Émile leaves the table and although it's still a little early, he starts to prepare the house for blackout.

He goes to bed before Letty that night and lies there in the guttering candlelight, waiting, the card beside him on the bedside table. Words on it that Letty can't even read, much less understand – *Purveyor of Fine Wines and Spirits* – but Maud would understand them, Maud would be intrigued, and dammit, he hadn't gone through everything he had for Mr Jean Le Lacheur, Esquire to turn up now and start interfering. He thinks about what he could have said out there in the kitchen.

'The trouble with your ma, girls, is that she's always had a struggle keeping her legs together.'

'The trouble with your ma is that she gets her head turned easy.'

'The trouble with your ma . . .'

The trouble with Letty is that she is Letty.

The bedroom door opens with a burst and the flame falters, borders on extinction, survives. She doesn't look at him as she strips – blouse, skirt, stockings, brassiere, fall to the floor in a pile. Naked, she yanks the pins from her hair, then reaches under the pillow for her nightdress. Émile can smell her now, a dense, briny scent like the beach at low tide, stronger than usual, more potent.

'Wha'?' She frowns at him, pulls her nightdress over her head.

Émile picks up Le Lacheur's card and tosses it at her. 'Surprised he can still get it up,' he says. 'Surprised he's still going at all, if it comes to it.'

That moment when people know they've been found out. Almost a kind of power in it. Like cleaning up in a

game of poker – and only those with money to lose will
risk playing with Émile; they say he's got second sight,
when all it is is thirty years of watching people, not hearing
them, seeing into their hearts. There is no poker face that
he can't see through and his wife has never been one for
card games.

'You're disgusting!' She turns away and starts folding her
clothes, hanging her blouse in the wardrobe rather than
leaving it on the back of the chair as she usually does.

'It's true, isn't it?' Émile pauses. 'What people are saying.'

He knows Letty's weak spots as well as he knows the
contours and lines that map her body. Alarm flits across her
face.

'What people?'

'Folk talk when there's something up.' Émile picks up the
card again. 'I hope he gave you more than a packet of
biscuits for your trouble.'

Letty lunges at him, clawing like an animal and he has to
hold her wrists to keep her off. She writhes in his grip and
he gestures towards the girls' bedroom and tells her to keep
it down. So he was right, he was right and he feels filled up
with the misery of it and he lets Letty go. Wiping her eyes,
she reaches for his notebook.

i did what i had to

Like the first time, was it, he says, and the time after that
and the time after, when you did what you *had* to!

His hand is shaking as he points at her. His body is not
his own anymore, his blood surges as if whipped by the
wind. Letty backs away.

'How often?' he demands. 'How many times?'

Letty shrugs, mumbles. Three, she says, just three.

Double it, triple it. His wife is not to be trusted.

'Not good enough for you, am I?' Émile says. 'Good enough when it suited you, when you needed me. Good enough then.'

He wrenches it out, this long-buried truth, and it lies between them, like a twitching half-dead animal that neither want to touch. The pounding in his head lessens as he watches Letty struggle to respond. Placate or attack? She pauses, then seizes the notebook.

you never wanted her, she writes, scoring out the words with force. *you tried to get rid of her.*

She underlines this last sentence twice and Émile has to walk away. He cannot bring himself to look at her and he understands suddenly how it might happen, that first crack of a palm against a cheek.

'I wanted to help you, woman!' He wants to bellow it out, to make the house shake. He repeats it and silence echoes back at him, and Letty starts to cry.

The bedroom door opens and Maud appears. Long, pale legs disappearing into a lemon-yellow nightdress, dishevelled hair, thick as gorse; a sharpness to her features, which are neither his nor Letty's.

'Go to bed,' he barks, and Letty gives a quick nod.

Maud doesn't move. 'What's going on?' she says. She picks up Le Lacheur's card, and this time, neither of them stop her.

'It's about him,' she says, 'isn't it?'

She looks from Émile to Letty and back again. For a moment, Émile's mother is there standing next to him; he can smell the sour milk of her breath, see the knowing curl of her bottom lip, the silver scythe-shaped scar on her temple. *Did you really think she'd never find out? Smart girl like her, and no question where she's got her brains from, that's for certain.*

'No.' The best he can do is to pretend it never happened, it is a game that he and Letty are so used to playing that at times he almost believes it. 'Go to bed now.'

In his head, his voice is soft, soothing, the voice of a father. But Maud doesn't like to be taken for a fool any more than he does and as she leaves, she gives them a look as if to say this is the start of the matter, not the end. Letty snuffs out the candle and climbs under the covers and when Émile joins her, he feels the bed tremble with the rhythm of her sobs, and he is not far short of stuffing his fist in his mouth to prevent himself from yelling at her to stop.

Émile had wanted to help her, the pretty housemaid from Mount Durand with eyes the colour of iris, whom he found crying in the barn where they stored the apples. It was late September and the air smelt fecund, of overripe fruit on the cusp of rotting. Wasps dipped and hovered in the buttery gold light. He was on a delivery and had taken himself outside to have a smoke while the driver sweet talked the cook in the kitchen. Something had drawn him into the barn, a listless curiosity, and there she was hunched up against the wall, partially obscured by towering boxes of apples. She looked up with alarm when she saw the door open, then slumped back when she saw it was him.

Yes, it's only the deaf man, Émile thought. He'd been back from Canada for five years now and was used to being treated as if he didn't count. He walked over and knelt on the ground next to her. Her face was puffy and mottled from crying. At first he imagined that she'd been scolded by the cook for some minor misdemeanour, fingerprints on the crystal wine glasses her master was so fond of or a mishap with a tray. But they bred them tough in Mount

Durand; people joked that babies came out of the womb with their fists curled and their teeth bared, besides which the cook was a good-natured woman from what he had seen, jovial and patient.

He asked her what the matter was. She looked at him as if he were speaking a foreign language and he took out the notebook and pencil that he carried everywhere and wrote the question down. She hesitated as he handed her the pencil. She was 'in trubbel', she wrote. And then someone must have called her because she scrambled to her feet and ran off. When he came out of the barn, the driver was waiting and spent the rest of the day ribbing him about what he'd got up to in there with the housemaid.

Letty, her name was, or Juliette in full, though no one had called her that ever, she told him the next time he saw her. Letty's leaving us, the cook announced as he unloaded the groceries, you'd best say your goodbyes. Émile found her starching sheets in the laundry room; she was dry eyed but pale as chalk and somehow he knew. There were some girls who you could imagine at it and others who you just couldn't, and Letty was firmly in the first category. His heart quivered as he asked her if she'd be getting married, and he realised he had already started to construct a fantasy around Letty and how absurd it had been to hope that she didn't have a sweetheart. Her mouth had formed a tight hard line and she shook her head.

'He has to,' Émile said.

She said nothing but, for the first time, she looked at him with something approaching tenderness, as if he were a small child incapable of understanding.

That evening, when his mother had gone to bed, Émile took down the red cloth book entitled *Household Remedies* and thumbed through the yellowing pages, until he found what he was searching for. It was as simple and straightforward as a relief for a sore throat or a bad chest: juniper berries crushed to a pulp, a handful of dock leaves, three wild thistle flowers, all boiled for five minutes, then drunk down in one go.

Letty lived with her aunt and uncle and multiple siblings in a cramped tenement at the top of Mount Durand. Her cheeks blazed with shame when she answered the door and saw Émile standing on the landing. The smell of unmade beds and the privy had been impossible to ignore. She told him to leave, but he said he had something for her, offered her his arm. He took her for tea at the kiosk by the bathing pools and gave her the weeds and berries wrapped in newspaper, wrote down what she should do with them. Letty bit her lip and nodded. She took the pencil. *It werent sposed to happen*, she wrote. *He sed he wood see to things*. She paused, knowing the question that Émile couldn't bring himself to ask.

Mr Le Lacheur, she wrote. *The master*.

She couldn't look at him then. She stared out to sea, her expression as opaque as the milky horizon, daring him to judge her. Old enough to be her grandfather almost; it was obscene, disgusting. Émile had seen the man from time to time. He looked like the type who wouldn't take no for an answer. Letty's face was fierce, her hands clenched, and Émile felt consumed with admiration for her: this tough, proud girl with a dead mother and a father who didn't want to know, who nonetheless had worked hard, found herself a position, only to be taken advantage of in the worst way imaginable. He felt at that moment as the waves frothed over the rocks, surging in and out of the pools, that he understood her perfectly.

He asked if Le Lacheur knew. She nodded, the curl of her lip telling Émile everything. So, Letty had been dismissed, seen off the premises before any blame could be laid at Le Lacheur's door. Émile's outrage at the injustice of the situation increased. He walked Letty back to Mount Durand and said he'd call on her in a few days' time to see how she was doing. He went home happy, happier than he had been in a considerably long time.

When he next saw Letty, he took a bunch of freesias, put oil in his hair. Letty looked wan and ill and cross. She stared at the flowers as if they were a trick. The herbs hadn't worked, she said; she'd been sick as a dog for a week was all. Émile said he was sorry; he was just trying to help. It didn't help, said Letty, not one bit. Her aunt was going to go spare when she found out – Letty grabbed his notebook and scribbled when he said he couldn't understand – she'd belt her, more than likely, maybe turn her out. Then the tears came and Émile put his arm around her and they sat that way on the cliffs, and after a while he felt her body lean into him and that was the start of it: the daring to hope.

Émile proposed a month later. It was rash, reckless, and made more sense than anything had since he lost his hearing. They would bring up the child as his own. They would have more – two, three, four. Giggling, the two of them scribbled down the numbers. He would rent them a cottage with a backyard for the children to play in, next to a vinery where there was work to be had. They wouldn't be rich but there'd be food on the table and a roof over their heads. And Letty? Émile couldn't hear her say the words of course, but he knew she loved him: she drew hearts in his notebook with his initials and hers in the centre. And if there were doubts that niggled at the back of his mind, Émile ignored them. The only story he needed to hear was the one he was telling himself. He was getting married to a young, beautiful woman and their child was coming. He would stop going to bed lonely and waking up the same way. What he had never thought conceivable, not after Isabelle, seemed to have happened: he was in love again.

'Get something for tea, will you?' Her mother hands Maud coupons from her purse, her eyes a little puffy, a little pink. 'Try and be first in the queue when the market opens – we'll end up with scrag ends not fit for an animal, otherwise.'

Maud nods, says she will. Ma is pulling on her coat now, knotting the turban she wears to clean in. She reminds her daughters to clear away the breakfast things, tells Stella to get her skates on or she'll be late for work. The words are coming out in a rush, and she pauses suddenly and looks at them both.

'You mustn't mind your pa's mithering,' she says. 'You know what he's like. Gets the wrong end of the stick about things.'

Maud and Stella exchange looks. The argument had been bad, even by their parents' standards, and when their mother had started crying, an uncommon enough occurrence in itself, Maud had done something she had never dared to before: she had intervened. She was part of this row in some way that she wasn't quite sure of yet; she was responsible for it, and she had felt sick to the depths of herself as she stood outside their room, her hand on the doorknob, suddenly afraid of what she might discover. They had treated her like a child, of course, and sent her back to bed, but not before she had taken back what belonged to her, the thing that had started it all: the wine merchant's card. Now it sits securely in the inside pocket of her skirt and it feels dangerous, like having a gun in a holster, and makes the queasy lightheaded feeling she woke with worse than ever. But she can't stop thinking of it – or of him.

The door slams, and their mother has gone.

Stella glances at Maud. 'What was last night about, do you think?'

Maud looks at her sister. Stella hasn't styled her hair today as she usually does and she seems listless, uneasy. The instinct to lie overtakes her.

'Money, probably.'

If Stella doesn't believe her, she doesn't say so. She puts on the lipstick Ma insists she's too young to wear, even if she does work in a beauty parlour, then blots her lips on her handkerchief.

'You teaching today?' she asks.

Maud shakes her head.

'All right for some.' Stella pouts and blows her a kiss, as she leaves. 'See you later, Lady Muck!'

The door slams for a second time.

Maud does the dishes, then wanders into the hall. The door to her parents' room is ajar and on impulse she goes in. The bed is unmade, a tangle of sheets and blankets pooling onto the carpet. Candle wax has spilt from the holder and onto the varnished wood of the dressing table. Maud moves a pile of clothes from the stool underneath and Pa's notebook falls to the floor. It surprises her to find it anywhere other than in the side pocket of his serge overalls – he must have forgotten it – and tentatively she flicks through the pages. It is a catalogue of minutiae, of instructions and directions, of misunderstandings clarified – *I'm deaf.* She turns to the last entry, sees Ma's handwriting, unmistakeable, each stumpy, misspelt letter groaning with effort.

i did what i had to
you never wanted her
you tryed to get rid of her

A chill steals through Maud. She re-reads her mother's words, tries to make sense of them.

you never wanted her.

The translation is painfully simple, impossible to escape: her father never wanted her. Doesn't she have evidence as old as she is to give it weight? Racing Stella down to the greenhouse at the end of the day so that she could be the one to tell him that tea was ready and getting little more than a nod. Bringing home her school exercise book so that he could see for himself the 'Excellents' and 'Very goods' that peppered the pages, achievements which may have earned her a humbug from the jar on the dresser but which failed to make his eyes crinkle at the sides, the way Stella could. It was always Stella who seemed to be scooped onto his lap after she'd twirled around the kitchen pretending to be a fairy, Stella who got the last humbug (which Stella, being Stella, unfailingly shared with Maud); Stella, who somehow appeared to be the daughter he really wanted. Ever since the bombing, three months ago, Maud has not been able to quash the notion that if it had been Stella's turn to help with the tomatoes, he would have been more alert to the danger in the circling planes and insisted she stay at home.

Maud stares at herself in the mirror. She is not pretty like Stella is or Ma used to be and is the only one in the family with dark eyes and darker hair. She has always felt different, inside as well as out. People say she has inherited the musical talent Pa once had, but she is not sure if this is true: her love affair with the accordion is a complicated one, borne of a desire to please him, before realising that he would rather she stop. Yet she has kept playing regardless, year after year, all the while knowing he will never hear her, knowing he will never be truly proud.

He never wanted her; he tried to get rid of her. She does not want to understand what these last few words might even mean, but she must. Maud slips the notebook into her pocket. She will go to the French House and return it to him and there, away from Ma and Stella, she will ask him to tell her what he wouldn't last night, and what her mother refuses to. She will demand that, for once, he is honest with her.

Émile is hoeing when Maud arrives, decapitating nettles and bindweed with a vigour that makes his back ache. He is surprised to see her yet by the same token he is not; he had bolted from the house not long after sunrise, the prospect of the morning after around the breakfast table worse than any hangover. But you can't hide from bad news, he thinks, and this is no social call. Maud is flanked by Isabelle, who is pointing in his direction, and Émile bends his head and takes a swipe at a thistle, will not look up until Maud is standing there in front of him.

She is holding his notebook and Émile pats his right pocket and finds it missing. He holds out his hand, but Maud won't give it up. She is breathing fast as she opens it and points to Letty's scrawled half-sentences from the night before.

'She means me, doesn't she?' Maud is saying. 'You never

84

wanted *me*.'

Émile leans on his hoe and tries to suppress his growing panic as he meets her eyes. He didn't know her then, he wants to say, and sometimes the truth is hard to tell straight when it's as gnarled and tangled as hundred-year-old roots. From the corner of his eye, he sees Isabelle watering the pots of parsley and sage on the window ledge. She ducks her head and he knows she is listening.

He tells Maud that if she's come to start a row, she can go straight back home again. She ignores him and takes out Le Lacheur's card, then turns to a fresh page in the notebook. *Who is he?*

Émile says nothing, his thoughts spinning. The truth that Maud wants so badly would crush her. A man who'd have left her and her mother to the mercies of the poor house, or worse, a man who took as much from people as he could get.

'He's just a man your ma used to work for,' he says eventually. 'No one who matters.'

Maud glares at him as if he's the enemy, when all he has ever wanted is to protect her. He remembers the first time he held her, in the bedroom where she had just been born, breathing in the iron tang of blood. He had sat there, rocking her gently to and fro, waiting to be hit by a rush of love, praying for it, but all he could see was another man's baby, and a wife who, he was rapidly discovering, didn't love him as she should. As if sensing his misgivings, Maud had screwed up her tiny eyes, opened her tiny mouth and let out what Émile could only assume was a huge wail. Letty had gathered her up protectively. Dispatched from the bedroom, a deep loneliness had engulfed him along with a terrible sense of shame, for what kind of man was jealous of a baby?

But by the time Stella was born two years later, he had learned to love Maud almost without trying. Yet from her first smile, Stella enchanted, whereas Maud infuriated; Stella loved to please and Maud to disrupt.

He looks at her. 'I'll speak to him myself,' Maud is saying. 'I'll find out.'

'No,' Émile says firmly. 'You won't.'

'You can't stop me.'

'Go near that man' – Émile jerks the hoe at the card – 'and you'll not be welcome at home.'

As soon as the words are out of his mouth, he regrets them. This is Maud after all, never one to leave a gauntlet for someone else to trip over.

She stares at him, her hands trembling with anger. 'You're throwing me out?'

No, Émile says, she doesn't understand, that's not what he means, but she will not listen, because the girl never listens and he finds himself shaking in turn.

'I understand perfectly,' Maud says, with a thin crease of a smile.

She thrusts the notebook at him and marches down the path, ignoring Isabelle, who looks up with concern as she passes, and despite everything Émile wants to yell at Maud to mind her manners. It matters more than he cares to admit that Isabelle might think he's brought up his children to behave as they like.

When five o'clock comes, Isabelle cannot settle with her book as usual. The exploits of Flora Poste prove to be an ineffective distraction from the story that had unfolded in front of her a few hours earlier, and it doesn't matter how severely she tells herself it's none of her business, the fact remains that she wants it to be. When she answered the door to Émile's daughter, her first thought was that someone had died; the girl was as tightly wound as a spinning top.

'Is he here?' she'd said, and it had taken Isabelle a moment to place her, to understand who she was talking about.

Your father? Isabelle said, yes, he is, and was about to go and fetch him, when Maud had stepped into the passageway, set to follow her. They'd gone to the garden, where Émile was weeding, and she wished then she had told Maud to wait outside because it was clear by the way she marched up to him that she was spoiling for a fight, and Isabelle hated rows. She had busied herself with watering the herbs and although she'd tried not to eavesdrop, the row seemed to be about some man whom Émile was forbidding Maud from seeing. It didn't last long but after Maud had gone, Isabelle caught Émile staring at the dog-eared notebook that he carried everywhere with such despair that she had to go upstairs to the office, which overlooked the street not the garden, and immerse herself in that month's accounts.

Isabelle puts down *Cold Comfort Farm* and goes outside, checks under the stone by the back doorstep where Émile often leaves notes for her when he's finished for the day. There is nothing there. She finds herself lacing up her shoes with the intent of going down to the shed and checking on him. She searches for a decent excuse – she will tell him she needs the spare set of keys to the shed, or some such, in case he's ever taken ill.

As she approaches the enclosure, she hears a series of grunts followed by a low cry of pain. She stops and reminds herself that Émile is not the man he was – she should be careful. Instinct has her tapping on the door before she realises her error. As the groans continue, she almost turns away. Then chastising herself for being no better than a coward, she lets herself in.

Émile is leaning against the wall with his back to her; one hand splayed against the brickwork for support as he swings his right fist into the rough granite, over and over again.

'Stop!'

Isabelle runs towards him, seizes his arm as he raises it. He stumbles when he sees her, tries to shake her off. He is red-faced, panting, and she can smell his sweat. His knuckles are raw and bloodied but the look in his eyes distresses her more: they are dark with hopelessness. This is not the first time he has done this, she would swear to it, and there is a briskness to her as she addresses him: he does not need sympathy from her of all people.

'Come to the kitchen.' Isabelle jerks her thumb towards the house. 'Your hand needs cleaning up.'

Émile shakes his head but he has turned away from the wall now, and the fight seems to drain from him. Isabelle holds open the enclosure door. He hesitates then lumbers past her, holding his right hand gingerly in front of him as if he has only just started to feel the pain.

Isabelle makes him sit at the kitchen table. She fills the washing-up bowl with soapy water and, while he soaks his hand, tears a strip from an old tea towel for a bandage. She leaves him to wrap up the wound and goes to Corbeille's office, where she fetches the bottle of cognac from his filing cabinet. If it comes to it, she will tell him that Émile had some kind of accident and needed it for the shock. When she comes downstairs again, she half expects him to have bolted, but he is still there, straight-backed in the chair, his knuckles bound tight in the white cloth. He is staring at the pot of red cyclamen on the windowsill.

'Lifts your spirits to see a bit of colour,' he says.

'I think so.' Isabelle takes two teacups and pours them each a glug of cognac.

Émile regards the bottle with scepticism. 'Get in trouble, will I, for drinking this?' he says, but he takes the cup without waiting for her reply.

'If anyone gets into trouble, it'll be me,' Isabelle says and Émile lifts an eyebrow as if to say they both know how the world works – and takes a couple of sips.

He squints at the bottle. 'Good stuff. Not that I'm an expert.'

'Nor me.'

He gives her a shadow of a smile. She is three mouthfuls bolder and nods towards his bandaged fist. 'Why?' she asks.

Émile pauses. 'You try your best,' he says, 'and turns out it still ain't good enough.'

Isabelle thinks again of the way Maud blew into the passageway like her own weather system; how she commandeered the room when she played her accordion at Candie, Occupation or no Occupation. The kind of girl teachers refer to as headstrong, wilful.

'I'm sure you're a fine father,' she says. 'Better than many.'

Émile examines a chip in the rim of the teacup. 'Maud don't think so. She's got a notion in her head and now she's not content with what she has.'

'How old is she? Nineteen?'

Émile nods. 'This April just gone.'

'Isn't that normal? To want more?'

Like you did, like we both did. She sees the two of them reflected in the windowpane and it is like squinting at an alternative future, one where they are sitting discussing their own children over a glass of brandy, the one she had once hoped for.

'Don't always turn out the way you think, is all.' Émile's gaze drifts to the bottle and she pours them both a little more. The wild look from earlier has gone now, and his gaze is cool and steady.

'You never had children.'

It is a statement, delivered as a question, and one that over the years Isabelle has become adept at answering, peddling untruths in an attempt to quash the curiosity of the neighbourhood busybodies. She wasn't that interested in children; she didn't have the patience; she had her work and a husband who needed looking after and that was enough. But this is Émile. In this matter, at least, he knows her.

'Yes.' Her voice comes out in a croak, as she holds up a finger. 'One. A boy.'

Émile frowns. He looks confused, he is getting out his notebook, he wants clarification and she knows what he is thinking: they may live in different parishes, they may have taken great pains to avoid each other, as if they were debtors unable to pay their dues, but a child – this news would have carried.

Isabelle goes to the dresser, takes down the black leather Bible that neither she or anyone else ever reads, pulls the gold ribbon from its centre and removes the photograph she keeps there. It hurts her to look at it for too long; it is like a horsewhip to the face, and she has no words to say as she passes the picture to Émile.

He looks from the photograph to her and then back again. She has never shown it to anyone outside her home, and she worries now that Émile will be repulsed, as her husband was. It is clear of course, as it was when the boy was born, but in this photograph, taken on his seventh birthday, there is no room for ambiguity. His eyes bulbous, the lids heavy, the left eye drooping a little. His imperfect, perfect face, the nose a little flatter than it should be, his mouth open, tongue protruding slightly. He isn't smiling, of course – they'd told her children like him didn't, they weren't capable. She hadn't believed them then, and she didn't now. Dark hair, a similar shade to her own, full of static and standing on end, as if it has been brushed quickly and without care. His hands are clenched into small, tense fists –through fear or frustration, Isabelle can't tell. He was, after all, no longer hers.

Émile lays the photograph on the table with care, like liquid he is determined not to spill.

'What's his name?' he asks simply.

Isabelle picks up a pen.

Peter.

Émile studies the name with intent, as if it is the word rather than Isabelle that will provide him with answers.

'I gave him away,' Isabelle says, but he looks at her uncomprehendingly. Unbearable to mime – she writes it down. The horsewhip returns; her eyes smart.

Émile is quiet for a moment, then nods towards the picture. 'He looks like a good lad,' he says.

There is no reply that she can give to this. She takes the photograph and returns the Bible to the top shelf and when she turns, Émile is up and putting on his cap.

'Till tomorrow, then,' he says. It is the first time he has done anything more than mumble with his head down when he leaves for the day, her first reminder of the depths of warmth to be found in the unyielding greyness of his eyes.

'Till tomorrow.'

Isabelle washes up the teacups, then takes a sliver of carbolic soap. She froths it up as best she can then mashes it roughly against her teeth and tongue, takes a gulp of water, swills, and spits, almost retching. She repeats the process three times, telling herself it is to rid her breath of any trace of brandy: it will only cause trouble. Then she heads home, almost a full hour later than usual, to where her husband is waiting.

Nightdress, toothbrush, three changes of underwear – no four, even five – who knows how long she may stay away? Maud shoves her possessions into a pillowcase and ties a loose knot. She will be gone for as long as it takes her parents to realise that whatever lies they have told each other will not hold with her. She sits on Stella's bed and scribbles a note.

Gone to Old Mum's for a few days. Don't worry about me. M x

Maud imagines her sister's response. She will wrinkle her nose and say rather you than me; Stella's visits to their grandmother's are rare – she complains that the house reeks of cat and Old Mum's tobacco smoke makes her sneeze. And although Old Mum is far too prickly to have favourites, she has let Maud use her musty back bedroom for accordion practice for years now, when Ma can't take any more of the 'racket' – she says it keeps her company while she's smoking her pipe.

'Almost as good as your Pa was,' her grandmother tells her sometimes, which makes Maud feel proud and sad at the same time, although sympathy is wasted on Pa, and Old Mum has told her that too. She is fond of saying that he should never have gone gallivanting to the other side of the world in the first place – 'and he knows it. That's why he gets in his rages. No point in feeling sorry for him – it just makes him worse.'

Maud fetches her accordion and goes into the kitchen, takes her keys from the hook. Locking the back door behind her, she loads the front basket of her bicycle and sets off through the lanes.

When she arrives, the sky is darkening and it is starting to spit with rain. Old Mum's cat sits at the front window and fixes Maud with an amber-eyed stare. Maud goes around to the back of the house and knocks on the kitchen door. She hears the creak of the rocking chair, then an inaudible muttering as her grandmother draws back the bolt.

'Oh, it's you,' she says. She peers at Maud through her spectacles, then notices the pillowcase. 'Arguing again, are they?' She draws a few wisps of wiry hair away from her forehead, revealing the faint scar on her right temple. Maud has a sudden memory of a baby crying, raised voices, her hands holding tightly to her mother's stockinged leg, a saucer with a blue rim breaking into fragments around her. Then later, being sat high, high up on the kitchen table and being told to stay there as her mother swept with a dustpan and brush.

Maud opens her mouth to speak but there is a huge lump in her throat where the words usually are, and nothing comes out.

'I think I've found out something,' she says eventually. 'Something important.'

Old Mum tuts softly and draws open the door. 'Come inside, girl, before that one from next door sees you, or the whole island will know your business by blackout.'

Maud hesitates. One time when she was a child, she had walked into the sea at Cobo and for once, she hadn't swum across the bay and back as she usually did, but instead had headed in a straight line horizon-wards, not looking back until her body ached and the people on the beach were just specks in the distance. All she had wanted then was to be back to where she had been only ten minutes earlier, paddling in the shallows with just the inconvenience of the sun in her eyes to trouble her. She feels the same now but it is too late: she cannot unhear her parents' fight, or forget she has ever made the acquaintance of a man called Le Lacheur.

She picks up her accordion case and follows Old Mum into the long shadows of her cottage.

8

Isabelle casts off the last row of the scarf she is knitting and, frowning, examines it under the lamplight. The fringe had been more fiddly than she'd expected, but it has turned out well and any thoughts she might have had about giving it to her husband as a Christmas gift disappear: she will make him socks instead with the wool that remains. She fetches brown paper and string from the bureau, then makes a gift tag from an old Christmas card. Her pen hovers, before she writes.

With very best wishes, Isabelle.

She looks at the clock. There are still two hours until curfew. Ron is playing cards at a friend's, and Peter – as she privately calls him – is always out on a Wednesday. Isabelle takes the package, collects some freshly laundered towels from the airing cupboard, then goes upstairs to the attic, tapping lightly on the door for form's sake, just in case. She always does this; it is part of the imaginary game she has started to play with herself.

Isabelle lets herself in, turns on the light. As usual, it is neat and orderly, almost eerily so. His grey tunic hangs on the back of the door and a pair of polished boots stand poised at the foot of the bed. On the dressing table, a half-empty bottle of cologne, a metal comb, a shaving brush. She puts the Christmas gift on his bedside table, next to the photograph of his mother, and lays the towels on the end of the bed. Then Isabelle sits in the armchair next to the bookshelves, closes her eyes. She knows it is ridiculous, this flight of fancy, that she is the woman in the photo in the summer dress, depositing clean laundry in her son's bedroom while he is out for the evening – with his new sweetheart, perhaps – and she hopes she is a nice girl, intelligent, polite; someone with whom she might share a book recommendation, accompany on a shopping trip into Town. It is ridiculous and it is treacherous and it is callous, because even if her son had survived, even if he had lived beyond the first ten years of his life, the only thing that he and Leutnant Schreiber would have in common is their age and their first name, and to wish otherwise is a betrayal to Peter's memory.

Isabelle shivers, gets up, runs her fingers along the book spines, like the keys of a piano. If she hadn't been able to have children at all, it would have been easier. If she and Ron had heeded the warning signs and stopped trying . . . The grim frequency of her miscarriages, so much pain and blood and disappointment that the two of them could hardly believe it when it appeared she was carrying a baby to full term. What a fuss had been made of her then; everyone so pleased with her, even her parents. She would sit reading in this very room with her feet up, book propped against the mound of her stomach, and she would thank the baby inside her for saving her marriage. And then the birth itself, the searing, ripping terror of it, before the anaesthetic wail of the baby. The midwife had placed him on her chest and as he wrapped his perfect tiny fingers around her right thumb, Isabelle's heart had hurt with how much she loved him. Peter.

But he wasn't perfect. His tongue lolled, his eyes didn't focus. In the days that followed, he was away from her more than he was with her – for health checks, the nurses said. There were no flowers or gifts. No one visited, other than her parents and Ron, and he couldn't even look her in the eye.

'He's not right,' he said, and her mother and father had been quick to agree. Then a few days later, a doctor had told them everything that wasn't right about their son. His eyesight was poor, his reactions slow: he was subnormal, he said. He would need special care for the rest of his life. The doctor had paused. There were places, apparently, institutions on the mainland that were well equipped to do this.

No, Isabelle had said. No, no, no, no. She had wailed as if she were Peter, as if it were her they were sending away. Her mother had demanded that she calm herself; her father and Ron had left the room. And then her mother had got to work. It was the best thing, the kindest thing, to be done. Isabelle would thank her later – and besides, there was her husband to think of.

'Ronald needs you, Isabelle,' she had said sternly, and Isabelle had said what about Peter, he was five days old, didn't he need her more? You're not capable, her mother had snapped, and Isabelle had turned on her side and cried some more and when she stopped, her mother was gone. But she was back the day after and the next, along with Ron, one either side of her bed, force-feeding her the particulars of a care home in Inverness, leaving a sheaf of papers on her bedside table.

Isabelle takes a Thomas Hardy from the top shelf and flicks through it, the words glazing over her. She had felt as if she was being buried alive, and she had lost her fight. She had signed the papers. Her name in ink next to Ron's, and how she had hated him at that moment, the way he patted her shoulder afterwards. Good girl, he'd murmured. Well done.

She sighs, returns to the safe territory of the bookshelf. Stories are her sedative, she cannot do without them. Here too is one of the Brontës – *The Professor*, well-thumbed with a cracked spine: it is her favourite too. At the end of the shelf, the books lose their neatness, they slump and topple as if recently disturbed, and Isabelle sees that there is something lodged behind them. Don't you have anything better to do than snoop, she chides herself, but it seems that she doesn't as now she is reaching up and easing out what looks to be a sketch pad. She begins to flick through the pages. A fisherman in overalls and wellington boots, emptying nets from a trawler at the harbour. She turns the page. Another fisherman – the same one, she thinks – bending over a bucket, naked to the waist. A taut ridge of muscle runs down his torso, a tideline of dark stubble shadowing the side of his face.

Isabelle hesitates. The sketches pulse with the energy of a diary and she knows she should stop right away and put it back, but she can't. The page turns and she gasps, catches her reflection in the wardrobe mirror, her hand clamped to her mouth. It's the fisherman again, casting out a line from the side of a boat, but this time he's completely naked apart from a pair of wellington boots, which somehow make it worse. She can see his . . . thing, and the hair around it, and she may be a prude, but really, yes, Isabelle is a little shocked, she cannot deny it.

On the next sheet, the same man is naked again, but lying on his side this time, knee bent, so one's eye cannot help but be drawn to what's between his legs, which the artist has rendered with studious attention to detail. The man smirks at her and Isabelle flips the pad shut, returns it to its hiding place behind the copies of Trollope. Her first thought is that her husband must not find out; her next one that she has read Peter Schreiber wrong. Life drawing, isn't that what it's called? She'd have been startled enough to see portraits of a woman in the nude, but at least that would have fitted better with the story she's been concocting around his Wednesday evening absences.

The back door slams and her name bounces like an order through the hall. Quickly, Isabelle turns off the light, hurries to the door. Ron stands at the bottom of the stairs, still in his hat and raincoat.

'What you doing up there?'

'Just dropping off some clean towels,' Isabelle says lightly. She comes downstairs and takes his wet things.

'Hope he's paying extra for laundry.' Ron slips his arm around her and roughly squeezes her waist. He smells faintly of alcohol. 'Is he out over Christmas, then?'

'I expect so. He mentioned a lunch at the Soldatenheim, some party or other.'

'All right for some.' Ron follows her into the sitting room, sprawls on the armchair. 'Word has it they're bringing the wireless sets back for Christmas.'

'Oh. Good.'

It is better than good. It's been two months since the Germans confiscated every wireless on the island, and Isabelle has been wondering how they will get through Christmas without it. She gives him a small smile, tries to forget the sketches and what they might mean, reaches for her pile of sewing.

'So what have you got me for Christmas, Is-a-belle?' His legs are splayed on the footstool as he regards her lazily.

'It's a surprise,' Isabelle says, but there's no mistaking the look in his eyes, and now he's on his feet and upon her, planting dry kisses on her neck, unbuttoning her blouse, his hand crawling towards her breasts. Isabelle tells herself she'd rather have it this way than the other, and it will be over quickly – or at least quickly enough. She puts down her darning and turns towards him.

'Let's go and lie down, shall we?'

The rumours about the wireless sets arrive long before the sets themselves and this additional absence in a house that already has one spare place too many at the table on Christmas Day, adds weight to the gloom in Émile's household. Letty declares that they've been missed off the list and it's only the posh folk up in St Martins and the Forest who'll get them back. Stella has spent the best part of the day huddled in her coat and scarf at the top of the lane, ready to flag down anyone who might look as if they are from the Controlling Committee and have lost their way.

'It doesn't feel like Christmas,' Letty grumbles as the three of them eat lunch and Stella's bottom lip juts out, just as it used to when she was little and about to cry. Letty gives Émile a pointed look and Émile takes a mouthful of dark bitter beer, wondering how it is that the whole Maud problem had become his fault and not Letty's or Maud's herself or even Old Mum's, because Lord knows she isn't helping matters by indulging the girl and letting her stay. Every day, Letty asks him to go and fetch Maud back and every day Émile tells her that there's no point in bringing someone somewhere they don't want to be. Then the silent name calling begins, underscored for emphasis in his notebook: he is 'stubborn', apparently, 'pig-headed'.

And through all of this, when he isn't thinking about Maud and Letty, or the war, or whether he might pay a visit to Céline, just one, just for comfort, something curious is happening. Isabelle has started to occupy the spaces in his thoughts: she is putting down roots, refusing to move. Ever since that day when they'd sat in the kitchen with his smashed knuckles and the bottle of brandy and she'd given him a piece of her sorrow in exchange for his own, the questions have started. Has this bank clerk from the mainland made a better husband than he would have done a father? Did Isabelle want to give away the child? Why did she keep his picture in the kitchen dresser at the French House? Her fingers had trembled as she handed him the photograph and in spite of everything, he had felt the urge to cover her hand with her own, to reassure her that it wasn't for him to pass judgement.

Stella touches his elbow and he starts, rabbit stew dripping down his chin. She points to the window, her face illuminated, and Émile sees two men walking down the path, carrying the wireless. It had taken him months to save up for and he is glad to have it back (privately he'd agreed with Letty and thought they'd seen the last of it). Letty and Stella usher in the men and for a moment the energy in the kitchen soars. Émile senses laughter, and wishes he could join in. The wireless is returned to its spot on the dresser and Stella fiddles with the dial and says something that makes the men laugh afresh. They turn to him as man of the house and shake his hand and speak so close to his ear that he can feel the gust of their breath as if by bellowing at his deafness, they might shatter it.

The men go and Letty gestures for Émile's notebook.

Tell Maud, she writes, pointing at the wireless and then at him. *Tell her we got it.*

Émile gets to his feet, takes his coat from the hook on the back door.

'You tell her!' he says with more force than perhaps he intended, for Stella looks up in concern, and Letty's mouth sets into a grim line, and he leaves in a bit of a temper, thinking that it comes to something when a talking box starts to matter more to his family than he does.

The sky is already darkening when Émile arrives in Town. He props his bicycle outside the Caves and steps inside. The place is heaving with fellows who, like him, have no place better to be, and his spirits lift as he goes to the bar and orders his first pint, enjoying the bank holiday drunkenness, the backslaps and Christmas greetings. He is dealt into a round of euchre and for a while he is in his element, with his fan of cards, reading the faces of those around him, knowing when to play and when to pass. They are playing for money, just the shrapnel of coppers and the occasional sixpence, but losing is losing for certain types and the man in the corner, a fellow with a distinct absence of festive cheer (and who Émile would take a guess earns three times what he does) throws down his cards in a huff as Émile pockets another round's winnings.

The man is muttering something and the others in the circle glance at each other and shift uncomfortably, and Émile finds himself out in the cold again.

'What's the matter?' He looks at the man more closely. He thinks he's something special, no doubt about it, as he slouches loose-limbed in his suit, glowering at Émile as if he'd like to hit him but can't quite summon up the energy. And it is this curdling of his features that releases the memory for Émile and he remembers that afternoon at the North Show, years ago, before Letty, and the man in front of him with a ridiculous moustache stepping out with the woman who should have been Émile's.

Isabelle's husband flicks his wrist, shooing Émile away. He leans forward, brings his face close to Émile's, tells him to play with someone else, somewhere else. Émile looks at Le Galley, the man who dealt him in to begin with, but he hands the cards to Larch to shuffle and will not meet his eye.

Émile gets up. 'I know your sort,' he says.

It is not much by way of a comeback and Émile himself doesn't know exactly what he means by it, not until he has drunk another beer in an opposite corner of the pub, and the realisation distils like sediment at the bottom of his glass: the man is a bully. He buttons up his coat and heads out into the cold.

The route home takes him up through Hauteville. The darkness is thick now, the moon a single nail clipping of light. As he approaches the French House, Émile slows down, remembers that he has the keys in his coat pocket. They start to weigh heavy, like a physical presence, forcing him to stop. She is fond of the house, attached to it; her books sit in the kitchen dresser. He can picture her there reading by candlelight, one hand playing with her hair, just as she does at the end of the day when the work's finished. It's Christmas Day, Émile tells himself, no one goes to sit like a lemon in the place that pays their wages when they've got time off from it, but the French House means more than that to Isabelle and he has only just begun to realise why. Leaving his bike against the railings, Émile lets himself in through the side entrance.

A faint, watery light is coming from the kitchen window and as he draws closer, he sees her through a gap in the curtains. Drawn up to her full height, Isabelle is moving in careful semicircles across the room, her right hand clasping a glass of something, the other flexed at the wrist, the rhythm of her movements precise as if she is counting out loud. Right, forward, side, close; back, side, close . . . and repeat. One, two, three, one, two, three – it is some kind of waltz, like the one they taught each other at dusk on the sands at Pembroke, just them and the oystercatchers and the surging waves. He remembers the angle of her shoulder blade under his palm, the thrill at being melded so close to her, the feeling he had that they'd fitted, even when they didn't, when they stumbled or trod on each other's feet. He had wanted those dance lessons to last forever, dreading the time when the days would shrink and shorten, and they would be left with nowhere to go.

Isabelle twirls expansively, her skirt flaring out, and comes to a standstill in front of the window. They stare at each other but she doesn't seem as surprised to see him as she might have been and this Émile attributes to whatever she's just knocked back from her glass. She takes another sip and gestures rather impatiently towards the back door.

The door is unlocked. Émile takes off his boots and goes inside, feeling his way through the unlit passageway to the kitchen. Isabelle stands in the centre of the room in stockinged feet and a wine-red dress, smiling like a hostess receiving her first guest. The remains of a fire gutter in the grate; the brandy bottle is on the table, open.

'Drink?' She reaches for a glass from the cupboard and pours him a generous measure.

Émile takes a sip and looks nervously towards the window. Isabelle's tipsiness is doing a good job of sobering him up – they are on the premises when they shouldn't be, drinking what he knows to be their employer's cognac, with a disregard for blackout that would give the slowest elementary school child reason to tell them off. He needs this job, even if she doesn't, and he's about to tell her as much but she is taking his arm as if it's the most natural thing in the world and leading him away from the table.

'Dance with me,' she seems to be saying. 'It's Christmas.'

She grasps his left hand, places his right on her shoulder. He is close to her now, close enough to smell the ripeness of her breath, to feel the row of buttons running down the front of her dress press against him.

Émile pulls away. 'I can't.'

'Rubbish.' She draws him back to her, laughing, and holds up her fingers. 'Just count. One, two, three. Like you taught me.'

He is glad it is dark. He feels clumsy and awkward and is grateful for the beer and brandy muffling the questions in his head. He closes his eyes and lets his body remember, and they move across the kitchen, slowly at first, like the first time when he no more knew how to waltz than she did, but he'd been there enough times to understand how the swell of a tune, the rhythm of it, stitched everyone in the room together. His thoughts drift. He is in Davy's on Keefer Street in downtown Vancouver, playing a breezy valse-musette on his accordion to a packed bar. He is back on the slipway on Pembroke, playing for the godless on a Sunday afternoon, when he sees Isabelle for the first time, in a cream bathing dress, long brown legs flecked with sand, chocolate-coloured hair whipping across her face, as she returns a tea tray to the kiosk. He smiles; she does the same and he feels himself rushing to the finish as she approaches so that he doesn't miss his chance to speak to her, before this moment dissolves.

The pressure on his left hand increases and he looks up, opens his eyes. Isabelle is smiling.

'It's that song, isn't it? The one you used to play.'

It takes him a few moments to understand her, to realise that the song in his head had come out into the open. He stops, pulls away from her.

'That's enough.'

'Oh, Émile.' Her lips purse in disappointment.

Oh, Émile, nothing. It's been a mistake. She has softened him up, she is playing with him. She ignored his letters; she married another man. It is time for him to leave. He goes to the table and drains his glass.

'Dance with your husband, if you're so set on it,' he says.

Isabelle says nothing, then she takes the candle and puts it on the table between them.

'I don't want to dance with my husband.'

Émile thinks of the shame of his tuneless humming, the shambling deaf man who thinks he can still dance. He doesn't need her pity. 'You married him,' he says.

'My mother,' she begins, gesturing for his notebook. 'My mother married me to him.'

Because YOU stopped writing. She puts down the pencil, her smile gone.

Émile stares at her. Her features blur and bleed in the candlelight. She is a stranger, indistinct, grotesque.

'I wrote,' he says. He excavates the words with effort, his breath coming in short, painful bursts. 'Week after week.

Even after the accident with my fucking collarbone in plaster. I waited and waited for you, Belle.'

'No.' But her fingers play doubtfully on her lips and she becomes herself again as she sees he is leaving and asks him not to, reaching for his arm, as she did when he arrived, but with less courage this time, less nerve. Then he is gone, before they can do each other any more damage, Émile thinks as he cycles home, head down against the sharp easterly wind.

9

Letty has used the extra ration of suet and sugar from Christmas to make a small pudding for her mother-in-law. She covers it with a tea towel, puts on her navy head-scarf and practises being pleasant in the mirror.

'Hello, Gwendoline. How are you keeping? Just brought you a little something.'

She buttons up her coat, telling herself it must be done, that it doesn't matter how rude the old bat has been to her over the years – she has to come home with her daughter. They cannot enter the new year with Maud's place unlaid at the table; their marriage will not survive it. The longer Maud is gone, the worse Letty's betrayal becomes – it has become this huge, wordless space between her and Émile. God knows things weren't perfect before but there was a safety in the way they were together, and Letty no longer feels safe.

As she walks through the lanes, she rages against the unfairness of it all. Was she the one who had drunk the housekeeping money away the night of the bombing; was it her who took weeks and weeks to get a job after the Germans arrived? How did Émile expect them to live – on fresh air and dandelions? It wasn't as if she'd taken any pleasure in it, on her hands and knees on that rough rug in Le Lacheur's office with her underwear around her ankles and the smell of his filthy cigars everywhere. She had just kept her mind on what she might get afterwards in return. As far as she was concerned, there had been little difference between what she had done with Le Lacheur and getting a bit extra for polishing the silver at one of her cleaning jobs. The way Émile had carried on, it was as if she'd been planning to run off with the man.

An icy wind whips across the fields and Letty shivers. She cannot deny, though, how much the whole business has shaken her, even without Maud running off, which was just the final straw. She has, she realises, throughout the long years of their marriage as much taken it for granted that Émile is on her side as she has the rising and setting of the sun. She'd need several hands to list his faults, but in fairness, he has never mocked her for her bad spelling or slow reading, as some would, and she's known him to tear a strip off the girls if they don't do their fair share around the house when she comes home after a day cleaning. And then there was that time just after Stella was born, when she overheard Old Mum ask him if he was sure Stella was his – how could he be certain after the last time, she said – and Letty had taken a saucer and hurled it across the kitchen at her departing mother-in-law. Her aim was more effective than she had intended: it had hit Old Mum on the forehead and blood had begun to trickle and then to flow, and Letty started to worry that she had really hurt the old boot. The cut was deep and had left a scar, yet Émile had never blamed her.

His mother had no right to say those things, he told Letty when she was working her way up to some kind of apology a few days later; let it be. But the night of the argument had changed everything – he had looked at her as if he thought the same as all the others. Letty Baudains, can't keep her legs together; no better than she should be. She had hit back hard, said and written things she shouldn't, and words you'd taken the trouble to write were even harder to take back. No, Maud must see sense and come home.

As she approaches Old Mum's cottage, Letty hears the sound of the accordion leaking from the back bedroom. Another chip to bargain with; she should never have made a fuss about Maud practising at home all these years – she's played right into Old Mum's hands. Clutching the pudding, she tries to sweep her mind of unpleasant thoughts and knocks on the door.

The latch lifts and Old Mum peers out. 'Oh!' she says. Her eyes glint behind the smear of her spectacles. 'Well.'

She fingers the scar on her temple, her lips twitching. Nothing wrong with her memory, Letty thinks, losing the few shreds of patience she came with and thrusting the pudding towards her.

'Are you going to let me in?'

It is more statement than question and where her mother-in-law is concerned, Letty has a reputation to live down to. Before she can be stopped, Letty has pushed past her and is inside the sallow gloom of the kitchen. The cat yowls and jumps from the windowsill with a thud, wrapping itself around Letty's legs. She shakes it off irritably and turns to Old Mum, who is settling herself in her rocking chair.

'Get her out here, would you?'

'Maud!' Old Mum's voice is surprisingly robust. 'There's someone to see you.'

A few more bars play before the accordion falls silent and Maud appears in the doorway. She is thinner than Letty remembers, and a pink flush veils her daughter's cheeks as their eyes meet. She is almost ashamed of me, Letty thinks. I've come just in time.

With reluctance, Old Mum gets up from her chair and shuffles past them. 'Don't take any guff,' she mutters to Maud, closing the door behind her.

'Is she listening?' Letty glares at the door. 'I'll bet she's listening.'

'And what if she is?' Maud shrugs, examines her fingernails, and this is not how it is meant to be, Letty thinks, wondering how Maud can bear it here as she looks around the dismal kitchen, which could do with a bloody good clean.

'It's time you came home,' she says firmly. 'Enough of this nonsense. Your sister misses you.' She pauses. 'We all do.'

'Really?' Her daughter cocks her head to one side, her eyebrows raised, a mannerism that is both very Maud and very irritating to Letty. It was so much easier, she thinks, when she could just slap her girls on the back of the legs and send them to their room.

'Does that include Pa?' Maud goes on. 'Because he made it quite clear that I wasn't welcome.'

Letty sighs. 'He didn't mean it. He gets angry – you know how he is. You have to make allowances.'

'Maybe I'm tired of making allowances.' Maud walks over to the fireplace and stares at her mother. 'If you tell me the truth,' she says slowly, 'I'll come home.'

'You're part of this family.' Letty stares back at her, wills herself not to look away. 'We want you back.'

'Who is he – this Le Lacheur man? Old Mum said you used to work for him before you met Pa.'

So her mother-in-law has been stirring the pot, although it seems that Maud hasn't sought Le Lacheur out as yet. That at least is some comfort. Letty sniffs. She cannot bring herself to say it, she will not.

'Men can't be trusted,' she says shortly. 'Doesn't matter how much money they've got or how many long words they use. I learnt my lesson and you should learn from it too.'

It is as much of a confession as she is willing to make and she holds up her hand as the questions come again. 'I mean it, Maud. What's past is past. You have a father, the one who's fed and clothed you since the day you were born. There's many that don't – you should be grateful.'

'Then why hasn't he come?' There is a tremor in Maud's voice.

'He said it was better if I spoke to you. Mother to daughter, like.' Letty reaches out and gives Maud's hand a tight squeeze. 'You can bring your accordion back. Practise whenever the fancy takes you. No point in dragging yourself down here in all weathers.'

Maud glances towards Old Mum's rocking chair with a small smile. 'You've never liked her.'

'And nor would you if you'd had someone looking down their nose at you for the best part of twenty years.' She gives Maud a sharp look. 'I hope it hasn't rubbed off.'

'Don't be silly.' Maud reddens with discomfort and Letty knows then she has won.

'Well, then.' Letty nods brusquely. 'Get your things together and we'll be going.'

Isabelle counts out Émile's wages for December and slips them inside a brown envelope, writes his name neatly across the front. She looks out of the window across the desolate garden. There are spring tides and the weather is foul; she'd got drenched cycling to work and had to push her bike for most of the way up Hauteville, the winds were so strong. Now, torrents of rain course from the gutters, the apple tree wrestles tirelessly with the wind; upstairs a door slams, floorboards creak and groan. The house is as unsettled as she is herself, and she looks again at the clock and tells herself firmly that if Émile isn't here by quarter past to collect his wages, she'll have to lock up and go. It has been thirty years after all; what she has to say to Émile – and she doesn't even know if she can find the words for it – will keep until the New Year, but she is scared of what she has found out, afraid that Ron will notice her preoccupation and winkle out its source.

Yesterday, when she had returned from her mother's, Isabelle had attributed her puffy eyes and balled-up hanky to an argument over 'something and nothing' and Ron had told her with a dripping condescension that if she asked him, it was high time Isabelle stood up to her mother. Well, that was exactly what had happened, but he must never know it.

Isabelle had made the journey up to St Martins under the pretext of helping her mother navigate the settings on her wireless set, which she complained had been impossible to tune since the Germans returned it. Within minutes, Isabelle had tuned the radio into the BBC and then they had sat together in the cramped parlour, listening to a turgid organ recital. Isabelle had felt her courage draining, until her eyes landed on the photograph of her and Ron, taken in a studio in Town the day after their wedding, in front of a badly painted backdrop of the Austrian Alps (Isabelle had always loathed it – she had wanted something plainer, a side table with flowers) and she could bear it no longer. She had turned off the radio and confronted her mother, asked her outright.

'Émile who?' her mother said at first, before her lips pursed in recognition. 'Oh, him. The deaf man.'

'He wasn't always deaf, was he?' Isabelle snapped. 'He wasn't deaf when he came here and asked Father if he could marry me, and the two of you treated him as if he was some kind of cheap salesman.'

'And that was better than he deserved. The cheek of the man.' Her mother had frowned, sat up in her chair. 'Isabelle, have you quite taken leave of your senses? What on earth's the matter?'

'Did he write?'

'What?'

'Were there any letters? From Canada?'

Her mother tutted, but didn't meet her eyes. 'Why would you ask such a thing? It was a lifetime ago.'

'I want to know if you and Father stole my letters.'

Isabelle is back there on the window seat of her bedroom, every morning at ten, waiting for the post. *I waited and waited for you, Belle.* The truth was written in the lines in her mother's face, in the murmurings behind closed doors, in the paper knife with the ivory handle, so prized by her father, which he used with overblown ceremony to open the morning mail.

'Isabelle, for heaven's sake, you're behaving like a child. Steal your letters! Your father and I wanted the best for you, that was all.'

'He did write, didn't he?'

'That man was not your equal!' For a frail woman, her mother's voice had surprising strength. 'If ever anyone had ideas above their station, it was Émile Quenneville. The man could barely spell.'

Isabelle hadn't been able to help herself: she had grasped her mother by the shoulders and shaken her, demanded to know what had become of the letters. The shock in her mother's watery eyes jolted her and she had let her go, her body hot with shame. She was no better than her husband, she thought, as the carriage clock on the mantlepiece whirred and began to chime four. Her mother took her stick and eased herself from the couch.

'Your problem, Isabelle,' she said, 'is that you don't know how to be happy. Father warned Ronald that he'd have his work cut out with you, and he wasn't wrong. The grass is always greener, isn't it? If you really want to know what kind of life you'd have had with that so-called suitor of yours, look at his wife. He did get married in the end, I believe?'

Isabelle had nodded dumbly.

'Scrubbing floors for a living, being refused credit in front of half the neighbourhood, scrimping to put food on the table. Is that what you wanted? Is it?'

Then she had taken a small key from one of the bureau drawers and tossed it towards Isabelle. 'Bottom drawer, back compartment. Your father should have burnt the lot of them when he had the chance.' She began to hobble towards the door. 'If you've got even a modicum of sense left, I suggest you start counting your blessings and go home to your husband.'

The letters were delicate as moth wings, the wafer-thin paper fragile with age. There was her name, repeated carefully and patiently over and over. *Dear Isabelle. Dearest Isabelle. My dear Isabelle.* He wrote of the neat clapperboard houses with the front porches and steps where the men sit and smoke when it's warm of an evening, his long night shifts at the dairy with the blokes from Ireland and Japan and China, the savings account he has opened for them both; then as the winter comes, the snow, the damned snow, more grey than white. *I miss you. Please write.*

Then the letters stopped. For a month, there was nothing. When they started up again, the handwriting was that of someone much older, shaky, at times, barely legible. He was writing from hospital; he had had a fall – a bad one – while he was on nights at the dairy. His collarbone was broken and it hurt like hell, but that was nothing compared to the main problem, which was that he couldn't hear, not a peep. Every night, he dreamt that he was lying at the bottom of the lift shaft, bellowing for help, and sometimes the nurses sedated him because the racket he made disturbed the rest of the ward.

Isabelle forced herself to go on. He was angry now – with the doctors, the dairy, particularly the dairy. He had taken advice from a lawyer and would be suing them, he will have the money to buy three homesteads then, should the fancy take him, and get his hearing fixed. He was angry with her too, she was no longer 'Dearest Isabelle'; he had stopped asking her to write. The final letter was postmarked on the day she got married to Ron and it was brief.

Isabelle,

There might be thousands of miles between us, but I haven't gone soft in the head – I know when someone's taking me for a fool. That said, I never reckoned it would be you, so that makes me more of a fool than I think.

Do what you want with the ring – Ingrouille on the Bridge should give you a good price for it.

E

If she had just kept the faith. If she hadn't allowed her mother's judgement to pollute her own, if she had kept writing no matter what, if her father hadn't been such a bully. Isabelle runs her finger across the underside of her chipped front tooth. She has always been too scared to take risks and this is where she has landed. It is of her own making. Outside, the wind howls. An idea forms from the silt of this bottomless afternoon and for her, it is audacious. She will deliver Émile's wages to him personally; she will cycle up to his home in L'Islet, and the new year will be her alibi. She was just passing, she will say, and what with tomorrow being a holiday, she didn't want him to have to wait for his wages until he was back at work.

Isabelle thinks for a moment, then taking a pen, she writes a short note, puts it in the envelope with the wages, and licks it shut.

So Maud is back. The kitchen smells of meat, for once, not boiled potatoes, and Letty has bought him some beer from somewhere and set it at his place at the table. Stella has been instructed to get out the pack of cards.

'I thought we could have a game of whist before tea,' Letty says to Émile and he thinks that there aren't enough coupons in the whole of the parish to pay for the buttering up she's doing. Letty hates cards; she doesn't have the patience for it.

'Decided to come home, then?' he says to Maud and she lifts her head and says, hello, Pa, as if she has nothing to be sorry for, and he thanks his lucky stars for Stella dancing along to a tune on the wireless, as she shuffles and re-shuffles the cards. He always knows where he is with his youngest daughter.

They play one game and then another. He and Stella are winning. Then Letty looks up, frowning, and Stella says, 'Who's that?', and Émile half-expects to see his mother at the door, ready to make trouble. But it is a woman in a waterproof headscarf and a green mackintosh, like the one Isabelle wears, and it *is* Isabelle, soaked through from the rain. But why is she here? Why does he feel both glad and furious that she should turn up like this? Letty is looking at him, not Isabelle, frowning as if he's expressly invited the woman without her say so, and he gets to his feet, but to do what, he hasn't the first clue.

Isabelle takes an envelope from her pocket and hands it to him across the table, rainwater from her coat sleeve speckling the playing cards.

'I was just passing,' Isabelle is saying. She smiles at the girls, at Letty, at the clock on the mantlepiece – anywhere but at him. 'Happy New Year!'

Then she is gone, and Letty goes to the window and lingers there, looking out. When she takes her place at the table, she says something about Isabelle that Émile suspects is less than charitable, because Maud remonstrates with her, nods towards the envelope.

They continue playing but Émile can no longer concentrate, loses this game and the next, until Letty with a bit of a temper on her tells the girls they should call it a day – their pa, she informs them, is bored.

Later, when Letty is getting ready for bed, Émile opens the envelope. Somehow he is not surprised to find a slip of paper, discreetly folded underneath his pay. He holds it to the lamp and reads.

I should never have doubted you.
  Belle

Letty appears in the doorway in her nightdress. 'All there?' she asks, pointing at the envelope.

Émile nods.

Come to bed, she says, or at least he thinks that's what she says – it is not a phrase he has seen in his wife's mouth for some time and he remembers the look Letty gave Isabelle when she came into the kitchen. His wife might not be able to spell but she knows when something's up; she smells it like blood. He stuffs Isabelle's note in his pocket and tells her he won't be long.

When he comes into the bedroom, he is surprised to find Letty still up, brushing out her hair at the dressing table. He undresses down to his long johns and vest and gets into bed. He catches Letty's reflection in the looking glass.

'What did you tell Maud?' he asks, jerking his head towards the girls' bedroom. 'To bring her back?'

Letty shrugs and turns to face him. 'Nothing much.'

'Does she know?' He can't bring himself to say Le Lacheur's name.

Letty pauses. 'You're her father. I told her that. That's the end of it.'

She puts down the hairbrush, then abruptly pulls her nightdress over her head. Taking the candle, she stands rather awkwardly opposite the bed, shivering. She wants him to look at her, Émile realises, desires it. It is so long since she has let him take pleasure in seeing her naked body that he is unseated by it; it almost feels wrong. He looks away. He doesn't want to, he's not in the mood. He thinks of her again with Le Lacheur, parting her legs for biscuits and loose change.

Letty climbs under the covers and places a cold hand on his penis. As her fingers curl around him, his body starts to respond, although his mind wanders. Was the note from Isabelle some kind of apology? Is that why she cycled through the storm? Well, it's too late now for sorry and brandy and dancing, war or no war. Émile runs a hand over Letty's behind to distract himself and she takes this as a sign that he is ready, and pulls him on top of her. His erection flails, subsides, and he sees the disappointment etched across her face. She is still his wife. In her own way she is trying, and he must try too.

Émile closes his eyes. He thinks of the last time he visited Céline, how Isabelle's sadness had clung to him until he could bear it no longer and all he wanted was a transaction, quick and easy, two shillings in the tea caddy and Céline's musky scent, her nonchalance as she slipped off her nightgown, positioned herself in her usual place on the bed. He calls up the memory. It had aroused him at the time, but not now, not with Letty; all he feels is shame. He is like a drowned man washed up on a bank of cold shingle, he thinks he may have to give up, but then another image floats in his head and once there it refuses to clear. Isabelle grasping his left hand, the swell of her breasts under her dress, the arch of her neck, the old pathway for his kisses – collarbone to earlobe and back again. He has never seen her naked, and it is a long time since he has let himself imagine it. He is hard again and inside Letty almost without knowing it; but then it is only a few strokes before it's finished, and he feels as if he's betrayed her all over again.

Letty turns on her side, snuffs out the candle. Émile reaches for her, rests his hand on her hip, but there is nothing natural in it – they sleep apart, not together – and after a few minutes, he rolls away, stares into the darkness. If he could only have his time over again. If things had worked out the way he'd planned, if he'd found a job on a homestead, not Vancouver, not the dairy, if he'd followed the cycle of the seasons, sowing and reaping and trading at market. Or if the two of them, he and Isabelle, had been braver, if they'd gone to Canada together as newlyweds and told anyone who didn't like it to go to buggery. Those parents of hers had thought they were so fine when anyone could see that they were just jumped-up country folk; her mother spoke patois as well as the next person.

So she hadn't received his letters – well, no more had he had word from her and he hadn't started looking around for someone else to marry. But Isabelle had not been free to love who she chose. In his heart he had always known that, but it had taken that brute of a father of hers to tell him, standing by the mantlepiece in that dusty parlour, where they hadn't offered him so much as a cup of tea – and there was Émile, all trussed up in a borrowed suit and waistcoat, boots shining like mirrors, as if it was the wedding day already come.

'You must be out of your mind, Mr Quenneville,' her father had said. 'You must be out of your mind if you think that I would allow my daughter to go to the other side of the world with someone like you.'

The man had smiled, almost pleasantly, after he'd said it, and then called for the maid to show him out.

No, he should never have left her. Émile thinks again of her husband, the way the man had shooed him away in the pub, dismissing him in much the same way Isabelle's father had. He has an inkling then of the person she has married and how it came to be, for why wouldn't her father choose someone he recognised, in whom he saw something of himself?

The darkness with its own heavy silence presses upon him, second upon second, minute upon minute, until the old year is smothered by the new one and Émile drifts towards sleep.

'Pubic lice, Mrs Quenneville. Regrettably.' The doctor pauses as Letty emerges from the curtained cubicle. 'Tiny parasites, barely visible to the human eye. Spread through close, usually sexual, bodily contact.'

He doesn't invite her to sit down so she stands self-consciously by his desk as he reaches for his prescription pad.

'Lousing powder, twice daily in the affected areas. Cool baths. A poultice might help relieve the swelling.' He hands her the chit and meets her eye for the first time. 'Your husband too, obviously. Has he complained of similar symptoms?'

Letty shakes her head. 'He's deaf,' she says, as if this somehow explains it. Now she thinks of it, he has been as restless at night as she has, grunting and moaning more than usual in his sleep. Her lips tighten. It'll be one of those tarts on Cornet Street – it's happened before, but she'd thought all that nonsense had stopped since the Germans came. She finds herself suddenly a little short of breath. How could he?

The doctor is holding open the door, now, and there is nothing polite about the way he does it.

'Wouldn't hurt to give the bedclothes a wash while you're at it,' he says and Letty is so embarrassed she almost forgets the itching. When she arrives home a little later, she could swear her cheeks are still scorched with the humiliation of it all.

It is late afternoon and everyone is out. She locks herself in the bathroom, takes a pair of kitchen scissors and cuts off as much of the hair down below as she can, then applies the powder. It stings and leaves her smelling like paint stripper. She goes to the bedroom and rips the sheets from the bed, puts water on to boil. No matter that it's not laundry day and the girls will ask questions. She will never forget the way the doctor looked at her, as if she was some slut, no better than the one who gave it to him. *Wouldn't hurt to give the bedclothes a wash.* The cheek of it, while Émile got away scot-free. She should have kept well away from him on New Year's Eve; the whole thing had been over in a matter of seconds, with precious little pleasure in it for her and him barely able to do what a proper man would.

Letty dumps the bedclothes in a steel drum of hot water, rolls up her sleeves and begins to scrub. When Maud and Stella get home, she packs them off to Old Mum's and tells them to come back after tea. She has just put the last sheet through the mangle when the back door opens.

'All right?' Émile calls through to the scullery. He wears the same bewildered look as the girls had earlier when he sees her up to her armpits in laundry.

Letty comes into the kitchen and yanks his arm, pulling him through to the bedroom. She smacks a packet of lousing powder against his chest.

'You're not fit to be a husband, nor a father neither.'

He stares at her, then looks at the packet.

'You gave me lice.' She is trembling, barely able to get the words out. 'Lice!' she says again, more emphatically. She points between her legs. 'Down below.'

Émile turns crimson and Letty can almost feel the heat coming from him. He looks anxiously towards the door.

'The girls are at your mother's,' she snaps. 'This isn't for their ears.'

Émile rubs at the greying stubble on his chin. His eyes are watery and full, but Letty isn't having any of it. To think that there were some that said that she'd done well for herself with Émile, that she'd married above her. She would rather sleep with Le Lacheur ten times over, she thinks, than open her legs for her husband again.

'Find somewhere else to go tonight, Émile,' she says. 'I don't want you near me.'

Émile has nowhere to go and so he finds himself in the Caves. He buys a half of beer and settles himself in a corner. Familiar faces haunt the bar, men he has known for most of his life. They nod at him and then get back to the business of drinking. He senses the quiet in the room, the unease. Six months since the Germans arrived and not a man among them who wasn't a few pounds lighter, or a touch greyer. Too old to fight and too young to die. He thinks of Letty, the way her hands were shaking with fury when she gave him the lousing powder, the smell of washday on her. She was right to be angry. He'd been sent half-mad from the itching himself; he should have realised what it was. He wondered how many of these silent arguments they'd had in nineteen years and whether they'd have had fewer if he'd been able to hear the viciousness in them.

He finishes up his beer and returns the tankard to the bar. The place is clearing now, the manager wiping down the tables; they are in the shadow of curfew. Émile slips unnoticed into the deserted street. A cold, prickly rain stings his face and he winces. He's gone soft, he thinks. He'd survived a Canadian winter without grumbling as much as some. His feet drag him up towards Hauteville and as he fingers the keys in his pocket, he wonders how he has allowed his world to become so small. The French House looms large before him, the oak tree still as a sentinel. There could be worse places than the shed to spend the night. He will bed down on the floor alongside the trays of potato seed, wrap himself up like a mummy in the old, creosote-splattered dog blanket.

The rain is getting heavier. He tries to remember the roar of it as it falls, the slippery, sluicing sound of a world turned liquid. He lets himself into the side passage, collects the torch from behind the pot of rosemary on the kitchen step then crosses the sodden garden towards the enclosure.

When Émile turns the key in the lock, there is no resistance: the door is open. A wave of unease consumes him. He always locks up – he takes great care to do so, turning back sometimes to double-check. He has a sudden image of Isabelle huddled up in the corner of the shed, before he tells himself not to be fanciful. On a filthy night like this one, she will be warm and dry at home, and even if for whatever reason that weren't the case, she has the keys to the house; she wouldn't need to take refuge in a shed.

He waves the beam of the torch back and forth along the length of the enclosure, then stops abruptly. There is a ladder – his ladder – removed from its brackets and extended to its full height against the outer wall. The sheer nerve of it paralyses Émile for a few seconds, then sensing movement from the shed, he turns. The door bursts open and a young lad bolts out, running directly for the ladder. As Émile moves to stop him, the man shoves him hard and Émile stumbles, slipping on the muddy ground. Swearing at the intruder who is now halfway up the ladder, Émile gets to his feet and shakes the lower rungs with full force. The man glances fearfully over his shoulder and for a moment his face is illuminated in the funnel of white torchlight and Émile recognises him. It's the Ozanne boy, Ozzy, as slippery a customer as the fish he sells under the counter, the one who makes a song and dance of flirting with Stella when he does deliveries. There's always been something off about him, Émile thinks, like he's hiding something, and he yells at the lad, calling him a thieving bastard, just as he reaches the top of the wall.

Émile is about to give chase when something or some-one grasps his shoulder, and it scares the life out of him to be crept up on. Cursing himself for not keeping his wits about him, he swivels and swings his fist, makes contact with the bridge of a nose. The man staggers backwards, holding a hand over his face, and as Émile shines the torch on him, his heart drops. He stares. Unless Ozzy's accom-plice has taken to dressing up like a Nazi for larks, it appears that Émile has just hit a German, bloodied his nose, to be precise, the blood now dripping onto his grey tunic, which is unevenly buttoned and loose at the neck.

He's in for it now, Émile thinks, and he doesn't know whether to scarper or say he's sorry, or both. Then as the German reaches for a handkerchief to stem the flow of blood, Émile sees his face properly.

'You!' He turns towards the shed, and it all slots into place – the spare set of keys that had gone from the hook and he'd assumed Isabelle had taken; this German shiv-ering in front of him, sitting in the enclosure in the autumn sunshine with his sketch pad and cigarettes. Nice spot, wasn't that what he'd said? It is Isabelle's billet, Schreiber.

Rain streaks Schreiber's face. His mouth moves, but Émile cannot make the words out, if indeed there are any to interpret, and before he can ask, the man has fled through the enclosure door, leaving it swinging back and forth on its hinges with the force of his departure.

It is the scene inside the shed that gives Émile the heart of the story, that and the smell of bodies and sweat and secret places, of cigarettes recently smoked. The blanket is rumpled and strewn across the floor; a silver hip flask sits next to the seeding trays; a pair of neatly folded spectacles glint at him from their place on the bench. One of them has left a scarf behind – it is thicker and warmer than his own, and Émile wraps it around his neck, takes a swig from the hip flask. Bloody idiot German creeping up on him like that. He was asking to be walloped.

He stares at Maud's portrait that Schreiber had given him, the paper yellowing a little now, and wonders how long it has been going on, this – thing – with Ozanne in his shed. The brandy soothes his mangled nerves, and he drinks a little more. There was something you wouldn't catch in the back of the *Press*, amongst the barter advertisements – *German leutnant would like to meet fisherman for exchange of conversation, bodily fluids, and more.* Émile shakes his head. Schreiber should have hit him back – they'd have been kind of even then – but anyone can see the man doesn't have it in him. He's a gentle type, and Émile feels sorry for him suddenly.

He shakes out the blanket and lies down on the floor, where the men were before him. He thinks of Letty, alone in their bed, sprawled in the centre of it, mouth open. His last thought before exhaustion overcomes the cold and the gnawing hunger is that a night apart from his wife isn't that much different from one spent together, and he buries deeper into the folds of the blanket, breathing in what remains of another man's passion.

Émile doesn't go home the next day, nor the day after. He washes in the water butt, survives on bread and raw carrots, applies the powder Letty gave him by candlelight in the privacy of the shed. He avoids Isabelle as much as possible, his body prickling with humiliation whenever he sees her. The spectacles remain on the shelf, along with the now empty hip flask; Émile supposes Schreiber can live without the flask, but not the specs, surely. It occurs to him that he, himself, might be under surveillance, that Schreiber might be waiting for him to leave. Then, on his third night, just as he has finished what passes for supper, the door to the shed swings open and Schreiber appears. He peers at Émile through the dim candlelight.

You're still here, he seems to say, and he approaches cautiously, as if half expecting Émile to hit him again.

'I'm sorry.' Émile gestures towards the German's nose. 'You gave me a fright, see.'

He hands Schreiber his spectacles and after a moment's hesitation, the hip flask. The German nods graciously, a little self-conscious as he puts on his glasses, before taking out his notepad.

'You're living here?' he asks, his brow creased, and Émile tells him no, that is, yes, only temporarily. 'Problems at home,' he explains. 'Letting the dust settle.'

'Ah.' The German gives him a quizzical look, then delves into the deep pocket of his greatcoat and passes him a small sausage-shaped package wrapped in newspaper. Émile can smell that it is meat of some kind and as he opens it, he feels almost faint with longing.

Blutwurst (Bavaria) Schreiber writes, and as he takes a bite, Émile thinks he doesn't really care where it's from, or the fact that it has teeth marks on it already – the stuff is delicious.

'I'm sorry,' the German is saying now. 'About the other night.'

No harm done, Émile says, wondering when the man will get to the crux of the matter, for he may have given him sausage, but he hasn't given him the keys back and he's beginning to think there's as much chance of that happening as there is of Hitler changing his mind and calling the whole thing off.

Schreiber starts to scribble.

Mr Ozanne is worried.

Here it comes. Émile wipes his mouth on the back of his hand and looks at him.

About his reputation.

Ozzy's reputation as what? A con artist or a ladies' man? Émile suppresses a smirk. But Schreiber is watching him intently, and Émile understands how much this matters, that he should forget what he saw, tell no one. He wants to tell Schreiber that he and Mr Ozanne aren't the first to meet in secret, Émile knows that better than most, and he's got enough on his plate without worrying about what the pair of them might be getting up to on the floor of his shed.

'It's your business,' he says. 'Not mine.'

Relief washes over the German's face and Émile feels awkward for being the cause of it. There would be some wearing that same uniform who would have Schreiber's type swinging from a lamp post, he supposes, but Émile isn't one of them. He wishes Schreiber good night, finishes the rest of the sausage, then braces himself for another night of penance on the floor.

Isabelle is in the upstairs office, typing up a monthly report for Grange Lodge, when the tradesmen's bell goes. Glancing out of the window, she sees that it is Émile's wife – Letty – standing at the side entrance in a navy raincoat, and the look on her face is far from friendly. Letty points at the door and then at Isabelle before pressing her finger against the bell another time for good measure.

Didn't anyone ever tell her it was rude to point! Isabelle steps out of view and slowly makes her way downstairs. So this is payback time, she supposes, and she wonders what had possessed her to write that note for Émile. She wouldn't be surprised if he passed his wages straight to Letty; he certainly hadn't mentioned it since and going to their house like that had just made her miserable, seeing them all sat around playing cards, like a scene straight out of Laura Ingalls Wilder.

As she goes outside to the passageway, she feels the same churning sick feeling she gets when Ron has come home in one of his tempers. Actions have consequences, Isabelle, she tells herself, as she unlocks the door, but it's so unfair when she hasn't really done anything other than a bit of daydreaming, and since when is that a crime?

'Mrs Quenneville,' she says.

Letty is made up in a rather slapdash way, her cheeks daubed with rouge – which she doesn't need as her colour is high already – and orange lipstick, faint in some places and not in others, feathering chapped lips.

'I wanted to check he's come into work,' Letty says without preamble, looking at her sharply.

'Émile?'

'Not got any other husbands, last time I looked.'

'Oh!' So she is a conduit for Letty's rage, rather than the target. Isabelle regains her composure. 'Come through to the kitchen. I'll call him.'

Letty doesn't move. 'There's no need. Just tell him to get his backside home tonight, will you?' She stares over Isabelle's shoulder into the far distance. 'The rent's due.'

So the lipstick and the rouge is all front; Isabelle feels a wave of sympathy for the woman.

'I'll tell him,' she says. 'Don't worry.'

Letty nods curtly and bolts off, her footsteps echoing down the street.

Isabelle goes back to the kitchen. She had got in early that morning and gone down to the shed to fetch some paraffin, where she had been surprised to see Émile bent over the water butt, dousing his face. Now it seemed that he hadn't been home at all last night, perhaps not for days. She glances at the clock and sees that it's almost time for elevenses, and she brews up some acorn tea and fills a flask to take down to the shed.

When she gets to the enclosure, the shed door is ajar. Inside, Émile is hunched on the bench, smoking. He looks up in surprise and sits up a little straighter, hesitating when she asks if she can come in. He nods and clears the potting trays from the bench to make space.

Isabelle hands him the flask. 'Pretend it's real tea,' she says with a small smile. 'Not that I ever can.'

He thanks her and pours the tea, gulps it down with gusto.

'Letty was here,' Isabelle says.

'Letty?' He looks at her warily. 'When?'

'Just now.' Isabelle swallows. 'She says you haven't been home. She needs you there.'

When he says nothing, she repeats it, and he grimaces and shakes his head. 'She don't need me.'

Isabelle looks around the shed, spots the blanket wedged under the bench, the stub of a candle on top of the toolbox.

'Have you been sleeping here?'

'Just a few nights.' Émile gives her the faintest echo of a smile. 'You want to charge me rent?'

'A few nights!' Isabelle stares at him. She must have been blind not to notice, but she sees it now: the grainy pallor of his skin, the bloodshot eyes. 'Why?' She hesitates. 'Is it because of me? Coming to the house?'

'No.' He looks away, mumbles something about an infection.

'Are you ill? Is Letty or one of the girls?'

He will not answer her. Isabelle takes his notebook and pencil, and turns to a new page.

You look dreadful!

She thrusts it at him and Émile studies it, then throws back his head and laughs. The sound swells around them, like the first sweeping chord of an accordion polka; it is as if he has saved it up for this moment, and she doesn't know what she has said really, other than insult him, but she is glad in any case and, after a moment, she joins in.

He grins. 'I feel it,' he says. 'I'm not eighteen anymore, that's for certain.'

'Nor me.' Her hand goes to the frizzy grey hairs at the crown of her head, which she used to remove with tweezers but recently hasn't bothered. She gets to her feet, suddenly self-conscious.

'I'll arrange an advance on your wages,' she says, 'so you can take care of things.'

She gestures for the notebook but he has understood and is shaking his head. 'No need.'

'I know.' Isabelle thinks again of Letty. She is Occupation thin, and the weight loss doesn't suit her. 'But I'm sure you'll find a use for it.'

Émile hands back the flask.

'Best be getting on,' he says, putting on a scarf that draws Isabelle's attention. It is not the one he usually wears, which is grey and fraying at the edges; this one is navy with three tassels at each end and a cable knit detail running through the centre. It has been made with care, and she should know because it is remarkably similar to the one she gave Schreiber for Christmas.

'Where did you get that?' She regards him closely, but he will not look her in the eye.

'Found it.' Émile's colour seems to rise. 'Some folks don't take enough care of their things.'

Isabelle pauses. 'I suppose you're right,' she says.

She returns to the house and the report for Grange Lodge, but she cannot settle. What would Émile be doing with Peter's scarf? She must be mistaken. And yet, when she enquired after it, he had flushed. She thinks of the sketches again and a strange, unsettling notion occurs to her. She tells herself not to be ridiculous, and gets back to the accounts.

That night, once Isabelle is certain that Ron is unshakeably asleep, she gets out of bed and creeps down the hallway into the living room. She takes the small copper key from the pencil pot on the bureau and unlocks the bottom drawer, where Ron keeps their rainy day money. There could be no advance on Émile's wages – the Hauteville accounts were stretched as it was – but she had known it was the only way he'd accept any money. She takes out a one pound note and stuffs it inside an old, denuded lipstick, which she places in the zipped compartment of her handbag. Then, she tiptoes back to the bedroom. As she climbs into bed, Ron stirs.

'What are you up to, Izzy?' His voice is surprisingly crisp, unsoftened by sleep.

'Just went to the lav,' she says, drawing the covers tightly around her. 'Sorry to wake you.'

'I wasn't asleep,' he says, and the possibility of it is enough to keep Isabelle from sleep herself. She is still awake when a sallow dawn seeps through the blackout blinds, and she warns herself never to underestimate the man she married.

The next day when Isabelle takes Émile the money, she finds that he has shaved and the thick seam of grime has gone from under his fingernails. He is still wearing the scarf which, regardless of how he acquired it, suits him, bringing out the blue-grey of his eyes. He stops digging and thanks her, tucks the pound note in his back pocket. As she turns to leave, he calls out.

'Better looking today, am I?'

'Pardon?'

Isabelle looks back. He is smiling in the way she remembers when he used to tease her, when they first met. *Please don't tell me you're in the Temperance Society – you're not, well, thank the Lord for that!* No, she wasn't about to sign the pledge, but she was in a sewing circle and he should be grateful for it, because they met on a Wednesday afternoon, which coincided nicely with his half day off from the vinery. She always arrived to meet him carrying her tapestry bag, which contained the tablecloth she was making – it still remained unfinished at the end of the summer, when her alibi became her downfall and her mother found out where she hadn't been for the past two months. But the tablecloth had become a standing joke between them – Émile would enquire after its progress, in the same breath as he would ask after her mother's well-being – and she is reminded now, with a pang of sadness, of how the two of them used to be when they were together.

'A fraction,' she mouths back and he gives her a mini-salute, then gets back to the digging.

Maud walks down the darkening High Street past one barter shop after another and tries to remember what was in their place before the war started. The sweet shop has closed, and the haberdasher's next to it. Creasey's is one of the few places where there are still things left to buy, although the woman who just served her told her to treat her new pair of stockings with kid gloves as they were almost completely out of stock. Now it is almost teatime and Maud feels worn out and crochety, which is nothing new these days because her life has just flipped right back to what it used to be, and she has let it happen.

'We'll always be sisters, Mo,' Stella had said on her first night back after being at Old Mum's. 'Nothing's changed' – and a heaviness had settled on Maud as she lay in her old bed, trying to block out the sounds of what could only be copulation from her parents' room next door, and the black thought that her mother was showing her gratitude to Pa for letting Maud back in. As for Pa, he treated her absence as if it had been nothing more than some childish whim, something easily forgotten with a game of cards and a little bit extra at teatime.

She cuts down an alleyway and is some way from the High Street, before she notices a huddle of German soldiers in the gloom ahead of her. They form a line as she approaches and she sees that they are young, not much older than she is, and they wear a collective smirk. Her heart starts to thump and she has just turned to retrace her steps when one of them calls out to her.

'Halt!' The man bends forward and beckons to her with his index finger, as if coaxing a small child. The others laugh.

'Your papers, Fräulein.'

Maud hands him her identity card. His companions peer over her shoulder as he studies her photo. More laughter follows.

'The Fräulein is very serious, no?' The man moves towards her and chucks her under the chin.

Maud recoils and steps away. They crowd around her, backing her against the wall. She can no longer see the street: she can smell the damp wool of their tunics, the tar soap. They banter back and forth in German and Maud isn't sure if it's better or worse not to be able to understand. She jostles against them trying to get out but they just move closer.

'Maybe it's her monthly time,' one of them says. His cheeks are pitted with acne scars. 'Shall we find out?'

He forces his hand under her skirt. His fingers, rough and cold, crawl up her skin. Not to her, Maud thinks, this can't be happening to her. For a few seconds, she is frozen, reduced to an inch of copy in the *Press*. *Woman, 18, assaulted in Town. The German authorities are investigating the incident.*

Maud screams and screams again and suddenly the mass of uniforms thins out and she hears a man's voice, gruff with authority, bellowing down the alley.

'What the hell is going on?'

The soldier with the acne scoffs. 'Nothing to do with you, old man.'

The man *is* old. He walks with a limp and his stick makes a clipping sound on the cobbles, and Maud's heart sinks, for what help can he be? But there is something familiar about his gait and as he approaches, her breath comes faster. It is Le Lacheur.

'We'll see what Kommandant Maas has to say about that,' he says, and the mention of the Kommandant's name, the ease with which it slides off his tongue, acts like a gunshot amongst the men: they flinch, unsettled.

'I have a delivery of wine for Grange Lodge tomorrow morning, as it happens.' Le Lacheur surveys the group. 'Names, please.'

The Germans are silent.

'*Namen!*'

Slowly, reluctantly, the men mumble their names. They are like schoolboys about to be caned, Maud thinks, and it is almost as if she has imagined the whole thing. Le Lacheur repeats the names back, then shakes his stick at them, as if they're a flock of pigeons that have got in his way.

'Off with you!'

He watches as they hurry down the deserted street. 'I'd horsewhip the lot of them myself if I could,' he says coldly. 'I hope they didn't hurt you, my dear.'

He is solicitous but distant and for a moment, Maud thinks he hasn't recognised her.

'I'm all right – thank you.' Her hands tremble in time with her voice, which quivers and shakes and doesn't sound like her own.

'It's Maud,' she adds, and he gives her a small smile.

'I know,' he says. He offers her his arm and it's a second before Maud realises she is expected to take it. 'Now, how about an early supper? I, for one, could do with a drink.'

They go to the People's Friend in the Pollet. The manager greets Le Lacheur by name and gives them a table by the fire. Le Lacheur orders beef broth for them both and a bottle of claret. Maud watches as he swirls the wine around the glass, breathing in the aroma, while the waiter stands attendant. Rolling back the sleeves of her yellow sweater to hide the tea stain on the cuff, she wishes she was wearing any skirt but her ancient plaid one, which is faded and worn and makes her feel about twelve years old. She feels as if she has just been hatched. She is shy, her head empty of anything that might be worthwhile to say. She has imagined this encounter or similar a hundred times over since they first met, has longed for it, but in her fantasies, there was never this awkwardness. Conversation had flowed like the tide, like blood through veins . . . like father to daughter. Could he be? Is she right? Maud takes another sip of the wine she isn't sure she likes, and thanks Le Lacheur again for intervening.

He tells her he'd been checking up on a delivery of Burgundy to the Soldatenheim and was on his way back to the office when he heard her screams.

'Call it providence.' He takes a mouthful of soup. 'To tell you the truth, I've been hoping our paths might cross again.'

His tone is casual but it holds the weight of a question. Maud stares at him and then down at her broth.

'Your card caused quite a row at home,' she says evenly. 'Pa said I wasn't to contact you. Ma said the same.'

'You always do what your ma and pa tell you, do you? You surprise me, Maud!' Le Lacheur chuckles and reaches for the bottle. 'Look' – he leans towards her, lowers his voice – 'I don't know what you've heard but Letty – your ma – used to work for me, back in the day. Don't mind saying I had a soft spot for her – she wasn't scared of hard work, not like some – and I respect that. She was courting your father, got herself in a spot of trouble, and my late wife, God bless her, couldn't keep her on, not in her condition.' He shrugs. 'As I recall, your father was rather angry about it.' He wipes his mouth with a napkin. 'If you ask me, the past is the past. Does no good to hold grudges.'

So it is not what she thought, after all. Maud looks at him blankly. The truth she has craved is mundane, ordinary. She could have been born the wrong side of the blanket, but her father had seen to it that she wasn't. He had married her mother and resented the reason for it. *You never wanted her.* She forces down more wine.

Le Lacheur studies her. 'And you, young lady, have done very well for yourself by all accounts.' He wags his finger. 'Matriculated top of your class at the Intermediate, I hear? Not often that happens with a scholarship girl. You should be thinking of teacher training college, not wasting your talents at Amherst Infants.'

How does he know so much about her? For an instant, she is not sure if she has thought the question or said it out loud, because he is answering her now, saying he has his sources, he likes to keep abreast of who's who, and what's what on the island, and while he's about it, how's her French?

'My French? Passable, I suppose.'

'Ever been?'

'No.'

'Would you like to?'

'Yes, especially Paris.'

A smile creeps across his face, and Maud suspects him of making fun of her. 'You're inviting me, I suppose?' she says, archly.

However the sharpness in her tone appears to delight not offend, as Le Lacheur laughs and says in a manner of speaking, he might be. He is petitioning the Controlling Committee for another trip in a few months' time and an assistant would be helpful, especially at his time of life. Not just for the trips, come to think of it, but in the office too – to run a few errands, do the accounts.

'I need some young blood around the place,' he says, leaning back in his chair. 'A couple of afternoons a week.'

'I can't.' Maud drains her wine glass, this time without needing to grimace. 'My parents would never agree, I'm afraid.'

'Then don't tell 'em!' Le Lacheur gestures for the bill, rifles through the notes in his wallet. 'You're not a child. This war won't last forever, and when it's over, you need to be ready. Paris doesn't come cheap.'

She looks at him. He believes in her, this man who has made something of himself, he has seen in her what she sees, what she knows has been there all along. Her heart skips. She will remember this moment always, the black-berry taste of the wine, the blue-black shine of his eyes in the firelight, urging her to be bold. He understands what she wants, she thinks, in a way her parents never could.

'I want to,' she says. 'I do. I just need a day or two to think it over.'

'Of course. Shall we?' He beckons to the waiter to bring their coats.

Outside, it has started to rain. Le Lacheur puts up his umbrella and glances at her. 'You're not planning on getting married, are you?'

Maud frowns, a little startled. 'No, of course not.'

'Sensible girl.' Le Lacheur pats her shoulder. 'Let me know by Monday. I'll put an ad in the *Press* otherwise.'

Maud is halfway to the tram terminus when the first wave of nausea hits her and she vomits the beef broth into the gutter. She attributes the churning in her stomach to the wine and the shock from earlier, and she is just thankful that Le Lacheur isn't there to witness it. Leaning against the wall, she wipes her mouth with her handkerchief. She will tell no one about today, not even Stella, ask nobody's permission for what she is about to do next. It is time for her life to begin.

Le Lacheur's offices are gloomier than Maud expected and smell of stale cigar smoke and dust. A brisk, severe-looking woman in a lavender cardigan, who introduces herself as Miss Guille, leads Maud up a narrow flight of steps and into a poky room that is stuffed with filing cabinets and one large desk. From the manner in which Miss Guille slams down the pile of ledgers, Maud understands that she is not wholly complicit in Le Lacheur's desire for young blood around the place, particularly when this involves having to share her desk.

'Mr Le Lacheur tells me you're good with figures,' she says stiffly. 'You can start with these.'

Maud takes a seat on the rickety chair and opens the first ledger. Columns of numbers sway before her. She can hear no sound from the room next door. 'Is Mr Le Lacheur in today?'

'He's out at meetings.' Miss Guille plumps herself down at the desk and reels a sheet of paper into her typewriter.

'No need to concern yourself with the whys and the where-fores. Now, check the numbers tally and try not to blot.'

Maud fingers the pearl buttons on the red blouse she borrowed from Stella. As far as her sister and parents know, she is giving singing lessons to a pair of nine-year-old twins who live in a big house on the Grange. Twice weekly, she'd told them, and the money was good. Le Lacheur will be in later, she tells herself; he can't just leave her here with this guard dog in a cardigan on her first afternoon. Trying to block out the repetitive clatter of the typewriter, she takes a ruler and begins to inch her way down the rows of figures.

At around four, just as Miss Guille is putting on her coat to leave, the front door slams and there comes the sound of Le Lacheur's cane knocking against the stairs. He pokes his head around the door of their office, wheezing a little.

'Ladies.' His gaze skims Maud, but does not settle. 'And how is our new assistant coming along, Miss Guille?'

'All satisfactory, as far as I can see,' she says with a tight smile. 'I'm leaving early today, as we agreed.'

'Splendid.' He tips his hat at them both and then disappears into the room next door.

Miss Guille waits for a moment and then lowers her voice. 'No need to stay late, if he asks, Miss Quenneville. I can pick up anything that doesn't get done tomorrow.'

Maud shrugs. 'I don't mind doing a bit extra.'

'Suit yourself.' The woman gives her a stark look. 'I don't suppose you put on that pretty blouse for nothing, did you?'

Then, she is gone, closing the office door with a certain assertion behind her.

Maud stares after her. But how ridiculous! She hopes the woman isn't a gossip – the last thing she needs is someone feeding her to the rumour mill and her parents finding out.

She sighs, reaches for another ledger, waits impatiently for Le Lacheur to call her in. And then, just as the Town Church is striking five and she is considering packing up and going home, he does.

His office smells as Maud imagines a gentlemen's club might, of leather and stale tobacco and the underlying sweetness of alcohol. There is a yellowing map showing vineyards of France on the wall and a rather grand mahogany desk with a silver inkwell and a green leather pad laid into the wood. Le Lacheur takes a bottle of cognac from his desk drawer and pours them both a measure.

'It's a little early for me.' Maud pushes the glass to one side and Le Lacheur shrugs and tops up his own.

'Thought you might need it after an afternoon of arithmetic,' he says. Maud notices the slide of his belly as he sits back in his chair, the middle button missing from his waistcoat. She wonders how long he has been a widower, if he spends his evenings at home entirely alone.

'It has been a bit dull,' she says, tentatively, and Le Lacheur laughs and says he doesn't doubt it.

'You mustn't mind Miss Guille,' he says. 'Bark's worse than her bite, and so on. She's competent but she lacks flair – unlike your good self!'

Taking a key from his waistcoat pocket, he unlocks a drawer and takes out a sheaf of headed notepaper that bears the address of a vineyard in Bordeaux.

'Got a few hundred pounds worth of foreign exchange from the Jerries for my last trip. The wine I bring back – the bulk of it's for them. So, I'm keen to put the prices up a little for our German friends. What they don't know won't hurt them.'

Maud stares at the notepaper and then at him. 'What do I have to do?'

'Just fill in a few of the invoice sheets and the receipts. Add fifteen per cent to the prices. Scrawl a few signatures. Your best doctor's handwriting, Maud!' His moustache bristles at the joke.

Maud doesn't smile back. 'What if they find out?'

'The Germans? They won't. They trust me.' He leans towards her solemnly, making a steeple of his fingers. 'In fact, I was telling Kommandant Maas about your ordeal at the hands of his subordinates only the other day. He assured me that those concerned would be reprimanded.' He shakes his head. 'Have you fully recovered, my dear? It was remiss of me not to have asked earlier.'

He roots through papers, taking out a price list, a fistful of blank receipts. The word *crooked* pops into Maud's head and stays there. Le Lacheur glances at her; she has disappointed him, she sees.

'I'm sorry, Maud. I misjudged you.' He starts to gather up the papers. 'I shouldn't have presumed. Let's say no more about it.'

'I'll do it.' Maud gets up, smooths down her skirt, gives him a quick, brief smile. 'I can make a start now.'

'If you're sure?'

The mood in the room becomes spring cleaned and light: she can breathe again.

'Of course.' Maud thinks about the German soldier's hand, clammy and persistent, under her skirt, his friends egging him on. As she leaves, she smiles brightly as if she is on stage, taking an encore. 'There's a war on, isn't there?'

12

For the first time in years, a cluster of snowdrops has popped up in Isabelle's front garden and as she stands at the window, watching them being buffeted in the wind, their appearance feels nothing short of a small miracle. She hasn't had to hoard coupons or barter or go without to enjoy them – there is no sacrifice to be made in return, or deal to be done. It is hard to believe that spring is here, that the seasons have kept turning in spite of everything. Even the garden at the French House seems less desolate these days, with every patch of soil sown with the seeds that Émile had stored over the winter: beetroot, cabbage, leeks, carrots.

When the Germans first came and Émile had to rip up the plants and the rose bushes, turn the lush expanse of lawn inside out so that all you could see was muck and mud, she could hardly bear to set eyes on it. Émile said it looked the same now as it did six months ago. Dirt is dirt, he'd said, crumbling a handful through his fingers, and she'd replied, yes, but it was nice to think of what was going on under-neath. Behind the scenes, he said. Yes, she said. He had smiled and she had felt a little silly and then he said he hadn't thought of it like that, and she stopped feeling silly and felt pleased instead.

Isabelle hears the clip of the back door and sees Schreiber walk to the gate, attaché case in hand. He turns in her direction and smiles, half-raises his hand. Would he greet her with quite the same warmth if he knew that she was effectively spying on him, she wonders as she waves back, if he knew that one of her most absorbing pastimes when she was alone was to go up to his room, reach behind the volumes of Trollope and settle down in the armchair with his sketch pad. The same fisherman still populated the pages – usually naked, or in some state of undress – although recently, Isabelle has noticed that the tone of the sketches has changed somewhat. The man's face in candlelight, eyes half-closed and faintly troubled, hair dishevelled, a scene so still that she can almost hear his breathing. Another of him descaling a sea bream with a glinting knife, the straps of his overalls dangling low over his thighs, his muscled chest shadowed with a crucifix of wild, dark hair.

Isabelle knows the words people use for men like Peter. Fairy. Nancy boy. Queer. She supposes she should be revolted or appalled by what he is, but now she remains only deeply intrigued. To her, he is no longer a German. He is an artist in fancy dress. He is a man with a secret, whose life depends on his ability to act the part he has been allocated with conviction. He is a young man who desires another. Week after week, the pages fill. There are doodles too, squeezed in the margins: Swastikas, seagulls, sailing boats – and one which stops her heart with its audacity: the Führer, absurd as a kiss-me-quick postcard, knock-kneed, naked and cowering, covering his bits with his hands.

She is about to go and clear away the things from tea when there are two sharp raps on the front door. Peering through the net curtains, she sees a German standing on the porch and there is something about the way he is holding himself that makes Isabelle want to duck down and pretend they're not in. But it's too late; she can hear Ron in the hallway, muttering under his breath as he pulls back the latch.

Please make him leave, Isabelle murmurs to herself, but next thing her name is being called. Reluctantly she emerges from the living room. The German looms on their threshold, blocking out the light.

'My wife might know,' Ron is saying. He turns to her. 'Did Leutnant Schreiber say where he was going tonight, Izzy?'

She shakes her head. 'No.'

Ron's hand is on the door now, ready to close it. 'As I said, Leutnant, he keeps himself to himself.'

'Commander,' the German corrects him, then takes a step closer and looks into the gloomy hallway. 'Might I have a look around?'

His English is as good as Schreiber's but he turns every word ugly, Isabelle thinks: his accent is harsh, gutteral.

'A look around?' she echoes.

'Just Leutnant Schreiber's room.'

The Germans usually come in pairs, if they're doing searches; she's never heard of them snooping on their own men. She is terrified, suddenly, for Peter and those drawings and his rows of English novels. 'The thing is—'

'Please don't distress yourself, madam.' Somehow the man is inside their house now, crowding the hallway. He gives her a condescending smile. 'If you or your husband could kindly show me the way . . .'

She will not lead him there, but she cannot just wait and listen and do nothing either. Now Ron is halfway up the stairs to the attic with the Commander striding behind him. Isabelle hesitates, then follows in their wake. She wishes the room had a lock, and then in the same moment is glad it doesn't. It is less suspicious this way: he can walk right in, just as he is doing now. She and Ron hover on the landing. She hears drawers opened and shut again then, through the half-open door, she sees him approach the bookshelves. He pulls out a book and flicks through it, puts it back, does the same with another, mutters in German.

'They're mine,' Isabelle calls out. Her voice is as thin as a thread. She cannot look at her husband.

'You like to read, madam.'

The German glances at her coolly, then grabs an armful of books and tosses them on the floor, working his way along the shelves, swiftly and methodically, until he reaches the top. Isabelle stares at a stain on the rug, unable to watch. She hears the rhythm of her husband's breathing, the thud of books thrown to the ground, then silence. The German coughs, clears his throat. This room is so unlucky, Isabelle thinks miserably, but then so is this house, so is she. The floorboards creak and she dares to look up. The Commander's face is cast in a frown, his arms tightly folded as he stands amongst the tide of books. The top shelf is empty. There is no sketch pad, just a fine layer of dust.

'Thank you for your cooperation.' He nods brusquely. 'That will be all.'

He marches past them and down the stairs, slams the front door with vigour.

Isabelle wants to laugh with relief. She turns to Ron, says what is expected of her. 'Would you look at this mess!'

'Better tidy it up then, hadn't you?' Ron is looking at her suspiciously. 'Seeing as they're *your* books.'

'I just— '

'Save the lies for the Jerries, Isabelle.' He shakes his head and pushes past her.

Isabelle closes the bedroom door softly, stares at the vacant bookshelves. She knows a bully when she sees one. Peter needs to take care. She kneels on the floor and begins to gather up his novels, suddenly cold to the bone. She had been wrong, after all, to think that spring was around the corner.

Émile refills the watering can and gives the tomato plants another rinsing. It is one of his favourite smells, damp soil mingling with the earthy warmth of tomatoes ripening on the vine. He remembers Stella when she was tiny, coming into the greenhouse and saying it smelt of green, and he had known exactly what she meant even if Maud had told her not to be silly and that colours didn't smell. Sun slants through the open vents, warming his forearms, and he thinks about the afternoon ahead and what he might do with it. Wednesdays are a half day and he has a yearning to go up to the cliffs by the bathing pools, forage for some wild garlic and dandelion root, nettles for tea.

He goes back to the shed and locks up, double-checking the padlock, although he knows it will make no difference: Schreiber is still coming. He has started leaving small offerings – an egg in the watering can, a twist of tobacco tucked inside one of the seed trays, and once the last dregs of a bottle of cognac. At times, these gifts trouble Émile as they imply an agreement of some kind, but who wouldn't say no to a couple of extra smokes or a swig of the hard stuff at the end of the day? So he smokes the baccy and drinks the brandy and takes the egg home for the girls, and tells himself that the German's just taking comfort where he can, same as they all are in their different ways.

As he walks up the garden, he sees Isabelle on her hands and knees pulling up tufts of weed from between the patio tiles. She takes as much pride in this house as she might her own, he thinks, his eyes drawn to the jam jar of daffodils on the kitchen windowsill. He admires this – the way she keeps going, almost as if there is no war. She isn't someone who complains for the sake of it, not like some. She sits back as he approaches, shielding her eyes from the sun.

'You don't want to be weeding on your afternoon off,' he says.

She shrugs and tugs at a clump of chickweed, tosses it into a pile. 'What are you doing?'

'Going up to the cliffs. See what I can find up there, before everyone else has the same idea.' He stoops next to her and removes a couple of dandelions from the discarded weeds. 'You can eat the leaves from these. The roots too, if you cook 'em for long enough.'

'Really?'

'If you have to.' His turn to shrug. 'Come along, if you've nothing better.'

He stands up, avoiding her gaze, and sets off down the passageway. If she comes, she comes – he's not making a song and dance about it. He doesn't look back until he has wheeled his bicycle out from under the lean-to and he realises he must have set his mind for disappointment, because of the pleasure he gets when he sees her there behind him, knotting her scarf under her chin, brushing a spider from the saddle of her bike.

They take the wooded path that runs up the side of the cliffs and fill a basket with gorse flowers and nettles. They head into the woods, which will be carpeted with bluebells in another month or so, and pick bunches of wild garlic until their fingers are sticky with the sap. Through the trees, Émile catches glimpses of the silver sea. He calls to mind the keening of the gulls, the insistent hum of insects, the rustling of the leaves underfoot, tries to imagine them into existence. He does this sometimes if his humour is right, mining his memory for the feeling of a warm spring afternoon and the sounds that went with it. They have done this before, she and him, scouring L'Ancresse Common for the first blackberries as summer drew to a close, using that big sewing bag of hers to carry them. He still remembers Isabelle's face when she held up the table-cloth she was making, the white linen streaked purple with juice, but she hadn't cared, not really. She had hated that sewing circle, full of gossipy women from the church embroidering cushions and bedspreads that she said no one really needed.

She warns him off the mushrooms underneath the beech trees, which she tells him are poisonous, and points towards the headland. Let's go and sit for a while, she says, I think we have enough, and her mouth parts and he realises she is laughing. He tries to recall the sound of it but all he hears is silence and for a moment his mood takes a dip. They find a bench, set back from the path and out of the wind. Beyond the scrawl of barbed wire, the sea glitters in rebellion as if the war is mere rumour.

Émile yawns, loosens his scarf, lets the sun warm him. He is aware of Isabelle's eyes on him and it is the strangest feeling when you're not accustomed to it, both welcome and discomfiting, like a sudden blast of daylight after being cloistered in the dark.

She takes a notebook from her bag, then begins to write. *Can you hear when you dream?*

Émile considers this. It's like dreaming about eating, he tells her. You think you can taste it, but you can't, and you just wake up hungrier than ever.

She nods. *Roast beef!* she writes. *Warm bread and butter!*

Émile grins and gestures towards the basket. 'Not dandelions? Or a nice pot of nettle tea?'

'I won't be drinking that when the war's over!' She stares across the headland. 'If it's ever over.'

Émile thinks of Letty. The infection has long gone now and they carp and bicker and lie back to back in bed, just as they used to, but it seems to him that no sooner has one problem cleared up then a whole host of others jostle to take its place. Since Maud came back from Old Mum's, she's been more silent and secretive than ever. She's up to something, but Letty refuses to see it.

'Strikes me a lot of folks on this island have got the same problems they did before the war, but with Germans in their soup,' he says. He looks at her, wonders if she has any inkling of what her German gets up to of an evening. 'How is it with one of 'em living under your roof?'

'Schreiber? Oh, he's no trouble. In fact, I like having him around.' Her face clouds and she hesitates, before taking the pen.

The other day a German had come to the house and searched his room while he was out, she tells him. A thoroughly obnoxious fellow, too.

'What do you think he was looking for?'

At first, Isabelle doesn't answer. Absently, she takes a dandelion and starts to shred the stalk. 'Émile' – she turns to him, strands of hair blowing across freckled cheeks, and her lips form his name with such care, such attention that he can almost hear her voice – 'Peter – I mean, Schreiber – he's not . . .'

She looks back towards the sea. Émile remembers her quietness, and how he had loved the extra weight this gave her words when they came, how he would replay their conversations to comfort himself when he was away from her, over and over again.

'That scarf' – she reaches towards him and touches it lightly – 'it's his, isn't it?'

I won't be angry she writes. *I just want to know.*

Émile pauses. 'I found it,' he says. 'Like I told you.'

'Where?'

'In the shed.

'The shed at the French House?' Isabelle shakes her head, confused.

He takes her pen. *Schreiber left it behind.*

'He's . . . entertaining in there, Belle.'

'Entertaining?' She has a strange expression on her face, as she studies him. 'With you?' she asks quietly.

The bench shudders and shakes and she turns to him, startled. He is laughing, laughing until his belly aches, and when he looks up, Isabelle has joined in. Sorry, she is saying, her hand on his arm, she doesn't know what to think anymore. Her face wreaths and crinkles as she laughs, and she is young again, and beautiful, and he is surprised it has taken him this long to notice. Then who is it, she asks him, and says something about a fisherman; and this is how rumours start, Émile thinks, but it's too late now, and besides, he wants to tell her.

'Ozzy Ozanne!' Isabelle echoes, her eyebrows arched.

She reaches for the notebook and covers a whole page telling him about the German and his mucky drawings, although in fairness they're not all mucky, but the most shocking one was of Hitler without a stitch on him. She'd been so scared for Schreiber when the Commander had come, she tells him, and then so relieved that the sketch pad wasn't there.

'You must think I'm a terrible person.' She returns to the dandelion shredding. 'Going through his things.'

He doesn't, Émile says. It's just a puzzle to him as to why she would bother and Isabelle blushes as she scribbles in the notebook.

I like to pretend he's my son.

'I know it's wicked, after what I did.' Her knuckles grip the edge of the bench. 'But I never wanted to send Peter away.'

The urge to take her hand is so strong that Émile shifts on the bench, puts more inches between them.

'How old is he now?'

When Isabelle doesn't answer, he understands, her eyes telling him what she can't bring herself to say.

'He died?'

'Many years ago now.' She holds up both hands. 'He was ten, Émile. Just ten years old.'

Émile scratches his stubble. Minutes pass. A flotilla of fishing boats heads in the direction of the harbour, flanked by the German patrol. When they have disappeared, he turns to her. He takes care to speak slowly, as clearly as he is able.

She has to forgive herself, he says, she must. There is nothing now to be done about it; besides which he's sure there are others who should be shouldering the blame alongside her.

His words fall between them. He hasn't said the man's name, nor does he need to. Isabelle rubs her eyes, then takes his hand and briefly squeezes it.

'Shall we go?' she says.

As they walk down the steps to the road, a question swells inside Émile. He has wanted to ask it for some time, ever since that night playing cards in the Caves, but he realises he is afraid of the answer, and it is not until they are getting on their bikes and about to go that he blurts it out.

'Does he treat you right?'

At first she doesn't reply, carries on adjusting the pedals on her bike, and he can't decide if she hasn't heard or just doesn't want to hear. But when he reaches for his notebook, she makes a dismissive gesture.

'Mostly,' she says. She waves, unsmiling, then sets off, her back poker straight, as if she is forged from iron, Émile thinks, or tough, fired earth.

The next morning, when Isabelle sees Schreiber taking a late breakfast in the kitchen, she decides that the French House will have to wait. She pours herself some tea from the dregs of the pot, and draws up a chair at the table. His nose and forehead are pink from yesterday's sun and wind – he is too fair-skinned for island weather, she thinks, he'll fry when summer comes. She says as much and he smiles and tells her it's his penance for getting out of the office for an afternoon.

'It was a quiet day at the *Press*, so I joined the fishing detail.'

'The fishing detail? That's quite a change from the press office, isn't it?' Isabelle reminds herself to forget what she's seen, to forget what Émile had told her. She keeps her tone breezy. 'Come to think of it, I saw the boats come in yesterday when I was on the cliffs with a friend. It looked choppy out there.'

'Small price to pay.' He dusts his fingers clean of toast crumbs. 'It was such a wonderful feeling to head out to sea. I used to love being on the water as a boy – I have an uncle in Kiel who taught me to sail. Made it all the way to Copenhagen one summer.'

'Well, I have no sea legs whatsoever. Green at the gills at the first sign of wind!'

Isabelle swallows some more tea. The way he's sitting there, gazing out of the window, as if he's here on his holidays and has no more to trouble him than the direction of the wind – she must tell him.

'Mr Schreiber.' She pauses. 'A commanding officer came to the house the other night, while you were out. My husband said we should keep out of your business, but I wanted to tell you. He searched your room.'

He blinks several times, his full attention trained on her now. 'I noticed the books were a little . . .' He stops. 'I thought perhaps they'd been moved for dusting.' He rubs at a cut on his chin. 'Was he a big man? Tall? Built like a tree?'

'He was certainly imposing.' Isabelle sighs. 'And rather rude and unpleasant, if I'm to be perfectly frank.'

'It sounds as if you made the acquaintance of my Commanding Officer, Kassenmeier.' Schreiber gets up from the table and puts on his hat. 'Between you and me, the opinion you formed of him, Mrs Larch, is entirely accurate.'

'He was asking questions about where you were. As I told him, how would we know!' Her laughter is a little too forced. 'But I thought you should be aware.'

'Thank you.' Schreiber reaches for her hand, cups it for a moment between his. 'I'm grateful. Really I am. And I'm sorry you were inconvenienced. I don't want to cause you any difficulty.'

'Nonsense.' She starts to clear away the breakfast things. 'Have a good day.'

'And to you.'

As he leaves, his attaché case holds less swing than usual, his expression preoccupied under the blush of his sunburnt face.

After their afternoon on the cliffs, Émile doesn't see Isabelle until gone midday the following day and he worries that he went too far, offended her with his opinion on her son, his question about her husband. But she hadn't seemed offended. If anything, she seemed grateful – he cannot forget the way she grasped his hand. Nonetheless, he is pleased to see her smiling as she comes to the enclosure, carrying a yellow cushion and a thick plaid blanket.

'The nights are still cold,' she says, nodding towards the shed. 'Especially if one is entertaining.'

'I hope he leaves a tip,' Émile says, smiling back, and later, when he is alone, he buries his head in the blanket and inhales deeply. But there is no smell of her, no scent of fresh sea spray and the faint musk of marigolds, just the damp mustiness of an unopened trunk and a whiff of the secret they now share.

13

Maud has never been to Grange Lodge before. Until the Germans arrived, it was a hotel for visitors with money; now a large scarlet Swastika hangs above the entrance, which is flanked by two guards in helmets that look like pudding bowls. It is where decisions are made that determine whether islanders will have two ounces of butter a week or one, where arrest warrants are typed and filed, where the Kommandant takes a pen and gets to play God, requisitioning people's homes and authorising deportations to dank, windowless cells in France. Yet, Maud reminds herself as she approaches the guards, it is also where Le Lacheur delivers wine, and where the censor, Leutnant Schreiber, runs an eye over revue programmes, such as the one in her satchel, and decides whether there might be any potential for sedition in an Armenian polka or a limerick from Edward Lear.

'You'll be in and out of the place in five minutes,' Miss Le Noury had assured her. She was the organiser of the revue and an old hand at visits to the Lodge. 'He hasn't asked us to change anything for months.'

The guards motion her inside and a young clerk, not much older than Maud, painstakingly transcribes the details from her identity card onto a form, and tells her to take a seat. Maud looks around. It is just an office, she tells herself, that's all, populated by men in military uniform. From a nearby corridor comes the staccato beat of a typewriter. A telephone rings. The clerk gets up from his desk.

'Leutnant Schreiber will see you now,' he says.

Maud follows him upstairs to an office at the end of a long corridor. She sees the censor at his desk through the half-open door, remembers him from the dance at Candie, red-faced and uncomfortable from the heat, staring at her and that idiot Ozzy from the back of the hall. He looks up and motions her in, gives her a sympathetic smile as she passes him the programme.

'Please sit. Cigarette?'

'No – thank you.'

She feels slightly wrong-footed; Miss Le Noury hadn't mentioned cigarettes. Maud watches as the censor lights up and scans the sheet of paper.

'Nothing in here I need to waste ink on,' he says after a moment. He glances at the programme again before handing it back. 'And so . . . Miss Quenneville, you are the accordionist. I had the pleasure of hearing you play last summer at Candie Gardens.'

His English is practically flawless, like the men who read the news on the BBC. 'That's right,' she says, unsure whether to acknowledge the compliment or ignore it.

He exhales a plume of smoke. 'I always think it's impossible to give in to melancholy when an accordion is playing. I knew some talented accordionists in Berlin – London, too.'

'You lived in London?' Maud stares at him.

'I had an apprenticeship at a news agency, before the war. Lived in a little flat in Bloomsbury.' He smiles. 'There was a man who played outside the underground every Friday evening when I came home from work. I'd always stay for a while and listen to him. And then one day, a few months before war was declared, he wasn't there anymore.'

'What happened to him?'

The censor shakes his head. 'One of the drawbacks of capital cities. It's easy to lose people. And one of the pleasures too, I suppose. The anonymity, that is.'

'Yes.' Maud nods. 'I think I might like that.'

'I hope you are able to find out. Once this war's over and done with.' He studies her, then draws back his chair and shakes her hand. 'In any event, I look forward to hearing you play again at the revue.'

He escorts her out of the office and back down the stairs to the main entrance and as she says goodbye, she thinks that there are nice Germans, after all, and they're not all like the horrid men who pawed her in the alleyway in the half-dark.

As she comes out onto the Rohais, she hears a familiar voice behind her.

'Well, if it isn't Miss Maud.'

She turns to face Le Lacheur, smart in a dark suit, his bush of white hair mussed up by the wind. He pats his pocket and Maud sees the bulky outline of a bottle. 'Just delivering a little something extra to the top brass.' He lowers his voice. 'Hope it might stop the vultures circling.'

'The vultures?'

'Damn Germans have been nosing around the house again.' He makes a face. 'I'm blowed if I'm having them moving in just because I've got an extra room or two. Anyway' – he steps a little closer and smiles – 'what brings you here? I hope you're not snitching on me!'

Maud tells him she's just been to see the censor about the revue and Le Lacheur screws up his face.

'Funny fish, that one,' he says. 'Cushy job, no doubt about it. Making up lies in the *Press* that put the Jerries in a good light and the rest of us in a bad one.'

'His English is good.' Maud finds herself wanting to defend him. The few minutes spent talking in his office had been like skimming the first page of a novel that promised to be rather engrossing. 'Very good, actually. He seems rather . . . sophisticated.'

'Sophisticated, eh?' Le Lacheur's laugh is not altogether kind. 'Someone's had her head turned.'

She feels heat rise in her cheeks. 'I just meant—'

'Aren't I allowed to tease you, my dear, just a little?' He reaches forwards and strokes her cheek. 'Come now.'

He has never touched her before, not like this. Maud doesn't know what it means, nor does she understand why she isn't stepping away, recoiling, but staying right where she is, allowing it to happen. He would describe what there is between them as a 'soft spot', she supposes, if anyone saw them with his hand on her face; he has a soft spot for her, as he did for her mother. Maud thinks back to the beef broth and claret in the People's Friend, that moment when she'd thought she was close to the truth. She has the same feeling now. She opens her mouth to speak, but he talks over her, asking when the revue is and taking a diary from his pocket.

'It's next Wednesday at the Ozanne Hall.' Maud watches him jot down the details. 'You'll come? I think you might find it a little dull.'

'Not in the least,' he says, snapping the diary shut, and asking her to wish him luck, he winks again and limps energetically across the courtyard towards Grange Lodge.

★　　★　　★

166

The evening of the revue is chilly and grey. Cold for April, people are saying as they take their seats in the draughty hall and a fractious hum grows as the room fills. Meat rations have been halved again for the second week running; the Germans are short of bicycles, so guard yours with your life, before they swipe it. Everyone is hungry and tired and sugar and tea and coffee deprived – tempers are as short as the rations. Maud watches from the wings as the rows fill up. Le Lacheur will probably be late, she tells herself, he's that kind of man. She is dressed in the colours of the Union Jack in a white blouse with red piping and a navy skirt, and it is not a coincidence, although no one at home even noticed. Stella, pleading exhaustion after a day cutting hair, had asked if Maud minded ever so if she didn't come with her. For once, Maud is relieved; she isn't sure she is ready for the torrent of questions from her sister if Le Lacheur makes himself known.

'Is he here yet?'

Miss Le Noury comes up behind her and scans the audience.

'Sorry?'

'The censor.' She smiles and pats Maud's shoulder. 'With any luck, he'll leave us to it. I'm sure he has better things to do with his time.'

Miss Le Noury checks her watch and nods at the caretaker at the back of the hall. He closes the doors and Maud wants to shout that he doesn't have to shut them, what about latecomers, but a polite hush falls as Miss Le Noury takes her seat at the piano and the revue begins. Beverley Mahy squawks out the words to 'I'm Letting in the Sunshine', the grubby strap of her brassière slipping down her upper arm. The audience nod their collective heads agreeably in time to the music, and Maud thinks that perhaps it's best that Le Lacheur is a little late after all. Then it's a recital – 'You are old, Father William' – and as the words swirl around her, meaningless, Maud looks at the clock and considers where the dividing line might be between being late and deciding not to come at all.

The evening creeps on and as they reach the intermission, Maud cannot pretend otherwise: Le Lacheur isn't coming any more than the censor himself, a detail that has not gone unnoticed by the audience. Wasn't it nice not to have any Germans breathing down their necks for once, remarks one woman, and Maud agrees, yet she feels doubly disappointed, as if Schreiber too had broken a promise. There is more laughter than usual, the mood in the hall has changed, see-sawing with her own. As Miss Le Noury takes to the stage and announces that Maud Quenneville will provide them with a lively finish to a wonderful evening's entertainment, the applause is spirited.

Maud doesn't feel the usual quiver of nerves as she walks on stage, and this she knows is a bad sign, but there is nothing she can do about it because at this moment she would rather be anywhere than here, an amateur playing to amateurs. Even the 'Beer Barrel Polka' cannot lift her and each note she plays feels bloodless and bland, but no one seems to notice or care. As she draws out the bellows, she worries that this is all she will ever be, that in twenty years' time she will still be here, playing lively finishes at church hall revues.

Robust applause. The hall stirs as a few people get up to leave. From the wings, Miss Le Noury holds up her forefinger – her cue for an encore. Maud is on the verge of declining – all she wants is to go home and forget this evening ever happened. Then an idea occurs to her, a way of shaking off the mediocrity of the evening. She will have to play it from memory, but the tune is predictable and repetitive, easy to master. She plays the establishing notes. A woman in the front row recognises the first bar and twitches uncertainly. By the second, a ripple of recognition has passed through the hall and as her fingers move across the keys, Maud waits to be stopped, for Miss Le Noury's hand on her shoulder, for someone to stand up and tell her enough now. But no one does. Maud has never really cared for this particular piece – she finds waltzes old-fashioned, and the words of this particular one, which some of the audience are now mouthing, are sentimental in the extreme – but she plays the island's national anthem as she never could have done when she was free to play it, before the Germans came, before it was banned.

She stops after the first chorus. No one claps; there is no need for it. An elderly man tips his hat at her as he leaves, a woman in the front row wipes away a tear.

As Maud leaves the stage, Miss Le Noury grasps her forearm. 'Don't you ever try something like that again, do you hear?' she hisses. 'What if the censor had slipped in at the last moment?'

'But he didn't,' Maud says with a nonchalance she doesn't quite feel.

'And that is why I let it pass.' The woman's tone is crisp now. 'Go home and we'll say no more about it.'

When she gets back, Pa is sitting alone in the grey twilight of the kitchen and everyone else is in bed. His gaze settles on the accordion case in her right hand and he stares at it with a kind of longing, as if Maud is a mere appendage to the instrument itself.

'All right?' he asks.

She nods.

'Good turnout?'

'Not bad.'

It seems, after this, there is nothing left to say.

Her father rubs his hand over his face and gets up, goes to the door. He is about to leave, but then he points to the hem of her sleeve.

'Those colours,' he says. 'You should be careful.'

The door closes behind him, leaving Maud alone in the gloom. She takes off her shoes and sits in Pa's place at the table, fingering the piping on her blouse. Of course Le Lacheur hadn't come; why would he? She was just his employee, two afternoons a week. And yet ... She hopes that news of the revue will somehow make its way to him, that next time they are in the office he will pour her a small brandy and tell her, with a certain pride, that he heard she brought the house down with her impromptu performance of *Sarnia Cherie*.

14

Émile knows something is up when he sees Stella at the top of the lane, scouring the road, waiting, just as she used to when she was younger and he was coming back from the harbour in the lorry, and she wanted a turn up front with him before he returned it to the depot. He brakes and draws into the kerb and she almost falls upon him, her lips moving in a muddle of words. He imagines a bombing he hasn't heard, fighter planes he has failed to noticed, but Stella is saying something about Germans at the house, and he can't begin to think what he might have that they could want. Then he has a vision of Maud in her red, white and blue, and the way she'd breezed in last night after the revue, drunk on something that wasn't liquor – and he starts to feel afraid. He freewheels down the lane with Stella following in his wake and there is Letty standing at the gate in her blue housecoat, her face streaked with old tears and fresh ones.

'It's Maud,' she says and suddenly she is in his arms and shaking, her body shuddering against him as she sobs. Gently, Émile lifts her head from his chest.

'What's happened?'

'They've taken her.' For once, Letty takes care to speak slowly.

'Who?'

'Maud,' she says. 'The Germans.'

He can join the dots. They may make the wrong shape but the start and the end point are clear. Ever since that trouble at Christmas, Maud has reminded him of a foal about to bolt. He turns to Stella and passes her his notebook, saying he wants the truth, he can't help her sister if he doesn't have the truth.

Stella scribbles frantically. It was the revue, she says, and Maud played *Sarnia Cherie*, just a verse, Pa, no more than that – she glances fearfully at her mother; Maud had told her in bed last night. There were no Germans there, or she wouldn't have risked it, but word must have got out and they had come, three of them, just a short time ago, when Maud got in from work.

Letty wipes her nose on her sleeve. 'Pushing and shoving her into the car,' she says. 'As if she's some kind of criminal.'

'They're trying to scare her,' Émile says. 'She's just a girl.' But this seems to exasperate Letty who stops crying and starts shouting.

'Do something, Émile!' she seems to be saying and Émile wonders if his wife has forgotten who he is, if she thinks that he with his stained hands and way of talking that makes some folks screw up their faces as if he might as well be speaking in Chinese; as if he could just saunter into Grange Lodge and say a few words to the right people and make everything fall into place.

Émile falls into the silence which surrounds him until Letty and Stella are frozen, out of focus, as he thinks. He remembers Maud sitting at the breakfast table in her best clothes a couple of weeks ago. She had an appointment at Grange Lodge with the censor, Stella had told him, to get the all-clear on the programme for the revue. And that was part of Schreiber's job, wasn't it, to be there at these public gatherings, to keep them all in order, but last night he'd had something better to do than listen to schoolgirls sing 'Daisy, Daisy' and Émile knew more than anyone what that was. When he'd gone into the shed that morning, there were two cigarettes on top of Isabelle's cushion; Émile had smoked one straight away, pocketing the other for later when he really needed it.

He puts a hand on Letty's shoulder, asks her to heat some water so he can get himself cleaned up.

'You're going to talk to the Germans?' Stella asks and he replies that yes, he is going to try, and it touches him to see the relief in her face, and mirrored in Letty's.

What he is planning is risky, but the way he sees it, he doesn't have any other option. Émile follows his wife and daughter into the house and fingers Schreiber's second cigarette in his pocket, promising himself that he will keep it there for luck, and not smoke it until he has got what he set out for.

Had Émile ever tried to picture Isabelle's marital home, he would have imagined something quite different to Sarnia Cottage. Window frames shedding paint like leaves, weeds strangling the half-hearted flower beds, a starburst of splintered glass in one of the front-room windows. It hurts him to see it that way and to think of Isabelle inside it. Office fellows like Larch are all the same, Émile thinks, they don't know one end of a screwdriver from another. He hopes the man is still at work – he has no desire to explain himself to him of all people.

He walks around to the back porch and knocks on the door. A shadow falls across the frosted glass and as the door opens, Émile's heart sinks. It is Larch, in his work clothes, shirt and braces, and he looks at Émile as he might a mange-ridden dog he has half a mind to kick. When he speaks, his lips barely move, but whatever he says isn't very friendly and Émile has no interest in hearing it. He tells him he needs to speak to his billet.

'It's urgent,' he says and Larch's lips move just a fraction before the door begins to close. Émile takes a step forward and wedges his foot in the door jamb.

'Like I said, it's urgent.'

Larch turns and calls out into the kitchen and Isabelle comes to the door, wiping her hands on her apron, her eyes widening to see him there.

'It's my eldest,' he says. 'She's in a spot of trouble. I need to speak to the censor fellow, if he's about?'

Isabelle starts to reply but Larch silences her. He points at his watch and seems to be telling Émile that this is his house, not an office, that it's almost seven in the evening and he's imposing, but Isabelle murmurs something – and they to-and-fro before Larch reluctantly opens the door.

'This way,' Isabelle says, but Émile stops to take off his boots first, fumbling with the laces while Larch sprawls in his seat at the kitchen table, watching. He is one of those men, Émile thinks, who is impossible to ignore, who takes up all the oxygen in a room, all the space.

Émile follows Isabelle into the hall.

'What happened?' she mouths.

'Trouble at the revue. The police have got her.'

'Oh no.'

Émile supposes Isabelle sounds as horrified as she looks, and this does little to settle his nerves as she shows him into the sitting room. Although it is still light outside, the curtains are drawn and it smells faintly of tobacco. On the mantle-piece, two china dogs with floppy ears gaze plaintively into the distance. There are a pair of worn armchairs on either side of the fireplace, and she removes a tapestry sewing bag from the one he assumes is hers and indicates that he should sit.

'I'll go and get him,' she says. She stands helplessly for a moment, glancing at his notebook, which he has laid on the coffee table. 'Do you want me to stay?'

Her husband's slippers protrude from underneath the chair opposite. Émile can't imagine they have too many laughs of an evening; there is a feeling about the place, as if everyone in it is holding their breath. He nods towards the kitchen and says her husband doesn't seem too pleased to see him here out of the blue, and he doesn't want to cause any trouble.

'Let me stay.' Isabelle touches his shoulder and leaves the room.

When she returns, Schreiber is with her. He seems at home here in this gloomy sitting room with him and Isabelle. He shakes Émile's hand with warmth, as if they are friends or something close to it, and the churning in Émile's belly subsides a little. Schreiber sits down opposite him, draws his chair in close.

'It's your daughter, isn't it?' he says. 'Maud.'

'You know about it?' Isabelle asks and Schreiber nods.

'I am also in trouble.' Schreiber repeats it and takes Émile's notebook. *My superiors,* he writes, *are angry. I should have been at Ozanne Hall. Or arranged for someone to attend.*

'I suppose you were busy,' Émile says. 'With something more important.'

In another world, another life, Schreiber would have made a formidable opponent in a game of cards, Émile thinks. He has the face for it. Isabelle stares at the floor, at her sewing bag. No one speaks for some time.

'What will they do to Maud?' Émile says. 'Will they let her go?'

'It is a small thing, what she did.' Schreiber makes a circle in the air with his fingers. 'But small things lead to bigger things. This is the problem.'

Isabelle jumps in. Émile can't catch it all, but she appears to be defending Maud. She gestures towards Émile. A good family. A lesson learnt. A young girl, just nineteen – she holds up fingers for him – isn't that right, Émile?

The censor looks at them both with a sympathy that chills Émile. He pities them, because they have gone to him for help, which he can't give. He pities them because they are powerless.

'It is not my decision.' Schreiber puts his hand on his chest. 'I'm sorry.'

For a moment, Émile feels overwhelmed. It is an old tune, this one, first heard in a courtroom in Vancouver. He is poor and always will be. He doesn't matter and the people above him know it. He will always be easy to overlook.

He is not aware that he has lowered his head, his eyes closed, until Isabelle taps his shoulder. He looks up and Schreiber passes him the notebook.

Sometimes, I am slapdash, Mr Quenneville. I don't pay attention to details as I should.

'I was tired,' he says. 'The morning Maud came to see me.'

I should have checked her programme more thoroughly, briefed her with more rigour.

'It should never have happened,' he says and he is very serious now; it is as if Émile is the superior whom he has to convince. 'I take responsibility.'

He writes it down and Émile stares at the words. He is aware of Isabelle beside him, thanking Schreiber with an appreciation that seems to make him uneasy and Émile understands why. He will do what he can, just as Émile himself is doing now, but the rest is down to chance. It occurs to Émile that in a cock-eyed way, Schreiber has little more control over his life than Émile does over his own. He is a man who has to creep around at night to take his pleasure, someone who would rather use his censor's pen to draw cartoons than to write headlines in the *Press* about the Germans winning the war.

Émile gets up, holds out his hand. 'I'm grateful,' he says.

'As I am to you both.' Schreiber dips his head respectfully and takes his leave.

Émile looks at Isabelle. He wants to take her hand – more than that, he wants to hold her close, as he did when they were dancing at Christmas. He wants to get them both out of this sad, unloved little house in which, he has only just noticed, there doesn't seem to be a single one of her books.

'You have to go.' She points rather urgently to the front door. 'Go out the front way.'

He wants to ask her to come with him, just for a few minutes, to walk him to the gate. But she wants him out before Larch throws him out – Isabelle is scared, Émile can smell it, and as he says goodbye, he hopes fervently there won't be any trouble in it for her. He wants it to be tomorrow already, with Maud home and Isabelle there in the kitchen at the French House to share the news with. He will get her a little something as a thank you, he thinks, as he sets off on his bike. He'll pick some wild flowers from the hedge, tie them up nicely with a ribbon if he can find one, or, failing that, twine.

★   ★   ★

Isabelle stoops and brushes up the shards of dull glass into the dustpan. She had jumped at some phantom noise as she was drying up after supper and dropped a tumbler: she is all fingers and thumbs since Émile left. It hasn't helped that Ron hasn't spoken one word to her, and she had almost hoped that the sound of the shattered glass would provoke him into leaving his armchair in the sitting room to take the opportunity to reprimand her. She hates his silences more than she does his put-downs. They leave her with no recourse other than to wait.

Carefully, she wraps the glass in an old copy of the *Press* and puts it in the bin, glances at the time. Schreiber had been gone for almost an hour. If Maud were her daughter, she would be in pieces; she can't imagine how Letty must be feeling. But Letty is lucky – she has Émile. It was brave of him to come here, to talk to Schreiber privately away from Grange Lodge, although Isabelle had hated every minute he was in the house, bearing witness to the spareness of it. She had barely been able to look him in the eye when he left.

'Where's the Kraut?'

Isabelle jumps and looks around to see that Ron has crept up on her, quiet as a cat. He stands in the doorway, arms folded.

'Out.'

'The Kraut's out.' Ron chuckles and Isabelle suppresses a sigh and wishes he had remained silent after all. 'What time can we expect him back?'

'No idea.' Isabelle hangs up the tea towel.

'You're thick as thieves, the two of you, these days, aren't you?'

'I wouldn't say so.'

'No?'

'No.' She wrings out the dishcloth, gives the draining board another wipe it doesn't need, hoping that when she turns around, he will be gone.

'It's quite the harem you've got going on, Isabelle.' He pronounces it *harram*. 'Never know who I'm going to find in my armchair next.'

Suddenly Isabelle feels very tired. She pulls out a chair and sits down. 'Mmm.'

'Is that all you've got to say for yourself?' His tone has changed as she knew it would. '*Mmm. Mmm.*'

She knows what will come next. It has been building since Christmas. It doesn't matter what she does or doesn't say. She looks straight at him. 'It's har-*eem*,' she says. 'Stress on the last syllable.'

For a man with so little flair for spontaneity, he moves very quickly. Isabelle is flung to the floor, the chair yanked from under her, as he grabs a clump of her hair and half-drags her down the hall to the living room.

'You think you're so clever, don't you?' He pinches her earlobe and a sliver of pain, a premonition of what's to come, pierces her. 'Think you can get one over, without me noticing.'

Isabelle finds herself shoved roughly towards the bureau in the corner.

'Anything you want to tell me?' His grip tightens on the back of her neck.

As Isabelle opens her mouth, he slaps her hard. For a moment, she sees sparks and she worries for herself, tells herself to toughen up because this, she knows, will not be over quickly.

'Spending our savings. Did you think I wouldn't notice? What have you done with our money?'

Another slap, one that makes her cry out.

'A friend was in trouble.' She tries to look at him, but she can't move her head. He has her by the scruff of the neck, shaking her by it as he might an animal.

'I'll pay it back,' she says, but now he is asking who, who, which one of the 'har-*eem*' – 'Did I say it the right way this time, did I, did I?' – *slap*, which one of her men did she give it to?

He kicks her left shin. Does she think he hasn't noticed, he says, that something's going on, with all her mooning around the place? If he didn't know better, he'd think she was having it off with the Kraut. The man would have to be desperate, desperate anyway to look at an ugly bitch like her – he must fuck her from behind with his eyes shut, he says, and then, when did it start, Isabelle, when did she go panting after this man who was young enough to be her fucking son?

'Let me get up.' Her voice comes out in a croak. She is crouched on the carpet, her hands protecting her ears. 'I'll tell you everything if you let me get up.'

There is silence. His feet are braced apart as she picks herself up, but he makes no move to stop her. Her ears are singing, the sinews in her neck burn. She rubs her collar bone and forces herself to look at him.

'There is nothing going on between me and Schreiber. I promise you.' She pauses. 'And the money – just a pound, Ron' – she searches his face for a speck of compassion but finds none – 'was a loan. Émile had medical bills to pay.'

'Émile!' He spits out the name. 'I don't give a fuck about "Émile". That man's got trouble written all over him. His damn fool daughter gets taken in by the Jerries and you're getting involved, inviting him over, jeopardising –' he pauses

as he always does when he uses a word he's proud of –
'jeopardising our safety, Isabelle.'

'His daughter's in prison. He needed help.'

'Still holding a candle for the handicapped,' he says
mockingly. 'After all these years.'

It is too much. Isabelle hears the smack of her palm
against his face, almost before she knows she has done it –
and it is both a glorious and a terrible sound, and the shock
in his eyes, the splinter of pain makes her feel peculiar, as if
she's discovered a new talent she's not sure she ever wanted.

Ron cups his reddening cheek. His breathing is as heavy,
as ominous as the ticking of a clock.

'You shouldn't have done that,' he says.

And then he lifts his fist and swings for her and as she
falls, the last thing Isabelle sees are the china spaniels on the
mantelpiece staring at her with their pathetic expressions,
and she has a premonition that one day, if she survives this,
she'll pick up each one of his hideous ornaments and let
them slip through her fingers onto the tiled hearth until
milkmaid's pail is indistinguishable from spaniel's ear and
they are just a pile of shattered porcelain, to be swept up,
dumped in the rubbish and forgotten.

15

Maud sits hunched on the thin, lumpy mattress, watching rays of mid-morning sun slope across the wall towards the metal door. She smells of old sweat and new fear, and every footstep that echoes down the hallway past her cell makes her body tighten, both with hope and anxiety. She tries to maintain a sense of perspective. They are trying to scare her, nothing more. She is nineteen, just a girl, like her mother said. She hears Ma's voice again plaintive and pleading, yesterday morning when they took her away.

'She's just a girl. Please don't hurt her.'

One of them had a magenta birthmark covering his left cheek and Maud had felt some relief upon seeing it, as if it might make him more human, more kind. But he had gripped her hard, his fingers pressing into her upper arm with such force that today pale lilac bruises are beginning to form.

They took her to the German wing of the prison and sat her in a stuffy room in the basement. There she was asked question after question by an unsmiling officer who seemed permanently on the verge of yawning, a technique Maud could only assume was designed to lull her into a false sense of security. How did she spend her evenings? Who did she spend her time with? Some of the civilian population seemed to think it was amusing to deface German property with childish propaganda signs – was she one of those people? Or her parents, perhaps?

No, Maud said, not at all. She told him she had made a foolish mistake – *Sarnia Cherie* had always been part of her repertoire and she had forgotten herself. She had meant no harm.

The scratch of the pen as the boy with the birthmark took notes. The whirr of the fan chopping up the stuffy air. The quiver in her own voice, which made the truth sound like a lie. What kind of work did she do, they asked. She was a music teacher she said, her hands shaking under the table, not knowing whether or not to mention Le Lacheur, and suddenly all she can see are his offices looted, the filing cabinets overturned, Miss Guille looking on in horror when they discover Maud's handwriting on the forged invoices. Maud asked then for a glass of water and in the time it took to bring it, she had calmed herself. Le Lacheur had influence, he took bribes of brandy to the 'top brass' at Grange Lodge, the mere mention of his name might be enough to get her out of this place. And so she told them she did some bookkeeping for a local wine merchant two afternoons a week, and Le Lacheur's name was noted down, but the boy spelt it wrongly even though she spelled out every letter, and it felt like a bad omen somehow.

The officer said something in German and the boy passed him the notes and the whole thing was so procedural, so drained of any emotion, that Maud had felt sure they might let her go. But then she was marched through a maze of corridors and taken to a cell that smelt like a public lavatory and then she was the one asking the questions – they tumbled out of her – but no one listened or answered and the key had turned with a solid sound in the solid lock.

After the first night, they let her see Stella. She came, she said, because Ma was in no fit state and Pa was working. She brought her a large dollop of homemade toothpaste and held Maud's hand across the table, all the while eyeing the guard who stood sentry by the door.

'You can't stay here, Mo,' she said, looking very much as if she were about to cry.

Maud had looked steadily at her sister. 'I need you to do something for me,' she said. 'There's a man I know who might be able to help.' And Stella had nodded slowly, saying nothing, as Maud told her to go to the wine merchants on Trinity Square and let Mr Le Lacheur know the reason for her absence from work. Once back in her cell, Maud felt a sense of deep relief: he would 'deal with the matter' – she can almost hear his voice, can see him laying his hat on his lap as he sits in the Feldkommandatur's office, explaining in measured and reasonable tones that he is sure Miss Quenneville didn't intend any offence, that she is of excellent character.

But it has been two days now and nothing has happened. Maud creates a hundred different scenarios. Le Lacheur wasn't in the office when Stella called. Or he was there, but Miss Guille wouldn't let her see him. Or worse, he refused to see Stella, sent her away with a flea in her ear before she could explain. Maud paces to the window. For the first time since they brought her here, she feels the familiar twist of hunger and it makes her feel human again. She leans against the wall and closes her eyes.

A man clears his throat outside her cell, then the lock turns. This German is higher ranking – two chevrons mark his shoulder pads. He is carrying a clipboard and forms. The appetite falls out of Maud and a high-pitched buzzing starts up in her ears. She will be tried and sentenced, sent to smash rocks in a French prison until her fingers bleed and her spine is as crooked as an old woman's. But the German hands her a pen and tells her that she is free to go. Maud can barely see the form through her tears and she is still crying when she collects her accordion from an office next to the entrance and signs another form. Then she is out in the bustle of the bright May morning, with the housewives and their shopping trolleys and the Germans on motor-bikes, and for the briefest of moments, she considers going straight to Le Lacheur's office to thank him. The filth under her fingernails and the unwelcome reflection of her wild, unbrushed hair in the grocer's window opposite prevents her. Maud picks up her accordion and heads in the direc-tion of home.

Mrs Larch is indisposed.

Émile sits on the step outside the shed and reads and re-reads the feathery handwriting of Mr Corbeille in his notebook, as if the act of concentration might reveal some-thing he's missed, give some more concrete reason as to Isabelle's absence.

'Just carry on as usual,' the man had said, looking a little awkward as he stood in the vegetable patch in his nice suit, hands clasped behind his back. 'Good man.'

Émile has a bad feeling about the whole business. Bad luck comes in threes, he should know, and you were lucky if it stopped after that. Lost his hearing, lost his woman, lost his savings, up to his neck in debt. And Maud still in prison, for two days now, and he's not sure if he might have made things worse for her, not better. Letty refuses to leave the house for fear of tongues wagging around her and now

Isabelle, who he's never known to miss work, has been absent since Wednesday. Indisposed.

The enclosure door eases open. It is Mr Corbeille. As Émile gets to his feet, the man does an elaborate mime that seems to indicate that he's off home and will Émile be so kind as to lock up?

At least he's not one of those who shout themselves blue in the face and still expect him to hear. Émile nods solemnly and shows him his set of keys, by way of reassurance.

'I'm sorry about your daughter,' Corbeille goes on. He presses his palm against his heart. 'I hope they let her home soon.'

In that moment, Émile warms to the man. You can smell the goodness in some folk, he thinks, it's like the scent of honeysuckle wafting from a hedge. Then he remembers something.

'I'll get that money to you soon,' he says. 'For the advance on my pay, like. Wife needed medicine, you see.'

Corbeille looks puzzled. He shakes his head. 'You must be mistaken, Mr Quenneville.'

What he says next cannot be acted out, it seems, because he is gesturing for the notepad, but Émile understands enough. He remembers taking the pound note from the envelope Isabelle gave him and noticing in a vague sense that it felt different to usual; the note was crumpled, not crisp, and curled at the edges.

He looks at Corbeille. 'Must have got my wires crossed,' he says with an attempt at a smile. 'Mind's all over the place.'

Corbeille nods with a grave sympathy, as if offering his condolences, and turns to leave.

★   ★   ★

Émile cycles home. The hosing on his tyres is wearing thin, but this evening the jolts in the road barely register. The money came from Isabelle. He thinks of their house and its peeling paint and faded curtains, the worn armchairs, no better than his and Letty's when it came to it, but he was just a grower, not an office man like Larch. The notion that he keeps her short, that he makes her life smaller, drabber than it should be, flattens Émile. He pictures their living room again. He had imagined bookshelves, brightly coloured rugs, a silver tray with a cut glass decanter and glasses.

He turns into the lane, freewheels into the yard. He sees Letty through the kitchen window, and there is something looser about the set of her shoulders as she chops carrots at the table. Then Stella comes into view and she smiles when she sees him as if all her birthdays and Christmases have come at once, and Émile thinks that either peace was declared while his back was turned or Maud's home. And there she is, sitting on the back doorstep in the fading sunlight, shelling peas and tapping her foot to some music he can't hear.

Maud looks up. 'Hello, Pa,' she says.

He places a hand on her shoulder and she lets it rest there. She is pale, tired and too thin, but she is still Maud. And she is home.

'Did they treat you right?'

The circles under her eyes are dark violet. If they'd wanted to scare her, they'd succeeded, Émile thinks; she looks both older and younger than her nineteen years.

'Lots of questions,' she mouths. 'Then they let me go.'

'It's good to have you back.'

She smiles briefly, then leans forward to reach for more pods and slips away from him once more.

Inside, the table is laid for tea. Letty tosses carrot peelings into the colander and jerks her head towards the corner of the kitchen. On top of the basket where they store kindling and bits of twigs for firewood, Émile sees his accordion.

Letty's words scatter like fragments of a plate hurled across the room. *That thing. She's not to play it. Told her.* Émile glances through the door at Maud, who is pretending not to hear. He feels a familiar tug of irritation towards his wife. As if getting rid of the accordion is going to wipe out what Maud did and why she did it, like a neat row of figures. He picks up the case, feels the worn leather handle in his hand. There is a tightness in his chest. He remembers the man in the pawn shop looking it over with a careless eye. You'll buy another one, Émile had told himself, a better one. Once you're settled in Canada, once the money's coming in. And then Isabelle had hunted it down, bought it back for him.

He looks at his wife. 'It's mine,' he says. Maud comes to the doorway now and for once she is listening as if she cares deeply about what he might say. 'It's not going anywhere.'

Later, when Émile sits smoking in the back garden, as the last light leaches from the sky, Maud seeks him out. She stands awkwardly in front of him, twisting her hands. They must always confront each other, Émile thinks, this is the problem. It can never be a word in an ear, their eyes fixed on the horizon as they lean against the wall.

'Thank you,' she says. 'For the accordion.'

Émile studies her. She is moving further away from them every day, he thinks, and whatever the cause, it's not making her any happier than she was before.

'Why?' he asks. 'Why did you do it?'

She shrugs. 'I don't know. It just happened.'

'To impress someone? A lad?'

'No!' She blushes fiercely. So, there is someone.

'He ain't worth it,' Émile says and Maud rolls her eyes, and they are back to normal again.

'I'm sorry,' she says. Her lips move slowly. 'I know Ma was very upset.'

'You're home now, anyway,' he says and she nods and escapes inside, and Émile resumes his fretting, the pleasure he should be getting from Schreiber's cigarette numbed by his anxiety about Isabelle, and the feeling he can't shake that something is very wrong.

16

Isabelle sits in bed, swallowing mouthfuls of watery soup, while her husband watches her. From time to time, she catches sight of her reflection side-on in the dressing-table mirror, and adjusts herself so it captures her right side, her good side, with the eye wide open, watchful and alert, and nothing more untoward than a sunken dark circle and the kind of puffiness that comes from shallow, restive sleep. Ron has pulled the dressing-table stool up to the end of the bed and he leans on the bedpost, his chin propped on his knuckles. It reminds Isabelle of the time she had bad pneumonia as a child and was in bed for a week, and her mother would come up every lunchtime, accompanied by their maid, Phyllis, who brought her lunch on a tray. Her mother would gently but firmly take whatever book Isabelle was reading and hold it ransom on her lap.

'You know the rules. A nice clean plate and you can have your book back.'

And then the silent tussle between them would begin and there were many afternoons when Isabelle didn't get her book back, when the cold meat rissoles, congealing under a lake of gravy, would prove to be more repellent than the magnetism of *Anne of Green Gables*.

'How is it?' Ron clears his throat.

The soup needs salt. And meat. He has overcooked the vegetables. Isabelle says nothing. They both register the thud of the back door, then the sound of Schreiber's footsteps in the hallway. She waits for the creak of the stairs as he goes up to the attic, but there is quiet and then they hear him call out.

'Good evening.'

Ron bristles and gets up. He puts a hand on the doorknob, waits until he hears the rhythm of boots on the stairs, the sound of him moving around in the room above.

Ron exhales deeply. Isabelle puts down her spoon.

'I've had enough,' she says.

He nods and takes the bowl into the kitchen, returning with a wet flannel folded into a small square. He looms over her, gently pressing it to her swollen left eye, so close her fingers curl into tense, tight fists. When he has finished, he steps back and makes to stroke her head, but Isabelle shrinks away.

'Please don't,' she says and he looks at her mournfully, then tells her to get some rest.

Over the following days, Isabelle has more rest than she knows what to do with. The violet bruise on her face creeps towards a dirty yellow. Schreiber comes and goes, more quietly than usual as Ron has told him she is suffering from a migraine. She sits in her dressing gown in the kitchen with the curtains open a crack so that she can see the spray of white blossom on the hawthorn tree. Then one lunchtime, she hears boots on the gravel path and before she has a chance to gather herself, to take refuge in the bedroom, Schreiber appears. He is carrying a small dish covered with a tea towel, and the delicious aroma of thyme and pork fills the kitchen.

'Mrs Larch,' he says. Isabelle notices how he takes care not to stare as he sets the casserole on the table. 'There were leftovers at the Soldatenheim. Hunter's stew. My mother's cure for all ailments.' He pauses and this time, he looks directly at her, and although she tries her hardest not to, she feels her cheeks flood red with shame. 'I thought it might help your recovery.'

He busies himself with plates and cutlery and chatter. There had been a consignment of French pork; an official's birthday; some leftovers no one would miss. He lays a place next to her at the table and they sit side by side, like passengers on a bus. Isabelle watches him dish up and thinks that if Ron saw the two of them now, he would black her other eye, finish the job.

The casserole is topped with mashed potato, which someone has taken the time and trouble to pipe into small peaks. Small pats of butter have been stirred into the potato with the sole purpose of providing pleasure for whoever is lucky enough to eat it, with complete disregard for rationing and making do. Isabelle knows she should feel angry at the waste, at the decadence of it when the islanders have so little, but in the moment, she can only feel thankful. She takes another mouthful.

'Is there any news of Maud?' she asks. 'Mr Quenneville's daughter.'

'They released her,' he says. 'I've been waiting to tell you.'

'Thank goodness.' She closes her eyes. 'Thank you. A million times over.'

'It was the least I could do.' Schreiber turns to her, takes in her bruised face. 'How often does this happen?' he asks softly.

She looks away. 'It's not usually this bad.'

Schreiber rubs his wrist against his forehead. 'Is there anywhere you can go?' he asks. 'Somewhere you'll be safe? Your family perhaps . . .'

'Leave him, you mean?' Isabelle lets herself imagine what her mother might have said, if she'd seen her afterwards, her half-closed eye, the left side of her face all the colours of a sunset. *You must have provoked him in some way, Isabelle. Lord knows, you're capable of it.*

She shakes her head. 'No.'

Neither of them speak for a moment, then Schreiber takes out a twist of newspaper from his pocket. 'Tea?'

He gets up and fills the kettle. 'You must forgive me, but I've met many men like your husband. The Third Reich is stuffed with them.'

'Like your superior? The one who came to the house?'

'A classic example.' Schreiber nods. 'One leaves school and thinks that's the end of it, but of course it never is. Show me the boy and I'll show you the man, isn't that what they say?'

'You didn't enjoy school?'

'I liked learning, but not what went with it.' He gives her a small smile as he puts milk into teacups. 'Having to explain to my mother why my trousers were ripped or my glasses were broken.'

Isabelle thinks of her own son, how it might have been if they hadn't sent him away. 'Children can be terribly cruel,' she says.

Schreiber fills the teapot, reaches for the crocheted tea cosy. 'I liked books and sketching, not football. I detested summer camp – I was scared of the dark, used to shriek like a girl if I saw spiders! I didn't fit in.'

'It must be difficult' – Isabelle chooses her words carefully – 'if you feel different.'

'Yes.'

His eyes are clear and blue, bottomless, and as he stares at her, she feels as if she's been caught red-handed thumbing through his sketches. She must be as honest as she can; it is only fair.

'Mr Schreiber, as you know, Émile – Mr Quenneville – and myself are friends.' Isabelle puts down her cup. 'He told me. About the shed.'

'He did?' Schreiber fiddles with the frame of his spectacles; he cannot meet her eye. 'You must think I'm—'

'It's really nothing to do with us,' Isabelle says gently. 'I just worry that you could get into trouble.'

'We're discreet,' he says.

Are you really, Isabelle wants to say. How did you meet in the first place, was that being discreet? And what about going out with the fishing detail, don't tell her that it's mere coincidence? But she has said enough, he is already embarrassed, and her left eye begins to throb as the pain returns. She touches it gingerly.

'You should rest.' Schreiber looks at her with concern. 'I'm assuming it wouldn't help matters if I spoke to your husband?'

The look on her face seems to give him answer enough.

'I thought so.'

He tells her he has to fetch something from his room and goes upstairs. A few minutes later, he reappears and now he is all business, as if the conversation about the shed had never taken place.

'I've lent you something,' he says. 'It's in your sewing bag. My mother used to tell me to stand up to bullies. But I've realised that to do so, one must learn their language.'

'What do you mean?'

'You cannot let him do this again, Mrs Larch.' He gestures towards her face. 'Next time it could be much worse.'

He wishes her a peaceful afternoon then leaves for work, the back door clicking shut quietly behind him.

Isabelle gets up and walks slowly into the sitting room, pulls out her tapestry sewing bag from under the armchair. As she picks it up, she notices that it is heavier than usual, and she rummages amongst the balls of wool and pieces of assorted fabric, the socks she has still to darn. Her hand encounters something cold and metallic and instinct makes her glance towards the windows as she withdraws it, checking that there is no one outside.

He has given her a gun. She recoils, drops it back in the bag, her heart racing. Then she takes it out again, feels the fit of it in her hand. She could never. Then, she remembers the rage she'd felt when Ron had belittled Émile and called him handicapped of all things, knowing how much that word would hurt her. There had been an intense satisfaction in hitting back for once, even if it had got her nowhere.

Thoughtful now, she puts the pistol inside an old sock and places it in the bottom of the bag. It is the last place Ron would go snooping; it was clever of Peter to think of it. She will never turn a gun on her husband – the notion is ludicrous. But there is a comfort in having it there, like a cat dozing on her lap. It means that she is not alone anymore, that even when Peter is out, he is with her, he is on her side.

Isabelle goes back into the kitchen and heats water for a bath, then de-tangles and washes her hair. She applies a thick layer of powder to her bruised cheek and puts on coral lipstick. Then she sits in the kitchen with all the windows open to rinse out the smell of Hunter's stew and waits for her husband to come home.

Isabelle waits until after dinner, when she and Ron have retired to the sitting room. She fingers the bruised side of her face and reminds herself that while the marks are still visible, he is weakened.

'I've been thinking,' she says, taking out her darning needle, 'that I could go into work tomorrow.'

Ron puts down the *Press*. He smiles and nods. 'I was thinking the same.'

Isabelle frowns. There is barely any wool left. He will have to live with holes in his socks if the war lasts another winter. Her husband never thinks the same. Carefully, she threads the needle and waits.

'I could go in on your behalf, I suppose,' he continues, 'but it's better coming from you.'

'What do you mean?'

'Your resignation.' His tone is patient. 'You need to let Corbeille know, don't you?'

Isabelle wills herself to stay calm. 'But I don't want to resign,' she says. 'I want to keep on working.'

'That place isn't making you happy, Izzy, I can tell.' Patient is hardening to firm. 'And I don't like you working for the Germans, either.'

'It never bothered you before.' She works the needle, back and forth. 'Anyway, I'm not working for the Germans. If anything, I'm working for the French. We're keeping the Germans from getting their hands on the place.'

He harrumphs and lowers the newspaper. 'You've changed. I see it. I see *you*, every day. You come back from there and you're jumpy as a box of frogs.'

She tuts. 'Oh, nonsense.'

'You turned the colour of a ripe tomato when Quenneville turned up here the other night. You're doing it now.'

He laughs as her hand goes to her face.

'Is this about the money again? Because I told you he'd pay it back.' She can hear herself becoming shrill. 'You're being ridiculous.'

'Am I?' He lets the question hang.

She opens her sewing bag and brings out some more wool. 'I'm not resigning, Ron.'

The clock ticks. Isabelle feels out of breath, as though she's been running uphill. Outside in the gutter, a pair of wood pigeons ruffle and coo.

Ron gets up. He walks to the mantlepiece and adjusts one of the spaniels slightly, so that it faces towards the door.

'All these years I've been patient with you, Isabelle, wouldn't you say?' He looks over at her. 'All those false alarms at the start. Then you start to accept it. No kids. No grandkids. That's it for the Larches. Soon to be extinct.'

'We had a child,' Isabelle begins and his face changes and they are back to where they were a week ago, except this time she knows he won't touch her.

'He doesn't count!'

Isabelle flinches and tries to focus on the needle, moving up and down, row upon row, as her husband starts listing her crimes.

'You creep about at night and steal money from our savings. You suck up to the Kraut any chance you get. You invite some deaf man who was sweet on you once to come and sit in my house and hob-nob with the bloody German, without so much as a by-your-leave. And these are just the things I know about.' He shakes his head and returns to the

Press. 'I'll ask around, find you another job,' he says. 'Let's say no more about it.'

Her left cheek throbs, her mind whirring. She hasn't gone through all of this to be in an even worse position now to when she started; she won't have it. Peter was right – you have to stand up to bullies, and she has been too silent for too long. She stares at the sewing bag, calls to mind its contents.

'Ron' – she begins.

'Izzy?' There is a thickness to his voice and when he lowers the newspaper, she sees to her surprise that his eyes are red. He gropes in his pocket for a handkerchief. 'All I'm asking for is some ... cooperation to make things more pleasant around here. Do you think I enjoy this?' He sniffs.

'I don't know,' she says coolly. She snips and knots the wool, picks up the next sock from the pile. Perhaps, in spite of it all, it is possible that Ron has suffered more than she realised. He married a woman who turned out to be as good as barren, and he has stuck with her; she has never suspected him of playing around. She glances at him. The job at the French House could end at any time, she supposes. Corbeille doesn't need her. He could easily do the administrative work himself, hire a girl for the cleaning – she has long suspected he is just being kind by keeping her there. And Émile? She has reproached herself a hundred times over for going to his house on New Year's Eve, for slipping that note in with his wages like a lovelorn schoolgirl. He has a wife who needs him, a wayward daughter, a family. What did she think was going to happen? That they would have some kind of affair, like Schreiber and Ozzy, bedding down in the shed? Émile tolerates her because they work together. He has forgiven her – that is all. He no more has feelings for her than she does for those ridiculous dogs on the mantlepiece.

Isabelle sets down her darning. 'I'll go and see Mr Corbeille tomorrow,' she announces, and her husband smiles at her in a way that makes her want to slap him all over again.

'Good girl,' he says.

She is back. There is her bicycle with the diagonal tear in the saddle and the stuffing frothing out of it – and there through the kitchen window is Isabelle herself, sitting at the table with her back to him. It is relief Émile feels first, before pleasure kicks in. He is inordinately glad to see her. It has been a whole week. Normally, he would go straight to the shed, but he finds himself tapping on the window, seeking her attention.

She raises her head, nods, and looks down again. As if she's operated by strings, Émile thinks, like some kind of puppet. She barely smiles. He cannot wait until later. He leaves his boots on the doorstep and goes inside.

'All right?'

Isabelle looks up. She holds a scrap of blotting paper, which she is pressing against the wet ink of her signature. Ink, blotting paper, signatures: these things make Émile nervous. Crested notepaper, lawyer's fees. Sign here, Mr Quenneville, that's right, there where my finger is.

'What are you doing?'

She doesn't reply. Or at least, she doesn't say anything. She reaches for an envelope.

'Are you better?' Émile says. 'Corbeille said you were sick.'

'Yes, thank you.'

Her hair falls loose around her face and her skin has a sickly tinge to it. Clouds the colour of charcoal block out the sun and the kitchen darkens then brightens again, illuminating her in sunlight. She looks up and squints and it is then that Émile sees it, the dirty yellow bruise under her eye socket, which she has tried to conceal with powder.

'What happened?' he says, knowing the answer, recoiling from the pointlessness of the question. And it seems that Isabelle thinks it's not worth the trouble of answering too, because she's gathering up her papers, and heading for the stairs. She cannot or will not look at him. There is a puff of air as the door closes behind her.

It is his fault. He can't know that, of course, but Émile senses it. Larch had looked ready to swing for him when he barged his way in; he remembers the speed with which Isabelle ushered him into the sitting room and then out of the house again, afterwards. And then there was the advance on his pay – he'd bet a month's rations that Larch had known nothing about that. There is a rushing in his ears as he takes the stairs two at a time up to the main house, out of bounds under ordinary circumstances for the likes of him, but he doesn't give a fig. He is going to find her, even if it gets him the sack. In the hallway, he catches his reflection in the fish-eye mirror on the landing; he looks like a burglar, he thinks, with his stubble and shabby Guernsey sweater, amongst all the fancy carved wood and dripping chandeliers. He goes up to the first floor and sees Isabelle sitting at a desk through the half-open door of the office.

'You shouldn't be up here,' she says, as he walks in. She is folding the letter with careful precision.

'What is that?' Émile points to the letter.

Isabelle hesitates, then hands it to him. It is addressed to Mr Corbeille and as Émile reads it, he can't imagine the words in her mouth. It isn't the Isabelle he knows, the one who loves this house, who – and this just occurs to him – takes refuge in it. She is leaving, offering notice with immediate effect. She is sorry for any inconvenience caused. Yours etcetera.

'I need a change,' she says. 'I've been here too long.'

She starts to tell him not to worry, that his job is safe, but he stops her. He can't bear it, all this talking around the houses.

'It's him, isn't it? He's making you do this.'

'He's my husband.' Her gaze is steady, almost challenging. 'We're married. You know how it is.'

'A husband who batters you.' It's out before he can stop himself.

She looks at him as though he has just uttered a string of obscenities. 'You shouldn't be up here,' she says, taking back the letter and sliding it into an envelope. She stares at him blankly and it is the dull-eyed gaze of his nightmares, when he loses her all over again. 'Please leave.'

Émile has the rest of the day for his temper to stew. He digs and plants and hoes until his shoulders ache and the sweat pools on him, but Larch won't be back from work until five, and he has to do something to fill the time. And when the time comes and he joins the trickle of workers cycling through Town, he feels resolute. His fists clench on the handlebars and through his eyelids, the sun seeps like blood. When had it started? On their wedding night, or a few years on, once disappointment had set in, when they'd sent their son to be raised by people who were paid to do it? Why did she stay, why did she let him? But marriages were like the iceberg that brought down the Titanic: it was what the folks around you couldn't see that was important, that soldered a husband and wife together.

He is in their road now, can see their cottage. Pebbledash and prim net curtains like a bad disguise. He'll kick the door in if he has to; he'll turn the house over to find him. Émile gets off his bike. Then he sees Larch walking down the road towards him, something furtive about the way he moves, as if he's dragging his secrets around with him. He gives Émile a look of terse enquiry but something passes between them as Larch approaches, a change of current that a deaf man like him is quick to register. Or a deaf cunt like him because that seems to be what Larch is saying, a scowl setting deep into the smoker's lines of his face. Émile is glad of the insult, it is the crack of the starting pistol, and the first swing comes easy, despite his bad shoulder, and he'd have given a lot to hear the sound of his fist making contact with Larch's jaw, the man's cry of pain as he stumbles and falls. He lies on the ground, arms curving around his gut and private parts as he catches his breath, and with a surge of anger, Émile imagines Isabelle cowering in a corner on their kitchen floor.

'Get up.'

Larch struggles to his feet and lunges at him clumsily, and Émile socks him on the chin again, right side this time, feeling a growing repugnance – the bastard can't even fight, not when it's man to man. Larch reels backwards then propels himself towards Émile. He fights dirty, of course – a knee in the groin, then a punch to his left eye, another on the bridge of the nose. Émile feels a sticky flow of blood running down his face and filling his throat. He coughs, hawking out the blood, a brush of panic as he feels close to choking, and Larch delivers a few kicks to his ribs, before pain drives Émile on – for Isabelle, for her bruised face, her chipped tooth, and all the times he doesn't know about, and he is back standing again. Larch is upon him but this time Émile is ready and he grips Larch's arm, twisting it behind his back. Larch's mouth gapes into a howl. How long to teach him a lesson? Five seconds? Ten? He releases him when Larch's face has turned the colour of quarry dust, when his eyes are beginning to roll.

'I'll kill you next time.'

Émile shakes himself free of the man and limps towards his bike. It is only then that he notices Schreiber standing on the front porch. He is staring towards where Larch is slumped against the wall, then back at Émile.

Émile nods at him. 'No more than he deserves,' he says.

And Schreiber seems to agree because he makes no move to help the man and when Émile reaches the end of the lane and looks back, Larch is still there immobile at the side of the road, and the German has disappeared.

17

It is the whispering Letty finds hardest, a low hum around her like a distant swarm of bees. It stops as soon as she swings around, daring just one of the women behind her in the queue for the butchers to say to her face what only seems intended for her back.

'Ignore them, Ma,' Maud says and Letty tuts and ignores her, because she is half of the problem and Émile the other half, and together they've given the gossips enough to keep them going for months. She had got to the market early especially, but being near the front of the queue hadn't saved her. The shop was late opening and Lord knows why; how difficult was it to be punctual when you only opened twice a week for two hours? She folds and unfolds the coupons in her hand.

Émile had got into fights before, but not for a long time, not since Stella was born. He'd slink in like a tomcat after a night out, cuts and scratches keeping company with his sore head. A misunderstanding in the pub, he'd say, avoiding her eyes. She'd never understood how a man who couldn't hear anything could take so much offence in the first place. But she'd never seen him as bad as he was on that Wednesday afternoon. He'd half dragged himself into the house, his face streaked with dry blood, and his nose, swollen and misshapen. At first she'd thought he'd got into a spat with the Germans and she had ushered the girls out of the kitchen, boiled water and fetched towels for a bath. But then the truth had come out, or a version of it, as bent out of shape as his nose.

'He was battering her,' he'd said, as he sat in the bathtub, rubbing at the sliver of soap.

'Who?'

'Isabelle Larch. Her husband was beating her up.'

And that woman's name had swelled and filled the room until there was no space for anything else.

Someone had to do something, Émile had said, and when she asked what on earth he thought he was doing interfering in other folks' personal affairs, Letty found the answer in his eyes. He had loved her once and now he loved someone else, and she found herself unprepared for the pain it caused her. She felt as if he had kicked her hard in the soft flesh of her belly, where faded stretchmarks, left behind from Maud and Stella, rippled across her skin.

'Ma.'

Letty feels Maud stiffen next to her and looks up. Walking towards them is Isabelle Larch. Such a high and mighty way she has of carrying herself, Letty thinks, although her shoes are every bit as scuffed and worn as Letty's own, and as Isabelle draws nearer, she can see that her coat has a tear in the sleeve.

'Mrs Quenneville.'

A hush descends on the queue, as if the curtain has just lifted at the theatre. Letty stares at her. The woman's a bag of bones; you'd cut yourself on her if you weren't careful. The image of her lying naked underneath Émile pops uninvited into Letty's head.

'Come to gloat, have you?' Letty says.

No, Isabelle says, she hasn't and she is calm as a millpond and the way she says even the simplest of words seems designed to mock Letty, to make her feel less than she is, more stupid.

'Why don't you just sod off then?' Let the back of the queue get their money's worth, Letty thinks as she yells, let them get a bit extra with their ounces of stringy mince. 'Go on!'

Isabelle reddens. When she speaks, her voice trembles. 'He broke my husband's arm, you know. You're lucky Mr Larch hasn't reported it.'

Maud's hand is on Letty's sleeve, but Letty won't stop.

'Don't give me that. He ain't gone to the police because of what you were getting up to with him.'

Isabelle's tone hardens. 'We haven't pressed charges out of consideration for you and your family. You should be thanking me, Letty.'

She is tougher than she looks, Letty thinks, and her heart races. 'You keep away from him.'

Isabelle gives her a quick, tight smile. 'I intend to.'

Her heels echo as she walks the length of the queue, murmurs of approval following in her wake. Letty has never felt so glad to see Mr Le Mesurier arrive not long afterwards with his cheery, 'Afternoon, ladies,' as he takes down the shutters and opens up.

'Your sister's a sweet little thing, isn't she?'

He takes her by surprise. Maud turns, banging her elbow on the open drawer of the filing cabinet, to find Le Lacheur standing there next to her. It is her first afternoon back since she was released from prison, and she feels herself flush with the pleasure of seeing him.

'Can't imagine she gets told no very often,' he goes on and she is about to launch into her thank-you speech – for seeing Stella, for intervening – when Le Lacheur nods brusquely towards his office.

'Can I have a word?'

'Of course.' Maud follows him next door, where he lights a cigarette and smokes it with his back to her, staring out of the window.

'Do you have any idea of the danger you've put us in?' There is a harshness to his tone and when he looks at her, his face is red. Maud realises she's never seen him angry before. She starts to apologise but he cuts her off.

'They'll have you marked now, you know. No smoke without fire. You can forget about the trip to France.'

He has a knack of making her feel like a schoolgirl at the Intermediate again. It is all she can do not to bow her head.

'What with that and your father getting free with his fists. Not sure it's even wise to have you in the office.'

'I'm not responsible for his behaviour.' Maud understands suddenly how Ma felt in the queue at the market, and her stomach knots and tightens. She is embarrassed to find herself on the verge of tears.

'Mud sticks, Maud!' A fit of coughing overcomes him and he bends over, clutching his sides.

Maud fetches a glass of water and he takes a few sips, then sits at his desk, fingers to his temples. She dares to draw up a chair.

'I don't know how I can thank you for what you did. Stella said you were most helpful.'

In fact, Stella had said nothing of the kind, remained frustratingly tight-lipped on the subject of her encounter with Le Lacheur, providing only the barest of summaries.

'He said he'd do what he could,' she had told Maud, with a small shrug, going on to say that that secretary of his was like one of those yappy dogs that nip your ankles, and she really didn't know how Maud could bear to work there, no wonder she had kept it a secret.

Le Lacheur closes his eyes, puts his bad leg up on the footstool. 'Leg's been giving me jip recently,' he mutters. He shakes his head. 'Sarnia bloody Cherie. Why you'd want to play it in the first place is beyond me. It's for old ladies and school children. I'd pay good money never to hear the thing again.'

'I hate it too,' Maud says soberly, and he looks at her, alert again, and throws back his head and laughs. Maud smiles back, the immense relief she feels at being back in his good books tinged with shame, as if she's found a lavatory just in time to avoid an accident.

'Maud, Maud.' Le Lacheur wags his finger at her. 'You gave me such a fright. What are we going to do with you, eh?'

The question seems rhetorical on the face of it, but he opens a drawer as if the answer belongs somewhere inside it and takes out a scrap of typewritten paper. He passes it to her.

'Know anyone who might fit the bill?'

It is an advertisement for a live-in housekeeper. *Comfortable room in Torteval farmhouse,* Maud reads. *Full board and lodging in exchange for light domestic duties.*

A stutter she didn't know she had threatens to trip up her reply. 'Do you mean . . . I . . . I'm not a housekeeper.'

'Don't look so glum, girl!' he says, wincing and massaging his foot. 'I'm not putting you in a pinny with a feather duster. But the Germans are still sniffing around the place and it would kill two birds with one stone, as it were.' He gives her a steady look. 'I need someone who understands the confidential nature of my work. You could carry on doing what you do here.'

Outside, she hears the zip of a motorcycle in the square, the collision of German and English voices. Soon, streams of cyclists will be returning home in single file on the right side of the road, hosepipe substituting for tyres. How quickly people adapt to change, Maud thinks, to live the unthinkable. She looks at this man who has taken such a shine to her, who understands that she wants more than to be married off by twenty, with a life that echoes everyone else's.

'How *are* things at home?' he asks rather archly, as if he has been privy to the silent supper times, the discomfiting quiet that has replaced the low grumble of bickering, which seeps from her parents' room at night.

Maud doesn't answer. Pa's face is still cut and bruised from the fight, and it is all she can do to look at him. He slept with another man's wife – that tall, thin, sad-looking woman with the chipped tooth – and then broke her husband's arm when he found out. It was hardly the stuff of Stella's *True Romance* magazines, although her sister refuses to believe it, tells her that the Larch woman must be exaggerating, that they shouldn't listen to gossip.

There are sounds of movement in the office next door – Miss Guille is back.

'I'd better go,' Maud says. Is she being fanciful or are his eyes the exact colour of her own, the same shape even?

Le Lacheur speaks softly. 'I thought you were grateful.'

'I am. I'll . . .' Her stutter is back again. 'I'll think about it.'

Maud closes the door firmly behind her, unsure if what he has just proposed is an opportunity or an insult, a debt she has accrued that now needs to be paid.

Over the next few days, Maud watches her family. Pa with his wounds now healing but buried deeper than ever in a fog of his own thoughts. Their mother, banging down plates and pots on the kitchen table with a vehemence that causes Maud and Stella to exchange glances, but that Pa fails to notice. And Stella, cooler with Maud than usual ever since her return from prison, her once ripe anecdotes about her travails at the hairdresser's now reduced to a pithy sentence or two, and she hasn't once asked Maud to be her partner when she's dancing to Glenn Miller on the wireless.

Maud cannot settle. The accordion gives her no pleasure; Le Lacheur seems to follow her everywhere, his voice whispering in her ear.

Aren't I allowed to tease you a little?
Just add fifteen per cent to the prices.
You deserve better, Maud. A girl like you.

She takes down the battered leather suitcase Pa took to Canada from the top of the wardrobe and imagines herself packing her things in it. Then she puts it back again, empty.

And then late one Friday afternoon, Ozzy Ozanne comes to the house. His face and forearms are tanned red-brown from the sun, his sleeves are rolled up and he is whistling as he saunters up the path. He blows the three of them a kiss through the kitchen window and even Ma smiles and tells Stella, it's her admirer back again. The back door is open and she beckons him inside, asks him what he's got.

He has two spider crabs needing a home, he says, or mackerel if they prefer. Ma sniffs the fish.

'Fresher than I am,' he tells her with a wink. 'Caught this afternoon.'

'What do you do, stuff 'em down your long johns when the Jerries aren't looking?' Their mother regards him suspiciously, but her eyes linger on the flailing crab.

'Not all of 'em are bad sorts,' Ozzy says, and their mother scoffs and says that's not what she's heard and how much for the crab?

Maud watches as the two of them haggle, then Ma asks her to fetch her purse.

'I'll take a bit less if you throw in a bottle of the hard stuff, Maud,' Ozzy says, smirking a little. 'Or a fine wine from Paree, now you're in the business.'

Maud concentrates on counting out coins. If she ignores him, he will shut up, start blathering about something else . . . How did he even find out in the first place? But when she looks up, there is silence and the spider crab is paddling frantically in her mother's grip.

'What's he talking about?' She turns to Maud.

'Nothing. I don't know.'

Sensing trouble, Ozzy pockets the money swiftly, tipping his cap as he wishes them a good weekend and hurries away.

'What did he mean?' Ma glares at Maud, and then at Stella, who is wearing the look Maud remembers from when they were children and got caught playing ghosts in the muddy garden with Ma's bedsheets. 'And what are you keeping so quiet about, miss?'

Stella says nothing.

Their mother tosses the crab into the sink and takes their sharpest knife from the drawer. 'Have you been seeing that man again, when I told you not to? Have you?'

And Maud can bear it no longer. She is tired of pretending, tired of secrets, tired of the voice in her head that won't let her be.

'If you mean Mr Le Lacheur, then yes, I have. I've been working for him a couple of afternoons a week. I didn't tell you, Ma, because I knew how you'd react.'

It has been many years since her mother slapped her. The sound of it resounds around the kitchen and Maud isn't sure if it's pain or humiliation that makes her eyes smart. She cups her throbbing cheek.

'Why don't you do as you're told, Maud Quenneville, just for once?' Ma is close enough for Maud to see the droplets of sweat on her forehead, the errant hairs on her chin. 'How many times do I have to tell you? He is not a good man!'

She throws the crab onto the chopping board. 'Just wait until your father hears about this.'

It is this that does for Maud, more than a hundred slaps ever could. 'Why don't you tell the truth?' She is yelling at her mother, shouting in her face. 'He's not my father, is he? *Is he?*'

Ma drives the knife into the back of the crab and plunges it into the pan of boiling water that had been destined for the potatoes.

'He's asked me to live with him,' Maud says, her voice unsteady.

Her mother's back tenses, but she doesn't turn from the stove.

'And I've decided I will.'

Stella stares at her as if she doesn't know who she is anymore, then rushes from the room.

The kitchen is quiet, apart from the bubbling water and the knocking of the crab's claws against the pot.

'Take that blasted accordion with you, while you're at it,' her mother says eventually. When she turns around, her face is streaked with tears. 'I've had just about enough, Maud.'

It takes Maud just shy of five minutes to leave the house in which she's spent her whole life. If she stops to think, to consider, she knows she will lose her nerve. She scoops up skirts, dresses, stockings, a couple of books, her toothbrush, flannel, half a pot of cold cream, and throws them into Pa's old suitcase, wishing it didn't have a dent in the side, wishing it was smarter. Stella watches her coolly.

'We're your family, not him,' she says. 'And I didn't like the man one jot. If you really want to know, he gives me the heebie-jeebies.'

Maud tells her she'll be back to visit and Stella says she can do as she pleases, she's just glad to have the room to herself for once.

In the kitchen, Ma is hacking at the crab with a knife. She will not look at her.

'Ma . . .'

'If he puts you in the maid's room' – her mouth is set in a thin, rigid line – 'give him what for.'

Maud straps the accordion to her back and goes outside, wedges the suitcase in the basket of her bicycle. A low fog is rolling in, blurring the top of the hedgerows and she can taste the salt in it as she starts to cycle up the lane. A man on a bicycle is coming towards her, slowing to a halt. It is Pa, and the look on his face as he stares at the suitcase and then at her makes Maud catch her breath. He has lost his fight, his spirit and she is the cause. The strangeness of it is almost enough to have her turn back. She is free and it is terrifying.

'I have to leave,' she says. 'I'm sorry, Pa.'

Her vision clouds over and her father turns to water, insubstantial as the fog. For a moment, Maud feels that she has stepped into his world of silence because she senses he wants to tell her something but the words don't follow; and it is better for both of them, she thinks, if she just goes.

The road both ahead and behind her is lost to the mist. Maud wipes her eyes, and heads for the coast.

18

'You'll have to clean the men's facilities. You know that, Mrs Larch, don't you?'

The landlord regards Isabelle with deep scepticism. Isabelle looks around. The sour smell of stale beer and musky male sweat seems to impregnate every surface of the deserted pub. She wonders how many filthy urinals she'll have to scrub before Ron goes easier on her. A month's worth? Two months? A year?

'Of course,' she says.

The landlord drums his fingers on the table. He is the kind of man who in peacetime would be lighting up his next cigarette from the butt of the first. 'Your husband said your last place let you go. Up the road at the French House, wasn't it?'

'That's right.'

'Fancy.'

'Not really.' Isabelle smiles tightly. 'I was just a housekeeper.'

He shrugs and hauls himself to his feet. 'Let's get you started, then.'

She cleans there three mornings a week, scrubbing yellow streaks of piss from the lavatory floor, mopping up vomit from the front steps. She sweeps up cigarette butts, empties ashtrays and rubs at ancient stains on the bar until her arm muscles ache. Sometimes, Isabelle amuses herself by imagining her mother's reaction if she could see her on her haunches in a common boozer, scrubbing floors.

Recent events have injected her mother with some of the vitriolic energy Isabelle remembers from her youth and she found herself summoned up to St Martins.

'Is it true, Isabelle, what people are saying?'

'What *are* people saying?'

'That you were carrying on' – her mother spat out the words with a shudder – 'with that deaf man.'

No, Isabelle said, it wasn't true.

Her mother doesn't believe her any more than her husband does, or the gossips in the queues at the market. Sometimes it feels as if the whole island is accusing her of the very thing that she has most longed for but resisted, allowing herself only the luxury of imagination, glimpses of a life that she now knows could never have been. Their ranch on the homestead, the crackle and spit of logs on the fire, shelves lined with books to see her through till spring. The children – Peter, their first, the special one, and then his brother and sister who came later – all sitting cross-legged at Émile's feet as he plays the accordion (she has given him his hearing back and herself a more reliable womb). He is patient with them, he lets them take it in turns to hold the reins in the wagon when they go into Town and at night, when the children are tucked up in bed, the pleasure that she and Émile take with each other is such that she is glad their nearest neighbour is several miles away, and that there are only the horses and the chickens and the new litter of pigs to hear their cries.

But Émile had shown himself to be a violent man, no better, some might say, than Ron. He broke her husband's arm, left him battered and bruised in a ditch. He has made everything worse, not better. At times, Isabelle is ashamed of him, but there is one thing she has been wrong about, and it is the reason Ron has her scrubbing toilet bowls and why women whisper as she passes: what Émile did to her husband is not the action of a man who doesn't care.

It is a hot, soupy morning towards the end of summer when she sees him again. She is sweeping the steps outside the Caves and he is cycling down the hill towards her. Her first thought is that if he has come to apologise, she's not sure she can accept it, her second that she hopes there are no wagging tongues to witness their encounter, because he is braking, dismounting from his bike, two feet on one pedal like the youngsters do. And in fact, there is something youthful about him today, his hair, lightened by the sun and in need of a cut, falling in wisps across his forehead.

He props his bicycle against the wall and takes her in – the stained housecoat, the broom. Isabelle's head is hot, sweating under her turban. She lifts her chin, tells herself she is the same woman he knew from the French House, that she doesn't need his pity.

'I heard you were working here,' he says. 'Wasn't sure I believed it.'

'Call it penance,' she says and he doesn't understand and passes her his notebook, but she bats it away.

Émile unrolls a note from his pocket. 'I brought you your money.' He reddens as he hands it over. 'It's late – I'm sorry.'

'It doesn't matter.'

Isabelle picks up the broom and goes back into the bar, aware of his footsteps behind her. She begins wiping down the pumps, although the last barrels of beer in the cellar were finished long ago and the pumps are oxidised with disuse. Émile puts his cap on the counter and watches her for a minute.

'Are you all right?' he asks. His eyes are a soft grey, translucent, and remind Isabelle of rock pools, warmed under the sun. 'Has he stopped?'

'He can't hit me with a broken arm, Émile.'

She turns to him, waiting for an apology, but Émile says nothing. He picks up a beer mat and flicks it over, flicks it back. Then he reaches into his back pocket and hands her a book. It is the last one she was reading at the French House before she left, an Agatha Christie novel, her bookmark still in place.

'I've been reading it when I finish up for the day,' he says. 'First book I've read in years. That Poirot fellow's a funny one, isn't he?'

Isabelle starts to stack the chairs. She wants to stay angry with him; she is scared now of feeling anything else.

Émile pauses, then helps her. 'Half a mind to read another one. Keeps your thoughts off the war, if nothing else.'

'There are lots on the kitchen dresser,' she says, wiping at a piece of grime on the bevelled window, and her heart contracts at the memory of the house and her easy chair in the kitchen, with the apple tree nodding in the breeze, and the view of the sea in the distance, the rows of potato plants and canes of beans, all ready now for harvest.

'Come back,' Émile says, and the look in his eyes makes her wonder if that is really why he is here, if he misses her as she does him. 'Talk to Corbeille.'

Isabelle looks at him sharply. She is sweeping now, left to

right, and back again, the broom knocking against the table legs. 'You know they think we're carrying on.'

She will not write it down; she repeats it until he understands.

'Who?'

'Everyone! Your wife for one. My husband.'

'They're wrong.'

'You shouldn't have hit him.' Isabelle finds herself alarmingly close to tears. 'It didn't help.' She looks around with frustration at the dingy pub. 'It's made my life smaller than ever, can't you see?'

Émile falls silent. He takes a step towards her. Her grip tightens on the handle of the broom and she doesn't know if it's for support or defence. She has had no breakfast, her head feels as light as a balloon, and all she knows is that she isn't ready for whatever is about to happen next.

'You're right,' Émile says, so quietly she can barely hear him. 'I'm sorry.'

She sees him retreat back into himself, becoming the deaf man again, the man she saw on the night of the bombing, staring up at the windows of Hauteville House.

She stoops to pick up an empty beer bottle from under the table and when she gets up, he has gone.

Later, when she is alone at home, Isabelle takes out the Agatha Christie. As she removes the bookmark, she sees Peter's photograph, pressed like a flower into the crease of the spine. Isabelle plays the events that have led to this in her head: Émile, taking the Bible from the dresser, removing the picture with as much care as he might if it was one of his own children, thinking of her and only her as he does so. The thought of this makes Isabelle feel as if she has just jumped from a very great height. She presses her lips thoughtfully to her son's face.

She gets up and goes into the sitting room, to the bureau where her wedding photo resides in its tarnished silver frame. Isabelle thinks of the gun in her sewing bag, her heart pounding as she unclips the back and slides in Peter's photo so that it partially overlaps her and Ron, making them three not two. Then she dabs a cloth with vinegar and polishes the frame until it shines, returning it to the top of the bureau.

Maud stands the sheet music on top of an old cider barrel, stamps her feet to get some life back into them and runs through the 'Pennsylvania Polka' one last time before the light begins to fade. Barely a week after she'd arrived, Le Lacheur had asked if she'd mind terribly practising her accordion in the barn, despite the fact that her room is two floors above his study – as her mother had grimly predicted, he has put her in the maid's room.

'It's warmer up there,' he'd said, that first night when she'd arrived, unannounced on his doorstep, exhausted from the long cycle ride. He'd looked at her as if she was a prize he'd won unexpectedly at the fair, but didn't know quite what to do with. Nonetheless, he had ushered her inside, given her leftovers to eat and quite a lot to drink.

'Good for you,' he kept saying. 'You made the right decision, you'll see.'

Yet a month has passed now and Maud is beginning to question this. She spends much of her time at home, working in his study, and she is bored and restless; and then there are the meals to cook and the chores to be done, and more recently a new duty on her roster: that of nurse, because Le Lacheur has taken to bed with influenza.

Maud glances at her watch. She'll need to get tea ready soon, take Le Lacheur up some broth. Away from his silver ink well and inventory lists, and in an old pyjama shirt with a soup stain down the front, Maud has seen a different side to him: he is querulous, demanding, fretful. He is constantly asking her to check his temperature, to take his pulse – his limbs feel like sea sponge, he says, the slightest exertion and his heart races like a greyhound. Maud has realised that he is afraid of dying and of dying alone, and that part of her job is to ensure that neither of these scenarios come about.

She gathers up her things and walks across the garden to the house. Pinned on the inside of the kitchen door is the list of occupants, with her name recently added to his. It makes her feel odd, the feud of their two surnames, when she is becoming increasingly convinced that he is her father; and increasingly unsure as to how she might feel about this, were it to be true. There is a photograph of him as a young man in the study and when she first saw it Maud was struck, not just with their likeness, the way his hair fell and the slant of the eyebrows, but also something in his expression, a sort of determination, which she understands in the manner of a half-familiar language. Many times after a glass of wine, she has been on the verge of asking him outright, but then loses heart. If he lies as she believes he did the first time they met, this will crush her. But if he tells the truth, there are other unsettling questions to be asked about him and her mother, and so each time she goes to bed in the room Ma slept in before her, resolving to broach the subject another day.

Upstairs, she can hear him calling. Suppressing a sigh, she fills a glass with water and goes to his room. Marooned in the large double bed and propped up with pillows, he looks frail and furious about the fact.

'Where did you disappear to?' He seizes the water and gulps it down. 'I've been calling you for the past hour.'

'Sorry. I didn't hear.'

'Deaf as your pa,' he mutters.

Maud says nothing. She is learning to bite her tongue. She tells herself to make allowances: he is an old man and he is ill. They are not used to each other yet.

She places a hand on his clammy forehead.

'You've got a temperature,' she says. 'I'll make you a compress.'

Later, after supper, Maud goes to her room. There is enough oil for an hour of reading by lamplight but tonight she cannot concentrate. The window rattles, and shadows shrink and lengthen across the jaundiced wallpaper.

She rummages in her suitcase for her winter pullover. Why haven't you unpacked yet, she hears Stella saying, what are you waiting for? As her hand runs across the silky plaid lining, fraying now and becoming unstitched, she makes contact with a slip of paper. She takes it out, unfolds it. It is a letter, written in a looped script of curves and flourishes and exclamation marks that flows like a river across the page. It is dated September 1912.

Dearest Émile,

Maud hesitates. But it's not like finding someone's diary, she tells herself, and she starts to read.

224

Dearest Émile,

You know when I said I'd hide the ring you gave me in my drawers if I had to? Well, this evening, I made a little pouch out of some scraps of velvet and I'm going to tie it to the inside waistband of my skirts. So never scold me again for being unromantic!

By the time you read this, you'll be afloat, hopefully equipped with a decent pair of sea legs and not a whiff of la mal de mer. You will also be reunited with your accordion – I had the devil's own job smuggling it into the house without Mother seeing. It's not the kind of thing you can hide under your coat or in the bottom of your shopping basket! I was so relieved to see that it was still there in the window of Ingrouille's and as it turns out, I was just in time. That funny man with the squint told me he'd had interest from someone in St Sampsons and he was coming to get it once he'd been paid at the end of the week. Maybe it was just a ploy to up the price. Anyway, it's of little consequence now and once I'd bought it back, I went straight to the jeweller's and had your initials engraved on the case. It's yours forever now, EQ.

I should be sad about you leaving – and I am, of course – but I'm also excited, because I know that this time next year, I'll be doing the exact same journey. I keep thinking about the house we'll have on the prairie, with a veranda overlooking the wheat fields and a swinging chair for two. I must admit that it's always either sunset or sunrise when I imagine it, and never cold! But actually, I'm looking forward to the winters. As you said, long winter nights are perfect for a bookworm, like me. Unless of course we are blessed straight away with an EQ junior or two (or three!), in which case reading will be the last thing on my mind!

Anyway, it's time for me to take some hot milk to Mother before she goes to bed. I just tell myself that I only have to do this 365 more times. Reading that sentence back, I sound like a prisoner crossing off the days until they are free, but now you're gone, that is exactly how I feel. A prisoner with a feather mattress who has a boiled egg for breakfast every day, but nonetheless!

I miss you. I love you. Remember to write.

Your Isabelle

Maud lies back on her pillow and stares at the ceiling. When she had seen Isabelle Larch in the market that day, she had found it hard to imagine her and Pa together in any sense and had it not been for Ma's conviction, Maud would have questioned the substance of the rumours. Now she understands her mother's distress. 'The Larch woman' and Pa had been secretly engaged. She had loved him and presumably he had loved her back, at least for a while; and then something had happened that had meant there was no Canada, no love seat on the veranda, and they had both married other people.

The lamp hisses, the flame gutters and sways. Maud wonders if Ma has ever come upon the letter, as she has just now. She reads it again, absorbing the air of breezy confidence. The truth is her mother would barely be able to decipher it, and she feels a deep sadness for both of them, for Pa as well as her mother, and the choices they have made.

19

Émile has taken to sitting where Isabelle used to at the end of the day, in the beige easy chair, worn thin at the arms. He is halfway through *Death on the Nile*, and it is almost like being able to hear again, following the lilt of conversation, absorbing the sounds of Cairo at sunset, the wail of the call to prayer. He is often late home now on account of the reading and the evenings not quite drawn in yet. Letty may suspect the worst, but he hands over every last penny of his wages, and there's a little more of that too than there used to be.

With Isabelle gone, Corbeille has given him the key to the back door and every Friday morning, he and the Frenchman meet in the kitchen to talk about what he's done and what needs doing. Émile supposes that in a manner of speaking, he's been promoted a notch, but there is no one now to share the pleasure of the harvest with him as he packs crates of beans and carrots for the Germans, picks tomatoes, their skins bursting with flavour. Every now and then, he looks up from the vegetable patches towards the house and the house stares right through him, and a strange feeling comes over him, similar to his first days in Vancouver when he didn't know a soul.

He doesn't know why it should be so hard to stay away from someone he has spent most of his life avoiding, but it is. He has started taking a different route to work so he doesn't pass the pub where Isabelle works: the last time they'd met her message had been clear, even for a deaf bugger like him. As they'd stood there in the gloom of the pub, with the smell of beer all around them, Émile had understood something. Isabelle could leave Larch but she doesn't; she won't. In some warped way, she must feel she deserves him and it doesn't matter how many of her husband's limbs Émile breaks, that will never change.

And so he reads now to forget, to escape, as he used to with drink, and it is on one such afternoon around five that he takes off his boots and settles into Isabelle's old place by the dresser. The day has been warm and a soft haze gilds the potato plants; the garden seems to shimmer. Émile is ten minutes in and engrossed, and so he doesn't see or sense her until she is there, standing in the kitchen doorway. She gives him such a fright – it is as if she's stepped right out of his imagination, but the smile she gives him is as real as the keys she places on the table. She is wearing a yellow dress, belted at the waist, which he doesn't remember seeing before. It suits her, falling in soft folds that ripple and sway as she moves.

She points to the book and the chair and then herself. Is it his imagination or does she wink?

'You're not coming back, then?' Émile nods at the keys.

Isabelle doesn't answer. She stands by the table, her hands twisting.

'I hit him back, you know,' she says. 'When he attacked me.' She writes it in his notebook, when he doesn't catch it. 'It was a long time coming.'

Émile is glad and he isn't. He looks at her, the nubs of her wrists, the delicate curve of her collarbone. She looks like someone who would be easily broken, but reminds himself that three decades of marriage attest otherwise.

'Be careful,' he says. 'Please.'

'You haven't made my life smaller.' She shakes her head. 'I was wrong. I think I understand why you hit him and I'm grateful.'

'I shouldn't have done it,' he says. 'I wasn't thinking straight. Or maybe I was thinking too much.'

Isabelle reddens and points outside. 'You've done such a wonderful job.'

Not as pretty as it was, when he first came, Émile says. He gets up and joins her at the window. The urn looks strange set there among the rows of runner beans; he keeps the wheelbarrow in the dried-up hollow where the pond used to be. When he spent that first summer, digging up the garden, wrenching up the lavender bush and clumps of hydrangeas, she could barely look at it, or him. She would avert her eyes from whatever he was doing, as if she wanted no part of it.

'I felt like one of the enemy,' he says, teasingly. 'When I was just following orders.'

'My orders!' Her face creases into a smile.

They turn away from the garden and look at each other, for longer than is normal or usual, longer even than that time on Christmas Day when she was drunk on brandy. But today, her eyes are perfectly clear, and the colour that used to remind him of horse chestnuts, polished to a sheen.

Émile isn't sure who kisses who first. One of them starts to speak; the other swallows the words. It is a long kiss and there is a roaring in his ears, as if someone has turned down the silence. He draws her to him and it feels like both surrender and possession, to have her arms circling his neck, with no space for a pin to drop between their two bodies. And it is she who tugs at the curtain to shut out the daylight, who draws the bolt across the top of the door, who then stops, frozen, and blushes to the roots of her hair and asks him if he wants to.

He wants to, he says and laughs and she does too, and they make a nest of cushions on the rug and lie on their sides, opposite each other, his fingers touching her hair, which is coarser than he remembers with more kinks and waves. He runs his hand over the length of her body, over and back again, in long sweeping motions and her dress rises up and her skin is cool and pale and tastes of salt. When he touches her in the damp, private centre of herself, she trembles, and he wants badly to hear her, to know if she likes what he's doing, but now she is pulling his overalls down and he hopes he doesn't smell too much of his day in the garden. She is lifting her hips and guiding him into her – and although the act itself is far from new for either of them, Émile still feels the skittish excitement of the first time and he worries about it coming to an end too soon.

They roll over and he sees the pleasure in her face as she moves against him and it is as if all the moments he once hoped for have merged into one: a coupling on the sand in the dunes at Port Soif, lit by a harvest moon; a wedding night on Vancouver Island in a boarding house by the ocean and all the times after that and in between. When he comes, there is a gust of static in his ears and it wouldn't have surprised him if he'd bellowed outright like a bull.

Isabelle sits up, re-arranges her clothes, fetches them both glasses of water. She covers her face with her hands, and there is a moment of fear, when he thinks she is regretting it already, but then she takes them away and he sees that she is smiling.

'I can't believe it,' she is saying. 'After all this time.'

'You like to make a man wait.'

Isabelle laughs, perches on the arm of the easy chair, and sips her water. She asks for his notebook and they talk for a while, about the slave workers from Poland and Russia that are arriving, more and more each day, and the sad shoeless state of them, ragged and filthy, trudging in a long, faltering line up the Val de Terres from the harbour. They talk about Roy Le Prevost who was done for stealing a bike outside the Town Church, and how he was sentenced to a month's hard labour, laying cement for the bunkers with the Poles and the Russians, though at least he could go home to his bed at the end of the day, which was more than could be said for the other poor fellows.

Then he tells her about Maud, not just that she's gone, but the reason for it, and there is such relief in unburdening himself of the secret that he wishes he had come clean sooner.

'You're her father in all the ways that count,' Isabelle says. 'Not many people would take on someone else's child.'

She looks sad for a moment and he takes her hand, presses his mouth to her wrist. She stirs then glances at the clock – it is almost six.

'What will you tell him?' Émile asks.

Held up in Town. I'll blame it on the Germans! she writes. *You?*

He doesn't reply. Letty already knows. It was there in the eye that Larch had blackened, in the cuts and bruises on his body after the fight.

'Will you come back?' He knows he must be prepared for her to say no, or she isn't sure, or she wants to but can't.

But Isabelle takes the keys from the table and slips them in her handbag, and Émile's heart surges. It is all the answer he needs.

20

'I'll be home just after six,' Isabelle tells her husband as she buttons up her raincoat and locates her coupons in the kitchen drawer. Outside, yellow leaves swirl in a gust of wind. The trees have begun to look skeletal; the islands are approaching the dead season. 'I told Mother I'd stay for tea.'

'You're seeing a lot of her recently.'

'She's finding it difficult up there on her own. She gets lonely.'

A pause. Ron's newspaper rustles. 'I should pay her a visit myself some time,' he says. 'See if she needs any jobs doing around the place.'

Isabelle brushes some fluff from her coat. It is without doubt a warning, but her husband doesn't scare her quite like he used to. His arm has healed, but he has lost some of his swagger. He is careful with himself, his movements, slower.

'She'd like that,' she says lightly. 'Well, cheerio, then.'

'Cheerio.'

Is it her imagination or is he mocking her? Isabelle feels his eyes on her back as she leaves, not wholly able to relax until she is out of sight of the house.

It is a crisp, cold day. The sun is low and the sky a watery, wistful blue. In less than four hours, after the shopping is done and she's finished her shift at the pub, she will be with Émile. It will be the tenth time now since that day in the back end of summer, when Isabelle had found herself wanting him in a way she'd never thought possible, behaving like someone she barely recognised. And Émile is so different to Ron in that way, not to mention every other. He touches her for her own pleasure, not just his own, and each time they make love is better than the last. When she has to leave, it as if she is sinking a little deeper into wet sand, making it harder and harder to prise herself free.

She tells herself it's the honeymoon they never had, albeit with all sightseeing restricted to the French House itself. Émile had never seen any of the rooms, apart from the office, and now she has shown him each one, told him the stories that used to amuse visitors. She has shown him the large sash window in Hugo's bedroom, where he used to stand and perform his ablutions at the same time every morning so that his mistress could sit at her drawing-room window in the house across the road and watch. They have sat in the glass room at the top of the house, holding hands and watching German planes streak across the sky towards France. The salon rouge gives him a headache, he says, with all that grand furniture and so much to look at that your eyes never get a rest. His favourite room, he told her with a mischievous glint, was the kitchen down below; and he was surprised she couldn't guess that really and might he suggest – his arm around her waist now – that they drop in there again, before it was time to go.

Isabelle turns into Smith Street. There seem to be more Germans around than usual and she is just wondering whether this is her imagination or not when she notices Schreiber a little way ahead. His cap is lopsided and he looks in a tearing hurry. As she gets closer she thinks that he seems distracted, harassed as if he is trying to get away from someone or something and she is reminded of what he said about ripped trousers and school yard bullies.

The trickle of people down the High Street all seem to be going one way. Keeping Peter in sight, Isabelle ups her own pace. She sees the two women from the haberdasher's counter in Creasey's come out of the shop, pulling on their coats, and heading towards Town Church Square. A butcher, still in his bloodied apron, does the same and the barter shop on the corner of the Pollet has also emptied, the door swinging on its hinges.

Outside the church, a small crowd is gathering. The square holds the chilly hush of a crypt. Someone is sobbing quietly. Peter has stopped hurrying and Isabelle sees him inching slowly through the group of locals. Her instincts tell her that she should walk on, go to the market while there are no queues, but she cannot. She is drawn towards whatever has just caused someone to cry out in horror, towards this thing that has made the women from Creasey's bury their heads in each other's shoulders.

The crowd thins as she inches her way to the front. The men have taken their caps off and the women cluster together for comfort. Blood has stained the cobbles a rusty brown around the place where the man lies. At first, she doesn't recognise him, because she cannot bear to look for longer than a second or two. He is – was – young and probably handsome before his nose was smashed, the side of his face pummelled into a raw, bleeding mess. A dark flower of blood blooms across his singlet from the bullet wound in his chest. His eyes are wide open and staring. This is someone's son, Isabelle thinks, murdered and dumped, and she wants to scream. To halt the impulse, she turns to the man next to her and asks who it is.

'It's the young Ozanne lad who goes out on the boats,' he tells her, shaking his head. 'All he did was try to make a bit extra on the side. He ain't the first to do that.'

Isabelle looks back at the body and recalls Peter's sketches. There is a tideline at the base of Ozzy's neck where the sun had left its mark. A murmur rises through the crowd as a truck pulls up outside the church and two soldiers and an officer get out. The sound of jackboots echoes across the square as the soldiers march with purpose towards the body. The commanding officer barks out an order and as she looks more closely, Isabelle sees that it is Kassenmeier, the man who raided Peter's room. She scours the crowd for Peter but sees no sign, then spots him a few feet away, standing apart in the shadow of the church door, the horror on his face reflecting that in the square around him.

The Germans hoik Ozzy under the arms and drag him through the crowd. The man beside Isabelle calls out 'Shame!', a cry that is taken up across the square. Kassenmeier strides to the spot where Ozzy's body had been dumped and turns to address them.

'The shame was all his.'

He spits out the words then follows the soldiers to the truck, where the body is deposited under the tarpaulin. The smell of diesel fills the air as the engine starts up and the Germans drive away.

Isabelle finds herself unable to move. Around her, there are calls to fetch soap and water; they will scrub the cobbles until their hands are raw, a woman from the barter shop says through her tears. Filthy German scum, says another, everyone knows they use the Black Market as much as the next person.

'One can't help wondering if there was a little more to it,' an elderly man says thoughtfully, and Isabelle looks back towards the church, to where Peter had been standing. She is the only person who can begin to know how he must be feeling and why. Gripped with worry about what Kassenmeier might do next, she walks towards the church and an impulse draws her inside.

Peter is there, as she thought he might be, a hunched figure, tucked away in a corner pew. He looks up, agitated, at the sound of her footsteps.

'Mrs Larch,' he murmurs, and in the gloom, his face is white, corpse-like. Isabelle sits next to him and after a moment takes his hand. His fingers are freezing cold.

'He should never have listened to me,' he says.

'What do you mean?'

'I always used to say that we weren't hurting anyone.' Peter sniffs. 'Tell that to his mother, his brothers. Christ, his brothers.' He sinks his head in his hands.

'This is not your fault.'

'I should have stuck to clifftop views and Guernsey cows.' His foot judders on the flagstones. 'I signed his death warrant with those bloody drawings.'

Isabelle fixes her gaze on the altar. 'Drawings?' she says.

'Kassenmeier's been on my trail from the first day he met me,' he says. 'Waiting for me to trip up. He raided my office yesterday evening, found some sketches I'd done.' He pauses. 'They were private, not meant for anyone but me. He called me a degenerate, a disgrace to the Third Reich.'

'So he knows . . .?' Isabelle trails off.

'He has made assumptions. Of course, he has no real evidence. But that didn't help Ozzy.'

'The man's an animal.'

'They're sending me to Russia,' Peter says slowly. 'To the Front.'

'Russia!' Isabelle scrabbles around in her mind for the little she's gleaned from the World Service. The advance of Hitler's troops on the Soviets. The raids on Leningrad and the siege of the city, as the bitter winter begins. The hundreds of thousands of casualties on both sides. 'When?'

'Saturday. I'm to report at the White Rock at nine.'

She gasps. 'But that's only three days away!'

'No time to waste, when there's a war to be lost,' he says with a grimace. 'The truth is I'm a coward, Mrs Larch. Ozzy was the brave one. He was always reminding me that he was the one who'd be strung up by the balls, as he put it, if anyone found out – but he was fearless. Me? Scared of fighting, scared of pain. I'm scared of getting frostbite and losing all my toes.' He bends over, covers his face with his hands. 'I'd rather they just finished me off quickly with a bullet.'

'Peter . . .' Isabelle puts her arm around him and strokes his back. She thinks of his mother, the pleasant-looking woman in the photograph in his room. She will imagine her son is quite safe in the Channel Islands; she will expect him back when this wretched war is over. She pictures the pistol in her sewing bag and has a terrible premonition that one evening, she will take out her darning and find the gun gone, and the next morning, someone walking on the cliffs out in Jerbourg will step on the broken glass of Peter's abandoned spectacles, while their dog, scenting blood, burrows in the undergrowth for his body.

'Let me help you.' Isabelle's voice is so faint she can barely hear herself.

Peter looks up, his eyes puffy and red. 'Help me?'

'Escape,' she says. 'Don't tell me it hasn't crossed your mind.' She pauses. 'Didn't you say that your uncle taught you to sail?'

Peter sits up a little straighter. 'I'd have to row,' he says slowly. 'Most of the way, anyway. And all the boats have been requisitioned. They're locked up.'

'And I bet the boathouses down at Petit Bot are rotten and old and easily broken into, if one had a hammer.'

'I don't have a hammer.' He stares at her. 'Or a compass. Or maps or civilian clothes . . .'

'But you do have friends, don't you, in London, in England? People who could help you once you'd arrived?'

'If I arrived.' He chews on his thumbnail. 'I can't put you in danger. It isn't fair. I'd never forgive myself if—'

A flare of sunlight illuminates the stained glass in the apse, Jesus dying quietly in a mosaic of colours on his cross. Everywhere she looks, there is pain and violence, Isabelle thinks, people inflicting indescribable cruelty on each other. This man, shivering next to her, is the same age her son would have been had he survived, had she not sent him away to be raised by people who were paid – rather poorly – for the inconvenience of doing so.

'And I would never forgive myself if something happened to you, and I stood by and did nothing,' Isabelle says firmly. She shifts on the hard bench. 'I'll talk to Émile. We can get you what you need. No one has to know.'

'Are you sure?' He stares at her as the church clock starts to chime in feeble, rusty strokes.

'I'm sure,' Isabelle says. 'I'll go straight home when I've finished at the pub, get a few things together, check the tides.'

She picks up her shopping basket and tells him she'll see him later.

Outside, the square is deserted. There is a dark, damp patch where Ozzy's body had been in the centre of the cobbles. A pair of grubby pigeons peck insistently at whatever is left behind and Isabelle feels sick to her stomach at the sight. She shouts at the creatures to get away, striking out at them with her umbrella, like a mad woman, she thinks afterwards, like someone who has completely lost their mind.

21

'I'm not sure, Belle.'

Émile tears out the most recent page of his notebook and takes a match to it, not moving from the kitchen grate until every last word of Isabelle's handwriting has been reduced to ash. When he gets up, she is looking at him as if he's burnt her faith in him along with it. He tells her that what she's proposing has to stay in their heads and nowhere else – no lists, no nothing, otherwise they might as well go straight up to Grange Lodge and ask the Jerries if they had a small sailing boat they wouldn't mind lending out for a night-time excursion across the Channel. And look at what the bastards did to Ozzy. If that wasn't a warning, he didn't know what was.

'It's dangerous,' he says. 'For us and the lad.'

'He's an experienced sailor,' Isabelle says.

She goes on to tell Émile the same as she had the day before. That all they need to do is leave him a saw and a hammer in the shed on Thursday evening; she will bring a compass and some old clothes of Ron's that he won't miss. She has checked the tides and the conditions are perfect for an evening sailing, and if the easterly wind keeps up then so much the better because it will bring the mist in and he will have less chance of being seen.

Émile points out that if the easterly wind keeps up at the rate it's going, the man will be lucky to make it past Jethou

– he almost got knocked off his bike coming down the coast road this morning.

Isabelle says nothing. She goes to the sink, pours herself a glass of water.

'It's a death sentence,' she says. 'Sending him to Russia.' She makes the outline of a wireless, cups her hand to her ear. 'I listen to the news, Émile – I know!'

Well, isn't she lucky, Émile says and they glare at each other from opposite sides of the kitchen table, upon which only a few days ago they had made love. He'd forgotten just how single minded Isabelle could be, and how he had loved that about her.

'He's being punished for being different,' Isabelle says. She takes his notebook and writes it down. 'It's not fair.'

Émile sighs, paces to the window. It is just after five and black as your hat outside. Not long after the Germans arrived, a group of men from St Sampsons had done what Schreiber was planning and reached the mainland by all accounts, but there had been four of them, and they were from fishing families, going back generations, practically born at sea. Émile wouldn't be surprised if Schreiber's idea of sailing was puttering around a lake in Northern Germany for a few hours on his summer holidays. But he had to hand it to the man for wanting to try, and he can't forget how Schreiber helped him when Maud was in prison, when he needed it most.

Émile puts his arms around Isabelle, strokes the downy nape of her neck.

'Don't have much use for the saw anyway,' he says and her body loosens into his with relief. It touches him how much she wants to help the man. Then he thinks of the boy

242

in the photograph, tucked inside the Bible, and suddenly understands.

The following morning, on the way to the French House, Émile goes to the Caves where Isabelle is cleaning. She hands him a large moth-eaten overcoat, the collar spotted with dandruff, and a grey sweater that has seen better days.

'Put them on. Over your clothes. It'll look suspicious otherwise.'

Émile does as she says, although it occurs to him that he looks as suspicious wearing three layers of clothes as he would carrying them, and now he smells like a Sally Army jumble sale to boot.

'There's a map in the inside coat pocket and a compass front left,' she tells him. Her face is pale and he can tell she hasn't slept well. 'He'll need water too – can you see to it?'

Émile nods. He'll fill up some old containers he uses for watering the tomatoes, he says. He takes her hand briefly, tells her not to worry. Yesterday, he had taken Schreiber's portrait of Maud and burnt it, burying the ash deep in the ground – he wasn't going to take any chances.

'He's coming at six,' Isabelle says, holding up her fingers. 'Make sure you're gone by then.'

He'll be out by half-four today, he says, and Corbeille's not due in until Friday.

'Good,' she says, and he makes a move to kiss her, but she steps away, glancing anxiously at the pub door. 'Not here.'

Outside, the wind is getting up. The sky is gunmetal grey, casting the entire street in shadow. An image flits through Émile's mind of a fellow they'd found washed up on the rocks when he was a boy, out on his uncle's boat fishing for conger. The drowned man's legs were white and swollen, as bloated as blancmange, his eyes bulbous and blue-veined like marbles.

Émile walks up the road towards Hauteville, hands sunk deep into the mildewed pockets of Ronald Larch's old overcoat. His hand makes contact with the compass, which sits cool and smooth as a pebble in his fingers. He hadn't had the heart to tell Isabelle that with the storm that was forecast, Schreiber might have been better packing his kitbag for the frontline. It will be nothing short of a miracle, Émile thinks, as he approaches the French House, if the German makes it across the Channel. Hail stones in Hell would stand a better chance.

When Émile arrives at work the following morning, he is drenched to the bone and later than he should be for his Friday meeting with Monsieur Corbeille. His employer is sitting at the kitchen table, studying the contents of the beige folder he always brings with him. He smiles in a friendly manner as Émile comes in and passes him a hand towel.

'Foul weather.' Corbeille grimaces and Émile looks out at the muddy garden as he dries his hair, and thinks that at least the German's footprints will have been washed away. He had slept badly and imagines for every hour's sleep he'd had, Isabelle must have got half. All night he could feel the force of the storm, even if he wasn't able to hear it, and when he'd left the house that morning, the old elm tree from across the way had fallen, blocking the lane, the tough roots exposed like innards. It had felt like a bad omen, and thinking about Schreiber had distressed him more than he cared to admit. He keeps imagining his gold-rimmed specs entwined with seaweed on the seabed, the tattered great-coat fluttering from the uneven rocks.

Émile tries to turn his mind to potatoes and compost as the two of them get down to business. Corbeille has applied for a permit to gather *vraic* from the beach at L'Erée. The Germans have requested more of everything for the coming spring – carrots, onions, potatoes – especially potatoes. There is a blocked gutter around the side of the house, which needs seeing to. Corbeille transcribes all of this information in his neat, looped handwriting, with a little dot before each point, and when they have finished, he shakes Émile's hand as he always does, and asks him if he needs any help bringing the potatoes up from the shed.

No, Émile says. This, too, is one of their rituals – Corbeille doesn't really have the footwear for a muddy garden, but he always asks and Émile, in turn, refuses.

'Good man,' Corbeille slaps his shoulder and tells him he'll be upstairs in the office if he's wanted.

Émile puts on his boots and walks down the garden to the enclosure, unlocks the gate. A robin, perched on the roof of the shed, cocks its head at him then takes flight suddenly as if it has heard something Émile cannot. He takes out the key and unlocks the shed door.

He knows Schreiber is there, even before his eyes become accustomed to the gloom and he can make out the hump of a body, folded underneath the bench and covered with a grey blanket. It isn't just the man's sweat he can smell, it is his terror – the trip-wire tension of breath sucked in and held, the denial of life itself. Émile takes a step towards him. His first thought is relief that Schreiber is still alive, swiftly eclipsed by panic at the danger he's putting them both in.

'Get up!' he says, prodding the blanket and slowly Schreiber eases himself out, his face contorting as he stumbles to his feet. There are patches of straw-coloured stubble speckling his chin and his slight frame is drowned in Larch's overcoat. As the man fumbles for his spectacles, Émile sees that he is trembling. He gestures for Émile's notebook.

Just two nights, he writes, *until the storm has passed. I'll leave on Sunday evening.*

He draws his hands together. 'Please.'

'Does Isabelle know you're here?'

'No.' Schreiber shakes his head vigorously. 'No one knows.'

Well, now I know, don't I? Émile thinks angrily, his nerves so tangled he can hardly get things straight. There's Corbeille just a stone's throw away, not to mention the Germans who'll be coming to collect the potatoes later. The saw, the hammer, the jerrycan of water he filled before he left yesterday all lined up like pieces of evidence in the corner of the shed.

Schreiber follows his gaze and touches his chest, saying how sorry he is, that he had nowhere else to go. The man must be either very stupid or very brave, Émile thinks as he looks at him, although not brave enough to go to Russia, and God knows it would have saved a whole load of trouble for the three of them if he'd just followed orders. But in part, Émile understands that this is Schreiber's last chance to make the life he wants, not the one he's been told to live. And Émile should know, because isn't that exactly what he tried to do himself when he took the steamer to Canada all those years ago? He can't throw him to the wolves – he won't have a man's life on his conscience. Besides, he'd never be able to look Isabelle in the eye again.

Émile takes the notebook.

SUNDAY EVENING. NO LATER. DO NOT LEAVE SHED!

Schreiber's hand moves to his chest again and Émile nods sharply, as he picks up the sacks of potatoes, taking care to lock the shed door firmly after him.

'"Local man found dead in Town Church Square."'

Maud glances at Le Lacheur. He is poorly again and in bed. He pulls up the blankets around him, and tells her to read on.

'"A man found dead in Town Church Square on Tuesday morning has been identified as Mr Paul Ozanne of La Chaumière, L'Ancresse. A local fisherman, Mr Ozanne, aged twenty-five, was said to have been known to the authorities for some time as a profiteer. The death is not being treated as suspicious."'

Maud puts down the *Press*. Her head is hot and she has the same sick feeling that she did when she went into the office to fetch some papers on Tuesday morning and found Miss Guille weeping and drinking Le Lacheur's brandy at her desk. A bullet to the chest, Miss Guille had told her, and went on to say how the Germans had dragged his body through the square and dumped it in the truck as if he were a piece of rubbish.

'No one deserves that,' she had sobbed, and Maud had found herself in the unusual position of comforting her.

'Got cocky, I imagine, rubbed their noses in it.' Le Lacheur takes a sip of water. 'So-called newspaper. That Schreiber character must think we're all idiots.'

Maud folds up the paper. 'He's still missing,' she says.

She had been unprepared for the shock of seeing the censor's face on the Missing poster taped to a lamp post by the old bus terminus, earlier that day. It was definitely him, stiff in his uniform, a slight reflection from the camera flash on his glasses, a hesitant smile turning on his lips. She discovered that he was exactly ten years older than her, that at the time of his disappearance, he was thought to have been wearing an overcoat and lace-up shoes, and that his eye colour was blue.

Missing meant deserted and deserted meant execution if they caught you, and starvation if they didn't. She remembered the day she had gone to his office with the programme for the revue, his quiet interest in her music. In different circumstances, she imagined they might have been friends.

'And all he had to do all day was print lies in the *Press*!' Le Lacheur says, shaking his head. 'No backbone, some of them.'

'Maybe he didn't like printing lies.'

'That, my dear, is a rather naive notion.'

Maud wanders over to the dying fire and prods it with the poker. Something has been nagging at her ever since she saw the poster. 'He might have got into trouble. After I was released from prison.'

'Mmm?'

'He should have been at the concert. Or at least sent someone in his place.' She returns to her chair by the bed and hesitates. 'When you spoke to the Kommandant, did he mention him at all?'

'What?'

'I know you don't want any thanks and you'd rather I didn't talk about it but . . .'

Le Lacheur struggles up onto his pillows. 'You don't need to thank me, Maud, because I didn't do anything.' His tone is irritated.

'But – but Stella said you'd do what you could.'

He tuts, regards her sternly. 'It may have escaped your attention but I am an old man. I can't go running up to Grange Lodge, doing deals with the Germans every five minutes. And you should never have sent your sister to ask. Oh, don't look at me like that.' He wrestles impatiently with the blankets. 'Long and short of it is that they let you go.'

'You let me believe it was you,' Maud says slowly.

'I did nothing of the sort.' He jabs a wrinkled finger at her. 'Your trouble, my girl, is that you're fanciful. I've come to learn that about you.'

Maud stares at him. The other morning, after Miss Guille had stopped crying, the woman had patted Maud's hand and told her she was a nice girl, and she was sorry she'd misjudged her. It was none of her business, she said, but it was a shame Maud had fallen out with her family and was living elsewhere – she was sure her mother hadn't had an easy time of it over the years.

'You know my mother?' Maud had asked, surprised, and Miss Guille had flushed and said not really, she'd just come across her a couple of times.

'Here? At the office?' Maud said, at which Miss Guille became even more flustered.

'Once or twice,' she had said, adding that she assumed that her mother's acquaintance with Mr Le Lacheur was how Maud came by her position.

Outside the wind gains momentum, shrieking down the chimney.

'Has my mother ever come to your office?'

Le Lacheur frowns. 'Why would she do that?'

'Miss Guille mentioned she'd seen her.'

'Oh!' He stares into the fire. 'She might have come in to clean a few times, I suppose. I can barely remember.'

How convenient. Maud has a sudden and strong impulse to be back in the cottage at L'Islet in the crowded kitchen, listening to the wireless with Ma and Stella, as Pa turns the pages of the *Press* at the table.

'Why don't you just admit it?' Her voice is low, spiked with resentment.

'Admit what for heaven's sake?'

Maud marches downstairs and into the study, fetches the photograph in which they look so alike. When she returns to the bedroom, Le Lacheur is pink in the face and fidgeting.

'Look!' Maud thrusts the photo towards him. 'Look at you and look at me and tell me honestly that you're not my father.'

Le Lacheur's mouth twists. He splutters and coughs and asks for more water but Maud ignores him.

'You'll tell me,' she says, 'or I'll leave. Right away. Don't think that I won't.'

'Maud . . .' He closes his eyes. 'It's possible. It's certainly possible.' He holds up a hand to silence her. 'I haven't told you out of respect for your mother's wishes.'

'She was your housemaid.' Maud looks at him, at the pouches under his eyes, the lines and furrows of old age. 'And you had a wife.'

'I'm not a saint, Maud, and no more was your ma.' He lets out a small sigh. 'Your mother could be very persuasive when she wanted to be.'

For a moment, Maud imagines pressing the pillow down hard on his face. All he ever did was persuade people – a squeezed palm, a tot of brandy, a threat here, a bribe there. Ma had left school at fourteen and struggled to read; they were hardly equals. She remembers her mother's tear-stained face when she'd told Maud that Le Lacheur was not a good man, and feels a deep surge of guilt.

Le Lacheur takes her wrist. 'Maud, I've done what I can, given the circumstances. I've found you work, put a roof over your head.'

'I already had work. And a roof over my head,' she murmurs.

His eyes shine in the firelight and outside the wind drops like a stone. The room is suddenly quiet.

'But it wasn't enough for you, my dear, was it?' he says.

Leeks and carrots and big chunks of potato. Beef, the best bits, with the gristle cut off. Isabelle chops and she stirs and the lies whistle through her teeth as Ron sits at the kitchen table and scrutinises her.

'Still cooking for three?' He wanders over to the stove and peers into the saucepan. 'Did we get double rations this week, or something?'

'Mother's in bed with the flu,' Isabelle says. 'Dottie Le Lievre told me at church this morning. Thought I'd take her some soup for lunch.'

'Can't stay away from your mother these days, can you?' Ron gives the string of her apron a little tug. 'I remember the times when you couldn't stand the sight of each other.'

Isabelle stops stirring and turns to him. 'She's old, Ron. She needs looking after.'

He shrugs, resumes his place at the table. 'At least the wind's dropped. Not that a bit of bad weather would stop you, I'm sure.'

The mixture starts to bubble. She doesn't like his tone.

'I'll be back as soon as I can,' Isabelle says, and for once, she means it.

Isabelle bundles herself up in her scarf and raincoat and places the beef casserole in the basket of her bicycle. As she sets off, she sees the shadowy figure of her husband behind the net curtains at the front window, and she waves for appearance's sake, still limp with relief that he didn't suggest accompanying her. She had prepared a host of excuses – that her mother was infectious, that she hated people seeing her indisposed – but when it came to it, Isabelle hadn't had to use them. Ron had been in an exasperatingly chirpy mood all weekend, even when the Germans had turned up first thing on Friday morning to search the house when Schreiber had failed to report for duty.

'Belly as yellow as a dandelion, that one,' Ron had said with satisfaction after they'd gone. 'He'll be shitting himself now, wherever he is.'

And in a perverse way, Isabelle had hoped he was right, because that would mean Peter had survived. The weather on Thursday night had been atrocious and she hadn't been able to sleep for the shriek of the wind, and the thought of him being tossed around in that tiny rowing boat had made her feel as nauseous as if she were there with him. And then, just as she was finishing her shift at the Caves, the next day, Émile had appeared, and she had known from the look on his face what had happened even before he told her. He had urged her to keep away from the French House – he would do the same, he said – but Isabelle couldn't bear to think of Peter alone in the shed all weekend with barely enough food.

She sets off. She sees one German, and then another. Good God, it's a Sunday and the weather is miserable;

haven't they got better things to be doing than strutting around the place, looking for trouble? Then it occurs to her that they might be out searching for Peter, and she stares at the casserole as if it's an unexploded mine shell, and pedals twice as fast. She leaves her bike in a side street some distance from the house and walks through the back streets gripping the handle of the basket, her hands clammy in her gloves. Hauteville House looms ahead of her; the street is swept free of people. Isabelle breathes, takes the keys from her pocket. In less than a minute, she'll be inside. She is fine.

'Mrs Larch!'

She turns, startled, steps in a puddle and feels icy water seep through the cracked sole of her shoe, as she looks into the bloodshot eyes of the landlord from the Caves. He is holding a rolled-up copy of the *Press*, which he taps on the side of her basket.

'You're too kind,' he says, with a wink. 'Wouldn't say no if there's any going spare.'

'Me, neither.' Isabelle shrugs. 'But there's someone in the family way in Cornet Street with three little ones to feed who needs it more.'

'Always someone worse off than us, eh?' He sniffs. 'Though some might say breeding like a warren of rabbits, when there's a war on, is just plain selfish.'

'They might.' Isabelle stares at him. The phrase 'in cold blood' flits through her mind. If I had the gun, she thinks, I would make you move.

He gives her an odd look, then claps his hands together. 'Anyway, I won't keep you. See you back at the coal face. Regards to Ron.'

And he walks on down the road.

Bloody man. As if it's not bad enough cleaning his stinking pub. Isabelle waits until he is out of sight, then continues to the French House and lets herself into the side entrance. It is strange to be here without Émile, to pass by the kitchen where he is usually framed in the window, waiting. She will come tomorrow when it's all over, she tells herself, and surprise him. She will bring the half-bottle of sherry she keeps at the back of the cupboard for Christmas and they will raise a toast to Peter Schreiber and to each other. She goes into the enclosure and taps lightly on the shed door.

'It's me.' Her voice is a hoarse whisper.

When she goes inside, Peter is sitting upright on the bench, wrapped in a blanket, his breath visible in sketchy wisps of cloud. His kitbag is at his feet and he is pale and drawn with anxiety. He has the air of a thing that is hunted, ready at any moment to bolt.

'Mrs Larch. You shouldn't be here.' His gaze lingers on her basket, and his body seems to droop in surrender as Isabelle sits down next to him and begins to unpack.

'You need to get your strength up.' She takes the lid from the casserole and hands him a spoon. 'It might be a little cool but it's edible at least.'

He hesitates, then takes the spoon, eating slowly to begin with, then with more vigour as hunger overcomes him.

'They're looking for you,' she says. 'You must be careful. Don't leave until dark. High tide's at eight – you'll still have plenty of time.' She glances at the kitbag. 'Do you have enough water? Did Émile give you the tools?'

Peter wipes his mouth. 'You mustn't worry about me,' he says.

'But what about when you arrive? You don't have any papers. They might think you're a spy.'

The plan that had taken form with such fluidity a few days ago now seems to have more holes than a paper doily. She is encouraging him to cross mine-infested waters in a tiny sailing boat in the middle of winter, with little more than a torch and a compass. She must be out of her mind, she thinks.

'Mr William L. Hardy, a spy! Whatever next!' He shakes her hand as if meeting for the first time, all German inflection crushed from his accent. He is the man she found in her kitchen on that warm July evening, over a year ago, Oxford-educated, more English than she is.

'Covering the war for Reuters, got into a spot of bother travelling back from Cairo,' he goes on. 'Identity card, everything, lost at sea.' He smiles, leans back against the wall. 'Cut me open and I bleed red, white and blue.'

Isabelle shakes her head. 'They may not believe you.'

'I've been acting most of my life, Mrs Larch,' he says, serious again. 'It has to be worth a try.' He stands up and takes her hand. 'Will you promise me something?'

She has run out of promises; she has run out of faith. She can make him a hot meal and go home, that is as far as she is able to go to keep him safe.

'If I can.' She moves away, begins to clear up all evidence of her visit.

'That you'll find a way to make yourself happy.'

Isabelle pauses. 'I want to,' she says. 'But I'm afraid it may be too late.'

'It's never too late.' Peter leans forward and kisses her softly on both cheeks. 'Please go. I don't want to put you in any more danger.'

Isabelle picks up her things. '*À la perchoîne.*'

'*À la perchoîne.*'

As she closes the door, she feels a deep sense of relief to be outside again, breathing in air that is fresh and sharp and cold. The smell in the shed had reminded her of a trapped animal – it had made her want to cry. For the first time in a while, she thinks of her father, yellow-skinned and old, the vials of morphia on the bedside table as he lay dying of an unnamed illness that had branched through every part of his body. And yet even in the weeks it had taken for him to go, she had never felt as close to death as she had just now in the shed. It was like warm breath down the back of her neck. She hurries through the garden and tells herself not to be morbid. The sky is thick with cloud, the night sea will be calm. She hears the rhythmic splash of the oars, sees Peter, his eyes knitted on the horizon. He will endure, just as she has, and Émile in his turn. What other choice is there?

That evening, Isabelle cannot settle. She drops stitch after stitch as she knits, has to undo a whole section of the gloves she is making from one of her old scarves. She craves a cigarette, thinks of Émile, paces imaginary lengths of the living room. She jumps as the log crackles in the fire and Ron puts down the paper.

'You're twitchy tonight, Izzy,' he observes. He nods at the ceiling, towards Schreiber's old room. 'Seems they still haven't found him.'

'No.'

'He won't have got far. They never do.'

'No.'

Later, he brings her acorn tea that is bitter enough to make her wince, but nonetheless, she is startled by this kindness. He usually only acts like the husband she'd imagined she might have when he has just behaved like the man he truly is. She drinks it all in small, delicate sips. She longs for sugar, longs for him to go to bed and leave her alone, longs also for Émile. But Ron sits and watches her with the rapt attention he might give a newsreel at the cinema and her eyelids feel as if two penny bits as heavy as church collection plates are weighing down upon them. She struggles against it. She feels unsafe, suddenly, as if she is slipping down a slope, gathering speed, but her shoes won't grip and there is nothing to hold on to – and she can't seem to find her knitting needles and they would be useless anyway. There is a rushing in her ears and she can hear his voice – 'Isabelle, Isabelle' – hissing like steam from the kettle, before she surrenders and lets herself fall.

22

Émile takes the front page of yesterday's *Press* from the ledge in the privy and wipes himself. He had woken feeling as he used to in the days before Isabelle, as if a dead weight was pressing against his chest, and it was only his churning guts that had given him the momentum he needed to haul himself up and run outside. He doesn't want to go to work; he doesn't want to open the shed door and find the lad still there, cowering and half-starved and full of excuses. Friday was torturous enough with Corbeille just a few feet away and only the bad weather to keep him out of the garden; usually he did a circuit around lunchtime to check up on things. Émile had never felt so relieved to get out of the place, but the thought of a German hiding in his shed was not one that was easy to shift, and Schreiber's spectre had shadowed him all weekend.

He buttons himself up and walks across the frosted grass to the kitchen. Letty and Stella are already up and having breakfast, separated by Maud's empty place. When he came across Maud that day at the end of summer, pedalling down the lane as if her life depended on it, his suitcase wedged in her basket, Émile had known that there was nothing he could say at that moment to stop her. And when Letty told him that Maud had been working for that low life Le Lacheur on the sly, what remained of Émile's anger was replaced by a deep sadness. Living in that man's house might make Maud feel as if she'd escaped at first, but she'd end up trapped, Émile was sure of it. As he said to Isabelle afterwards, he wished then that he'd listened a bit harder to what Maud wanted when she graduated from the Intermediate, rather than what his wife wanted for her. It was time for Maud to earn her keep, Letty had said, not get into debt doing more studying on the mainland that she didn't need to do anyway, not when Amherst Infants were desperate to have her teach music there.

'Perhaps it's time to tell Maud the truth?' Isabelle had said. 'You don't want to lose her, do you?'

And Émile had thought and thought about this. Because what he and Letty had feared the most had already happened. Maud had gone and the only version of the truth she had was Le Lacheur's and that man was as slippery as a conger. He resolves to talk to Letty about it that very evening, try to make her see sense.

Émile sits down and starts to spoon in mouthfuls of watery porridge. Stella, in the blue dressing gown the colour of her eyes, yawns into the crook of her elbow, a habit adopted in childhood, and smiles at him. Letty presses her hand to her breast to suppress a belch; she has a crease down her left cheek where she has slept on her side. It touches him, in a way he can't explain. She sees him staring and turns away angrily, and he sees it there in the set of her shoulders, the creases in her forehead, the daily reminder of the price she pays for his time with Isabelle. Letty is hurting, but the longer it goes on, the harder it is for him to stop.

Outside, the sun is pale as a pearl, sunk deep in cloud. Émile gets on his bike and starts to cycle. If Schreiber is still there, he will turn him out, send him up the ladder and over the enclosure wall. It is harsh, but he can't have him taking advantage. There's many that would have grassed him up the first time they caught a whiff of him using the shed. He nods to the newspaper boy who he overtakes every day at the same spot at the bottom of the Charrotterie, swerves past the pothole that did in his last tyre. Everything the same as it ever was, Émile assures himself, and he tries to focus on the tasks of the day, more hoeing, more bagging of potatoes. But the closer he gets, the worse his nerves, until the only thing stopping him from turning back is the knowledge that it would look even more suspicious.

Émile turns into Hauteville and freewheels to the kink in the road, beyond which the French House is visible. As he turns the corner, he blinks several times in the hope that what he is seeing is a falsehood, a trick of the mind or the light, but each time he looks, he sees the same: the beetle black carapace of a Nazi vehicle straddling the street, a flock of soldiers with rifles gathered on the pavement. He brakes and skids. An officer in a pale grey overcoat and peaked hat is walking towards him with intent. Émile suppresses the urge to run, and his hands shake as he reaches for his identity card. The officer glances at his photo and gives a peremptory nod and for a moment, Émile thinks he is safe, but the nod is not meant for him and he finds himself seized by the arms and marched towards the car. He curses Schreiber for not having the balls to escape when he had the chance, curses himself for ever getting mixed up in this mess, when the door to the side entrance opens and two soldiers emerge, one of them holding a grey Army-issue blanket.

The officer in charge strides over and examines the blanket closely. It is all the evidence they have, Émile begins to realise, as a hand on his head pushes him into the car and he is wedged between two of the soldiers. There is still no sign of Schreiber, so he must have got away after all, unless they came for him last night. The car judders as the engine starts up. The officer takes the front seat and says something to the driver, and they pull away from the kerb.

A small group of onlookers has gathered, a blur of faces peering into the car. Poor bugger. No smoke without fire. Émile can almost hear the rumble of speculation. Insulting a German, assaulting a German, petty theft, non-petty theft, Black Market, remember poor Ozzy – who wouldn't be tempted when their bellies rattle hollow as half-empty piggy banks. But who gets taken away in a car stuffed full of Germans just for selling a bit of something extra on the side? Then, he sees a man standing a little apart from the rest, arms folded, and his demeanour has none of the hushed shock of the others, but rather that of someone who has come to oversee, to inspect. Émile leans towards the window. Staring straight at him, wearing his revenge as smugly as a three-piece suit, is Ronald Larch, and Émile realises then that he, Émile, is the evidence, that he is more valuable to the Germans than any blanket. Larch is not here by mere coincidence; he knew what was going to happen when Émile arrived at work, because he arranged it. Somehow he must have found out about Schreiber and tipped the Germans off.

The air in the car is stifling – stale cigars and body odour and damp wool. Émile puts a hand over his mouth and retches. By the time they stop, it is too late and he feels the violence of the swear words that must accompany the shove they give him as they open the doors. As they stand, waiting for the car to air, he catches the driver's eye and sees himself reflected, a man, wiping flecks of vomit from his mouth, whose luck, what little he ever had, has run out, who by sunset will be willing to trade in the boots he walks in for a glass of water, who by the week's end would consider giving up his hearing all over again for the chance to see fifty, to survive the war.

He is taken not to the prison, but to the grey building at the bottom of St Julian's Avenue, which used to belong to the States and is now the headquarters of the Gestapo. Inside it is as dingy, as colourless as any office, and Émile finds himself treated with both supreme indifference and brisk vigilance as he is marched down a flight of steps to the bowels of the building, and left to wait in a small, dark room that smells of mould. There are two metal chairs and a table, and a rust-coloured stain on the wall and once he's seen it, he can't unsee it, and his heart cartwheels with fear. His body keeps time for him, the pincer movement of hunger never quite eclipsing his need for water, the roof of his mouth furry and sandpaper dry. He begins to think they will keep him here forever, drying him out until his body is a mere husk, and so when the officer returns with another man, he is almost glad, before he sees the coil of rubber hosing looped over the guard's arm and the way they look at him as if he is no more than another article of furniture.

The officer sits down and indicates that Émile should do the same. He lays a slim, sludge-coloured file on the table, and several sheaves of blank paper.

'You can read?'

So he thinks he's stupid, as well as deaf. Yes, Émile says, a touch grudgingly, he can read.

The man holds up the photo of Schreiber they'd used on

the Missing posters and starts to write. His handwriting is as regimented as if it had come from a machine, each letter the same height, the same weight.

DO YOU KNOW THIS MAN?

'No.'

Impatiently, he writes another question.

WHERE IS HE NOW?

'I don't know.'

DID YOU HELP HIM ESCAPE?

'No.'

The officer nods to his subordinate and Émile sees the hose twitch and rise. His ears start to sing and the air prickles like electricity, like a charge, as the hose is brought down hard upon his back. The force of it knocks the wind from him, felling him like a tree and he is on the ground now, panting, sweating, before he is dragged back up and made to sit. The German opens the folder and passes a sheet of paper to Émile. It is a drawing of a man digging up potatoes or some such, a wheelbarrow next to him, the outer walls of a large house just visible in the background. The officer watches him intently. Émile turns back to the sketch, and then slowly begins to see himself. It's the Guernsey he wears for working in, the one he's wearing now with the holes in the sleeve, details the artist has not cared to omit, no more than he has the five days' worth of stubble or his dirty hands.

'Mr Quenneville.' The officer picks up his pen with some distaste. 'Are you a homosexual?'

Married, Émile writes, *19 years!* He looks the officer in the eye, his nerves momentarily replaced with indignation. What the man is implying is ludicrous. 'I have two children,' he says.

'Ah yes.' The German consults the folder again. 'Your daughter Maud. She was held in prison not so long ago.'

Émile shakes his head and reaches for the pen. A misunderstanding, he writes.

'Your family doesn't have much luck.' The officer reaches for Schreiber's photograph again and holds it up. 'Have you ever spoken to this man?'

'I don't remember.'

'Let me remind you.'

The officer's writing this time is less pristine.

On 2 July, the first day of your daughter's incarceration, you went to the lodgings of Leutnant Schreiber at Sarnia Cottage, Cambridge Park, St Peter Port where you blackmailed the officer in question so as to secure the release of your daughter.

Émile hesitates, before pointing to Schreiber's photo. 'Someone told me he was the man to go to. Above board, like, no funny business.'

'Someone?' The officer takes out another photograph. 'Mrs Isabelle Larch, perhaps?'

It is her identity card photo. Émile remembers the day she went to have it taken. She'd put on lipstick, saying that she wanted the picture to be passable if she had to look at it every day, but they wouldn't get a smile out of her. And it seems to him now that it might have helped if her expression were a little more neutral; there is more than a hint of confrontation in her gaze.

'Mrs Larch was on good terms with her lodger, would you say? She liked him?'

'She don't like the Germans no more than any of us do.'

Émile tenses, waits for the twitch and sting of the hose. But the officer leans back, as if he might just as feasibly be in his own living room with a tumbler of brandy at his side.

'Mrs Larch gave you the job at Hauteville House, correct?'

'Well, her and Monsieur Corbeille.'

'How would you describe your relationship with Mrs Larch?'

Émile does his best to look confused. He tells him he doesn't understand.

'Are you friends? Do you share confidences?'

Émile stares at the wall. The rust stain is the exact shape of Vancouver Island – he had had plans to take Isabelle there on their honeymoon, all those years ago.

'I looked after the garden, she looked after the house,' he says. 'We hardly saw each other.'

The German waits for a moment, then gestures to the guard. As he is yanked to his feet, Émile doesn't know what to do. He has had the last word, but it is not as he intended, not at all – and the thought of Isabelle being put through the same, marched through the corridors and shoved into a small cell with no more than a filthy mattress and a bucket to piss in, torments him as he lies on what passes for a bed, imprinted with the fear of those who were there before.

23

Isabelle dreams. Isabelle nightmares. Isabelle searches for a way out of the fog that has invaded her, clogging her synapses, turning her doddery and foolish. She is a child again, rocked in a cradle, but the rocking is too violent, too irregular to soothe. It is more a boat than a cradle, she is at sea, tossed from wave to wave, and she knows this thought is important somehow, but she can't remember why. Occasionally the fog thins and people or things appear. Chevrons on a uniform. A man's hand with hairy knuckles, holding a peaked hat. Her husband's voice, distorted, like the crackle of an untuned wireless. *She. My wife.* Isabelle listens. He is telling her or others what she needs. *My wife needs to rest. She needs to sleep. Not to be disturbed.*

She can remember nothing of the present so she is hurled backwards, years and years. Her trousseau laid out on the bed on the morning of her wedding, the pale lemon dress with the white trim and a matching cloche for the honeymoon in Jersey. The wedding dress itself splayed on the orange bedspread like a snowfall, the silk drawers she leaked all over as she was saying her vows, thanks to the early arrival of her monthlies. She didn't know who he was, this man she was marrying, not really – 'Oh do stop fretting, Isabelle,' her mother had snapped. Trussed up in her dress and veil, all Isabelle had wanted was to run.

There is someone, one person whom she trusts. In between times, between the fragments of dream, she searches for him, tries calling but she has forgotten his name, and he can't hear her and she can't hear him back and so the wrong people come and whisper around her.

A German in uniform.

A girl with a fuzzy cloud of dark hair.

Occasionally she wakes. The man she lives with is usually there, sitting at the foot of the bed. Her head is always pounding, her vision frayed at the edges. He gives her water to sip, holds the glass to her lips. In those moments, one lucid thought emerges from the froth: it is his fault, his fault that she is here, his fault that she is so confused. There is evil in the room, it moves with him, she can hardly bear it when he comes near.

'Try to rest,' he says and the questions she wants to ask him dissolve. She can only remember the beginnings, the Wheres and the Whats, and as she closes her eyes, she knows it is only a matter of time before those will be lost, too.

They get Émile up in the middle of the night and take him to another room for questioning. At least, it feels like the middle of the night, but how would he know? He hasn't seen daylight for hours, his cell is permanently lit by a flickering electric light. A different officer and this time there is no hose, just a typewritten sheet of paper with space at the bottom for his signature, telling him what he's supposed to have done.

He has assisted Leutnant Schreiber in the desertion of his post, the document says. He has used an outhouse at his place of work, Hauteville House, to harbour a fugitive, supplying him with food, water and various pieces of equipment to facilitate his escape, including a saw and a pair of pliers, property belonging to his employer, Monsieur Corbeille.

His first feeling is relief that Isabelle's name is nowhere to be found on this confession, quickly followed by the fear that for all he knows, she may be about to sign one of her own in a room a few doors down. Émile stares at the pen. If he signs, he will be shot. A silent bullet puncturing his heart, his body wrapped in a sack and left to Letty to deal with. A casket of cheap wood, splintered and flimsy. She'd send the girls to pick flowers, bunches of wild garlic that make Stella sneeze, dog rose from the dunes at Port Soif. He'd have a pauper's funeral – what else would it be? – and there'd be some who'd say it was no more than he deserved. A collaborator, bribed with tobacco and brandy, who put the enemy before his own family.

He pushes the confession across the table. 'I didn't help him,' he says. 'I'm just a grower.'

The German's expression is blank. He looks at Émile for the longest time. 'You are in a lot of trouble, Mr Quenneville. Do you understand?'

Yes.

'If you didn't help him, who did?' The officer scribbles on a scrap of paper.

GIVE ME NAMES

Silence as thick as pitch.

GIVE ME NAMES

The officer glances at his watch, then takes up the pen. He is telling Émile that he has a choice. A simple choice. He writes on a slip of paper, which he folds in half and hands to Émile, casually as if he is passing on a recommendation, like the name of a good cobbler or a farmer who won't charge through the nose for chicken feed.

GIVE US NAMES AND WE WON'T KILL YOU.

'Sleep on it,' the officer says.

Letty shifts her buttocks on the hard metal chair and glares at the clock, which she is sure must be broken. A prison minute feels like five normal ones, and Lord knows it must be worse when you're locked up by the Germans and you don't know what's going to happen from one moment to the next. On the street where she grew up, the men around her always seemed to be flitting in and out of prison, her own uncle included. He would return to Mount Durand, thinner and meaner, and you knew to keep out of his way. Stay out of trouble – that was the mantra that came from her aunt as she sent Letty and her siblings off to school. No 'work hard, do well, aren't you clever'; their school reports lay unopened for weeks under old copies of the *Racing Post*.

Yesterday morning, before Émile left for work, he had kissed her – lightly on her right temple, just as he used to do when they were first married – and this deviation from the furrows of their routine had made her instantly suspicious. Isabelle Larch was there between them and she had turned away from him. Now she wishes she hadn't. A small, uncomfortable notion takes root, of all the years, all the time, they have wasted. He couldn't hear her; she couldn't understand him. This was an excuse she had used over and again – but it hadn't stopped Isabelle, it hadn't stopped her daughters. Daft about their Pa when they were little, both of them, even Maud, before she shut herself away with that blessed accordion and all the trouble started, although

Maud was here now, at least, and that counted for something.

'How much longer will we have to wait, Ma?' Stella says, so quiet Letty can barely hear her, as if they're sitting in a church waiting for the service to begin.

'As long as it takes.' Letty's voice echoes through the hall.

That gangly man in the nice navy suit, all arms and legs, too tall for his bicycle, had turned up at the cottage just as she'd got back from her cleaning shift. A French name, Corbeille. He reminded her of a funeral director. He shook her hand and said that there had been a most unpleasant business at Hauteville House, involving her husband and some German who had deserted his post. She had sat there in the kitchen, crumbs and dirty teacups still on the table from breakfast, feeling like the stupidest girl in the class, as she listened to him because she couldn't understand what any of this had to do with Émile. But Corbeille had told her that it looked very likely that Émile had helped the man – at the very least, let him stay in the shed – and that there were indications that he and the German had known each other for some time.

'There may have been an arrangement of some kind,' he said, explaining that Émile may have been bribed with small gifts. 'Tobacco or small measures of brandy, perhaps.'

She told him that the whole thing sounded like the biggest pile of nonsense, that she'd never seen any 'gifts', and he looked at her in a kindly way and said he would do everything in his power to help her husband, that he would vouch for his good character – he was a decent, hardworking man. Then, as she started to cry – she hadn't been able to stop herself – he had sent word to Stella and Maud.

'*Kommen mit mir.*'

271

Maud takes her arm. 'Come on, Ma.'

She gets up and the three of them follow the guard though the prison. '*Drei Minuten*,' he says, making a slashing motion with his palm as he unlocks another gate, and then they are there, outside a barred, cage-like cell with four bunk beds and her husband lying on one of them, facing the wall. When he turns, he seems distressed rather than pleased to see them. His mouth parts but no sound comes and as he walks across the cell, Letty has the curious sensation that it is she who is behind the bars, that it is she who has made a terrible mistake.

'I'm sorry.' His voice has an early morning croak to it. He looks at her as if there is nothing more that could possibly be said, letting the filth of the cell, the attendant guard, the desperation of it all speak for him.

'It's them that should be sorry!' Letty nods angrily towards the guard. 'Locking up an innocent man.'

'Oh, Pa.' Next to her, Stella starts to sob, slips her hand between the bars to touch him.

'Is there anyone who can help you?' Maud asks. When he shakes his head, she repeats the question. They were making him a scapegoat, she had told Letty on the way to the prison, just because he was poor and deaf.

'Think, Pa, please. Any information you can give them?' Again, no.

Émile's hands curl around the bars, his knuckles and fingertips creased with dirt, stained with tar from a lifetime of working with tomato plants. Letty remembers how in the early years, she had recoiled from the sight of them, even though he scrubbed them every night with a pumice stone. For a time, she had become a little obsessed with men's hands – the smooth pale palms of the clerk at the post office, the pharmacist in the Pollet whose fingernails were always trimmed into perfect half-moons. She has always wanted what she couldn't have and it has made her miserable. She is a fool. Letty reaches out and cups Émile's hand with her own. His fingers lie cold and unresponsive under hers. He looks at her, his eyes bloodshot with exhaustion, puzzled for a moment, before slowly he returns the pressure.

If he could only hear her. If he could only hear her, she'd say that it hadn't been so bad, had it, and that all couples had their spats, all families, and God knows they'd had it harder than most. Remember the time we went to Sark with the girls when they were little, she'd say, when they'd ridden their bikes across the Coupée, just for the thrill of it. Or the four of them eating fish and chips on Pembroke beach, watching the tide creep in, shielded with a turquoise windbreak from the breeze. Or watching Stella dressed up as a fairy at the Battle of Flowers, twizzling around on the top of a float made out of pink and white chrysanths, tossing handfuls of sweets to the crowds. Remember? Remember?

The guard rattles his keys, speaks assertively in German. Maud's hand is on her shoulder, telling her they have to leave.

'If we make a fuss, they won't let us see him again,' Maud says and Letty knows she's right, but still Maud has to prise her fingers away, and it is only the sound of Stella crying that brings her to her senses and she snaps at her to stop, she can't bear the commotion.

This is what it means to love your husband, Letty thinks, as they follow the guard, and she clamps her hand over her mouth and keeps it there, afraid of the sounds that will come out if she lets it fall.

★   ★   ★

273

'Do you think he did it?' Maud winds the tassels on the bedspread around her finger. She is back in her old bed and it has never felt so comfortable. She hadn't intended to stay the night, but Ma was in such a state, and Stella not far behind her; she couldn't just leave them. When she told Le Lacheur the news about Pa, he had turned back to the letter he was reading and said she must do as she wished. Their parting had been cool.

'Helped the German escape? Of course he didn't.' Stella climbs into bed and snuffs out the candle. 'It's like you said, they're just looking for someone to blame. What about that Mrs Larch? Seems like she's got off scot-free.'

'She stopped working at the house a few months ago,' Maud says. 'She couldn't have known.'

The bed frame creaks as Stella sits up. 'You know he was billeted with her? The censor. The girls were talking about it at work. Said their house at Cambridge Park got worked over by the Jerries when he went missing.'

Maud's mind turns. She thinks of the thirty-year-old love letter in the lining of a suitcase, of Ronald Larch's broken arm.

'Do you think Pa was still seeing her, before all this happened?'

'I don't know.' Stella's voice wavers, then gains strength. 'What does it matter anyway? I don't know why we're talking about Isabelle Larch when Pa is stuck in that awful place.'

'I'm sorry.' Maud reaches between the beds and squeezes her sister's hand.

'S'all right.' Stella sniffs, turns over, then turns back again. 'How long are you staying for, Mo?'

'Until Pa's home,' Maud says, the foundations of a plan

settling in her mind, leaving her unable to sleep until the sound of her mother crying in the room next door has ceased and it is time to wake up again.

It is a grey, desolate morning, damp and overcast, weather that matches Maud's mood as she draws up outside Isabelle Larch's home. It is a cottage like any other, pebble-dashed front and a trio of windows in the roof, although there is a shabbiness in the peeling paint and weed-choked front garden that reminds Maud a little of Isabelle herself. On that day in the market, she had noticed that her front tooth was chipped and although Maud had thought little of it at the time, she now finds it strange that the woman who thirty years ago had thought nothing of buying back an accordion from a pawnshop should find herself in such reduced circumstances.

Maud walks to the back of the house and taps on the kitchen door. There is no response, which in some ways doesn't surprise her, and after a moment's hesitation she turns the handle and lets herself in. The kitchen is gloomy, the curtains drawn. She calls through into the hallway and a man appears, thin, wiry-looking, an unsprung tension in the way he carries himself.

'What do you think you're doing?'

And he is rude. Maud tries to be Stella: she gives him a wide, guileless smile. 'I'm sorry – the door was open. I'm here to see Mrs Larch, if I may.'

'You may not.' He is already striding towards her, ready to usher her out. 'My wife is indisposed and is not to be disturbed.'

So she gets to lie in bed with a headache while Pa rots in a cell? Maud keeps smiling. 'It really is rather important, Mr Larch.'

'Look,' – his voice rises, he has a temper on him, Maud sees. 'I don't know who you are but—'

'I'm from Hauteville House.' She nods towards her hand-bag. 'I've taken over Mrs Larch's former position and there are a couple of queries on the accounts. Things that don't quite add up.' Maud makes a sympathetic face. 'I would come back another time but the Germans are doing an audit and it just won't wait.'

'Are you stupid or something?'

'I—'

'I don't give a fiddler's fuck about your audit.' His fists tighten and he is close enough now for her to smell the last cigarette he smoked. 'Get out before I throw you out!'

Maud flinches as he yells. She is about to go when she hears a voice – fragile, querulous – carry down the hall.

'Ron . . . Ron! Hello? Hello?'

A woman in her nightclothes stumbles barefoot into the kitchen, her hair matted and unkempt. She bunches up the hem of her nightdress in her fist, as a child might, and regards them both with a dazed, startled look.

'Have you come for the dogs?' she says to Maud. 'Is it time for them to leave?'

Larch takes hold of Isabelle's arm. 'Come on, Izzy,' he says, much as if he were talking to an ageing family pet. 'Let's get you back to bed.'

He looks over his shoulder at Maud. 'You still here?'

The triumph in his voice rings like a slap. Isabelle will remain indisposed until Pa had been dealt with, Maud sees that now. Larch deserved to have both arms broken, she thinks, and that was just the beginning. As she cycles back along the road, she considers going up to Le

Lacheur's for lunch at least, but for the first time, the prospect of the farmhouse with its rugs and drapes and book-lined shelves chills her. She changes her mind and heads back home.

24

They let him out now into the exercise yard, a small rectangle of concrete, which Émile walks around clockwise with the other prisoners, like heifers at market. There are thieves and thugs, profiteers and vandals, driven by desperation or anger or the thrill of the forbidden. What they all have in common is that their luck has run out and they are a sorry bunch, Émile thinks, as they shuffle around the yard, all hollows and angles and shrivelled bravado, their trousers held up with string. When they ask what Émile is in for, what he's done, he says he hasn't done anything much and they look at him oddly and walk on. Nonetheless, it is an honest enough answer. He set out some tools and then chose to turn a blind eye to the German in his shed, and for one woman that meant everything. And even now, in spite of the daily interrogations, the shitting in a bucket, the meals that are the consistency of baby food and eaten from a rusty tin can, Émile doesn't regret it. Recently, his regrets are of a more overwhelming nature; they refuse to be reduced to a single act.

It starts to rain. Not heavy enough to bring them in, but his feet are dragging. He is easily tired these days, although all he seems to do is lie on his bunk and think. It gave him a start when Letty came with the girls, to see all three of them standing there, Maud too, their faces pressed against the bars. He couldn't remember the last time he had been on the receiving end of their focused attention, and he'd felt embarrassed and sorry and short on words. And Letty – it would have been easier if she'd railed at him for shaming them all, if she'd been more the woman he'd lived with for two decades than the girl he'd rescued all those years ago. When she clutched his hand, he'd wanted to shake her off. He'd felt numb, guilty, trapped by her fear.

And still Isabelle has not come.

Émile tells himself that of course she can't come. She must lie low, do nothing to arouse suspicion. She may have tried to visit and been refused. For all he knows, she may have come every day and been turned away. And yet. It is not the first time he's been in trouble and Isabelle has disappeared; it has happened before. He cannot shift this thought – it is chiselled afresh in his memory, the rhythm of it enveloping him as he paces about the yard. Where are you where are you where are you.

A younger man he hasn't seen before drops into line beside him and starts to speak. He mutters, his head lowered so as not to attract the attention of the guards, before another prisoner taps his shoulder and shakes his head. The man stares at Émile, then quickly moves on. Émile is used to this – his deafness might not be catching, but his bad luck could be. He supposes word has got round: every night he is woken and marched to a room where he is asked the same questions, and every night he refuses to give names. Yesterday, the officer had used his first name and offered him a cigarette, which Émile declined, and the German had become angry. It was his last chance to cooperate, he said, did he understand? Yes, Émile had said and he sat there watching as the German smoked, and it was as if his own life was being sucked away with each puff, each dribble of ash, until the butt hit the ground, extinguished with the heel of a boot and with a shrug, the German nodded to the guard.

The circle slows to a halt, and the men line up and go back inside. There is a German waiting outside his cell. He is low-ranking, no chevrons on his collar, a clerk of some sort, Émile guesses, as he is handed two slips of paper, one yellow, the other blue, the clerk's gaze skimming over him, before he walks away. The paper is light, insubstantial; it flutters in his hand as the cell door slams shut. There is his name at the top, like the star attraction in a variety show, enmeshed by long German words he doesn't understand, the spidery scrawl of someone's signature. He flips onto the blue paper. English this time, the words jumping out at him like blows to the head. *Trial – German Military Court – Harbouring a Fugitive – Accused.* It was on Friday 15 November at eight a.m., which was tomorrow, less than twenty-four hours from now, which was too close, too soon and he wasn't ready, he would never be ready.

Émile squats on the floor, looks up at the grubby skylight, at the glide and fall of the raindrops. Canada had taught him all about courtrooms. They made up their minds beforehand and men like him were hung out to dry, no matter if you had a fancy lawyer whose fees would make you weep. Émile had been nervous, his hands had left ghostly imprints on the polished table and the smell of his lawyer's cologne had made his head ache. All he'd wanted was his hearing back and as he sat there, he was already spending the compensation money his lawyer had assured him he was entitled to: he would purchase a small homestead, seek out the best doctors in Vancouver. He didn't care how many operations it took – it was the twentieth century and if they could send men above the clouds in planes and to the depths of the ocean in submarines, how difficult could it be to return his hearing after a bump to the head? Back then he was still young and foolish enough to believe that there was no problem that couldn't be solved if you had the money to throw at it.

His old life, the man he had been, died in that courtroom. It had taken three days for the judge to come to the conclusion that it was all his fault. There was no payout, no money at all, and the bigwigs from the dairy left with relief on their faces. The lawyer took him to a bar around the corner, bought him a large whisky and told him he could pay his fees in instalments. He'd cupped Émile's shoulder and repeated the same sentence several times, until Émile understood that he was telling him to go home, back to his people, his island.

It is raining harder now, the pane of glass has turned liquid. Émile lies on his bunk and closes his eyes. He sees an accordion in its death throes abandoned on an empty beach, the skin of the bellows ripped and torn, piano keys sticky with wet sand. The sea approaches, the waves are frisky, they thrash and foam, and he delves deep within him to bring to life the sound they make, the ssh-roar rhythm, but he cannot. The tide laps around the accordion until it is an island in shallow seas and it seems of utmost importance to Émile that he stay awake and guard it, but his eyelids are heavier than his will and he sinks into sleep.

They come for him early in the grey half-light, when the streets are deserted, while curfew still hangs low. He sits in the back of a comfortable car, in the clothes that smell far too much of himself, and he wishes they'd lent him a razor at least, let him smarten himself up a bit. The car pulls up outside the court and the door is held open as he gets out, almost as if he's royalty or some such, a notion that would have made him smile if he weren't so eaten up with nerves.

The courtroom is warm; heat pours from two fat radiators underneath a row of windows, which flood the room with light. Émile is given a glass of cold water and told to sit and he sips and waits and stares at the photo of Hitler that sits above the line of empty chairs opposite him. There are five chairs, five of them and one of him, but courts aren't made for fair fights – it's all about talking, smooth and clever enough to tie whoever who is sitting where he is into knots.

The door opens and the Germans file in. Their buttons and belt buckles gleam, and one of them has a Swastika on a band around his arm. A man draws up a chair next to Émile and sets down a sheaf of paper. For a moment, Émile thinks that by some miracle they have provided him with a defence, but then he sees that the papers are blank. The man's fingernails are dirty and Émile sees him emit a sigh as he picks up the pen. He has been brought to transcribe for him, nothing more.

The judge raises his hand and Émile's ears start to ring.

For the first time in many days, Isabelle wakes up feeling normal. She looks at the alarm clock and can't think why she would be lying in bed at ten o'clock in the morning and gets up, her legs unsteady as she takes down the blackout blind. Sunlight streams through the window and she stands in it for a moment, her eyes closed.

She goes to the kitchen and heats up water to wash in. She takes off her nightdress and checks her body for bruises, finds nothing. Apart from the background thrum of a head-ache and a gnawing hunger, she feels well, unhurt. But her reflection in the bathroom mirror horrifies her – it takes her forever to comb out her tangled hair and her skin has a sour, chemical smell to it. She hears the slap of the newspaper on the door mat and she goes to collect it, pausing as she sees the date. Friday, 15 November. Then it all returns in a sudden hit of memory – Peter in the shed; the weekend storm; the casserole she made. She has been in bed for almost a week.

A jolt of panic seizes her. She runs to the back door and, as she expected, finds it locked. She roots around and finds the spare key buried under a pile of knives in the cutlery drawer. Quickly she dresses, hunts for her identity card, which is not in its usual place in her purse, and is brought up short when she goes into the living room and sees her knitting, the half-finished gloves, the clump of navy wool lying in a messy heap on the hearth rug, as if she had thrown them across the room in a temper. Isabelle picks them up, returns them to her sewing bag. To her relief, the pistol remains undisturbed, just as she left it, wrapped in the sock. She thinks back. Knitting and acorn tea and an unsettling expression on her husband's face, her head full of Émile as the fire crackled in the grate. And after that, nothing. She must have fainted, spent days in bed with a fever; there can be no other explanation. She grabs her coat and steps outside.

Isabelle cycles to the French House, her mind whirling. She has to see Émile. She needs him to calm her, to feel his hands on her shoulders as he tells her that Schreiber is gone, that it is over. There is no need to think the worst, she tells herself, but it is like telling a child that the nightmare that terrified them was only a dream: her imagination overpowers her logic.

She stops outside the side entrance, takes out her keys. But the lock sticks and refuses to turn. She tries again. The wood must have swollen after the storm, Isabelle thinks, although it has never happened before.

'Mrs Larch!'

She turns and sees Mr Corbeille on the steps of the main house. There is a strange expression on his face as he looks at her – and then at the keys. Isabelle feels herself flush.

'Mr Corbeille.' She gives a little wave, to which he doesn't react. 'Is Émile in today? The gutters at home are completely clogged with leaves and I thought he might be able to help.'

He hesitates, then walks down the steps and joins her. 'What are you doing with those keys?'

'These?' She laughs. 'They've been rattling around my handbag for months. I keep meaning to return them.'

'You should have handed them back when you left your position, Mrs Larch.' Corbeille pauses, frowning. 'I should have made sure of it.'

'So sorry.' She gives a forced smile. 'Can I see Émile for a minute or two? Just while I'm passing.'

For the first time, she notices the shadows under his eyes, the knitted lines of his brow. He looks, she realises, with a cold fear, as if he might cry.

'Mr Quenneville got mixed up in some rather underhand business, I'm afraid.' He looks at her gravely. 'Are you quite well now, Isabelle? We heard you were very ill.'

Isabelle stares at the lock. 'Émile's not here, is he?'

Corbeille swallows. A vein throbs in his temple. It looks like a translucent blue worm trapped under his skin. Isabelle feels faint, nauseous.

'A German leutnant went missing earlier this week and if the authorities are to be believed, there is strong evidence that Émile was instrumental in helping him escape.'

'But what nonsense!'

'When I came to work on Monday morning, the place was crawling with Germans. Clearly, someone had tipped them off.' He grimaces. 'And it didn't help Mr Quenneville's defence that the man's blanket was in the shed. They were absolutely livid that he'd got away.'

Isabelle's mind races. She had been so careful! Outside the three of them, no one had known. She leans against the door. *Mr Quenneville's defence.* What has she done?

'Did they take Émile in for questioning?'

'They arrested him, Mrs Larch. I did what I could, spoke of his good character and so on. But it's caused untold problems for the House, as I'm sure you can appreciate. A loss of trust for one thing.' He shakes his head sombrely. 'I spent all day at Grange Lodge – a ghastly experience. Wanting to know all the comings and goings at the house, names of staff. It was fortunate I had your letter of resignation to prove that your employment here ended some time ago. If you hadn't been so ill, it's extremely likely they would have called you in too.'

'And Émile?'

'He's awaiting sentencing. Not that the poor man will get anything approaching a fair trial. It's a sorry state of affairs and I can't think why he would let himself get caught up in such a thing. War changes people. One never knows.' He stares at her then gestures towards the keys. 'You should give me those. They've changed all the locks but, nonetheless, it wouldn't be helpful to be found with them about your person.'

The French House

She makes no move to hand them over. 'There must be something we can do.'

'Go home, Isabelle.' He is sharp, sharper than she has ever known him to be. 'There's nothing more to be done here.'

At first, Émile does his utmost to concentrate, to follow who's speaking, focusing on each twitch and purse of lips in the hope that words will tumble out like pebbles and roll into a neat, cohesive line. But the men in front of him don't even try; they mumble amongst themselves, directing their questioning to the clerk not Émile, as if he's little more than an onlooker, a spectator at his own trial.

The questions they ask are the same. How does he explain the disappearance of the spare set of keys to the shed? How had he procured luxury items such as the bottle of brandy they'd found there? They frown and grimace when he replies, screwing up their faces, as if he is an old Guern from the country parishes speaking patois.

Émile looks at each of them in turn, weighs them up. The one at the end tapping his index finger impatiently on the table. The judge peering through his glasses at his papers. The fellow next to him who keeps glancing towards the window, as if he'd rather be anywhere than where he was. This is just a job to them, the first case in a long day; they'll struggle to remember who he was by this time next week. And Émile is suddenly tired, so sodding tired of being overlooked.

The next time he speaks, he makes no attempt to enunciate. He turns each sentence into a landslide of sloppy vowels and ragged consonants. He'll give them everything they think he is and more. He grins at them, scratches

287

compulsively at a patch of bristly stubble, yawns and slumps forward on the table, like a bored schoolboy. He digs deep to show them what he is not; it is all he has left to save himself.

The men withdraw from the courtroom, leaving just Émile and the guard on the door. Sweat pours from Émile. He shakes. He is consumed by the fear of what will come next. There was a time when he'd believed himself to be better off dead, but now the thought is absurd. He can't die, he isn't ready. He has a sudden and violent longing to hold his daughters in his arms. It is Letty who has made him a father, Letty who, in her own way, has stood by him for twenty years, but it is Isabelle who has his heart. He has never loved in the same way neither before nor since he met her, that is the plain truth. It is why he's landed up here and it is rotten for Letty and the girls, there is no doubt of that; he can't forgive himself.

The door opens and the Germans file back in. It seems to Émile that the judge looks at him differently this time, a thin layer of pity skimming his contempt. He gestures to Émile to stand and he begins to speak, with the interpreter at his side – and what is the point, Émile thinks, they are too far away for him to lipread properly, they are talking for their own sakes, not for his, and he lets out a moan or a grunt, he doesn't care how he sounds, and the judge recoils. He passes a sheet of paper to the clerk, who in turn passes it to Émile.

Émile reads.

He has been found guilty of aiding and abetting a deserting leutnant, providing food, shelter and facilitating his escape. There are other crimes listed – bribing a representative of the Occupying Forces in order to secure special privileges; theft of German property – and there is the blanket again, the fucking blanket. They'll be accusing him of stealing German air to breathe with next. He scans the page for the bit that matters, finds nothing, and the clerk turns the paper over and points to two short lines.

Sentenced to four years' hard labour in Freiburg prison, Germany.

Émile stares, reads and re-reads. There above the Feldkommandatur's signature, the type smudged with the ghost of a thumbprint, are a few bald words of explanation.

(Reduced sentence due to mental impairment of the accused.)

Time slows and stops. It is a curious sensation, like plunging underwater. He can barely see for the sun in his eyes as it streams through the windows. He has survived. He has fooled them. He feels bruised, battered, his breath comes in short rapid bursts like a sick dog, but he is alive.

25

Isabelle sits with her husband at the breakfast table, waiting. She has not boiled water for tea; she has not washed up the dishes from last night's supper, which he ate with gusto and she could barely swallow. The only thing she has done this morning is to dress carefully, for both warmth and smartness in her navy serge skirt and thick yellow pullover. The clock is like a chatty but tedious companion, tick-tocking from second to second, but it is not far from nine now, which is when the *Press* usually comes, which is what she is waiting for. And if Ron tries anything to stop her, she fantasises about taking the carving knife and holding the glinting blade to his private parts until his face blanches white as a maggot.

Ron's fingers drum on the table. His hands, like every other part of him, are ugly, with broad, purple-red knuckles, born to be fists. She has barely spoken to him since she resumed consciousness a few days ago. She is busy stacking up the facts, arranging the evidence, as a lawyer might. He drugged her, that much is clear – slipped something in her tea on that Sunday night after the storm had passed, the night Peter was planning to escape, and then kept on doing so, probably, enough to keep her out of the way while Émile was being interrogated. And the only way she can make sense of why her husband might do this is if he had found out about her and Émile, or at least got wind of their plan to help Peter. She remembers the Missing posters. There may have been no reward offered in exchange for information, but Ron didn't need a financial incentive to take revenge on Émile.

The letter box snaps in the hallway and they both jump to their feet.

'I'll get it,' he says, but Isabelle ignores him and dashes into the hall, aware of his footsteps behind her.

'Isabelle! Calm down.' Ron seizes her arm.

'Don't tell me to calm down.'

She shakes him off and snatches the *Press* from the mat. The headlines, the columns of text blur and sway. If they have killed Émile, she will kill herself. She will throw herself into the sea from the rocks at Pleinmont, and try not to struggle as the waves push her under. She closes her eyes. She will not drown herself, there will be no jumping from cliffs. She doesn't have it in her.

Ron follows her into the sitting room as she scans the front page.

Man, 49, sentenced to four years' hard labour

She sees Émile's name and feels sick to see it there, before the kick of relief as she re-reads the headline and reassures herself that he is still alive. And there are the crimes, which should have been hers too: harbouring a deserter from the Occupying Forces, aiding and abetting his escape.

'No less than he deserves.' Ron stands with his arms folded by the fireside. 'He's lucky they didn't shoot him.'

'You knew, didn't you?' Her voice is husky with disuse. 'About Peter.'

'I know you, Isabelle.' He shakes his head at her. 'And I also know you like to play me for a fool. Your imaginary Kraut son goes missing' – he grimaces – 'and next thing you're running around Hauteville at Sunday lunchtime with food for the poor. You must think I'm stupid.'

She stares at him. *Give my regards to Ron.* The landlord from the Caves must have told him he'd seen her. She looks again at the *Press*.

'It was you, wasn't it? You told the Germans about Schreiber in the shed. You let them think it was Émile's doing.'

'You didn't think you could carry on fucking that deaf cunt forever, did you?' He chuckles, then regards her sternly. 'You were getting yourself into all kinds of trouble. I was protecting you.'

'You put me in a coma!' Her voice shrieks like a tin whistle.

'If it wasn't for me, your name would be there too!' Ron grabs the newspaper. 'For Christ's sake. You needed saving from yourself.'

She cannot bear to look at him. It was all her fault. And Émile would have sat there in prison, day after day, thinking that she had deserted him. A sharp pain twists in her abdomen and she picks up her sewing bag.

'I'm leaving you,' she says.

'I don't think so.' Ron leans back against the mantlepiece, looking mildly amused. He wets his finger and removes a speck of dust from one of the spaniel's ears, and Isabelle digs her hand deep into the bag. He is talking now about how if she spent more time at home and less time chasing after married men, they might find they could get along quite agreeably, although he was going to have to pull her up on her cleaning; when was the last time she'd dusted in here?

Her hand curls around the handle of the gun. 'I'm leaving you,' she says again, and as he takes a step towards her, she pulls out the pistol and points it at him. It is easier than she thinks to do so and the shock on his face acts like a round of applause. He tells her to calm down again, but this time, his voice is tremulous.

'Give me the gun,' he says, 'you're not thinking straight,' and she sees her son's photo on the bureau and remembers all the times Ron has taken advantage of her 'not thinking straight'. If you give up the gun, he will kill you, she hears Émile whisper, then Peter Schreiber echoes the same. Isabelle takes aim at the spaniels, just behind Ron's left shoulder, and pulls the trigger.

The room bursts with sound. Flaxen-haired milkmaid and rosy-cheeked suitor, each dust-ridden fold of the spaniels' ears shatter into hundreds of unidentifiable pieces and tumble to the hearth where her husband crouches, his hands clamped over his ears. He looks up at her, his lips moving, but all she can hear is a high-pitched ringing sound like a distant siren. There is a bullet hole in the wall almost directly behind where Ron had been standing, and looking at it, Isabelle honestly wonders if she had intended to kill her husband after all.

Magwitch, he seems to be shouting as he gets to his feet, backing away from her, *madwitch, mad bitch!*

Isabelle's hearing slowly returns as he grips the edge of the mantelpiece for support. He is shaking but then so is she, as, still clutching the gun, she grabs Peter's photo from the bureau. What else does she need? Toothbrush, underwear, a change of clothes. No one to see her now or to care;

she'll wear the clothes she stands up in for the next four years and think nothing of it.

She goes to the bedroom and packs her things. When she comes back out, Ron is waiting for her.

'I'm your husband,' he says. He swallows hard. 'I love you.'

Isabelle stares at him. His fists are clenched but hang loose by his sides. He looks small, grey, scared.

'Well, I don't love you. How could I?'

She takes her coat and scarf from the hatstand. Her hand is on the doorknob when he calls out to her.

'Walk out now and I won't let you back. You'll lose everything.'

The words sound more like they come from the husband she knows, but the delivery lacks conviction. There he is, standing at the foot of the stairs in his socks, the peaks of his forehead shiny where his hair is receding. Odious man. She cannot even bring herself to say his name.

Isabelle steps outside and shuts the door firmly behind her. She doesn't hesitate as she collects her bicycle from the shed, doesn't look back once as she cycles down the lane, not stopping until she has put at least a mile between herself and the life she is leaving.

Every morning, Maud goes down to the harbour and waits. Sometimes her mother and Stella come with her on the days they're not working, but mostly she goes alone. Each time, before she leaves, Ma asks if she has remembered 'your father's things', the 'things' in question being a thick horsehair blanket, a navy scarf that was left dangling helplessly on a hook on the back door on the day he left, and a pair of sheepskin gloves donated from a kind soul at the Sally Army. They both know that the chances of Maud being allowed within fifty feet of Émile are slim in the extreme – they have been told in no uncertain terms that as a convicted prisoner due for deportation, he has forfeited the rights to see any family members – but all it takes is one Jerry who's a bit softer than the rest. It is worth a try.

'Tell him to keep his pecker up,' Ma says or, 'We'll be thinking of him, he can be sure of that,' but these instructions are always thrown from the safety of the kitchen sink or the scullery where Maud can only see her mother's back and not her face, and the only thing that betrays her emotion is her brittle tone.

This morning when she arrives, there is a grey cargo ship docked in the harbour. There is more activity than usual with lorries arriving and departing, a thicket of Germans milling around, but so far no prisoners, no sign of Pa. Her heart quickens. A part of her is afraid of seeing him, afraid of what they might have done to him. She hugs the blanket to her chest.

'Maud!'

A few feet away, a woman dismounts from her bicycle and hurries towards her. As she approaches, Maud sees that it is Isabelle Larch. You're too bloody late, her inner voice – Ma's voice – growls and she ignores Isabelle and looks away.

'It is Maud, isn't it? I'm so glad I've caught you.' She lays a hand on Maud's arm and Maud recoils.

'What do you want?'

'You're angry, you have every right.' Isabelle is out of breath and agitated, her eyes alert and unblinking as if she can't bear to close them, not even for a second. 'He drugged me, you see – my husband, I mean – I think he put mushrooms and God knows what in my tea, day after day. I remember parts of it though I get so horribly confused. You came to the house, didn't you?'

Maud nods, relenting a little.

'You did the right thing. I would never' – Isabelle jerks her head angrily – '*never* have let Émile go through what he did alone. You must believe me.'

What does the woman want – forgiveness? Maud fixes her gaze on the quay. 'It makes no difference now, does it?'

Isabelle doesn't answer. They stand in silence for a few minutes.

'They haven't let you see him, I suppose?' Isabelle says.

'Not since the trial. No.' Maud's eyes stream with the cold, and she takes out her handkerchief and hopes that Isabelle doesn't think she's crying. 'I don't think my mother could have taken it anyway.' She sighs, looks properly at Isabelle for the first time. 'I can't say I liked your husband much.'

'I've left him.' Isabelle shakes her head as if she can't quite believe it herself. 'Just this morning, actually.' She lets out a little laugh.

'Oh!' For the first time, Maud notices the bulging tapestry bag that is looped over her arm. 'Where will you go?'

'To my mother's. If she'll have me.' Isabelle's mouth twists. 'We've never exactly seen eye to eye.' She looks down at the churning sea. 'I know you and Émile have had your differences, Maud, and you can tell me to mind my own business. But I was there when he heard you'd been thrown in prison and I thought then how lucky you were.'

'Lucky?'

'To have a father who would go to the end of the earth to keep you safe.'

Maud stares at her. 'It was him?' she asks, her voice faint. 'It was him who got me out of prison?'

Isabelle gives her a small smile, then her face drains of colour and seizing her arm, she points to the jetty opposite.

Across the harbour, a truck has pulled up and a line of men are being corralled towards the cargo ship. Maud spots Émile immediately; he is in his navy Guernsey, he holds himself upright, he takes one last look around as the prisoner in front of him is pushed onto the gangway.

'Pa!' The wind carries her voice and she calls again; she cannot just stand silent even though she knows he can't hear her. And then, as her face is wet with tears, just as she thinks he is about to be swallowed up into the hold, he turns and stares straight at her, then raises a hand before stumbling inside.

Isabelle's arm creeps around her shoulder. Maud hesitates, then lets herself be drawn in. Together they stand huddled against the wind until the ship departs, a consort of squawking seagulls wheeling in its wake, as it dissolves into the grey December sky.

26

Germany: June, 1942

There is room for twenty men in the truck and there are thirty of them, packed together on the hard wooden benches, knocking against each other like dominoes as the truck swerves and jolts its way to wherever it is taking them, because as usual they are never told; they are left to surmise, to speculate, to dread. And it is dread that seizes them all today, the inhabitants of Gang 5, Block B, even Émile's cell-mate, Ernest, who has a reputation for toughness, and whom the night before Émile had found huddled under-neath the table in the middle of the night, visibly shaking. The table legs were trembling along with him – it was another raid – and for once, Émile couldn't muster up enough energy even for fear. His limbs felt like cast iron, his teeth ached – dammit, every part of his body ached and throbbed and passed complaint at its current situation – and he was both too hot and too cold, so he had just lain there, thinking of all the things he missed like fresh air and clean towels and the smell of the earth after a downpour, and when he'd next looked over, Ernest was back on his mattress.

Émile fingers the disc bearing his identity number, which hangs on filthy string around his neck. It makes them look like overgrown kids, he thinks, glancing around the truck at the row of identically dressed men in their prison-issue blue dungarees. No one speaks; they stare at the floor, the roof, the tarpaulin billowing in the breeze. They lost three men yesterday, clearing out one of the bomb craters. Everyone around Émile had thrown themselves to the ground when it happened, guards included, and only he had been left standing. The white light of the explosion had repeated again and again for the rest of the day, whenever he closed his eyes.

The truck slows and halts. A strip of blue sky emerges as the tarpaulin is untied, along with the now familiar chalky smell of crushed buildings. Émile can taste the grit as he clambers outside. It is the same scene as the day before: a landscape populated with mountains of bricks and rubble. In the distance he can see a warped iron girder, clawing at the sky. He looks around. They are in the middle of nowhere, far from the city itself. It's another factory, most likely, like the one yesterday.

More trucks arrive, spitting out a raggle-taggle trail of prisoners. Poles, Czechs, Russians, even some Germans. From time to time, Émile thinks about Schreiber and wonders where he is now, whether he made it, or if he got caught and shot. When the other men ask what he's in for, he is economical with the truth. A friend was in trouble and I helped him escape, he will say, and for the most part it convinces. He has learnt that people hear what they want to hear. No one quizzes him on who or why – it is inconceivable that anyone in this stinking latrine of a prison might be there because they had actually helped the enemy. Occasionally, on days like today, when he is feeling weak and sick and broken, Émile struggles to believe it himself.

He lines up with a group of others and they are marched to a far corner of the bombsite. With relief, Émile sees that the guards carry no shovels or pickaxes, so there will be no digging, no furrowing for unexploded bombs. A guard extracts a brick from the rubble and issues some orders, and Émile finds himself in a chain of men passing bricks from one to the other.

As hard labour goes, he's known worse. After a while, others start to complain of sores and blisters, but his hands are lumpy with callouses; he can handle a few bricks. His trouble seems to lie in what has hitherto been the simple act of staying upright; he sways as if keeping balance on a tug boat in a Force Nine Gale, he gets dizzy, the sunlight stings his eyes. He experiments with closing them, just for a moment, and receives a shove in the ribs from the man next to him.

'You all right?'

Émile nods. If he is too sick to work, he will be sent to the prison hospital and he hasn't known anyone ever come out of there alive.

His companion glances nervously at the guards. 'Take the fucking brick, then.'

They break for a lunch of hard black bread and a sliver of sausage. Émile leans against the side of the truck as he eats, worried that if he sits down, he will never get back up. The guards line them up again and this time Émile is handed a spade and told to head further into the rubble. He joins the small circle of prisoners, dislodging bricks from the debris. Just two hours until a break, he tells himself, then the afternoon's half gone. He has a touch of fever, nothing more. Sunday is only a day away and then he can rest up, sleep off whatever it is he's caught. But as he bends to pick up a handful of bricks, his head yo-yos and his legs give from under him – he falls face down into the rubble, spluttering and choking with the dust as a sharp pain sears his temple.

Hands grab Émile under the armpits and stand him up as a guard approaches. He has a pronounced limp and is almost scrawny enough to be a prisoner himself. Émile can almost hear his sigh as the guard looks at him, before gesturing towards the truck. He finds himself being half dragged, half carried from the rubble by two of the other men who deposit him next to the salvaged bricks. One of them, a Pole with soft, doughy skin, passes him a broom, saying something in his native language that Émile might have interpreted as you jammy bastard or some such, had he not felt the world rolling him up like a carpet and a rough darkness descend.

The prison doctor is a small, serious man who warms the stethoscope in the hollow of his hand before pressing it to Émile's bare chest. There is an empty coffee cup on the table with a cigarette butt on the saucer. A small window looks out onto a scrubby patch of grass populated with daisies. Despite the bars and the cutting pain in his lungs when he breathes, Émile feels an inch closer to who he used to be in this room, as if he is just a sick man visiting a doctor, who has only his best interests at heart.

Once he has examined him, the doctor lights a cigarette and leans back in his chair. He glances at Émile's notes and says something unintelligible. He frowns, tries again.

'Hol-i-day,' he mouths, then points at the file. 'Me. Guernsey.' He gives Émile an encouraging look. 'Very nice place. The beaches!' He brings his fingers to his lips, as if blowing a kiss.

Émile hesitates. If it's chit-chat the man's after, then it

might get him an aspirin at least. 'I live near the Common,' he says. 'L'Ancresse.'

'I know it.' The doctor smiles and mimes the swinging of a golf club. He scribbles down a name on a piece of paper and passes it to Émile. *Mr Le Pelley*, Émile reads. *Tea rooms – L'Ancresse.*

The doctor is watching him eagerly as Émile thinks for a moment.

'Ah yes.' Émile nods. 'I know him.'

Eugène Le Pelley who owned the tea rooms at Pembroke Beach was as odd as they came – a lifelong bachelor, with brightly coloured patches on his trouser knees and a monocle he used to tease the children with.

'He's my friend,' the doctor says with delight.

'Nice chap,' Émile agrees.

The man takes off his glasses and rubs the bridge of his nose, becomes serious again. His mannerisms, something in the way he holds himself, begin to remind Émile of somebody.

'You have three and a half more years here.' The doctor is speaking slowly, as if it really matters that Émile should understand, and Émile finds this extremely disconcerting. He is used to guards who slur and shout and make threats and crude gestures with their fists, and inmates who ignore him, who don't have it in them to bother with a deaf man.

'You need rest,' the doctor goes on. 'You need decent food. You need medicine.'

Next thing, he'll say he's sending him to the Ritz for a fortnight. Émile looks at him sceptically.

'You won't survive here.'

The man is playing with him. Messing with your mind; the Germans were good at that. Émile trains his eye on a sprinkling of freckles on the man's forehead.

'Do you have children?' the doctor asks.

Two daughters, Émile tells him, almost grown up now. He misses them, he says.

The doctor glances at the door and then at Émile's file. 'You helped a deserter. A German. Why?'

Émile says nothing, then shrugs. 'He needed help.'

The doctor looks at him for a long time. Then he takes a blank form from the drawer of his desk and writes on it. Émile's heart lifts. There is a possibility he is writing him a prescription. He will get aspirin for the pain, perhaps even be put on lighter duties for a few days. The doctor leans in close to Émile, his hand suddenly on his shoulder. It is a shock to be touched by another human being like this, and Émile stiffens.

'There is no medicine.' The doctor points to the half-empty cabinet, which contains a few rolls of bandages, a bottle of antiseptic. 'Not for prisoners. You know that.'

The doctor makes a swooping motion as if landing a plane, then mouths a word. Émile tries to make sense of it. Fresh. French. *France*.

Transfer. Prison. France. Transfer. Prison. France.

Again the doctor's eyes are on the door. 'Do you understand?'

Émile isn't sure that he does. Then the man presses his hand to his heart, and there is a gentleness inherent in this gesture, a glimpse of who he might be if there were no war, and for a moment Émile sees Schreiber again, hunched up on the floor of the shed.

'Closer to home,' the doctor says, before his face tightens and he backs away from Émile, calling for a guard. As Émile is hustled out, he can still feel the weight of the man's hand on his shoulder.

It comes to Émile a few days later, as he sits in a truck with his hands tied, a few hours into the long journey across northern Germany. It is a certainty, just as it is that Le Pelley from the tea rooms will never take a wife. The doctor was one of Schreiber's kind – and he has just saved Émile's life.

27

Even after six months of practice, the woman at St Martin's Stores still occasionally slips up and calls Isabelle by her married name. The first time it happened, Isabelle had corrected her in front of the whole shop.

'Just Isabelle will do,' she said, as she handed over her coupons. 'Or Miss de Garis, to be strictly accurate.'

Her mother would have been vindicated by the silence that had descended as Mrs De Carteret sliced the bread, the exchange of looks that flowed through the queue.

'People will say he threw you out,' her mother had said when Isabelle had turned up with her bulging bag and asked if she could stay. 'They'll say there's no smoke without fire.'

And then as the days turned into weeks, her mother's clairvoyance as to what the gossips might or might not say became interspersed with her own reflections on the matrimonial state.

'Marriage isn't a walk in the park, you know, Isabelle. You can't just run home at the first sign of trouble.'

Isabelle had caved in then. She said out loud what she had never told anyone. He hit me. Not just once, she said firmly, seeing her mother's mouth open in protest, often. If his tea wasn't hot enough, or his bath water wasn't deep enough, or if the cushions that she'd made for the armchairs clashed with the curtains. Her cheeks had scorched with shame, her eyes were fixed on the floor as she spoke, but when she eventually looked up, her mother was fiddling with the fringe on the armrest and couldn't meet her gaze. She had muttered something about how she could do with some company around the place, in any case, and it wasn't for her to interfere in the comings and goings of her daughter's marriage, and would Isabelle help her upstairs to bed, because she felt quite unwell suddenly, her heart was fluttering like a bird.

This morning, when Isabelle enters the corner shop, a group of women are huddled around the counter, poring over a copy of the *Press*. A weary symphony of tutting and sighing fills the air.

Mrs De Carteret nods at her. 'Oh, Mrs . . . Miss de Garis. Have you heard the news?'

The women make way for her, a couple eye her curiously. She has been talked about, Isabelle realises, her name arriving before she did, she smells it like a snuffed candle. Please not Émile, she prays silently, not him. While there was no news, there was hope and it was hope that kept her going as she sat every evening in her childhood bedroom, writing letters she has nowhere to send.

Someone passes her the newspaper.

By order of the German authorities, all inhabitants aged 16 to 70 years not born on the island, will be evacuated and transferred to Germany.

How terrible, she murmurs, as she looks up at the sea of faces. Yet this does not apply to her; she is as Guernsey as they come, five generations back at least. And the same as far as she knows for Mrs De Carteret and the others, none

308

of them mainlanders, and then she sees Eileen McCulloch, who's turned white as paper, and remembers her husband, Seamus, and his accent, which rolls and lilts like the hills of Donegal.

'Eileen, I'm so sorry.' Isabelle clasps her hand.

'We've got two days is all,' Eileen says, weeping. 'We got the list of things to bring this morning. Blankets and a spare pair of shoes.' She cries harder. 'I'd be lucky to have one decent pair of shoes. Who do they think we are?'

One of the women passes her a handkerchief and Eileen wipes her eyes, throws Isabelle a cautious look. 'What about your Ronald? He'll be trying for a waiver or some such, I suppose, what with his job in the States.'

Your Ronald. She hadn't thought of him. For six months, she has done her utmost not to, even when at the beginning he would turn up unannounced at her mother's house and plead with her to come home. Ronald Larch of Enfield, North London, credentials that had impressed her parents no end when they had first met him – a Londoner no less – although Isabelle remembered looking up Enfield on a map and feeling a little deceived; it was so far into the suburbs it was almost in a different county altogether.

'I don't know,' she hears herself say. 'We're not in touch.'

Mrs De Carteret takes the *Press* from her with assertion.

'Poor souls,' she says. 'Wouldn't wish this on my worst enemy.'

There is reproach in her voice and the group murmur approvingly, and as Isabelle takes out her purse, she has the familiar feeling of being on trial for the crime of abandoning her husband. She still cannot understand why the change in her marital status should matter so much to people to whom she matters so little. As she leaves she calls out goodbye, but no one replies.

The lad in the bed next to Émile died in the night. Émile wakes early and sees that he has gone: his skin has the pallor of melted wax, his eyes are wide open, his stare deep as a pit. Calling out to a couple of the others, Ingrouille and Bisson, he closes the boy's eyes and fetches a stretcher. They carry him outside and across the frozen courtyard to the morgue, and Émile has lost count of the number of times he's done this now, since he arrived in Normandy – the winter is the worst for it, they drop like flies. Ingrouille's eyes are streaming and Émile looks away before it starts him off down the same direction. The lad is young, barely into his twenties. He had a girl whose photograph was stuffed in the underside of his mattress – he'd planned to marry her when the war was over.

The duty guard glances at the stretcher, takes the boy's identification tag and orders them to undress him. The boy's skin is smooth and practically hairless, his chest concave. There are no executions here, but death and sickness is everywhere. Émile has learnt to recognise when someone is on the way out and it's despair and loneliness that does for them mostly, not just the fever and the sickness and the nights spent shitting your guts out into a metal bucket. He watches hope drain from the new prisoners as weeks roll into months, and they spend each second of it living cheek by jowl, twenty to a cell, close enough to smell each other's sweat and farts and bad breath, but more alone than they could ever have known possible. The younger ones especially, like this lad René, just don't have the temperament for it. He would have been the same himself,

Émile supposes, before his accident. Over the years, he has had plenty of practice of being locked up with just his own thoughts for company.

They wrap René in a grubby sheet. Before they leave, Émile lets his hand linger on the boy's shoulder. Time was he'd have gladly swapped places; now, in spite of everything, he isn't so sure. This isn't the end for him, not even close to it. He will see the sea again before he dies, he will walk down the lane to the cottage and there will be his wife and daughters framed through the kitchen window, waiting, and he will be grateful just for that – and here he becomes stern with himself, and remembers Letty's fingers clutching his through the prison bars.

The three of them walk back to the hut. Émile averts his eyes from René's empty bed and reaches under the mattress for the letters that Maud and Stella have sent, rifling through until he finds the latest one from Maud. It is strange but it seems that the distance separating him and his eldest daughter is going some way to bringing them closer together. Her words on the page settle into a pattern in his mind, so that for the first time he can hear her.

She is back at home now and seems set to stay there. She and Letty must have reached some kind of truce, so his imprisonment has been good for one thing. He pictures her sitting at the kitchen table, Letty at her side, patiently transcribing her mother's fragments of news. Everyone says they'll be free by Christmas. Someone or other in Town asked after him.

He has read her most recent letter so often, he has committed it to heart. It has saved him in his darkest moments, like now when a boy the same age as Maud has just died on the bed next to him, before he even had a

chance to live. Émile smooths out the creases and reads it
again.

Dear Pa,

*We've missed two Christmases with you now, and
although the Occupation hasn't been good for much, it has
given me time to think.*

*Some time ago, I managed to prise out the truth from
Jean Le Lacheur about him and Ma. I had thought it
would make me happy to bring things out into the open, to
know who my real father was – but it hasn't.*

*Stella likes to tease me about how lucky I am having
two pas – 'the Torteval one and the L'Islet one'. The truth
is that it's just made me realise how much I miss you – the
real one.*

*My Torteval father is not in the best of health. I go to see
him when I can and he looks forward to my visits. I know
what you're thinking. He wants to know me now that he's
sick and old and finds himself with more enemies than
friends, but what about twenty years ago when it really
mattered . . .? For my part, I tell myself he's a businessman
through and through, that he can't help himself. Someone
who is incapable of giving without wanting something in
return.*

*I know now why you tried to stop me finding out. You
were trying to protect Ma, and keep me safe the same way
you always have, just like you did when I ended up in
prison. I behaved like a brat and I'm sorry.*

*I am on 'stop and say hello' terms now with Isabelle
Larch (if I'm out without Ma, that is . . .). I saw her on the
Bridge the other day. She heard you'd been moved to
Normandy and said she wanted to write. I didn't know*

what to say, Pa. Goes without saying that Ma wouldn't
like it. But I thought you should know.
We're waiting for you – come back to us soon.
Yours, with love
Maud xx

Émile lies back and closes his eyes. He remembers the shock
of seeing Maud with Isabelle at the harbour on the day he
left, side by side, like a secret come to life. The daughter
who wasn't his daughter, the fiancée who became someone
else's wife. He had felt an unexpected rush of elation, which
had remained with him even as he was shoved with the
other prisoners into the underbelly of the boat, with the
scampering rats and the smell of vomit and the assurance
from the guards that anyone who tried to move would be
shot. Whatever had happened in between his arrest and his
sentence, whatever her reasons for staying away, Isabelle
had not deserted him, and no more had Maud.

His family are waiting; that has to be enough. Later, he
borrows a pen and writes to Letty and the girls. He misses
them, he says. He's sure it's no barrel of laughs for them
either, three years into the Occupation, and never knowing
when it might be over. He hopes they are getting enough to
eat and tells Maud to be careful not to exhaust herself
cycling all the way up to Torteval. He promises Stella that
when he's home again, he'd like her to teach him to dance
the modern way, no matter that he can't hear. He hands the
letter to the duty guard.

In the days that follow, Émile is firm with himself. If
Isabelle writes, he will destroy her letter without reading it;
it is better for everyone that way. He tells himself that it is
like setting sail, the moment when you pull up the anchor

and wind in the rope, the freedom a man feels as he turns his back on where he's come from, until it shrinks to just the smallest of specks. But as the months pass and winter melts into spring, he finds that the land he's left behind him looms as large as ever, and he is no further forward than he was when he cut loose.

'Where you off to?'

Her mother's tone is sharper than usual. She is dusting the mantlepiece, which has become a veritable shrine to Pa's memory, with a sepia photograph where the clock used to be, flanked by assorted bric-a-brac, including his old tobacco tin and a chipped statuette of a Canadian Mountie.

'The hospital,' Maud says.

'You'll wear yourself out, cycling into Town.'

'He's dying, Ma.' Maud knots her scarf under her chin. 'And he doesn't have anyone else.'

'No one to blame but himself for that,' Ma says and Maud doesn't disagree as she calls out goodbye and sets off on her bicycle.

After Pa had been sent to Germany and she'd told Ma that she'd come home for good, her mother had hugged her and said she hoped they could put all the other nonsense behind them. She had looked at Maud so pleadingly that Maud had held her tongue, and waited, until one evening a couple of months later, when the first letter had arrived from Pa. Then she had asked the question that had been haunting her the most, that would determine whether or not she ever saw Le Lacheur again.

'Did he force you, Ma?' she asked and her mother's knitting needles had worked a beat like drumsticks, until eventually she replied.

'Not as such,' she said. 'No more than he forced you to work for him. But I didn't know any better.'

And that was the last word that had been said on the matter. Once Le Lacheur had forgiven her for leaving, Maud began to pay monthly visits to the farmhouse, Sunday afternoons that she senses her father derives more pleasure from than she does. When the conversation dries up, they play draughts together, and as she moves the pieces from square to square, she feels a curious numbness, as if she is watching herself from the outside. When the time comes to go and he presses his papery lips to her cheek, she has a sense of duty done, and little else.

Le Lacheur is in a ward on the top floor. The nurse on duty is a rounded middle-aged woman, whose broken spectacle frames are sealed together with parcel tape.

'Hello, dear,' she says. Her voice lowers. 'He didn't have a very good night, I'm afraid.'

Maud takes her place at her father's bedside. His eyelids quiver when she announces her arrival. Asleep and unshaven, with flecks of dried spittle coating the corners of his lips, he is practically indistinguishable from any other patient on the ward. The high-pitched whistle of his breathing grates on Maud and she tells herself that she is a terrible person, that this is her father, the man whose approval had once seemed important enough to leave her family for. She should feel sad, not irritated.

Tentatively she takes his hand in hers. The empty feeling remains. She thinks of Pa and wonders if Isabelle Larch has written to him. The day their paths had crossed on the Bridge, Maud had seen the depth of sadness in her eyes, as stumbling over her words, Isabelle had asked if anyone would mind if she dropped him a note. Maud's response had been deliberately cool. She had thought of her mother and the shrine on the mantlepiece and his letters, which Ma often asked her to read over and over again of an evening. A refrain of 'when-your-pa's-back-and-the-Jerries-have-gone' would inevitably follow these sessions. There would be no more crowding round the wireless every spare second, her mother said, it wasn't fair if he couldn't hear it too – they'd play cards instead. And when the Germans were gone and they were no longer half-starved to death, they'd walk up to L'Ancresse on a Sunday afternoon and have a cup of tea at the kiosk, all four of them, like a proper family. Maud knew there could be no place for Isabelle in that.

Maud releases Le Lacheur's hand. The wheezing has become more of a rattle, like dice in a shaker. He mutters something and his eyes open and stare blankly into her own, before closing again. The nurse appears with a grave expression and a thermometer. She takes his pulse, then pats Maud's shoulder.

'He's very poorly, I'm sorry to say. It's best you stay, if you can.' She pulls a screen around the bed.

Maud nods. When the nurse has gone, she goes to the window and looks out at the gardens below. A man in a dressing gown with a slight limp is walking across the grass with his two small daughters. One skips from side to side, her braids bouncing, swinging her father's hand in hers; the other trails behind, kicking at clods of earth. The man turns to ruffle her hair and she ducks from underneath him, her expression as she turns away one of undiluted fury. How was it possible to be so angry with the world when you were no older than six, Maud wonders. Then she thinks of the potency of the stories she told herself as she was growing up, the roles she attributed to her family, where she played the outsider and Pa was always the villain. She had wanted so badly to be proved right that she refused to see the good in him. Yet he had taken on her and her mother, when the man lying behind her had abandoned them.

Maud returns to the bed. Le Lacheur stirs and moans, his breathing ragged. She has loved the idea of him, not the man himself and this must be why the tears won't come and as he gasps for breath, she wets his lips with water, wipes sweat from his forehead, soothes as she might a child, because who else is there to do it? When the end comes, it is marked by a protracted gurgle that makes her want to stopper up her ears, but the silence that follows is like a gift and, calling for the nurse, Maud feels an overpowering sensation of release.

It is dark when she arrives back home. Ma and Stella are sitting at the kitchen table. Her mother clutches a much-used handkerchief in her fist and a typed form, rubber stamped, lies between them.

'What's happened?'

Ma sniffs and pushes the form towards her.

'Pa's coming home,' Stella says, and their mother smiles, and for a second, Maud can almost see the girl she was at the farmhouse, all dimples and wisps of hair and eyes as blue and innocent as a kitten's. 'They're letting him go.'

28

They bring Émile back on a small boat that was once used to transport cattle, their discontent smeared in grubby yellow streaks across the sides of the hold. It is a warm, bright morning in early May and before they leave, he stands on the quay at St Malo and looks up at the ramparts of the walled city, and the line of green helmets weaving amongst them. Even from a distance there is a dispirited air to their movements, as if they are prisoners themselves, which Émile supposes they are, more or less. Which one of them wouldn't rather be somewhere else, doing an honest day's work rather than parading around in a uniform, marching and saluting until they were half demented, fighting a battle that belonged to a madman with a funny moustache, who was safe and cosy and well-fed in a bunker somewhere and planned to keep it that way?

Émile is hungry. He is hungry and he is nervous and he is free. He is dressed in another man's clothes and he has had to use string to keep the trousers up and the sweater has more holes than it does stitching, but he is grateful, as he is for the crust of bread he was given before they set sail by a German who looked just as starving as him. He has a knapsack that contains two years' worth of letters from the girls, and one that arrived from Isabelle a month before they released him. It is wrong of him to keep it, he knows this, but he cannot bring himself to throw it away.

Ron is gone, Isabelle says, deported to Germany, and she is living with her mother. They rattle around like marbles in the house in St Martins, and it's both a trial and a blessing to be Miss De Garis again.

I left him, Émile, when I found out that he was the one who grassed you up to the Germans.

She had felt perfectly calm, she said, although for the first few nights, she slept with Schreiber's gun under her pillow. Not that she needed to, because when Ron did turn up, he was blubbing and carrying on, begging her to come back and promising her all sorts – '*even books! Can you believe it?*'

She reads and re-reads his letters, she tells him, the ones he wrote as a young man, and each time they make her more sorry. Sorry that she hadn't kept writing regardless, sorry to have let him down when he most needed her, sorry to have doubted him.

Émile rummages in his knapsack for her letter. Sometimes he is afraid that he has imagined her closing words, that he hallucinated them. But there they are, decisive, at the foot of the page and as he reads them again, they go straight to his head.

> *I have made many mistakes in my life. Loving you was never one of them.*
> Isabelle

The guard appears and gestures he should come up on deck. The fresh air is a relief, as is the sight of St Peter Port, which looms in the distance. He thinks of the last time he came back to the island, from Canada when he was first deaf, and how he had stared at the Weighbridge tower and thought he'd rather be dead than return like this, and with barely a halfpenny to his name. His mother had been waiting for him, I-told-you-so etched into every crevice of her face and she had nodded at his accordion – which he hadn't been able to bring himself to leave behind even though he'd have got some money for it – and then she said something he was glad he couldn't hear. Now the Weighbridge is partly rubble and he and Maud had been lucky not to be buried along with it on the day the Germans arrived uninvited. Émile thinks of the boy, René. He has seen enough death and misery in the past two years never to take life for granted again.

The boat docks. The harbour steps are slippery with seaweed and the sea, when he looks back, sparkles as if war had never been invented. No one pays him any attention as he walks into Town. Everyone is prisoner-thin, Émile notices with a shock, Germans and Guernsey people alike. It's in their faces you see it the most, cheekbones so sharp you'd cut yourself. He wishes he had money in his pockets as he has a sudden bizarre impulse to buy gifts – a box of chocolates for Letty, scent for Stella and sheet music for Maud, a selection of books, the pages crackling with newness for Isabelle. There's nothing in the shops of course and even if there was, who brings presents home from prison? And with two women in mind, not just the one he's wed to.

Émile walks to the terminus where the trams run from and finds it deserted. A street sweeper looks at him strangely and tells him they stopped the trams a while back.

'Shanks' pony for you, mate,' he says, glancing doubtfully at Émile's destroyed boots and Émile begins the long walk back to L'Islet. He stops several times along the way, feeling like a man twice his age. God help him, he wouldn't say no to a stick. The hedgerows are in bloom, hawthorn flowers nestling like snow amongst the brambles, the smell of honeysuckle teasing him. He should pick a bunch for Letty, but he thinks better of it – chances are she'll ram them down his throat. Chocolates, flowers, what was he thinking? Two and a half years, he imagines her shouting, almost three years you've been gone. Getting himself mixed up in all sorts, bringing shame on the family, leaving her and the girls as good as destitute. And for what? To save another woman's skin. He reminds himself that Letty doesn't know this, but people talk, that's all they do, with no wireless or anything else to distract them.

By the time Émile reaches the lane, the sun is lowering in the sky. The knot in his stomach pulls a little tighter. He may even find another man in his place at the table and who can say, perhaps that might be the best outcome for all of them. The cottage is exactly as he remembers, and he pauses before he walks up the path. There are no bikes leaning against the wall so the girls must be out, but he can see Letty's bowed head through the kitchen window. To his surprise, he sees that she is reading, her finger moving slowly across the page as she mouths the words. Letty looks up when she hears him, the book falling to the floor. The glass of water next to her spills as she scrambles to her feet but she can barely look at him as he comes in: she is shy as he has never seen her, her hand covering her mouth.

'The girls are at work,' she says and there is something different about the way she speaks. He can make out the words as he never could before and he realises that she is speaking slowly and with care, as if she's been practising.

Then she hugs him hard and she is like another woman in his arms she has grown so thin. He puts his hands on her shoulders and looks at her. Her hair is greying at the roots and temples, the shadows under her eyes are the purple of bruises. She smiles.

'You came back.'

'They let me out early,' he says, looking about the place. There is a photo of him on the mantlepiece that hasn't seen the light of day for decades: she must have gone through everything he owns to find it. The thought embarrasses him and he goes to the table, picks up the book she was reading. It is a treasury of fairy tales.

Letty reddens and goes back to her old way of talking, mumbling something that requires more guesswork on his part than anything else. Then she is pressing him down into a chair and going into the scullery to heat water for a bath.

Later, after Émile has scrubbed himself to the point of rawness and changed into the clean clothes Letty had pressed and folded ready for his return, Maud and Stella come home. Stella, more woman now than girl, half-squeezing the breath out of him; and Maud holding him for a long time, looking older too but in a different way to Stella. As the evening unfolds, he sees that it is Maud who has held the family together, that it is she who soothes Letty and stops her from fussing, who makes Stella giggle with asides that he can only guess at, who gives him a notepad and pencil, small enough to fit in his pocket. The paper is creamy and expensive-looking, with a lingering smell of cigars when he holds it close.

'He died,' she says. 'The Torteval one.' She takes the pencil and writes it down.

'I'm sorry.' Émile lays a hand on her wrist.

'No, I'm sorry,' she says, mouthing the words with precision. 'For everything.'

She nods to Stella, who gets up from where she is kneeling on the hearth rug and the two of them say goodnight, even though it is early, and there is a look of panic in Letty's eyes as the door closes behind them. Émile points to the chair next to his and she joins him at the table, picking at a seam of dirt under her thumbnail. The light is draining from the sky, a wisp of indigo cloud leaves a trail like smoke. Letty gets up and goes to the bedroom, returns, clutching something in the curve of her palm. She holds it out to him, uncurls her fingers. It is his wedding ring.

Émile takes it. He wants to tell her that she should have pawned it and that he's surprised she hasn't. He can't remember when he last wore it. As he slips it on, it rolls at the base of his finger as if it belongs to someone else. He feels clobbered with weariness and confusion, his dearest wish at that moment to throw himself on the floor and cry like a three year old.

Letty reaches for the notepad. She writes slowly, gripping the pencil between her thumb and forefinger. Émile imagines snatching it from her hand, yelling that he doesn't want the burden of her anymore, that the thought of just the two of them sitting like this night after night for years on end feels like a different kind of prison. He does none of those things. When his wife has finished, he smiles gently and takes the notebook from her.

Dont leave us again. Promiss?

Her features blur in the grey twilight. Her hands are cold as he holds them in his.

'Promise,' he says.

29

Isabelle has taken to waking at three every morning. She lies there, windows open, waiting for the birds to rouse themselves, listening hard. Sometimes she is sure she can hear the distant sound of shells exploding on the Normandy coast. Every day fleets of planes roar overhead, like strange migratory birds, and a current of anticipation crackles across the island and those that have them get out their crystal wireless sets from under the floorboards and inside lavatory cisterns, and those that don't, like Isabelle, sift through rumour and fact. Cherbourg is down, the Allies have taken Belgium, Paris will be next. Hitler is dead, Hitler is on the run, Hitler is in his bunker shitting himself. They say Guernsey will be made an Open Town, that they will be freed by the Red Cross, that there will be proper bread again and butter and sugar – great sacks of it – and tea, of course, real tea.

'It will be so nice to get back to normal,' her mother had said the other evening and Isabelle had snapped that the war wasn't over yet, not by a long way, and her mother chided her for being a killjoy, a position Isabelle couldn't find it in herself to defend. Now, she sits on the window seat in the rose-pink dawn and lets the wood pigeons in the eaves echo her own incontrovertible truths. Your husband is gone; Émile has come back. Your husband is gone; Émile has come back.

Jacquie Bloese

He is back and he doesn't want to see her. She sucks on her little fingernail, a childhood habit. A few weeks ago, she had taken her mother to the hairdresser's in Berthelot Street.

'I can hardly bear to look at myself in the mirror these days,' her mother had complained, casting a sideways glance at Isabelle's yellow turban, which she was rarely without. 'And it wouldn't do you any harm to get yourself tidied up.'

And so the pair of them had trekked into Town and had their hair washed with the same hard green soap that they used at home, and the girl who did Isabelle's was a bit on the rough side, yanking at the tangles until Isabelle's scalp ached. Unsmiling, she had pointed to the seat nearest the lavatory, and told Isabelle to wait there, and no, she didn't know how long Mrs Carré was going to be. The girl wore her curtness uneasily, like a pair of high heels borrowed from her mother and, left to sit with dripping hair, Isabelle was perplexed. She had stared at her reflection in the mirror, the fine lines around her eyes and at the corners of her mouth and thought, you are getting old, my girl, as eddies of conversation swirled around her. The barter shop on the High Street had closed, would Mrs Le Page like a shingle cut or plain, side parting on the left or the right; and then – 'How's your pa, dear, since he got back?' and for a second, Isabelle met the girl's bluebell gaze and recognised who she was.

Her pa was all right, she said. He had been ill while he was in prison, pleurisy or similar, and his cough was dreadful.

Poor man.

Yes.

Terrible.

Yes.

Bet your ma's pleased, ain't she, to have him back?

'She is, Mrs Le Page.' And Isabelle felt the girl's eyes settle on her. 'My sister and I joke that they're on a second honeymoon.'

A burst of harsh laughter from the woman. 'My old man wouldn't know a honeymoon if it came up and asked him for a smacker on the lips.' A pause. Silence, then the snipping of scissors. 'Not too much off the sides, Stella, love.'

Stella. His daughter. Isabelle's scalp had begun to ache afresh. She had got up and told her mother she would meet her outside the Town Church; she had changed her mind, she said, her hair was fine as it was.

Second honeymoon. The wood pigeons change their tune. The sky burns orange. And Isabelle takes a book from the bedside table and tries to connect words with meaning, to soothe herself with a story other than her own.

She sees him some two weeks later, the day after the Americans drop bombs on the harbour. As Isabelle picks her way through shards of shattered glass along the Esplanade, there is not a German to be seen and it is almost like the old days. There are workmen everywhere, repairing the damage. The air vibrates with the sound of hammering and there are a jumble of ladders in the High Street and men in overalls, joshing and cursing, all except one, at the top of a ladder outside Lloyds Bank and it is Émile. It is him.

Isabelle stops. She walks on a few paces, then turns back, looks up. He has not noticed her. She watches him as he hammers in the final nail, checks the board is secure, then slips the hammer in the pocket of his overalls. The soles of his boots are hanging off, she can see the dirt in his heels as he descends. His eyes are bluer than she remembers, his stubble greyer, his bare arms tough with muscle. A collision of thoughts: it is so long since she's been held, he is wearing a ring.

'Belle.'

He wraps her up. For a few glorious seconds, she is right at the heart of him, her face pressed to his chest, his arms locking around her back. She feels both wonderfully safe and terribly afraid. Then he steps back, and she is alone again.

Émile picks up his knapsack and points up Smith Street towards Candie Gardens. 'Lunch,' he says.

'Can I come with you?'

It seems to Isabelle that Émile hesitates before he nods, and they fall into step with each other.

The day is warm, sultry. Sun burns the back of her neck, the grass sings in the breeze. They find a shady spot in the sunken gardens near a ragged palm and sit on the low wall. The bread he shares with her sticks in her throat like sawdust.

'The stuff they gave us in prison was better,' he says, with a ghost of a smile.

There are no words for what has happened, Isabelle thinks, no language. She stands up and brushes the crumbs from her lap. *I'm so sorry.* Turning away, she tries on the words for size, and they sound just as trite, as inadequate as she feared. She draws back towards him.

'Ron's still in Germany?' he asks.

'Yes.'

'I'm not sorry.'

'No.'

'You hear from him?'

'Never.'

A blue tit lands on the paving and pecks at the crumbs. Isabelle watches it for a second, then sits down again. Émile nudges her with his elbow.

'We're still here,' he says. 'It's not so bad.'

She nods. She can't speak. His ring blinks at her dumbly. What had she expected? That he would come back and Letty would just conveniently disappear? When Isabelle is able to look at Émile again, he is frowning.

'She needs me,' he says. 'I didn't realise. But she does.' His hand settles on hers.

The woman's tough as old leather, Isabelle wants to say. She's done a job on you from the first day you met and you can't see it. You're too good to see it.

She moves her hand away. 'You look tired.'

Nightmares, he says, he can't sleep most nights. He's up at three every morning, nothing to be done but sit in the kitchen and watch the sun rise.

Isabelle looks up. At the far end of the garden, a young woman with a froth of dark hair stands watching them. Émile raises a hand and as the girl approaches, Isabelle sees that it is Maud.

'I have to go,' Isabelle says. She gets up and hurries down the path. Maud slows to greet her, and Isabelle can hardly bear it, not now, not anymore. Over the years, she has learnt that she can withstand many things – the put-downs of a controlling parent, the temper of a little man who wanted to make himself bigger. Far harder to stomach is the way Émile's eldest daughter is gazing at her now, with immense sympathy.

'You look out for your father, you hear.' Isabelle's tone comes out sharper than she intends. 'He's been through enough for a dozen lifetimes.'

She doesn't wait for Maud's response. But she feels their eyes on her, both of them, as she opens the gate and walks away, increasing her pace until she is stalled by a sharp stitch searing the right side of her body, the pain rendering her breathless.

30

May, 1945

'H itler's dead!'
Stella grabs Émile's notebook and writes the
words in block capitals, does a little twirl around the kitchen.
Letty puts down the dishcloth and scolds her. Keep your
voice down, haven't we had enough trouble, she is saying,
and Émile looks at his notebook and then back at Stella,
who is protesting that it's true, it's true, she was round at
Roddy's and heard it on his dad's crystal set.

'You can't believe everything you hear,' Émile says.

'It was the BBC!' Stella says indignantly, tracing the letters
in large strokes across the kitchen as if she's painting a wall.
The back door opens and she turns with relief towards
Maud, who slings her satchel on the table, and then his wife
and daughters become embroiled in the kind of slingshot
conversation Émile has no hope of following, so he stops
trying and returns to his book. He will have to ask Maud to
pick him up another from the library next time she's in Town
– he is on to Sherlock Holmes now, and some of them he's
read twice, just for the comfort of it. Émile likes to imagine
that he is being read to – a woman's voice – *her* voice –
breathing life into the words until they envelop him like the
London fog in the stories.

Maud taps him on the shoulder. Flanked by Letty and
Stella, their faces alert with curiosity, she is handing him a

square of paper. It came to the school with the Red Cross messages from the evacuees in Yorkshire, she tells him.

'Look, Pa – it has your name on the back.'

FOR MR ÉMILE QUENNEVILLE & FRIENDS

Émile flips over the paper. It is a drawing, an inked sketch of an imposing man in a waistcoat, with a full bush of a beard, standing beside some railings, a large oak tree towering behind him.

'Victor Hugo,' Maud mouths and Émile studies the drawing and remembers the photos Isabelle showed him in the office. Maud is right, it is Victor Hugo outside the French House.

Maud takes his notebook. 'We think it's from one of the art teachers,' she explains. 'Do you know anyone in Yorkshire, Pa?'

Émile looks back at the dedication, stares out of the window. 'He made it,' he mutters.

He had always imagined Schreiber dead, either snatched by the sea, or blown apart by a mine, and he had hoped for Schreiber's sake that it was the latter, over before he knew it.

'Who?' Letty is asking, over and again. 'Who?'

'The censor,' Maud tells her patiently, her eyes bright. 'The German, who Pa helped.'

Then his eldest daughter puts her arms around his neck and kisses him lightly on the forehead, and he feels his heart surge and swell with how much has changed, and he blinks hard to prevent the tears that no words could begin to explain.

Letty picks up the drawing and frowns. 'What's the point?' she seems to be asking, and then with a flounce, 'The war's not done with yet,' and Maud and Stella roll their eyes, and Émile smiles a little and turns back to the drawing. He sets it on the mantelpiece, next to the Mountie, and he thinks of how happy it would make Isabelle to know that Schreiber was safe, hidden away in the countryside, filling out on Yorkshire butter and cream, teaching Guernsey children how to draw cows.

Later, when Letty is pegging out the washing, Émile finds Maud in her bedroom and asks if she'll do him a favour.

'Take the drawing to Isabelle for me,' he says. 'Let her know he's all right.'

Maud puts down her paperback. She looks troubled. 'Don't you want to go, Pa?'

'I can't,' he says. 'Your ma wouldn't like it.'

'All right, then,' Maud says, picking up her book as if it makes no difference to her, but as he leaves the room, Émile feels her watching him. She understands, he realises, she knows.

Letty takes what has now become her place in a pew at the back of the Vale Church and dips her head towards the altar. The woman in front turns around and greets her.

'You coming down to the harbour tomorrow, Mrs Quenneville, to cheer in our boys?'

Oh yes, Letty says, she and the girls will be there. Maud, who she has persuaded to come with her to church today for this special service, nods obligingly.

'Oh, the tears,' their neighbour goes on. She can feel herself welling up at the mere thought of it, she says. 'Five years!' She shakes her head. 'It's tested my faith, I don't mind admitting it.'

The church quietens as the organ fades and the minister announces the first hymn, which Letty is pleased to see is one of her favourites. Three years ago, she could never have guessed what solace there was to be found in singing a few songs and saying the same prayer every week; she would never have believed that she might enjoy it, yet she does. The only reason she'd come in the first place was because Betty, who she cleaned for, had invited her and the girls for Sunday lunch afterwards when Émile was first in prison, and when they'd arrived it had been just as bad as she feared with everyone staring at them and knowing their business. But at the end of his sermon, the minister had made special mention of Émile and asked the congregation to pray for his wife and daughters, and he'd given her her full name of Juliette – and rather than feeling ashamed, for once, Letty had felt special.

So, the following Sunday, she had come along with Betty again, even though she had nothing nice to wear, but no one seemed to care, and there was something very soothing about closing her eyes at the same moment as everyone else and praying for whatever she wanted most, which was for Émile to come back safely. And then, when that prayer was answered and she knew he was being released, she had prayed and prayed that he wouldn't leave her for Isabelle Larch, whose husband wasn't even on the island anymore, so what was there now to stop the two of them, if they had a mind to? It is a question that still preys upon her.

'Let us pray.'

Letty lowers her head. Émile has been home for the best part of a year now, and sometimes she thinks he looks more like a condemned man than one that's been freed. He's started reading of all things and spends his evenings with his nose stuck in a book, and Letty knows it's silly but it makes her feel like a spare part. She's tried talking to him about his books, but she can't muster up much interest for something that isn't real, and he never has much to say so their conversations jerk and stall. Letty wouldn't admit it to anyone, but she almost misses their arguments because at least there was something truthful at the heart of them. And as for what goes on in the bedroom, they're like two rusting bits of machinery.

They're on their feet again, onto the next hymn. Letty lets Maud sing for the two of them, just joining in for the chorus, which she knows by heart. She feels tired out with all the excitement and coming and going. She and the girls had gone into Town earlier to hear Churchill's speech, crackling through the loudspeakers outside the Town Church. It had been hard to concentrate with all the whooping and chattering going on, but as a huge cheer went up, Stella had hugged her and told her it was over, they were to be freed. When?, she'd asked, and that was when the confusion started for some said that very day, and others said the Jerries wouldn't surrender, and it could be days yet. When Letty had relayed this to Émile, he said Churchill had a short memory where the islands were concerned and that while there were still Swastikas flying about the place, he wouldn't believe it.

After the service, she and Maud join the throngs of people milling around outside. Across the fields, sheets billow on a washing line outside a cottage: it is a fresh day, the air feels clean and new. The minister approaches and touches her elbow.

'Mrs Quenneville! And this is your daughter . . .?' His brow wrinkles as he looks at Maud.

'Maud.' Maud smiles and holds out her hand.

'Of course. The accordionist,' he says pleasantly. 'You're to be married soon, is that right?'

Maud's mouth twists in amusement. 'No, that's my sister.'

'Stella,' says Letty. 'She couldn't come today, I'm afraid.'

'Well, I'm very glad to see both of you.' He asks Maud what her plans are, after 'liberation', as he puts it, and really, Letty wishes he wouldn't encourage her.

'I want to study music,' Maud says. 'At a conservatoire. I'm planning to apply for a scholarship.'

'So we'll be losing you to the mainland, for a while?'

'To Paris, I hope!'

Letty has heard this before, and really, she despairs. No sooner is the war over and things look like getting back to normal, than Maud wants to go rushing off to a big, foreign city with all manner of unpronounceable dangers. She can't understand why it's not enough for Maud to stay at Amherst Infants, where she has a perfectly good job and everyone likes her.

'I'm sure your mother will miss you.' The minister looks at Letty kindly, and he does have a knack, she thinks, of picking up on how a person's feeling. 'But now we've survived the war, it's time to live, wouldn't you say?'

He blesses them both and moves on.

They walk home along the headland, following the trail of barbed wire that divides the path from the beaches. Letty looks out across the pebbled sand and wonders if they'll have cleared the mines by the summer. It will be nice to be able to get down there again, have a few picnics.

'I like your minister,' Maud says.

Letty gives her a look. 'Because he didn't tell you to do the sensible thing and stay at home with your family?'

'Ma!' Maud shakes her head. 'Stella will still be here. And it's not as if you and Pa are old.'

She feels it, Letty says grumpily, and prison has made Pa old before his time. 'All that reading!'

'There's nothing wrong with reading.' Maud glances at her. 'Is he coming with us tomorrow?'

'He doesn't like crowds, you know how he is.'

They walk on in silence.

'Does he talk to you?' Letty asks suddenly.

'Pa? Not really. Not as such.'

'What does that mean?'

'I don't know. He just seems . . .' Maud hesitates. 'A bit pre-occupied, or something.'

'All this moping around.' Letty tuts. 'I'm sick of it. As if it was easy for me, left here on my own, not knowing if he was alive or dead from one week to the next.'

'But you did it. Like the minister said, you survived.'

'Just because I did it, doesn't mean I liked it.'

'Well, it's over now.'

She can tell Maud is losing patience with her, but Letty can't stop. She sniffs and when she next speaks, she is embarrassed by how shaky her voice sounds. 'But it's not over, is it? It'll never be over.'

'Ma?' Maud stops walking and looks at her with concern. 'What's wrong?'

'Me and him.' She can feel the tears coursing down her face and she turns away, unable to look at her daughter. 'It'll never be over.'

Maud's hand is on her back as she sobs into her dirty handkerchief. After a while, Maud speaks.

'You and Pa have got a right to be happy too, you know. It's the same as me going to Paris, and Stella marrying Roddy.'

337

Letty wipes her eyes. 'You two are young, it's different.'

'It's not.'

'I suppose you're talking about him and Isabelle Larch,' Letty snaps. 'What am I supposed to do – tell him to leave? I'm not having people say he left me for her, Maud, I won't have it.'

'I thought you didn't care what other people thought anymore?'

Letty has no clear answer to this so she sighs and says nothing.

They reach the turning for their lane. The cottage on the corner has a Union Jack flying from the gatepost. Letty supposes it really is happening. It occurs to her that they haven't seen a single German on the walk home. She turns to Maud.

'Not a word to your father or sister about any of this, you hear?'

Maud shrugs, then nods, and together they continue down the lane towards home.

That night, Letty can't sleep. Earlier, Stella pinned her hair into curls and told her to be sure to lie still, or she'd mess it up, but tonight it's beyond her. She thinks about what Maud said after church, about her right to be happy. These youngsters and their notions! She has never really thought about it as her 'right' before – she has treated life as something to be dealt with, day by day, and if the good days outweighed the bad ones, then there wasn't too much to complain about. She turns onto her side and looks at Émile. He is snoring lightly, his brow creased as if he is concentrating very hard on a dream. He had not shared in the day's excitement in the way she might have hoped. He had tried for the girls' sake, clambering onto the roof and tying the Guernsey flag to the chimney pot, smiling as Maud and Stella, with their new hairdos with the roll at the front, danced to the wireless. But in unguarded moments, when he thought no one was watching, he looked downright depressed, and this made her feel low too.

Letty slips her hand into his – it lies there limply and after a moment, she removes it. She doesn't know what a happy marriage looks like but it's not this, ring or no ring. Sighing, she turns her back to him and closes her eyes.

When she wakes, the early morning light is pale violet and there is an empty space next to her. There is nothing unusual in this – ever since prison, Émile has woken early, and usually she turns over and goes back to sleep. But today, Letty gets up, moving quietly so as not to wake the girls, and goes into the kitchen. The back door is open and Émile is sitting on the porch in his pyjamas. He looks up at her.

'Can't sleep,' he says and Letty isn't sure if he's telling her or asking. She tells him to make space so she can sit.

What does he think about when he comes out here? Even if she asks, he won't tell her. Nothing much, he'll say, thinking that he is sparing her feelings when really they are torn and tattered as rags.

A large bird – a buzzard perhaps – soars high above them, and then swoops down into a nearby field. She hears the beat of its wings against the still air.

'It's the two of us together is the problem,' Letty says.

Émile frowns at her, and she repeats it.

'It isn't you,' she says. 'Or me. It's us.'

He shakes his head, stares at the ground. 'I haven't been a good husband to you, Letty.'

He's done his best, Letty says, and so has she. No one

can say they haven't tried.

Émile doesn't say anything for a long while. Then, tentatively, warmly, he slips an arm around her shoulder and holds her close and somehow she knows that this is the last time they will ever touch each other as man and wife. They sit there for a long while, watching the sky turn a yolky yellow, as the insects stir in the long grass.

Letty wipes her eyes on the sleeve of her nightdress. There has been no shortage of tears recently, but this is the first time she's felt a little better afterwards, not worse or the same. Before she goes inside, she points to his wedding ring.

'I don't think you should wear that,' she says. 'Not anymore.'

Her husband nods, his eyes watery, and begins to ease the ring over his calloused skin.

31

On the morning of the liberation, Émile and his family squeeze onto the wagon that belongs to the organist at Letty's church, and set off into Town. The sky is a deep hydrangea blue and it is warm enough to roll up your sleeves. Children lean over the sides of the cart, waving flags at passers-by, and the horses snort and skip and need firm handling at the reins, even though you could play their ribs like a xylophone, they're so scrawny. Émile is pressed between a woman with a wriggling toddler on her lap and a man in a flat cap and braces, who keeps taking swigs from a hip flask when he thinks no one's looking. The girls are up at the front and Letty is opposite him, wearing the yellow dress she keeps for church, her hair curled and pinned in a more elaborate style than usual. She is talking to the woman next to her and at one point, both of them throw back their heads and laugh and Émile is glad of it. He knows Letty and he knows it took courage to say what she did this morning, even if neither of them can be sure what is to happen next.

As they come down the hill towards the harbour, his neighbour passes him the flask. Émile takes a gulp, the strength of the alcohol making his eyes swim. The cart pulls up by the Weighbridge and they clamber out, Maud bringing the accordion along with her, and they walk through the assembled crowds until they find a place along the

Esplanade. The girls scramble onto the sea wall and Émile hoiks himself up alongside them, sits with his legs dangling, taking in the view as a visitor might: the green-backed hump of Herm island basking in the sun like a sea creature; Castle Cornet in the distance, with the damn Swastika still flying; the crumbling clock tower, the hands frozen at seven o'clock ever since the day of the bombing. If he were a cat, he'd be running short on lives by now, Émile thinks. He could have been blown sky high along with the tomatoes five years ago when the Germans first came, or shot in the head in the prison courtyard. He could have died in a stinking cell in the camp in Freiburg, or of slow, simple starvation when he'd been released.

Stella taps his shoulder and points towards the harbour. Two ships have landed and Émile senses the excitement of the crowd, like a wave about to break. The air vibrates around him and he has never seen so many people, there must be half the island here or more, and he thinks of Isabelle, and almost immediately catches sight of Letty, a few feet away, waving her hat in the air. Sees Letty; thinks of Isabelle: it is a see-saw motion he can't escape from, no matter how hard he tries – and God knows he has tried.

The crowds part as the first trucks with the British soldiers come on land and people surge forward. He and the girls slip down from the wall and follow in the wake of Letty and her church friends. Uniforms are everywhere now and it is strange to see men in brown, not grey-green, and with normal boots on, not those oversized wellies the Germans used to stomp around in.

The first soldier he encounters shakes him warmly by the hand and gives him a pack of Players. There are sweets and bars of chocolate for the children; a sailor hands Maud and Stella an orange each and receives a kiss on the cheek in return. A smart-looking press man approaches with a notebook, asking a tangle of questions, and although Émile tells him he's deaf, the reporter seems to find plenty to scribble down regardless, and Émile wonders what sense can ever be made of what they have all gone through by those who weren't there. He looks around miserably. He feels as flat as a horizon in a sea of coiling waves. There is only one acceptable way to behave today and that is to smile until you feel your cheeks might split like ripe peaches, but he can't do it.

Maud is talking to him, gesturing towards the accordion. She's going to find somewhere to play, she says.

'Will you come, Pa?'

There is pleasure in her eyes when he agrees. The four of them manoeuvre their way through the mill of people posing for photographs, and walk to Town Church Square. Maud sits on the bench in the shadow of the Albion pub, which had been one of Émile's favourite spots back in the day – folks were always more generous with tips when they'd had a few – and she begins to play. In barely a minute, the square is filling and by the end of Maud's first piece, there is a crowd. Maud introduces her next song and she nods towards where he and Letty are standing, and people look their way and smile and then as she pulls out the bellows, he sees that everyone has started to sing.

'*Sarnia Cherie*,' Letty says, raising an eyebrow, and he can't make out what she says next but years of marriage help him to fill in the gaps.

'Least she won't get locked up this time,' he says and Letty rolls her eyes, but he can almost taste how proud she is of Maud as she plays – it is like a meal that they share.

343

Stella is the first to set off the dancing, her and Roddy, and the lad is like an excitable puppy, Émile thinks, he's that besotted. They seem so achingly young, too young to know what they could possibly want, but a heart doesn't grow old in the way that the rest of a person does, Émile knows that, and there's no point in trying to trick it into going a way it doesn't want: it will find you out.

Émile's gaze slips through the dancers and it is then he sees her, nodding distractedly in time to the music, standing a little apart from the others. She is wearing a red dress and has a yellow flower in her hair, but the jauntiness of her outfit does not complement her expression: like him, Isabelle is not smiling. He has missed her, he has missed her and it is like a physical pain to see her again after so many months and to realise that his heart has not changed its mind. She turns and her gaze settles on him and Letty, like fine rain, and stays there.

A man comes and stands in front of them, blocking his view. It is the organist from Letty's church and he seems to be asking if Letty would like to dance, if Émile doesn't mind, that is. Give me a minute, Letty says, and then she turns to Émile. For a moment the crowd disappears and it is just the problem of the two of them again. The look on her face is full of both longing and fear as she gestures towards the far edges of the circle and tells him to go to her, go to her, over and again. Then she steps lightly into the organist's arms.

Émile's hands are suddenly clammy. He is wearing his one good shirt and he is sweating like a schoolboy underneath it. He starts to circle the crowd, weaving in and out of the dancers. Isabelle is no longer in his eyeline and he worries that she might have gone, feels horribly superstitious that if he doesn't find her again on today of all days, he will not have another chance. He brushes past Letty, the fullness of her skirt like a flower in bloom. And then he spots Isabelle, alone, standing back from the crowd, as if she's reserved a space especially for them.

Émile approaches. She smells of a bath, recently taken, and of the peeled orange she holds in her right hand.

'I've missed you.'

They both say it at the same time, their words in each other's mouths. Isabelle smiles at him, for him. Her face, in the morning sunshine, is full of light. And Émile wonders why it has taken him until now to understand that what happens in the silences between words is as important as the words themselves; and this is why when he is with Isabelle, he no longer feels that he is deaf.

They both look towards the swirl of dancers. Émile reaches for her outstretched hand; Isabelle rests her head on his chest. And they dance on the outskirts to their own rhythm, to the music only they can hear and that Émile now knows to be the sound of the woman he loves, welcoming him home.

EPILOGUE

Guernsey, 1950

'Isabelle Larch?' The landlady, in the bed and breakfast where Peter Schreiber is staying sets down his scrambled eggs with care. 'She works up in Hauteville, at the French House. She used to, at any rate.' She taps her lip thoughtfully. 'She re-married a couple of years ago. Lost her first husband to the war, I believe.'

It has taken him five years to come back to the island. Five years and the freshness of a new decade and the hope that this visit might in some way cauterise the night terrors and the daytime panic attacks that have known him to abandon his students and take refuge in the toilets, head pressed to the cold stone wall. He has even stopped drawing for pleasure, because he is afraid, after the last time, of what will come out. The art teacher who cannot draw, Peter thinks as he gets ready to leave after breakfast, packing his sketch pad, as he always does, unsure whether this reflects short-sighted optimism or nostalgia for the person he used to be.

It is the middle of May, and Guernsey is blooming, the hedgerows bursting with flowers, the insolent cry of birdsong following him wherever he goes. The island disguises itself well, Peter will say that much, but he still can't bring himself to walk across Town Church Square, and now as he walks up Hauteville towards the house, he finds himself sweating, despite the breeze. Ozzy has appeared, falling in line with his step, and Peter is

347

relieved to see that this time his imagination has offered his lover up without bruises and a hole in his body, although Ozzy seems to know what's coming. Look at you, all smartened up and smelling fancy, he is saying in his good-natured way; it's all right for some, isn't it? A bit of rowing, a few blisters and a couple of mouthfuls of sea water – I'd say you got off lightly. Did I tell you they kicked out my front teeth?

Peter stops, takes a deep breath. The house stands before him, the French tricolor flapping in the breeze as a group of tourists chatter outside. He is not sure if he can do this, but he must. First he must find Isabelle and then Mr Quenneville, and then Ozzy's brothers if he is able. The front door is open and an older man who introduces himself as Mr Corbeille ushers in the visitors. Peter joins them and waits in the dark vestibule for the tour to begin.

He cannot bring himself to look out at the garden until they have reached the second floor. There, in Victor Hugo's bedroom where Isabelle had once entertained him with stories of the writer's dalliances with the maids, he goes to the window and sees that the vegetable plots have become grounds again; plump white roses and beds of African lilies and hollyhocks, the magnolia tree in full bloom, the fountain, which used to be a depository for gardening tools, now trickling water. On the patio, at a wrought-iron table, he can see a woman pouring tea from a pot, and as she comes into view and crosses the garden, Peter recognises her. Isabelle's shadow falls across the hunched form of a man, on his knees in one of the flowerbeds, and as he gets up and steps into the sunlight, it is who Peter hoped it might be, and he finds himself smiling for the first time since he arrived. He watches as Émile puts his arm around Isabelle's waist and they amble towards the patio.

'Quite back to their former glory, these gardens.' Mr Corbeille is next to him now. 'There were times I thought this place would never see out the war.'

They talk for a few moments about the war and its aftermath, the slow, painful healing of Europe. Then Peter asks if an Isabelle Larch still works at the house.

'Oh yes,' Corbeille says. 'Or Isabelle Quenneville as she is now. And her husband, Mr Quenneville, too. The old guard, so to speak!' He looks curiously at Peter. 'They're in today, if you'd like to say hello?'

He would, Peter says, but might he first ask a favour? He is an artist, he says, a keen amateur anyway, and he would love the opportunity to do a sketch of the view from this room.

Corbeille is happy to oblige, if he doesn't take too long. And so Peter gets out his sketch pad and the pencil, which he still takes the trouble to keep sharp, and begins to draw. He thinks of Ozzy and the shed in the enclosure, and their desire for each other as the seasons turned, through the heat of summer to winter's core, when the ground crunched with frost and every leaf and branch was iced like a wedding cake. He thinks of the sadness that permeated every room in Isabelle's house, and how much he had wanted to help her and her friend, the deaf man, as trapped in his silent world as Isabelle was in her own. And he feels glad now that he came back despite everything. He will hold it close, in the dark times, this vignette of Émile and Isabelle sipping tea from china cups among the nodding hollyhocks, unharmed and in love.

Peter finishes the drawing, scrutinises it with a frown. Then he tucks his sketch pad under his arm and goes downstairs to find them.

Author's Note

The 'French House' of the title refers to Hauteville House, the French novelist Victor Hugo's residence-in-exile in Guernsey from 1856–70, and where he wrote some of his most famous works. Now owned by the City of Paris, the house and gardens are open to visitors and I was lucky enough to work there as a guide when I was a student, many summers ago. Located on a quiet street on the outskirts of St Peter Port, all four storeys of Hauteville House were decorated by Hugo himself, in truly eclectic and eccentric style with rooms ranging from the Versailles-inspired *salon rouge* to the glass 'look out' at the top of the house, which served as his writing room.

Hugo's personal life was as unconventional and vibrant as his interiors – a gift to any tour guide! - and visitors to the house used to love the stories of Hugo and his lifelong mistress and muse, Juliette Drouet, who moved to Guernsey with the rest of the Hugo family but who lived, for propriety's sake, on the opposite side of the street. Theirs was an intense and passionate relationship with Juliette writing thousands of letters to Hugo over the course of her life – and they remained lovers for fifty years until her death in 1883.

Needless to say, Hauteville House and the stories it held seized my imagination, but it wasn't until almost thirty years later, as I was in the early stages of planning this novel, that it found its way onto the page. It struck me that not only was 'the French House' on Hauteville the perfect setting for a rather different kind of love story, but that its legacy as a place of both refuge and exile, embodied some of the core themes of the book.

It remains unclear as to exactly what happened to Hauteville House during the German Occupation and the story I have written is fictional. Victor Hugo's atmospheric Guernsey home is such a special place that continues to inspire so many people in different ways – an inheritance from the man himself to every one who passes through the doors.

For more information:
www.museums.gov.gg/hauteville
www.maisonsvictorhugo.paris.fr

Acknowledgements

Writing a book is a wonderful mix of the solitary and the collaborative. I would like to thank the following:

All at Madeleine Milburn Literary Agency, in particular Giles Milburn, my agent, for his insightful editorial eye, calm direction and support, and passion for *The French House*.

The team at Hodder and Stoughton, including my first editor Thorne Ryan who, amongst other things, went to war on my semi-colons! Many thanks also to Olivia Barber for embracing *The French House* with such enthusiasm, as well as Kimberley Atkins, Amy Batley, Laura Bartholomew, Steven Cooper, Becky Glibbery and Natalie Chen.

The Priaulx Library, Guernsey; Nathan Coyde and the team at the Island Archives; the Guernsey German Occupation Museum; the Imperial War Museum archives.

The curators of Hauteville House, Guernsey, for answering my questions and letting me visit the gardens one chilly New Year's Eve, when I first spotted the walled enclosure and a ladder …

Derek Strange for so generously sharing his experiences of living with hearing loss; and the late Barry Paint for much-needed seafaring advice.

My friend Sara Sarre – writer, cheerleader, literary matchmaker and editor extraordinaire – whose belief in me and this book has kept me going through some sticky times.

Equally, huge thanks to Frances Merivale for reading drafts of *The French House* so attentively and for spot on editorial comments and suggestions.

My writing group, formerly of Curtis Brown Creative: Dan, Eleanor, Fran, Jayne, Jon, Karen, Lauren, Mariko, Sara and Tim: the best of company, the most discerning of readers. I'm so glad we met.

All the writing tutors who have supported and encouraged me over the years, especially my former mentor, Emma Claire Sweeney, and Curtis Brown Creative founder, Anna Davis.

Wendy Bough and the team at the Caledonia Novel Award for their ongoing commitment to new writers and their work.

My wonderful friend Ruth Dunn, there through the highs and the lows for almost as long as I can remember, and the other Dunns – Guy, Imogen and Sophie for cheering me on at every stage through the medium of song, video and home made cards – you're awesome!

The other Bangor gals, the brilliant Rachel Lyon and Xanthe Stokell, whose enthusiasm and support, not to mention ready supply of emojis and gifs, have meant so much to me – no one could ask for better friends.

All the friends, family and colleagues who have supported this book and my writing, who have never been too busy to ask how 'the Guernsey novel' was going and even listened attentively when I updated them – thank you!

My grandma, Doris Martel, for sharing her experiences of the German Occupation, never questioning that I was anything less than a writer, who would one day be published. This book wouldn't exist without her, and I'm sorry that she didn't live to see its publication.

My partner, Jeff Zroback. It can be no coincidence that the second draft of this novel morphed into a full-on love story around the time we met. Thank you for your on-going support and loyalty, for being chief cook and sommelier, and for making me laugh on a daily basis. I love you.

My parents, Val and Ian. Huge thanks and love for everything, not least for giving me a childhood full of books, travel and experiences, and an adulthood where there has always been space at home to write. I owe you so much and *The French House* is dedicated to you.

And finally thank you to the 'real' Émile (1893–1980) who I hope would take this literary imagining of his experiences as the tribute it is intended to be.

I am indebted to the following publications which have helped with my research for this novel.

The *Aspects of War* series by June Money; *The Book of Ebenezer Le Page* by G B Edwards; *Diary of the German Occupation* by J C Sauvary; *A Fair and Honest Book* by Ambrose Sherwill; *Guernsey Under Occupation: The Second World War Diaries of Violet Carey,* edited by Alice Evans; *A Peep Behind the Screens 1940 – 1945* by Beryl S Ozanne; *The Silent War* by Frank Falla; *A Model Occupation* by Madeleine Bunting; *Occupied Guernsey* by Herbert Winterflood

Reading Group Questions

1. What did you know about the German Occupation of the Channel Islands before reading this novel? What did you learn about daily life for the islanders? Did anything surprise you?

2. What are the most challenging elements of life under Occupation for the characters in the book? Does anyone benefit from the situation?

3. What is your opinion of the portrayal of the Occupying Forces in The French House? Did your thoughts change or evolve as the novel progressed?

4. Much of the story in the novel takes place at Hauteville House, the French author Victor Hugo's former house of exile. What is the significance of this setting do you think? How are the themes of exile reflected in the characters of Émile, Isabelle and Schreiber?

5. How did the island setting enhance the story?

6. How has Émile's deafness forged his character? How has it impacted on the choices he's made in the past?

7. How and why does Émile change during the novel? What does he learn about himself and the people closest to him?

8. From the outset, Isabelle and Ronald Larch have very different attitudes to their billet, Leutnant Schreiber. What does their treatment of him reveal about their characters?

9. Discuss the character of Letty. How much sympathy did you have for her?

10. *No one in The French House is truly free.* To what extent, do you agree or disagree with this statement?

11. The French House is described as a book about 'wanting to hear and learning to listen'. How is this theme manifested in the different characters?

12. 'Hearts don't grow old in the way the rest of a person does.' Do you agree with Émile's observation?

13. What have each of the characters learnt by the end of the novel? How have their experiences during the Occupation changed or re-shaped the people they are?

14. What did you think of the ending? Was it the ending you were expecting?